Readers love the Bonfires series by Amy Lane

Bonfires

"...I just adored this story. There is such warmth and love here between these men that you can't help but want everything good for them."

—Joyfully Jay

"I can't recommend this enough. It was sweet, exciting, romantic, touching, and also really, really relevant and thought provoking."

—Open Skye Book Reviews

Crocus

"Amy Lane does real life like no other author I know. Gritty, messy and hectic does not begin to describe the life these two men live with their kids."

—The Novel Approach

"Crocus is a story of family and love and acceptance. It's about overcoming obstacles and keeping what's important at the forefront. It's about love. So, so much love."

—Diverse Reader

Sunset

"If you thought the previous books were a roller coaster of emotions, well buckle up. This one will knock the breath out of you."

—Love Bytes

"... I am very happy to have been there for the end."

—Paranormal Romance Guild

By Amy Lane

An Amy Lane Christmas
Behind the Curtain
Bewitched by Bella's Brother
Bolt-hole
Christmas Kitsch
Christmas with Danny Fit
Clear Water
Do-over
Food for Thought
Freckles
Gambling Men
Going Up
Hammer & Air
Homebird
If I Must
Immortal
It's Not Shakespeare
Late for Christmas
Left on St. Truth-be-Well
The Locker Room
Mourning Heaven
Phonebook
Puppy, Car, and Snow
Racing for the Sun • Hiding the Moon
Raising the Stakes
Regret Me Not
Shiny!
Shirt
Sidecar
Slow Pitch
String Boys
A Solid Core of Alpha
Swipe Left, Power Down, Look Up

Three Fates
Truth in the Dark
Turkey in the Snow
The Twelve Kittens of Christmas
Under the Rushes
Weirdos
Wishing on a Blue Star

BENEATH THE STAIN
Beneath the Stain • Paint It Black

BONFIRES
Bonfires • Crocus
Sunset • Torch Songs

CANDY MAN
Candy Man • Bitter Taffy
Lollipop • Tart and Sweet

COVERT
Under Cover

DREAMSPUN BEYOND
HEDGE WITCHES LONELY
HEARTS CLUB
Shortbread and Shadows
Portals and Puppy Dogs
Pentacles and Pelting Plants
Heartbeats in a Haunted House

Published by DREAMSPINNER PRESS
www.dreamspinnerpress.com

Published by DREAMSPINNER PRESS
www.dreamspinnerpress.com

By Amy Lane (cont)

Published by DSP Publications

ALL THAT HEAVEN WILL
ALLOW
All the Rules of Heaven

GREEN'S HILL
The Green's Hill Novellas

LITTLE GODDESS
Vulnerable
Wounded, Vol. 1 • Wounded, Vol. 2
Bound, Vol. 1 • Bound, Vol. 2
Rampant, Vol. 1 • Rampant, Vol. 2
Quickening, Vol. 1
Quickening, Vol. 2
Green's Hill Werewolves, Vol. 1
Green's Hill Werewolves, Vol. 2

Published by Harmony Ink Press

BITTER MOON SAGA
Triane's Son Rising
Triane's Son Learning
Triane's Son Fighting
Triane's Son Reigning

Published by DREAMSPINNER PRESS
www.dreamspinnerpress.com

TORCH SONGS

AMY LANE

Published by

DREAMSPINNER PRESS

5032 Capital Circle SW, Suite 2, PMB# 279, Tallahassee, FL 32305-7886 USA
www.dreamspinnerpress.com

Torch Songs
© 2024 Amy Lane

Cover Art
© 2024 L.C. Chase
http://www.lcchase.com
Cover content is for illustrative purposes only and any person depicted on the cover is a model.

Trade Paperback ISBN: 978-1-64108-730-8
Digital ISBN: 978-1-64108-729-2
Trade Paperback published September 2024
v. 1.0

To anyone who has listened to a song under a velvet black sky and heard the howl of their own heart in harmony. And to Mate and Mary. My kids can sit this one out—but Mate and Mary absolutely.

AUTHOR'S NOTE

SO, THIS story can absolutely positively stand alone. That Linda Ronstadt song—the one that showed up in the zombie series—"Long, Long, Time"—was rattling around in my head, and suddenly I had this vision of a musician on stage, singing that song, and of a perfectly reasonable human falling desperately in love, just that quickly. And as I was writing what would become the second chapter in a ficlet, I remembered that I KNEW a guy who'd been desperately, unrequitedly in love, and that Guthrie broke my heart in *String Boys*, and that maybe he deserved a happy ending of his own. And as I was writing that ficlet, using it like stretches at the barre for what I was really writing—*Sunset*—I realized that I KNEW a guy, a steady, funny guy, who deserved an all-consuming love like the kind you could get from hearing a musician sing a song that embodied all of human heartbreak in a few lovely notes. In fact, he'd just slid down a hill with Aaron George back in *Sunset*. Hunh, I thought. Hunh. So this story can absolutely, positively stand alone, but if you LIKE any of the supporting characters—Larx and Aaron from *Sunset*, Seth and Kelly from *String Boys*, even the detective and his porn star from *Sean's Sunshine*—be sure to check out their books. Because any love story can stand alone, but sometimes it's fun to check out the entire group, right?

LONG LONG TIME....

"OH MY God," Roberta practically squealed. "Really? You want me to go as your plus-one?"

Guthrie Arlo Woodson tried to keep the melancholy out of his smile and mostly succeeded. "Yep, darlin'. The invite said I could bring someone, and I choose you!"

Roberta Querling sat across from him at the Washoe House, on the bar side, as the joint closed down, and now she lowered her voice even below the closing-time babble and murmured, "They, uh, know I'm just a friend, right?"

Guthrie worked hard to keep his laugh from being bitter. "Babydoll," he drawled, "these guys knew I was gay before I did." He shuddered. "I kept saying I was bi, and then I'd go home with a pretty girl and have a truly shitty time."

Roberta groaned. "I don't even want to know," she said—and she was right. There were things a man did to fake an orgasm that were a lie for the woman and not fantastic for a man's self-esteem. The taint of those days gave Guthrie a case of the cringes even two years after he came out to himself completely.

"And I don't want to tell you," he said, managing to make it roguish instead of ashamed, "but this is a bit of short notice. I appreciate it."

"What about the hotel room?" she asked. "Should we go halfsies?"

He shook his head and laughed a little. "No. Uhm, Seth is renting two houses next to each other, side by side. I told you he and Kelly are adopting Kelly's niece and nephew, right?"

She nodded, clearly as enthralled now as she had been two years ago when they'd auditioned for each other to form their little dive-bar band. Roberta was a violinist—and a good one—and she had better-paying gigs during the week, but she'd been a fan of rock and pop music her entire life. Since that's what Guthrie had been born playing, pretty much, she'd been happy to help him reassemble a band that had been torn apart by time and, well, his father's bigotry, so he could continue to do his favorite thing in the world.

There hadn't been a time in their acquaintance that Roberta hadn't appeared starstruck by Guthrie's friendship with Seth Arnold.

Of course, Seth Arnold was *literally* an international superstar, a young phenom who had taken the music world by storm in his first years in the conservatory by releasing a series of innovative videos featuring him performing multiple instruments and his own compositions or arrangements. Guthrie was pretty sure that now Seth had the hang of monetizing his channel (or more likely somebody had stepped in and started doing it for him and was being generously paid for their time), he was making roughly twice what Guthrie made in his day job *just* from YouTube, but that wasn't the sort of thing Seth paid attention to.

Guthrie had known Seth for six years, four of them playing together in Guthrie's dad's little honky-tonk band, Fiddler and the Crabs—with Seth as the Fiddler. During that time, Guthrie had learned Seth had two things that really caught his attention. One was music, and the other was his family, starring the love of his life, the boy he'd worshipped in high school and on through adulthood, Kelly Cruz. Kelly wasn't the *only* member of the family; Seth's dad was in his sights, Kelly's mom and sisters, and Kelly's late brother's two children, both of them suffering the effects of a mother who used narcotics during her pregnancy.

Seth adored the children like his own. Watching him play with them over Zoom calls was one of the things that gave Guthrie hope for the world, and he couldn't imagine a world in which his Fiddler didn't get a happy ending with Kelly as his husband and the two children living with them, cared for and beloved, in their happy home.

So hearing that Seth was renting two houses for his wedding in Monterey during the frigid-cold off-season didn't surprise Guthrie in the least. Being invited—and invited to bring a date—to stay in one of the houses and to attend the wedding and play with the family for a week—*that* was one of the proudest things in Guthrie's life.

What wasn't to be proud of by maintaining that friendship? Seth was a violin virtuoso who had brought the house down in Italy and New York and probably had a thousand other venues where he'd be invited as a soloist, and once he and Kelly were married and the adoption finalized, Seth would be bringing his husband and their children with him.

Guthrie loved that Roberta had a celebrity crush on his old friend, who had subsidized Kelly's struggling family with his income from Guthrie's father's band.

What he didn't love so much was that his feelings for Seth went way beyond crush, and he'd had them for six long goddamned years.

"So," Roberta said now, completely oblivious to the turmoil in Guthrie's heart, "we get to stay with the family in one of the houses?"

Guthrie shrugged. "Fiddler—erm, Seth and I go way back," he said. "He and Kelly had to overcome a *lot* of obstacles to have this moment in the sun. I'm proud that he invited me. But yeah. We're in with the family."

Roberta was a pretty young woman with long, straight brown hair that she pulled back from a long oval of a face with a band at her nape. She was a few years younger than Guthrie, right out of school, and still had some of the spots and the awkwardness that went with spending all her attention on her studies and very little on her fellow students. In a way she reminded Guthrie quite a bit of Seth, but Roberta had never had to hide in her own mind like Seth had. She still had some brain power left to observe other humans.

"You must be *really* good friends," she said softly, "for him to invite you like family."

Guthrie swallowed and looked out into the thinning crowd. He, Roberta, and two of her friends from her own conservatory/music days all performed at Washoe House three nights a week. They spent two other nights at a slightly more upscale place closer to San Francisco, and another night practicing, because they liked to play. During the day, Neil Chase, Owen Cuthbert, and Roberta all worked recording and teaching gigs in San Francisco, commuting from San Rafael, where Guthrie kept a small apartment as well. Playing with The Crabs was their happy place. It was fun music, with a lively, enthusiastic crowd, and while Neil, Owen, and Roberta were all top-notch musicians who could probably do *way* better, it was nice, Guthrie thought, for the three of them to play with an organization that didn't have reviews posted in the national press or frothing-at-the-mouth conductors who went on power trips designed to deconstruct even the strongest psyche.

Guthrie was under no illusions that The Crabs wasn't a step down for all three of them, just as he knew that for himself, it was the only thing that gave meaning to his life.

He hated to burden Roberta with the stupid, painful details of that life—but she was taking a week off from playing, practicing, and spending time with her family to be his plus-one so he didn't have to go in alone, and he thought maybe... just maybe... he could let her in a fraction.

But apparently she'd already seen a crack and shined her own light into it.

"Oh," she said softly.

"Oh what?" he asked, but he was watching Owen and Neil break down the instruments. The drum set was provided by the venue, thank God, because hauling around his own set was a colossal pain in the ass. He knew because he had to provide it for Scorpio, their other steady gig.

Her hand on his sleeve called him back to her, but he went reluctantly.

"Oh. You were in love with him," she said, like she knew for certain.

Well, it was a certain thing. "I was," he said, hoping the little lie would go unnoticed.

"Oh, Guthrie," she said, holding her hand to her mouth, her eyes watering. "No."

Apparently not. "Look," he said, touching her hand in return. "He knows. He's known since the beginning. For that matter, so has Kelly. They... they hung with me because I was a friend—and darlin', when I say friend, I mean *friend*. You can't get any better loyalty than Seth Arnold and Kelly Cruz. Don't ever doubt it. I do *not* want to repay that friendship by mooncalfing all over Seth during his wedding. He invited me—Kelly invited me—and I need to respect that means they both love me, and I am going to go hang out with their family and have the time of my life. Please come with me and make sure nobody gets hurt while I do that, okay?"

"Oh, Guthrie," she said again. "Nobody but you."

His own eyes burned. "And only you can know that," he said earnestly. "Please."

She squeezed his fingers and gave a watery smile. "Think he'll play for us?"

Guthrie laughed. "The boy plays like he breathes. Yeah. I think he will."

"Totally worth it," she said.

He was forced to agree.

AND DURING the ceremony, when Seth stood on a promontory at Pebble Beach, overlooking a thunderous winter ocean, playing a composition he'd written for his beloved and nobody else, Guthrie still agreed.

When Seth was done—and his best friend, Amara, had taken his violin and put it tenderly in a slightly heated case while Seth turned to Kelly to say his vows, Guthrie knew his face wasn't the only one freezing with brine.

Roberta clung to his arm and damn near sobbed, so he got to comfort her, and that was nice. Gay or not gay, it did make him feel a little more powerful to be able to comfort a pretty girl.

The vows were short, and equal parts foolishness and mooncalfing, as Seth would have said. And they were perfect. Guthrie and Roberta had played their share of weddings, but this one…. Guthrie was just as glad Seth provided the music here, because anything either one of them could have done would have made them both seem underaccomplished in comparison.

And that wasn't Seth's intention. That's what made him the boy Guthrie couldn't get over. Seth had written and performed that composition to make Kelly smile at him. Kelly, who was a year younger than Seth, was a short, compact boy with coarse black hair he pulled back from his face in a half-tail for the occasion, and wide, almost guileless brown eyes that practically sparkled with mischief and joy. He stared at his new husband with a fond look that said he knew he was stupid with love but didn't care.

For his part, Seth, who was tall and who never *had* managed the knack of wearing clothes that fit, had trimmed his blond corkscrew curls tight to his head and returned Kelly's expression of profound stupid love with green eyes that were only ever focused when he was looking at Kelly. Those eyes in Seth's pale brown face—his mother had been Black and his father was once a blond, blue-eyed high school basketball player—were striking enough, but the faraway expression in them made him almost otherworldly in his beauty.

The fact that Guthrie knew that the two of them had overcome more tragedy than people twice their age in order to stand on this ice-fucking-cold romantic cliff and stare hopefully into each other's eyes made their love even harder to resent.

Guthrie had no choice but to be happy and proud for the two of them. To love them like the small gathering of family and friends around him.

When Amara's husband, Vince, was done with the short ceremony, they turned toward their parents, Seth to his father and Kelly to his mother, who both held out their arms. Seth's father deposited an almost pitifully thin little girl into Seth's arms. She clung to his neck and laughed excitedly, talking a mile a minute about cold and wind and pretty coats and "Set'" and "her music." Kelly took a limp, placid little boy, bundled in a warm winter-blanket sleeper. Even from fifteen feet away, Guthrie could see the baby's arms weren't as active as most children's would be at eight months, and Guthrie's throat tightened. Kelly gazed down at this baby with affection and love. He and Seth were twenty-five and twenty-four, and they were embarking on their new life together with two children with special needs—and Guthrie could only gaze at them as they posed for a joyous, unself-conscious picture, and think about what a happy family they made.

"I present to you," Vince said, his handsome, boyish face wreathed in smiles, "the Arnold-Cruz family. They've already kissed, so now we all get to hug them and then bundle up and go back to the houses for a hot drink and some good food."

To general laughter, Guthrie jostled up with the rest of the family to kiss the babies and hug the men and greet Vince and Amara, who had arrived that morning along with Guthrie and Roberta and he hadn't had a chance to hug them yet.

The five of them used to hang out in Seth's dorms and watch movies and eat pizza and talk about their lives together. It was damned good to see them.

He expected Seth and Kelly to be distracted and generally high with happiness by the time they got to him, but instead Seth focused on him, and Kelly gave him a super tight one-armed hug while the baby drooled on his good suit.

"You came!" Seth said happily. "I'm so glad you came. We didn't give you much time."

"And miss an opportunity to freeze my balls off?" Guthrie asked, eliciting warm laughter from both men. "How could I?"

"Speaking of which," Amara murmured, coming up between them and holding her arms out imperiously for the placid baby, "let's load into the cars and go back to the houses. You guys, I can't wait to catch up." She kissed Guthrie on the cheek and gave Roberta a smile. "And you are...."

"His totally platonic plus-one," Roberta said cheerily. "He didn't want to make the drive alone."

"Roberta plays fiddle in The Crabs," he told Seth, who cackled with laughter.

"You kept the band name!" he said, like this made him unutterably happy. "I'm so glad! Are your dad and Uncle Jock—"

Guthrie cut him off with a quick shake of his head. "Naw. Just me and some of Roberta's conservatory friends. We do five nights a week— keeps me out of trouble and lets me hold down the day job without any corporate fatalities."

Seth blew out a breath. "You're too good to have a day job," he said seriously, which, Guthrie admitted, could be yet another reason he loved the guy. Then right on the heels of the one thing came another. "You brought your guitar, right? You're gonna play for us tonight? 'Cause I'm saying, I've got some prime musicians here—Amara, Vince, you—" He grinned at Roberta. "And you, probably, cause you wouldn't play with Guthrie if you sucked!"

Roberta grinned, obviously enchanted. "I'm not bad," she said primly.

"Good." Seth nodded, taking her at her word. "You guys, me and Kelly are going to talk to all the people, and we're gonna dance and we're gonna eat and we're gonna have us a helluva party." He sobered. "I got us a house all lined up, and we're moving at the end of January. I'm gonna miss the hell out of everybody until we get to visit again, so you gotta make it good."

Guthrie nodded, a solemn oath, and held out his hand for Seth to shake. "I promise upon my honor," he said soberly.

"God, you're fun," Seth told him, shaking his hand.

They all broke up then to load into cars and minivans and rental mobiles—Guthrie watched as Kelly chivvied Seth into the passenger seat of an obviously new SUV after Seth had put the kids in the back, and laughed.

"What?" Roberta asked after they'd climbed into the cab of his ancient pickup truck, a vehicle so ugly Guthrie had almost expected to be stopped when they'd paid the fee for the lot at the state park where the wedding had been held. Across the street a few die-hard duffers were struggling through the bitter wind to capitalize on the famed golf-course's available tee times, but Seth and Kelly had managed to reserve a spit of sidewalk with a fenced-in promontory over a shoal of storm-tossed rocks. Guthrie had to admit, the scenery was right out of a Brontë movie. Who *wouldn't* be moved to confess undying love when right below their feet was proof of the mutability of life and the ever-present threat of mortality?

"Nothing," Guthrie said, slamming his door hard to make sure it shut. He cranked up the heater after he hit the ignition, because Roberta had worn a dress and her knees under her black tights were practically blue. "Just that he's traveled the world, he's overcome hardships, he's married the man of his dreams and is adopting two precious children, and that boy *still* hasn't learned how to drive."

Roberta let out a half laugh, because in California, that was practically heresy. "Why not? Does he have some sort of disability?"

Guthrie shrugged his shoulders. "Let's say the opportunity didn't present itself when he was younger, and our Fiddler is highly distractible. He's a sweet kid, but practicality ain't his strong suit."

"And I got to hear him play at his own wedding." Roberta gave a happy shiver. "And the week isn't over yet. Guthrie, I know you're probably eating your heart out, but I have to say thank you again, for being the most awesome friend."

"You know what?" Guthrie said, steering the truck around the 17 Mile Drive, careful not to go too fast around the curves. The ancient Chevy pickup was not exactly known for hugging the road.

"What?" she asked, huddling deeper into her wool coat and lush wool scarf.

"I may not actually be eating my heart out." He felt the words as he said them, a sort of letting go, a freedom from the burden of heartache that had plagued him for so long.

"Really?" she asked, sounding sort of excited.

"Yeah, darlin'. I... I mean, I love them both. I love Amara and Vince, and given how absolutely adorable Kelly's sisters were and how kind his parents seem to be, I could love them all too. But... but that's not the same as being *in* love, you know?"

"Yeah," she said carefully. "I know."

"Well maybe, after this, I can just love them. I don't have to worry about being *in* love with Seth. That would be load off my heart, you think?"

Roberta nodded. "Yeah," she said softly. "But you know what would put the cherry on the being-free sundae, don't you?"

He grimaced. "Can't we be happy with my heartfelt revelation right now?"

"Honey, I'm not going to be happy until you get laid."

WELL, IT didn't happen that long, long weekend—but Guthrie wasn't looking for that. Instead, all the things Seth had promised happened.

People ate together, talked together, reminisced together. The musicians played together, and the friends and family danced together.

They even went to the aquarium together and on short, brine-tossed boat rides that made Guthrie feel like singing sea shanties and playing the theme from *Jaws*.

As far as he and Roberta were concerned, it was a sweet, happy holiday with people they came to regard as family by the time it was over.

On the last night—New Year's Eve—most everybody went to bed after the ball dropped, but the original core of movie-watchers from Seth's old school—Vince, Amara, Kelly, Seth, and Guthrie—all stayed up late, lounging in the front room in front of a gas-powered fireplace, drinking wine. The wine thing was new for Seth, and he only drank a little, but apparently Amara had been trying to teach him how to order and accept a glass of wine in a restaurant so it wasn't a production.

"Even if you hate it," she said soberly, "you're only sipping it anyway, so nobody questions if you don't finish the glass."

"Just don't order red," Seth said seriously. "Headaches. Oh my God."

Kelly snorted. "Hate to tell you all, but I've actually *been clubbing*. I order shots. I'm fine."

Seth grunted. "I tried once—it was in front of my conductor in Italy. He knocked it back, I tried to do the same, and I coughed so hard I threw up all over us both. It's a good thing we were in his kitchen. God."

"Which is why he came to me when we moved to New York," Amara said. Seth had been all over the world in the last four years, while Kelly had been forced to stay home to help take care of his family, which Seth had subsidized with his music. Guthrie could tell the stories were their way of making up for lost time, but they were fun nonetheless.

"Yeah," Vince said. "I was with a dorm of three guys, and they were like, 'pub crawl!' So I learned to drink beer. I can tell you *all* about beer." He shuddered. "So much."

"Like, draft or bottled?" Guthrie asked, because those were the kind of bars *he* played at, but Vince—a beautiful native Hawai'ian man with skin a pale teak color and brown, fathomless eyes—shook his head.

"No, brother. I wish. This is, like, thirty taps in a place, and you go in and get a ten-shot flight and taste all these beers, and you have to *know* things. Like, 'Hmm, taste of citrus with a hint of plum and coffee!'"

Guthrie stared at him in horror. "Who?" he demanded. "Who? Who does this to beer?"

"Fuckin' heathens," Vince said, and he clinked his Sam Adams bottle with Guthrie, who had enjoyed it as an exotic taste when apparently it was like Coors to the people Vince hung out with.

Everyone else laughed, and the conversation went on. At its end, Seth and Amara had crashed next to each other, head on each other's shoulders, because they'd been friends from high school as well, and Vince curled up on the end of the same couch, his head in Amara's lush lap.

Guthrie smiled at the three of them as he and Kelly polished off the last two beers.

"How you doin', Guthrie?" Kelly asked. His eyes were a little glazed, but his speech wasn't slurred, and Guthrie had the feeling that Kelly was the one who could drink them all under the table.

"Fine," he said. He'd been nursing *his* alcohol, which was a trick you picked up when you'd been playing in dive bars since you were way underage. It was either that or his dad's route, which was full-blown alcoholism, and Guthrie wasn't a fan.

"Mm?" Kelly's eyes had sharpened, and Guthrie was forced to shrug.

"I've got a band right now," he said. It was his one good thing—he knew that.

"What about a *man* right now?" Kelly asked bluntly. "God, Guthrie. I know you had it bad for Seth. I couldn't even blame you. But neither of us want you to live alone forever because you"—his voice dropped—"fell in love with a guy you couldn't have. That's... that's not fair. You're a good guy, Guthrie. We want you to have more than a band for a minute."

Guthrie glanced away. Kelly was more right than he knew. Kids like Roberta, Owen, and Neil were too *good* to stay in The Crabs for long. They had places to go, real performances, spots in orchestras to achieve.

"What do you want me to say?" he asked finally, knowing there wasn't enough alcohol in the world to soothe over this rawness inside. "I'm.... Kelly, you know what I am. If... if your boy hadn't come wandering into that dive bar, looking for a job, I could have lied to myself my entire life. I could have slept with girls and told myself I wasn't the type to fall in love. I could have gotten drunk every night with my dad and Uncle Jock, and they could have yelled at me to get my shit together, and I would have known they were right, but I wouldn't have had any way, anywhere to reach higher. Your guy comes along and suddenly I'm, like, 'Hey, I can learn piano and get better at guitar! I can go to school! I can get a job with health and dental!'"

"You can fall in love with a guy, and it can last forever," Kelly said. "Man, I've been to school. I got the papers behind my name. Just like you, this wasn't a common thing in my family. And I can tell you right now, it's not the job or the health and dental—it's the guy you love forever and ever. That's the difference in your life. That's what makes it special."

Guthrie tried for condescension. "Maybe, sweetcheeks, I'm not special enough to get a special guy."

Kelly didn't blink. He simply stared at Guthrie until he shifted uncomfortably.

"What?" Guthrie finally asked.

"We love you, asshole. Seth worries about you. We know how to have friends from far away—you and me never stopped contact, not even when he was all over the damned planet. I want to hear there's a guy in your life. And don't tell me they don't fall in your lap. Keep your heart open for us, Guthrie. Learn to let someone in."

Guthrie swallowed, beaten and done. His eyes were burning, and it was all he could do not to sob his heart out on the shoulder of the guy *married* to the guy Guthrie couldn't seem to get over.

"It's hard," he admitted gruffly. "I… I know what it feels like now, when it's real. In your heart. Just like you two—I can't settle for anything smaller or dumber now."

"That's real good," Kelly said, nodding. "But don't let it hold you back. A kiss won't kill you, buddy. It's the way to see if there's sunshine in the corners."

Guthrie could only nod. He didn't remember much more about that night. They *all* fell asleep in the front room in front of the fire, bundled in blankets. Kelly took a recliner, and Guthrie lay in front of the couch, and when it was time to get up and leave in the morning, the five of them hugged and cried a little, because they were all old enough now to know times like that didn't come as often as they should.

But he kept Kelly's words in his heart: *A kiss won't kill you, buddy. It's the way to see if there's sunshine in the corners.*

He knew what to look for now. He'd look for sunshine.

GET KNOCKED DOWN

"HEY, CHRIS," Tad Hawkins said to his partner, Chris Castro, a fellow detective in the Sacramento Police Department, Office of Investigations. "How's this weekend looking? Anything I might get called in for?"

Their police department had been modernized—twenty years ago. The detective bullpen featured sturdy desks, barely cracked linoleum, and computers from the last decade at least. Chris pulled up the schedule on his computer and shook his head. "Not seeing anything pressing," he said, scanning it. Chris was a good detective—and a good family man. In his forties, with his youngest kid entering college at the beginning of September, Chris was savvy enough to have ensured he and Hawkins had a lightened load by the end of April. They both had investigations pending, which they worked doggedly on during the week. But weekends were for Chris helping his youngest, Robin, study for her AP exams and going to see her softball games, and Chris had seniority. Since Tad's ambitions had been shoved aside for his *own* family considerations, he was good with this. He loved his job—had been on the force for a couple of years and had enjoyed his promotion to detective very much—but he… well, needed time.

Needed to be able to compartmentalize: job on one hand, his sister on the other.

"Looking good so far," Chris told him, cracking a smile. He frowned for a moment. "Ugh. We've got a series of Monday morning workshops, though—whole next month. What we can do to aid our forensics team."

Tad brightened. "That's actually interesting!" he said. "I mean, I'm not a science genius but… you know." He hummed the theme for the original *CSI*, and Castro chuckled.

"Yeah, I watched it too. You're right. It'll be fun, but—" He glanced around as though this was a state secret. "—me and Robin have started waking up early, having coffee together. I mean, it'll be summer soon, she'll have her summer job, then school. I'm gonna miss my baby."

Tad smiled wistfully. He and his sister had been raised by a single mom, a constantly *exhausted* single mom, and moments like a cup of coffee with their parent had been really important. "You're a good dad," he said, fighting the lump in his throat. "I'll cover for you."

"Look at you, fuzzing the line like an old pro." Chris grinned at him, and Tad thought for the umpteenth time that he was damned cute. He had the eyes that crinkled in the corners and sparkled, and the strands of gray in his black hair only added to the sex appeal. But Chris was too good a mentor to be a crush—being partnered up with him had been one of the best things to happen to Tad in the last year, and he wouldn't clutter that up with a hopeless infatuation.

"Well, just know I'll be out of town this weekend. I mean, I can get here, but I'll be in Bodega Bay, so, you know…."

"Three hours away," Chris said soberly. "How's she doing?"

Of all the people in the department, Chris was the one who knew where he'd be.

Tad held out his hand and wobbled it from left to right. "We're stuck right now," he said on a sigh. "She… she doesn't do well in cities. She really does need a smaller town. But she keeps running into her old crowd, and that's no good either. She won't leave the halfway house right now, and the thought of coming to Sacramento makes her cry." Or it had six months earlier. Maybe that had changed?

Chris blew out a breath. "How's the halfway house?"

Tad cringed. "Gross," he said. Some of those places were nice, clean, newer, with a staff that was young and idealistic and ready to care. This place was small, the house was old, the staff was apathetic at best. Tad had worked to find a better one in the area, but Bodega Bay was a beachside town, no matter how popular. Much of the population was seasonal, and the seasonal population wasn't excited about paying for other people's problems.

Chris nodded. "Well, I don't have a long-term solution for you, kid, but I can tell you that your weekend is yours. How's that?"

"Thanks, Chris." He hoped the gratitude in his voice was crystal clear.

"Good, now that *that's* settled, do we have the labs on the Reeves murder?"

Tad grunted. "No. And yes, before you ask, I tried to light a fire under the techs, but you know…."

"Backlog, backlog, backlog." Castro rolled his eyes. "Any leads at all?"

Tad bit his lip—a tell, but he meant it to be in this instance. "Well…," he said, "their cousin, the one who was *so* helpful in the first interview?"

"Yeah?" Chris held out both hands and made a "gimme-gimme" motion.

"Would you like to know how much gambling debt he has?"

"Ooh." Chris made a little moue of excitement. "Is it more than my salary? As big as the gross national product? I'm all aflutter!"

Tad chuckled, feeling the excitement of the hunt in his bones. "Yes to the first, no to the second. Think we should pull him in, or do we need to do more digging?"

"Let us dig," Castro said, waggling his eyebrows. "Could be the young man already has enough dirt for us to make a big ole hole."

Tad pumped his arm like he'd done in high school when he'd caught a pass in football. "Booyah! Forensic accounting. It's got me all atingle!"

Castro laughed, and Tad took his seat at the desk across from his partner, and together they moved on to their favorite part of the day.

"So you got everything you need?" Tad asked, trying not to glance around April's depressing room for the umpteenth time. He'd done everything he could for it. He'd gone shopping with her for curtains, helped her pick out a bedspread, all in shades of pink and pale yellow— even hit internet sales for crocheted afghans like their mother had made them when they were kids. Most of those blankets had disappeared after their mother had passed on, and April had… well, disappeared herself.

Tad took a deep breath and tried not to think of April's pink blanket with pink-and-purple butterflies crocheted in the center of pink-and-white granny squares, surrounded with a white border. Their mother had made it for her when she was, what? Seven? Eight? She'd loved it. It had graced every snuggle in front of the television, every blanket fort, every beloved book from that moment on.

April had dragged it with her when her drug addiction had taken her to the streets in search of a john, in search of a fix. By the time Tad had found her, wrapped up in its tatters, the thing had needed a ritual burning, along with her clothes.

And her hair.

He shuddered, hauled back to those terrible weeks and the things he'd done to get her clean. God, all that because of a blanket.

Fucking blanket.

Tad couldn't find *that* one, but he'd found others, in other colors. "Different," he'd said. "But, you know—Mom's heart is still here."

April had clung to them. She'd even learned to crochet, like their mother, in rehab, and, along with the curtains and the new bedding, the new clothes—and the ones sourced from thrift shops—a plentiful supply of super colorful yarn in boxes and bags were scattered around the tiny room with its hand-me-down furniture and scratched hardwood floor.

"You don't need more yarn, do you?" he quipped, trying to make his parting easier.

She gave him a droll look, the kind that used to make him smile when they were kids. "Always," she said, picking up the project in her lap. "This won't last me a month."

He chuckled, although she was probably right. She'd made a blanket for every one of her housemates—different styles, different colors. He'd even bought her stitch bibles.

"You say that, but I don't have that new one yet," he joked. His had been the first one she'd made as she was learning.

Her eyes changed. "You don't need another one, Tadpole," she said soberly. "Blankets are for comfort. You're very self-sufficient."

He swallowed, not sure which way to go with this. Should he go with the patented big brother "Of course I'm self-sufficient—I've got this!" schtick, or should he go with honesty?

"You can't crochet me a boyfriend, anyway," he said, winking. There. The joke, the wink… and the truth. God, he was lonely. His last boyfriend had been a closeted fireman. Jesse, the fucking two-timing jerk.

"I could," April said in mock earnestness. "But I don't think it would do the same things for you that a real one would."

He chuckled, so grateful for the joke he could have cried. She'd been in the halfway house for six months—had been in rehab for the six months before that—and so much of that time she'd been pale and withdrawn and afraid. Their mother had died two years ago, and April had gone from the occasional party use to a full-blown addict in less than six months. Tad felt like he'd been missing his little sister as long as he'd been missing their mom.

"Hell, I don't even know what I'd do with a real one," he said. "Except for, you know. The regular things."

She laughed gently, but her eyes went sad. "I'm sorry," she said. "You... you spend a lot of time with me. I know that can't be easy on your life."

He swallowed. "Just... just keep feeling better, April. Don't worry about me. I mean, I'm a cop. I'm supposed to have a crappy love life. I think it's in the bylaws."

She flashed a little tiny smile, but her expression was still sober. "I can't make that any easier either."

"I'm lucky," he said, meaning it. "My partner—"

"Chris," she said, because he talked about work to her all the time. She seemed to like his stories: the bust he and Chris had made the day before, getting the DA to issue a warrant to search on Friday morning so they could bring the suspect in for questioning before lunch had been a roller-coaster ride from first to last. Getting the confession before quitting time had felt like winning the lottery, and he and Chris had joked about which one of them needed to sacrifice a virgin on the roof of the department building in order to get another bust like that.

"Yeah, he's a good family man. He works hard for us to have a really productive workweek, so if we do catch a case over the weekend, it's important." Of course, that didn't always work, but Chris was good enough at letting Tad have enough weekends off to come visit April that the weekends he missed weren't overwhelming for her.

"Tell him I'm grateful," she murmured. Her smile flashed for another moment. "I might even make him a blanket."

Tad laughed a little, but before he could needle her again about *his* blanket, she added, "But I still take up your free time, Tad. I know it. Just... you know. You... I'm not supposed to be getting better at your expense. You know that, right?"

"It's not my expense," he said.

"It is," she argued, her eyebrows drawing in, her thin-lipped mouth pulling together mutinously. In the last two years, her face had sharpened, become pointed and hard, and what had seemed like a playful pout when she'd been in high school or college appeared dangerous and real now. "I'm serious, Tad. You... you would make me happy if you called one weekend and said, 'Can't come today, honey—gotta get laid.'"

Tad laughed shortly. "Sorry to break this to you, 'honey,' but even when I have relationships, they don't work like that." No, Jesse notwithstanding, Tad usually had relationships with overearnest closet cases, or guys who were looking for the poster boy for Young Professional Gay. "Yes, we've had the requisite three-point-two dates, the point two being coffee and/or flirtation over something innocuous, so we may now proceed to sex with the understanding that if the sex was satisfactory, we will move in within three-to-six months because neither of us can do better."

"That yuppie lawyer really scarred you for life, didn't he?" she asked, and he tried not to be surprised that she remembered Sam. That had been about a year before their mother had passed suddenly from a stroke, and she'd been in college then. Most college students were pretty self-centered, and April had been struggling with her own mental health as well. Tad and Mom had been clueless—until Mom had died and suddenly April's emotions were uncontrollable, and Tad was at a loss.

"Ugh," he said, with feeling. "I gotta tell you, all I felt when he left was relief!"

She eyed him curiously. "What made him leave?"

Oh, this was awkward. He was never sure what would wreck her, and he'd been eyeing the clock, thinking he had to leave soon.

"Was it me or Mom?" she asked astutely. Well, she wasn't stupid—just oversensitive to absolutely all emotional nuance and balanced on a razor's edge of recovery strategy and antipsychotics.

"Little bit of both," he said, shaking his head. "I was wrecked—you and me both, actually. He saw us crying on each other at the funeral, and it probably ended right then, but he didn't tell me until…."

Until Tad had gotten back from helping April get in rehab. He didn't tell her that; the sequence of events wasn't important, but the wording of Sam's goodbye letter *was*, and he gave the abbreviated version now. "*Sorry, Tad, but you seem too emotionally codependent on your family, and I need an adult.*" He blew out a breath, and April said what he'd been thinking.

"He needed an *automaton*," she snapped. "Good God, what a jerk! What happened to the last guy you were dating? The fireman?"

He shook his head and told her the Jesse story as he'd heard it. "And the worst part?" he said.

"There's worse?" She was horrified.

"He apparently broke up with this guy when the guy was *in the hospital*, then showed up at my place with a fifth of bourbon and *the other guy's movies*." He shook his head, furious all over again. "I told him to go away and come back sober, but *Jesus*."

"What a douche!" She chuckled a little. "Tadpole, I love you, but maybe you really *do* need me to crochet you a guy. It's got to be an improvement, right?"

He chuckled and then stood from his spot on the edge of her bed, stretching. That was his cue. "All things considered, honey, I'd rather have a blanket."

She rose and went in for a short, hard hug, which he returned with interest.

"Love you," she whispered. "Don't worry so much about me, okay?"

"Oh but I do," he whispered back. "Stay safe and sane for me, okay?"

"Yeah." She kissed his cheek, and he trotted into the dank hall and toward the rickety steps of the two-story house by the beach.

It was cold and foggy outside. He'd gotten her a space heater for her room, but he'd still been able to feel the dankness creeping in through the gaps under the door and the window frames, so it didn't surprise him. As he hopped in his Ford Escape (he'd enjoyed the name, swore that's the only reason he bought the car), he cranked up the heater and shuddered.

And then his stomach growled.

Oh hell. He'd taken April out to lunch, but the place she liked was… well, sort of icky. He'd enjoyed vegan food in the past—if nothing else, tempura vegetables were supposed to be delicious! But this place put a spice that he couldn't place on all its dishes, and he was *not* a fan. Suddenly he was in the mood for a steak and a beer. Before he pulled out from in front of the halfway house, he took out his phone and searched for a steakhouse of sorts.

He found one that seemed to fit the bill. It offered live music on Friday, Saturday, and Sunday, and he thought, *How bad could it be? The ratings aren't bad, right?*

Washoe House turned out to be sort of a regional treasure.

He followed a series of fog-ridden backroads, wondering if his GPS was full of shit or possessed by demons, and was relieved when the giant red-and-white painted farmhouse appeared by the light of soda lamps in the mist.

The place looked like it got a new coat of paint once a year, and as he mounted the stairs, he realized that it seemed to be divided into two sections—family dining on one side and a bar that served food on the other. He asked to be seated in the restaurant, but that didn't mean he didn't listen as, midway through a really amazing steak, the band started to warm up.

Was that a... a violin? He listened some more, heard some guitar chords that didn't sound dirty in the least, a keyboard that sounded practically operatic, and a bass that sounded... oh my God. That was a cello. The bass was a cello. And they were playing in a honky-tonk bar?

This felt serendipitous—like the bust he and Chris had made on Friday. No dirt, no shooting, no miserable slogs through piles of data, everything had just fallen into their lap.

But then a sweet tenor voice with the hint of a southern twang said, "Hello there. We're The Crabs, and you all are pissing the night away!" And with that, the band launched into a version of "Tubthumping" the likes of which Tad Hawkins had never heard before.

It was glorious. The song normally consisted of the chorus, shouted regularly, and a sweet female voice, usually echoing the intro. But in this case, the sweet female voice was replaced by a violin, and the keyboard player did what the guitar player usually did.

And the drums carried the show.

Tad signaled his waitress and asked if he could take dessert and a beer in the bar, and she grinned, taking his credit card and allowing him to start a tab.

"They're great, aren't they?" she asked. "It's Sunday. There's a small table near the back. I'll set you up there."

He grinned back and went to sit down, getting there in time to hoot and holler and whistle for the next song.

"Friends in Low Places" came next, followed by Van Halen's, "Ain't Talking 'bout Love." From Guns N' Roses to Taylor Swift, the band played a truly eclectic mix of pop, country, rock, and oldies. As the lead male vocal/drummer/guitar player launched into Sam Cooke's "Cupid," Tad wanted to clutch his chest. The guy was... damn. Cute. He had longish dirty-blond hair, pulled into a half ponytail away from amazing brown eyes, and a narrow, appealing face with a Roman knife blade of a nose—one that had been broken a couple of times, to keep everything from being too boring. He grinned through teeth that probably could have used some fixing when he was a kid, and sang about wanting some help from the god of love because his lover didn't know he was alive, and Tad thought, *I'm right here! Look at me*!

The song ended and the bar erupted in applause, and Tad managed a glance at the clock. Dammit. *Dammit.* It was getting late, and they weren't done yet.

From the behind the bar, he heard the bartender—a fortyish woman with her hair in a messy bun, wearing an oft-laundered black shirt and jeans—call out, "Hey, guys, it's been a *long, long time*, hasn't it?"

The lead singer chuckled from behind the drum set and glanced at his bandmates. "Guess that's my cue, ain't it?"

"You love it, Guthrie," said the violinist, giving him a smile.

"It's your solo too," he said, and she batted eyes at him.

He laughed, stood, and walked around the set to grab his guitar and a small stool, which he parked in front of the microphone at the front of the stage. "Okay, guys. I guess it *has* been a long, long time."

And with that he settled into an old Linda Ronstadt song, and proceeded to break Tad's heart into a million pieces.

GONNA HURT ME

GUTHRIE BOTH loved and hated "Long Long Time."

He loved it because it was beautiful—Linda Ronstadt had the right of it over fifty years ago, and he'd always thought it was one of the most beautiful songs in the world. He loved it because it was one of the first songs he'd learned on the guitar, and when it was dropped an octave, he could sing it passably with his father's C&W band since he was maybe fifteen. Singing this song as he'd learned the fretwork had made him feel powerful, because he could make people cry.

This song made people cry.

Which was why he hated it. Because it had made *him* cry, nearly five years earlier when his heartbreak over Seth had really been gaining traction in his soul.

Three years ago, right before Seth went to Italy, Seth had allowed himself to go out on a "goodbye" date with Guthrie, because Guthrie had wanted to give Seth something beautiful to remember him by as he went off into the world and made gorgeous music. Guthrie had done the unthinkable then—a thing for which Kelly had still forgiven him—and had begged for a kiss to set himself free.

Seth had given him a kiss—a perfect kiss—and had said goodbye regretfully. It had worked, to some extent, because Guthrie had been able to set his heart to rest. It hadn't been that Guthrie wasn't good enough for such an exquisite musician, and such a truly good young man, to love. It was simply that Seth was already in love.

At least that's what he'd told himself then. He'd needed to believe it.

A human thing. If Guthrie could overcome his own broken heart, he could love again.

He'd tried. He'd had two relationships since then, but the problem had been in that kiss. He'd kissed someone he loved—*loved*—with all his heart, and whether Seth returned that love or not, Guthrie knew now what it felt like to love somebody so much that it didn't matter if they loved you back. It only mattered that they were happy.

It was a difficult, almost impossible, thing to do, but now that Guthrie had done it, he couldn't make himself settle for anything less.

Even four months after the wedding, he was still holding desperately on to that hope.

He refused to forget the way they'd gazed at each other. The way they'd touched. Even the way Seth held the two children, like they were his own, like they were precious.

Guthrie knew what love was now. It wasn't his father's "Come back when you're normal" kind of love. It was Seth's father's "Come back whenever you can. I will always love you" kind of love.

With the wedding still fresh in his mind, he could hold out for that—but Kelly's words kept haunting him. To open his heart and see if someone could bring him the sunshine.

Too busy. Music. School. Work. Who needed to fall in love, right?

Until he played this fuckin' song. And the band loved it. The bass and lead guitar players used to be Guthrie's dad and Uncle Jock, but after Guthrie had come out, they'd gone off on their own to play the old bigot's home or whatever, and two of Roberta's friends from the music conservatory joined him. Owen and Neil were good guys, straight as arrows, decently talented, and the four of them made good music together.

And the other three loved this fucking song. Roberta wasn't nearly as talented as Seth was, unless she was backing Guthrie up playing "Long Long Time," and Guthrie wished he could hate her for that, but she still had his back. Even if she was getting pushier and pushier about his private life.

Tonight, with Kelly's latest email burning in his phone, one of the chatty ones that he forwarded to his and Seth's friends because he knew Seth wasn't great with communication, the song seemed to treble from his throat with extra fullness. Guthrie could swear he heard somebody sobbing in the back of Washoe House bar and grill when he was done, and for the briefest second, Guthrie wanted to join him.

Then the crowd started calling for their absolute finale, "The Devil Went Down to Georgia," which they *had* to play as a country western band with a fiddler, right? Guthrie swung back to his drum set, and the spiderweb of love and grief was broken, only the tatters of melancholy floating about the darkened room to brush their skin after their last bow.

"Good job tonight," Sarah, the bartender, told them, handing them the tip jar she'd passed around afterward. "Stay for a drink? Please?" She gave an exaggerated sniffle. "You guys make Sunday nights bearable here, and I'd love to serve you a meal and a beer, right?"

"Got any prime rib left?" Owen asked hopefully, and Sarah grinned.

"Saved you all some. How about you, Guthrie? You good for it?"

Guthrie nodded, thinking the food was almost as good as the money. Maybe better, because eating with the band was always fun.

"Maybe you'll even talk tonight," Roberta said softly. After being graceful and balletic on stage, she was falling back into her coltishness on the ground with the mortals. Guthrie appreciated the difference; he knew that onstage he had a confidence, a presence, that deserted him on the ground too, and it was good to work with people who didn't sit in the sun's golden glow without trying. As much as he'd loved Seth, the younger man had made him supremely conscious of how much Guthrie was *not*.

"I don't know, darlin'," he'd said to Roberta with a wink. "Talking's going too far, you think?"

She laughed a little, and they gathered their instruments and set them in the storeroom in the back before going to sit at the bar table Sarah had cleared for them.

As they crowded back there, Guthrie noticed a man—midsized, stocky but very fit, with hair that was probably auburn in the sun but looked dark blond in the darkened bar—nursing a beer at the end of the counter. Guthrie had seen him during the Linda Ronstadt song, his wide green eyes fastened hungrily on Guthrie's face as Guthrie had poured everything he'd learned about love and loss in his twenty-eight years on the planet into the rough and abraded hearts who'd gathered that night to drink.

As Guthrie walked by, their eyes met, and Guthrie saw a spark of something—hope, hunger, something—in those eyes, and he was so surprised he paused, lips parting as he searched for something to say.

Neil bumped him from behind. Neil was like Roberta in that he was only graceful onstage with his keyboard, although he was much smaller than she was, and somehow sturdier. Guthrie wondered if, like Seth, who had been gay and Black in a place where that wasn't always expected, Neil had learned to fight fiercely to defend his right to exist after achieving the offensive height of five foot four.

"Guthrie?" Neil asked. He was unfailingly polite unless someone was rude to him first.

"Sorry," Guthrie murmured, and remembered a Seth word. Mooncalfing. He raised his voice. "I'm probably light-headed. Low blood sugar, you know!"

Sarah laughed and called, "Extra red meat for our songbird here, guys. Gotta keep him in prime rib so he keeps coming back."

There was general laughter then, and they all sat down and ate fried pickles and talked about their week. Neil, Owen, and Roberta were all aflutter about new auditions for shows and a few for studio gigs, and he was excited for them, glad to be asked in on the fun. He was very aware that he was a musical step or six below the lot of them. He'd picked up his skills playing in a bar band with his father from the age of fourteen. They'd been classically trained from practically the cradle, showing aptitude and drive when Guthrie had still been hustling for a free lunch at school. The fact that they treated him as a professional, as an equal, that said everything about them and proved Guthrie was luckier than he deserved to be.

They were playing for pin money here. It mattered that they were friends.

Owen was their storyteller, and he launched into a hilarious account of trying to explain how *Hamilton* did *too* have musical salutes to hip-hop and soul only to be told that if he *really* wanted to hear cutting edge musical theater, he should listen to something like *Jesus Christ, Superstar*.

To people with musical backgrounds—and at this point, Guthrie was included because after working with Seth for over four years, he'd taken it on to educate himself—it was hysterical, but Guthrie thought sadly that nobody else in the bar would laugh at the joke.

Until Owen delivered the scathing punchline, and Guthrie heard a throaty, rolling sound and glanced up, only to catch the same green eyes of the man at the end of the bar.

Who was watching Guthrie like he'd never stopped.

Guthrie swallowed hard, a throb of wanting thundering in his chest that he almost didn't recognize.

Sarah moved to deliver their food, and the spell was broken. Guthrie sighed, investing himself in the conversation of his bandmates for the rest of the meal. He'd learned, right?

"He's cute," Roberta murmured. "I've seen him in here before."

Guthrie blinked, while Neil and Owen engaged Sarah with some conversation—and some wheedling for cobbler for dessert. Musicians: always starving, never rich. They should have had T-shirts warning the populace.

"I haven't," he murmured, although there had been something familiar about him. Had Guthrie just not noticed?

"He's been staring at you for the last three Sundays, Guthrie," Roberta laughed. "Geez, you'll never find someone if you don't let yourself look!"

Guthrie rolled his eyes. "I'm busy," he muttered, cutting a piece of prime rib and remembering another steak dinner he'd eaten, a long time ago.

"You're oblivious," Roberta argued. "By design. For God's sake, Guthrie—it's been four months!"

Guthrie glared at her. "I'm sorry I brought you," he muttered.

"I'm not," she said softly. "It was a lovely weekend. I'm glad I got to go as a friend. And seriously—" She did jazz hands, because she'd been a serious Seth Arnold fan "—it was a total rush for me, and I can't pretend it wasn't. But Guthrie…." Her voice sank quietly. "You'll never know if you're ready to fall in love again if you can't meet a guy's eyes across a room."

Guthrie sent her a bored look. "At the Washoe House?" he asked, his eyes traveling around the rustic piece of history placed outside of Petaluma, on the way from Doran Beach. Sarah and the crew were friendly, and they liked to feed the band, but Guthrie wasn't sure they knew he wasn't flirting with any of the girls for a reason. He'd learned caginess from Seth, and it had been a good lesson.

"That's snobbery," Roberta said loftily. "Lots of people like country and western music. There's *scads* of gay artists now."

Guthrie blew out a breath and tried to forget those hungry green eyes. He glanced to where the guy had been and saw that he'd left.

"Well, this one isn't getting laid tonight," he said, keeping his voice light. Inside he was wondering if the guy would be back. Had he been coming to see the band? Was this a stop on a route? Or had those eyes, fastened on Guthrie's face during that damnable song, really been *just* for Guthrie.

He tried to keep the hopeful shiver from twitching up his spine, but he couldn't. It had been so long since he'd even had *that*—it felt like hope was the least luxury he could give himself.

"Next week," she said with confidence. "I swear."

"Right," he said, keeping his hope to himself. It was less painful when it flamed out close to his chest.

They finished their meal and thanked Sarah heartily, then split the tips before they all trooped out to their cars, parked back on the decomposed granite lot out of reach of the lights. They were near enough to the ocean for the fog to be gathering, which made the parking lot even more sinister, and Guthrie was glad they'd had practice in keeping safe.

Guthrie, Neil, and Owen made sure Roberta got into her own car first and that it started and the whole deal. Neil and Owen—who roomed together—hopped into Neil's aging Toyota and left, leaving Guthrie to trudge to his beloved beat-up Chevy truck.

He'd been jumped after a gig enough times to hear the footstep on the gravel first, and lucky him, he was carrying a sturdy guitar case. He swung it wide around, clocking the first guy on the head, and then he used his elbow on the guy behind him. The first guy let out a howl and ran away, holding his hand over his jaw, and the guy behind him swore.

"Mother*fucker*! Give me your goddamned money!" he growled, and Guthrie turned sideways and kicked the guy in the kneecap just as a stern voice said, "Police officer—freeze!"

"Fuck me," Guthrie muttered, holding his hands up, the guitar hanging heavily from his left. Behind him, he heard the tear of footsteps as his would-be assailant took off into the dark.

"That's a bit familiar," said the voice, and near the last vestiges of the soda lamps by the old restaurant building, a now familiar figure emerged. He was wearing jeans and a studded shirt—classic C&W wear—and his shoulders stretched the fabric nicely as he held his gun in a wholly professional manner, still aiming at the empty space where the bad guy used to be.

"Sorry about that," Guthrie muttered. "Can I put my arms down?"

"Since you weren't the one mugging a poor musician, sure," the man said, lowering his gun. "You okay?"

Guthrie flexed his elbow and shrugged. "Been worse. I thought you left an hour ago."

The stranger's smile did flip-floppy things to Guthrie's stomach. "You noticed," he murmured.

Guthrie shrugged again, not wanting to admit he'd been disappointed. "You got nice eyes," he said, hoping he wasn't about to get jumped in the damned parking lot for a whole other reason.

"You've got a nice everything," the stranger told him, drawing nearer. He smiled, the tiny lines at the corner of those nice eyes suggesting maybe he wasn't in his twenties like Guthrie had first thought. Maybe he was in his early thirties, but he had a young-looking face. "But you've got a *really* nice voice. That song does me in every time." He turned and holstered the gun in a harness he must have donned for his knight-in-shining-armor bit.

Guthrie grimaced. "It's fucking sad," he said, and his new friend threw his head back and laughed.

"It is," he admitted. "But sometimes the sadness is important."

Guthrie swallowed, hard. "Takes a wise man to know that," he admitted and then tried to get his head to the here and now before the strangers who'd jumped him came back. "Which reminds me, what are you doing here again?"

His friend grimaced. "Goddamned flat tire," he muttered. "I was struggling with the jack when I heard them get you. Lucky me, my gun and holster were locked in a box in the trunk."

Guthrie gave a grunt. "So you *are* a cop?"

The man shrugged. "Guilty. Work up at Sac, but I visit my sister in Bodega Bay. Last month I caught your act on the way home."

Oh. Wow. "Where you parked?" Guthrie asked. "I can help with a tire."

"Sure," the guy said, turning to guide him. "Aren't you going to ask?"

Guthrie actually counted four steps before he couldn't stand not knowing. "What made you come back?" he asked, drawing near the battered blue Escape with the spare tire leaning against the back bumper. He and the stranger were nearly shoulder to shoulder now, and he could feel the man's body heat seeping through the fog. Even in April, nights got cold this near the ocean, but not here, where he was standing mere inches from a man who'd just saved his bacon.

"You did," his friend said, turning to look at him. "You sang that song, and I thought my heart was going to break. I thought, 'Fuck me, he's pretty, but he's pining after somebody else, and I don't have a chance.' And the thought hurt so much I had to come back for the next three Sundays to make sure."

Guthrie's laugh surprised even Guthrie. "God," he said, "I've been there." He turned slightly and offered the hand not clutching the guitar case. It was not the first time he'd been grateful that Washoe had their own drum set. "Guthrie Woodson," he said. "Auto dealership office manager and C-rated musician, at your service."

His hand was engulfed in a strong, warm grip, one with calluses and rough skin—and a surprisingly gentle touch. "Tad Hawkins," said the man who was no longer a complete stranger. "Detective in the Department of Investigations, Sacramento PD. And I think your voice is the most heartbreaking thing I've ever heard."

Guthrie's chest quivered and threatened to fly apart.

"Maybe that's just the song," he rasped.

Tad Hawkins's nice eyes lit up with kindness... and desire. "I'll have to hear you sing a few more times to decide," he said. Then he grimaced. "But dammit, I need to be at work in eight hours—"

"And you're miles away from home," Guthrie agreed. "I get it. Here, can I set my guitar in your back seat?" He was wearing a denim jacket in the chill, and while Tad set the guitar up so it wasn't on the ground, Guthrie took his jacket off so he could take off his best western shirt, leaving him shivering in his T-shirt but hopefully not about to get grease on one of his three good performance outfits. "Now let's see if we can break that bolt loose, okay?"

"Deal," Tad said. He paused, though, and added, "As long as I can get your number before I drive screaming into the night."

Guthrie's mouth flickered in an almost smile, but he hesitated before answering.

"Or," Tad added, his face falling, "maybe you're still pining for whoever you think about when you sing that song."

Guthrie swallowed and then, surprisingly enough, shook his head. "No," he said, hoping it was true. "He got married to the boy he's loved since they were both little kids with old man's problems. He never led me on, never played with me. And he let me say goodbye to my crush so I could move on. I'm good."

But Tad's gentle expression didn't change. "Sounds painful," he said.

"If it wasn't," Guthrie told him, "that song wouldn't hurt so good, would it? Now do you want my number or not?"

Tad's grin held a bit of triumph in it, but also a satisfying amount of hope. He pulled out his phone and said, "Number first, tire second."

"And then you walk me to my truck before you go screaming into the night," Guthrie said, making sure.

"You'll always be safe with me," Tad told him, and his grin was gone. In its place was a surprisingly earnest, very sober expression that made Guthrie's eyes burn.

"That's good to know," he murmured. He took a deep breath then and rattled off his phone number before settling down to the tire.

Between the two of them, it took twenty minutes, and Tad *drove* Guthrie to his truck, which was blessedly unmolested in the foggy dark.

Tad kept the engine running and the lights on, and Guthrie hesitated, his hand on the door, before he jumped out to grab his guitar.

"Thank you," he said. "For saving me from the bad guys."

Tad shrugged. "You were doing a pretty good job of fighting them off before I came along," he admitted. "Just… you know. Be as careful of yourself as you were of your bandmates."

"They're kids," Guthrie told him. "Music conservatory kids. They'll outgrow me in a year or two, and I'll have to find me another band." It hurt—of course it did. But Guthrie loved playing too much to give up because it hurt.

"Or maybe you can go solo," Tad said, and Guthrie laughed, his heart beating faster as Tad moved closer in the confines of vehicle.

"You must be listening to another musician—"

Tad leaned in quickly and kissed him, and Guthrie, caught by surprise, opened his mouth and let him in.

Oh, as kisses went, it was a good one. He tasted good—one beer and peach cobbler good—and he was warm, and funny, and God, he really did have nice eyes! Guthrie found himself being plundered, and he was clutching Tad's biceps and shaking, he wanted so bad.

Tad was the one who pulled away, breathing hard. "Goddammit," he muttered. "I have *got* to be at work early. You couldn't have noticed my nice eyes two weeks ago when I had an extra day?"

Guthrie laughed humorlessly. "Nope," he said. "Apparently, I wasn't on nice-eye patrol until tonight."

Tad's strong fingers grasped his chin. "Guthrie Woodson?"

"Yeah?" Guthrie asked breathlessly.

"I'll be back. I can't promise when. I wish I could say this weekend, but it doesn't always work that way. But I'll be back. I'll text you tomorrow. And if you don't reply, I'll keep doing it. I'm not above stalking now that you've noticed me, do you understand?"

Guthrie closed his eyes and let out a bark of laughter. "I'm pretty sure you were stalking me when I *didn't* notice you."

Tad kissed him again, and Guthrie was helpless to stop him. He wanted it too damned bad.

Finally he pulled away because his cock was aching just from kissing, and he wanted to start grabbing and ripping off clothing, and they were *in the parking lot of a redneck bar*.

"I'll answer your texts," he muttered before sliding out of Tad's front seat and opening the back door to grab his guitar.

"You'd better," Tad said, still breathing hard. "And maybe, if you *really* like me, you'll sing something else next week."

Guthrie laughed as he shut the door, but after he'd climbed inside his ancient Chevy Colorado, guitar by his side, and started out after Tad, turning the opposite direction when they hit 101, he thought about it. He didn't have an answer quite yet, but he had a question.

He could sing that heartbreaking song damned good by now.

What song could he sing that had some hope in it?

Now that was a question worth pondering.

HE WAS still pondering the next day, as he drank his quad-shot of espresso iced mocha and hauled his polyester-clad ass to work.

He parked his truck, which looked like a dirty-butter-colored sock full of rocks with gray and red primer spots *everywhere*, in the *back* of the auto dealership as he'd been asked to do *personally* by the owner of the dealership itself.

"It's not that we don't like you, son," the man said genially, although Guthrie was pretty sure he did *not*, "but you know, having one of our employees drive a piece of shit like that is *not* good for business."

Guthrie had dealt with good ole boys like this all his life. His father was one and his uncle Jock another, although Uncle Jock wasn't a bad guy. But the box-suit wearing, Brylcream-sporting, toothy, smarmy asshole who put his name on Guthrie's check was the worst kind—oily, disdainful users. Guthrie had needed to put out warnings to all the pretty girls in the office whenever Gene Calhoun of Calhoun Auto Dealership drove up. Guthrie had even taken one of his coworkers, who had since fled for a better job, through the building, finding exit points, recesses, and all the ladies' rooms so they could escape Gene's meandering hands.

The faintest whisper of "Operation Octopus" could empty out the reception area before Gene's heavy cologne wafted across the office.

But the job came with health and dental, and it paid the pricey rent on Guthrie's small apartment. He had other sources of income—his gigs, some residuals from a CD that he'd put out with Fiddler and the Crabs, plus some gigs as a studio musician that the kids in the band *now* got him—but this close to San Francisco rent was a nightmare, and needing a filling could put a crimp in your musical style right quick.

"You're late," sang Martin, the only other guy in the front office, as Guthrie walked in. Martin was supposed to be behind the desk, but he was vying for the next salesman position that opened up, so he was not necessarily an ally. Guthrie had heard him say more than once that "There was no room for two roosters in a hen house," and while he'd wanted to tell the man, acidly, that Guthrie was a different kind of cock, Guthrie also knew that would get him fired quicker than screaming "Operation Octopus" at the top of his lungs and throwing himself in front of Tracy, the tiny nineteen-year-old with the unfairly bodacious chest, who hadn't figured out yet that Gene Calhoun had been trying to get a good grope since she got the job.

Acid roiled in his stomach for the umpteenth time, and he wondered if, since it was his night off of gigs, he couldn't polish up his resume a little and try to find a job somewhere else. After Seth had left the band for greener pastures, Guthrie had used the proceeds from their CD to finish up his education with a BA in Liberal Studies. He'd already worked as a mechanic, a carpenter, and a construction worker, and he'd been desperate for something that wouldn't ruin his hands. It was damned hard to play a gig if your knuckles were swollen or you'd driven a nail through your thumb, and he'd had to do both.

But he was yearning for the smell of grease and a socket wrench about now, because he did *not* like being in charge of this place when the guy who ran it was a danger to all of his employees.

Except Martin. Martin and his straight white penis were safe from Gene Calhoun.

"I am, in fact, exactly on time," Guthrie said sourly, typing the security code into his computer to the minute. "I usually get here ten to fifteen minutes early, because unlike some people, I've got a work ethic. If you get here early ninety-five percent of the time, hitting traffic on 380 once in a while doesn't get you fired."

"Ooh," Martin mocked. "Did somebody get laid last night? Did she leave without getting your number?"

Guthrie rolled his eyes. "No, that's *your* weekend, Martin. I had a gig last night. Fought off a mugger. Strained my shoulder." He grunted and rolled the shoulder he held his guitar case with. He hadn't realized it when it had been happening, but clocking a guy with your guitar case twisted sinews and muscles and shit that were *not* meant to go that way. Of course, then there'd been changing the flat, and then there'd been....

He very carefully didn't think of the kisses, the way his mouth had opened under Tad's like he'd been panting for—*longing* for—kisses just like *that*. God, it had been so long since he'd had sex, he couldn't remember if it was supposed to be that good; where someone's smell, the look in their eyes, their *body temperature* for sweet hell's sake, had just clicked, like cosmic tumblers in the magic Guthrie opening combination that made him want to drop his pants, bend over, take the sex, and sob.

Right as he was yanking his attention to the here and now, his pocket buzzed. Checking the lobby, because being on your phone when there were customers was not allowed, he saw a text.

This is Tad. I'm at a work meeting and thinking about you. Text me back, okay, or I'll think you're a mirage I made up on the drive home.

Guthrie smiled to himself and texted quickly, *Not enough coffee in the WORLD.*

He slid his phone back in his pocket before Martin could glance up from his computer screen and took a sip of coffee before opening his file of customers to see who was due to bring their car in for servicing and who had (poor bastards) answered an automatic questionnaire about would they want to trade their vehicles up.

Thank God he made the big bucks so he could delegate that shit. He made a file of the customers, thought briefly about sending it to Tracy because she'd be happy to do it and she was a sweetheart, and sent it to Martin instead.

"What the—hey!" Martin groaned. "Why do you give this shit to me? Make one of the girls do it. They're not doing anything!"

"In fact," Guthrie told him, "Tracy's being trained on auto bay reception today, and Lana's doing the training. That leaves me to service customers and you to do the hackwork."

"Who died and made you boss?" Martin snarled, and Guthrie was in no mood for this shit.

"I'm your office manager, Martin—managing the office is my *job*. You, on the other hand, are an absolute dick to people, so you can either piss them off anonymously over a cold call, or piss them off face-to-face where they can complain to your manager—*me*—and I have to pass it on to Mr. Calhoun."

"Why can't I be trained in the auto bay?" Martin whined, and Guthrie rolled his eyes.

"Because they all hate you there," he said. "And Tracy has zero write-ups and you have three. Look, buddy, hate to go all power mad on you, but you're circling the drain. Take the crap assignment, do it with a smile, and you might get to keep your health and dental, okay?"

"Prick," Martin muttered.

"Four times," Guthrie said, pulling the paperwork on his computer. "You've been written up four times."

Martin made a sound like air escaping a punctured tire, but he did not make it five.

GUTHRIE DIDN'T mind helping people. He greeted them, asked them what they wanted, hooked them up with sales reps, if the reps didn't get them first. Put them in touch with the maintenance department—and said hi to Tracy, who was a smart kid and doing just fine—when they needed it, and made sure the coffee and donuts were fresh and the area was clean.

Which was something he had to nag Martin to do, because Martin felt it was beneath him.

He was in the middle of cleaning up the coffee station when a woman said, "Hey. You look familiar!"

He turned with a pleasant smile on his face, pretty sure he didn't know her. He was right.

"You're... wait!" Suddenly she blushed. She was a pretty woman, in her late thirties maybe, with a lot of thick, styled brown hair and bronzer. *Mercedes, silver, hangs on to it for sentimental value although could probably trade it in for a bundle.*

He knew he'd seen that car in the parking lot of the Washoe the night before as he'd been leaving.

For a moment, his body washed hot and cold as he thought, *Oh yeah. This is it. There goes my job.*

Then he remembered those kisses in the front of Tad's SUV: The gentle bump of Tad's bold nose along his jawline, the burst of breath in Guthrie's ear when Guthrie had massaged his chest.

Totally worth it. Would repeat. 10/10.

The thought let him relax. He'd done nothing wrong, and this woman wasn't remembering him from a moment in a darkened car—she was remembering him from his few moments in the light.

"You sang that *song*," she said excitedly. "That tragic Linda Ronstadt song. And then you did vocals for 'The Devil Went Down to Georgia' while that girl played the fiddle. Oh my God, your band is *great*. I mean, *unusual*. It's not often that a fiddle and an electronic keyboard and a cello are backing up the drums and lead guitar, but… good stuff!"

Guthrie shrugged and gave her his best self-deprecating stage smile. "We do enjoy ourselves. The kids from the conservatory are *there* to have fun, right? So yeah. We like to think we bring a good time."

Her eyes softened a little as she took in his bright blue polyester polo. "Day job?" she asked.

He shrugged. "Health and dental. Can't crap on that, right?"

She laughed. "Well, keep your health and dental, but my God, keep playing!"

From the counter Martin said, "Ms. Kuhns? Your car's done. You can find it in the service bay."

"Thank you!" she called over Guthrie's shoulder. Then to Guthrie she said, "It's been a pleasure to meet you, uhm—"

"Guthrie, ma'am. Like Arlo and Woody, right?"

"It's in your blood," she said with an impish little grin.

"It is indeed." He gave a small bow then, like a troubadour of old, and she threw her head back and laughed, sounding younger, maybe. Like he'd made her feel good.

He liked doing that.

Cheerfully, he finished cleaning the coffee station and went to wash his hands. On the way, he caught Martin's glare.

"What?" he asked.

"What was that all about?" Martin all but snarled. "What song?"

"What I do on my off hours is my business," Guthrie said. "I play in a band. We do gigs. She was at one. Why?"

Martin's expression grew complicated. "You...." His jaw went slack. "You, uh, ever know anyone famous?"

And oh my God, serendipity. Their overhead music was played softly—loud enough to listen to if someone was bored, not loud enough to impose on conversation. And there, just as Guthrie was about to answer, came one of Seth Arnold's signature songs, released on an album shortly before Seth and Kelly were married. Apparently, it was a surprise to Kelly, who heard the cut on the radio one day during the wedding weekend and said, "Oh my God, papi, this you?"

Amara had told them then that Seth had produced so much good stuff for his YouTube channel that summer that he'd been asked to cut a CD.

Seth didn't remember. "Me and Kelly were, uhm, sort of taking a break. He had family shit to sort, and I dunno. I guess. That *sounds* like me."

Guthrie had been impressed and appalled, both at the same time. On the one hand, the song was glorious. It had to be to cross over from classical to pop. On the other, all Guthrie had ever wanted was to be *that good.* That successful. And Seth had been so intent on the love of his life he hadn't even noticed. Guthrie had wondered if he'd ever be unselfish enough to be that much in love. He still wondered.

But there it was now, Seth Arnold, playing on the overhead speakers, right when Guthrie needed a good comeback.

He didn't say a word. Just smiled evilly and let Martin figure it out for himself.

Martin's eyes got really wide. "Seth Arnold? Like—like *Seth Arnold*! Oh my God. Next you'll be telling me you know Outbreak Monkey!"

Guthrie rolled his eyes. "No, dumbass, because they never played in the Bay Area when I was there." Although Guthrie had heard those good ole boys speak in interviews, and he had a feeling he and Mackey Sanders would get along fine.

"Seth Arnold did?"

Guthrie wasn't sure if he hated doing this or loved it. "Man, look up Fiddler and the Crabs plus his name. See what pops up. Now I'm gonna go check the bathrooms. Try not to shit where you eat for a whole five minutes, okay?"

And with that Guthrie stalked off. Behind him, he heard Martin squeak, "You were in a band together? No shit?" and wondered if he'd live to regret that or not.

It didn't matter. He rounded the corner into a booth, and after a cursory glance to make sure the place was pristine—it was, Tracy had done cleanup a half hour earlier—he closed the door, leaned against it, and pulled out his phone.

Did you get coffee? That was from two hours ago.

Still not enough. You still in your meeting?

Naw. Doing paperwork before we hit the streets and do interviews. You thought of one yet?

Guthrie blinked. *One what?*

A song! Something happier than "Long Long Time."

Guthrie smiled. This could be a fun game. *Journey, "Faithfully."* It was one of his favorites.

Ooh. Good choice for a musician. If you can sing Linda Ronstadt, you can sing Steve Perry.

Ooh. Someone who knew music—at least a little. *But can I sing David Bowie or Freddie Mercury?*

I don't know. Can you?

He thought of a duet he used to do with Seth's fiddle. *I can do the Bowie part of "Under Pressure."*

Nice. You always like music?

At that point, he heard someone at the door outside, and he slid the phone back in his pocket and let himself out of the cubicle, making sure to stop and wash his hands before he left.

He was surprised to see Eugene C. Calhoun there, waiting for the cubicle.

"There you are, boy. Do you know that kid at the counter was talking all sorts of nonsense about you and a band? What do you know about that?"

Guthrie stared at him, not sure how to answer this. "Nothing, sir," he answered, figuring if he was caught out, he was caught out, but he wasn't volunteering *shit*.

"Good. 'Cause if I catch you playing with people of bad reputation, I'm gonna have to let you go."

Guthrie squinted at him. "Bad reputa—"

"That Arnold kid he was talking about. Didn't he just marry another man? Did I hear that right?"

Guthrie nodded dumbly, remembering the bite of the wind, the roar of the sea, and Seth and Kelly's absolute adoration as they lost themselves in the other's eyes. "Yeah," he rasped.

"That's not our kind of business here, you understand me, boy?"

"Loud and clear, sir," Guthrie said and slipped numbly out of the bathroom. He slid onto the stool next to Martin and started drawing up the schedule for the coming week.

Next to him, Martin muttered, "Sorry, Guthrie. I had no idea he was that kind of prick."

Guthrie gave him a glance, suddenly feeling bad for the kid. "Martin, sometimes you've got to assume everybody's that kind of prick until they show you different. I know it's not fair, but there it is."

Martin nodded, his eyes red-rimmed. "You used to play with Seth Arnold. That's the coolest fucking thing I've ever heard."

Guthrie gave him a smile and threw him a bone. "Truthfully, kid?"

Martin nodded.

"It was the coolest fucking thing I've ever done."

Martin smiled like the sun through the fog, and together they started working, quiet in the office until the next customer came in. Martin took care of them without a word of complaint.

SAY YES TO HEAVEN

I'M SORRY—I won't be able to come to Bodega Bay this weekend. Don't give up on me, okay?

Tad's finger hovered over Send. He paused, put the phone back in his pocket, then took it out again, pulled up the text, and erased the last bit. *I'll try next weekend, I swear.*

God. That was worse. And not honest.

Please don't give up on me. I'll see you next weekend.

And he was going to press Send... going to press Send....

"Jesus, kid, shit or get off the pot, fish or cut bait. Shit, get off the pot, cut some bait, and go fish. This is killing me here. Are you going to text her or not?"

Startled, Tad pressed Send in sheer reflex and tried not to claw at the screen and moan, "Come back!"

Since that wasn't an option, he glared at Chris in the confines of their department-issue SUV. They had the window down in deference to the temp in the mideighties, and he was *still* sweating. He glanced up at the apartment, and no, his suspect hadn't moved.

"Goddammit," he muttered.

"What's the matter?" Chris asked, some compassion seeping into his voice. "You afraid she'll spook?"

Tad sent him another glare, and then realized the obvious thing, which was that after a year, Chris still thought he'd be texting "her."

Shit.

"What makes you think it's a girl?" he asked. "It could be my sister."

Chris shook his head. "You get a different expression on your face when you're texting April. Your brow gets all scrunchier, and you get this look like a soldier going into battle. This is... it's different. It's like you're afraid of being gutted like a fish, but you still want to swim."

"You are confusing me with fishing metaphors," Tad evaded, smiling a little because *Cloudy with a Chance of Meatballs* had been one of April's favorite movies in middle school.

Chris cocked his head. "No, it's definitely a girl"—and apparently reading Tad's microexpressions— "no, wait. Boy?" He was asking, but not like it was a bad thing. Like he was checking.

"You're a really good detective," Tad said sourly, waiting for... for anything. He'd really loved working with Chris this last year, and he hadn't seen or heard anything that would indicate this would be a problem. But you never knew. Just because Castro supported Jackson Rivers and Ellery Cramer, the legal defense/PI team that had worked so hard to defend the innocent and root out corruption in their area, didn't mean he wanted to actually *work* with a gay man.

But Chris just rolled his eyes. "Yeah, I'm such a good detective I've detected you haven't seen anybody in a year. Go me. So, boy? Nonbinary? Transhuman?"

Tad's eyes grew wide. "Wow. Uhm, boy. Aren't you, uhm, progressive."

Another eye roll. "Please. I've spent the last few years getting daily liberal lessons from my children. Believe me, nothing is more disdainful than a teenager who thinks you're not liberating like you should be. It's terrifying. I mean, I'll be honest. I have no idea what nonbinary means. But you know what? It is no fucking skin off my nose to respect someone's pronouns. It's like I prefer to be called Chris, and not Christopher and not Topher and not Christoph. But if I wanted to be Topher, then I'd expect you to call me Topher. If someone's not feeling the gender thing, then they're a they. Making that a scary thing would make me the weakest, most cockless wonder on the planet. So, now that you know my politics, who is it? He/she/they? I need a name here or my wife is gonna start fixing you up."

Tad laughed softly. "It's a he," he murmured. "But... but he's skittish. Tell your wife I don't need a fix-up, but I may need some ice cream and a weepy movie when it doesn't work out."

"I could take you out for a beer and pour you onto my couch," Chris offered. "I mean, that is the traditional male remedy for heartbreak."

"Don't drink much." Tad shrugged. "Ice cream and a weepy movie or you'll have to know I'm breaking my heart in my shitty apartment, alone."

"I'll take it," Chris said. "It's a hard bargain, but I'll take it. Now tell me why he's skittish?"

Tad grimaced, looking at his phone again. "Well, he's a musician with a day job, so part of it is he's busy. Like, he texts me from the john at work because his day job is not rainbow-flag friendly. I, uh, saw him perform about a month ago, actually *talked* to him last week, and I was going to go see him again on Sunday, you know, since our workshop was canceled and we've got Monday morning off, but…."

"Augh! We caught a hot one," Chris muttered, scanning the apartment complex they were staking out. Their guy was supposedly in there, doing *all* the drugs, and Chris and Tad were supposed to keep his sidepiece from going in to see him, since his wife and kids were in protective custody. They didn't have a warrant yet, but when they did, they were arresting him for shooting a night clerk in the corner convenience store. Caught dead on tape and identified by several of his ex-coworkers, the guy had danger written all over him.

"Yeah," Tad said in resignation. "We caught a hot one. I just… I was looking forward to seeing him. I don't want him to think I'm blowing him off or—"

His phone made the quiet bloop sound that indicated a text.

I'm not running off with anybody else between now and next week. You've got a real job. No worries. Keep texting. "Glycerine."

Tad had to read the word three times before he remembered their game, where they tried to find the love song Guthrie would use to replace "Long, Long Time."

Nobody knows if that's supposed to be a girl's name or a bomb. Why?

Because Gavin Rossdale in concert is hot enough to blow your balls off from the nosebleed section. Does there need to be another reason?

Tad chuckled. *The Cure—"Friday I'm in Love."*

Well I was, but somebody had to cancel. Chat later!

D'oh! But it was too late. Guthrie was already on the run at his job. That's okay. He'd gotten a dirty joke, a little bit of back and forth on their game, and a smart retort. He was going to call it a win and concentrate on the coked-out failed businessman in his mistress's crappy apartment.

"So," Chris asked in seeming idleness, "is he running?"

"Nope. He did suggest I should see Gavin Rossdale in concert."

Chris snorted. "Oh I bet!"

Tad, who was busy scanning his own side of the street, sent him a look. "What does that mean?"

"It means my wife and I have seen him in concert—about six, seven years ago. He's got this shirt that's all… holey, like, with holes in it. At one point in the concert he puts his shirt on, and he's soaking wet and sweating and oozing sex appeal, and he goes running through the crowd, urging people to reach out and touch him, and you know what?"

"You reached out and touched a rock star?" Tad was laughing, trying to imagine it.

"You're goddamned right I did. I got some of his sexy sweat on my fingers, and I'm telling you, that man almost converted me. Wife and I had some *rockin'* alone time when we got home that night."

Tad was still chuckling when he saw a girl—oh God, it was a girl, right? Nineteen? Twenty at the most?—cross the street in front of them, coming from a side alley that wrapped around the apartment and heading for a small entrance into the common area that needed a key to get into.

"Shit, Chris, that's her. Fitton's girl."

"Oh my God, she's a baby," Chris said, horrified. "Okay, you big brother or me daddy. What's it gonna be?"

"You, papi," Tad said, indicating the girl's Latina features. "She's had enough grungy White boys at this point."

"I hear ya. Let's go."

They quietly exited the SUV, both of them wearing jeans, sport coats, and sneakers. Not standard department dress code, but apparently Chris got away with a lot because he'd been there for twenty, and Tad enjoyed riding in the wake of his practical shoes.

"Heya," Chris said. "Claudia? Claudia Romero? Can we have a word with you?"

The girl took one look at them and went sprinting for the door, key in hand.

"Uh-oh," Tad muttered.

And then someone shot at them from a second-floor apartment, the bullet whizzing by like a steroidal hummingbird and thunking the concrete five feet behind where Tad stood.

"Shit," Chris said. "Get her or he'll kill us all!"

And the chase was on.

TWELVE HOURS later, after a chase through the apartment maze and a body tackle to keep Ms. Romero from bringing more drugs to her boyfriend, Tad and Chris finally emerged from the tiny alcove of the apartment patio where they'd hidden with her during the standoff.

Tad's knees were bruised, and his elbows and his shoulder hurt from breaking through the little wooden patio fence so they'd have a place to hide.

For that matter, his bladder was killing him, and he'd crossed over from thirsty to parched to the dry, dusty husk of a skeleton hours ago.

He was waiting to be checked out by an EMT (and to use the porta-john somebody had installed near the op center where the rest of the force had set up) when he thought about his conversation with Guthrie.

Oh God. He hadn't checked his pocket since two in the afternoon, and it was 4:00 a.m. now?

He looked and saw zero texts, and his heart fell. He accepted the bandages on his knees and knuckles, gulped the Gatorade gratefully, and finished using the john so he could even *think* straight before he rinsed his hands off and texted, *Good night playing?*

He got back an immediate text.

Wasn't bad. Got mugged for tips, though. Still at hospital—fine, but needed to bandage my hand. Hope your night was better. I'm assuming you're safe?

Tad's heart almost launched itself out of his throat. *Now, yes. Long night. Will catch you up tomorrow when Chris and I clear the paperwork. Still playing at the Washoe?*

Yeah. I can do drums, but Berta may have to get a fill-in for guitar for a week.

Oh hell. Tad wanted to haul ass down the road *now*.

I'll be there, he texted. *I can visit April Sunday.* Oh God. That was presuming a lot. *I'll crash on your couch, if that's okay.*

No worries. There was a moment of thought bubbles before Guthrie texted, *It'll be nice to see you.*

You too.

At that moment Chris wandered by, looking as dazed and out of it as Tad felt. Tad needed a shower and a meal and bed.

And to know Guthrie was okay.

"He still there?" Castro asked.

"He got mugged," Tad told him, sighing. Claudia Romero had been hysterical and angry and absolutely sure that if she, and nobody else, went to talk to the guy shooting a handgun from an apartment building filled with kids, then everything would be okay.

She'd broken free of them once, and Fitton had shot at her close enough for her to feel the wind of the bullet pass by her ear. She'd gone limp then, terrified, almost catatonic for the rest of the siege, which had ended with Fitton's death, but fighting with her—and fighting not to hurt her—had strained a lot of their muscles and resulted in a lot of bruises.

"Did you get some ibuprofen?" Chris asked.

"Need some food or it'll rip up my stomach. We didn't get lunch, remember?"

Chris stared at him, then pulled out his phone.

"Brother, it's fuck-you in the morning—not even DoorDash can find us food."

Chris shook his head and then smiled slightly when his phone flashed. "My wife doesn't sleep until I get home," he said softly. "I asked her very nicely if there was anything in the house to eat. Come home with me, sleep on my couch, and have some casserole and a beer." He met Tad's eyes. "It's not a night to be alone, brother. Until you've got a bird in your nest, you can come to mine."

"Thanks, Chris," Tad said gratefully. "So... when do they cut us loose?"

Chris flagged down their lieutenant, who was on-site and who had supervised the sniper shot that had taken Fitton out.

"You guys good to go?" Lieutenant Gresham asked. She was a tiny, weathered White woman in her late fifties with hair she was letting gray naturally and eyes that were still sharp and bright.

"Yes, sir," Chris replied. "Paperwork in the morning?"

"On my desk by two," she said and then gave a faint smile. "So we can all have a Sunday morning, right?" She winked at them both.

"Yes, sir," Tad murmured, and then he smiled a little. "Could you, uh, thank Lieutenant Johnson for that nice shot at the end? I was getting tired of all the fuss." Janine Johnson was the leader of the SWAT unit, and Tad wouldn't trust anyone else with a kill shot in a place so full of friendlies.

"Thank her? I'm buying her a bottle of wine!" Gresham laughed. "And maybe helping her drink it on Sunday. Today was a helluva thing." She sobered. "Nice work tonight, guys. Thanks for keeping the stupid civilian safe and not getting dead."

"That last one was our pleasure, LT," Chris told her, and then he went and claimed the department issue and shooed Tad in, calling dispatch to let them know he was keeping the vehicle so they could go home and get some sleep.

The next morning, Chris dropped Tad off at his apartment on the way to the precinct building so Tad could get his own vehicle, water his plants, take out his trash before it stunk, and pack a couple changes of clothes, as well as put on another pair of jeans and a button-down for work.

He tossed the sweats Chris's wife had given him in the hamper, with the resolution to return them sometime in the next week after he'd done laundry. On his way out the door, he paused at the threshold, glanced around, and sighed. He'd spent some time on the place when he'd moved in nearly three years before, when he'd taken the job as a uniform in Sacramento. He'd wanted to be a detective—was well on his way, in fact—but Bodega Bay, where he and April had grown up, had such a small force, the odds of him getting promoted before he was forty were pretty decrepit, much like all their detectives were getting.

Tad had been so optimistic back then. He'd put up curtains and contact paper since he couldn't paint or wallpaper anything. He'd bought a nice little dinette set—wood, with country-style cushions he'd picked out himself. His couch was leather and comfortable, with one of April's afghans on the back and one that his mother had made him when he'd been younger too. He had bookshelves with books and Lego models on them, area rugs that added color, and prints of some of his favorite movies or locations on the walls.

He particularly liked the one of a field of poppies in the Sierra Nevada mountains, with a white-topped peak behind it and a brilliant blue sky, along with a companion print of a view of the rocks off Doran Beach.

He did love his native state.

He'd done all the right things here to make his little apartment a home, but without another person to take up the downtime slack there, it was… sad. Lonely. Dark.

He thought of Guthrie, alone the night before in the hospital, and threw his backpack over his shoulder with some oomph.

He sure would like that to change.

PAPERWORK WENT long, and afterward he and Chris caught a bite to eat at a nearby teriyaki place—Tad's treat, to say thanks for letting him crash on the couch the night before. Then Tad was on his way.

He realized halfway there that the only landmark he knew related to Guthrie Woodson, musician and office manager, was the Washoe, and he wasn't sure when Guthrie's set started.

On a burst of hope, he headed there, and while the sun was still out at six o'clock, just barely lowering in the mist surrounding the still-green hills, he could hear the music starting as he pulled up to the place.

Walking up the wooden porch of what had once been a B and B and restaurant, he almost felt like he was coming home.

He smiled at the hostess and found his way into the bar, surprised to see Guthrie singing in the front of the stage, guitar in hand. His left hand—the strumming hand—was wrapped in a thick bandage, but he seemed to be doing an okay job in spite of the blood seeping through while his right hand worked the frets.

He was doing "Little Suzi," a song made famous by a cover done by Tesla, and as Tad watched him sing, he became so focused on Guthrie's complete immersion in the song's dilemma—whether or not to let a lover go and fulfill her ambition of stardom or to hold on to the notions of hearth and home any young lover would want—that if there were misses or flubs he didn't hear them. He was singing along with the rest of the bar not to bring her down because she just wanted to fulfill her dreams.

As Guthrie wrapped up the final chords—mostly heartbroken cries—the crowd went nuts, and Tad put two fingers in his mouth and whistled.

Like dark river stones, Guthrie's soulful brown eyes were suddenly focused out in the crowd, and something sweet happened to Guthrie's narrow, intent features when Tad waved.

Guthrie gave a little wink from across the room and segued into the intro for a Cage the Elephant standard, "In One Ear."

For the next forty-five minutes, Tad was lost in the music. Guthrie's band didn't discriminate between time or place, or even genre. Roberta's violin often did the vocals for Beyoncé or Lady Gaga, and Guthrie sang everything from Harry Styles to Eminem to John Legend.

Depending on what was needed—and whether a song could live on a keyboard version of the guitar melody—Guthrie would play percussion or lead guitar, and only because Tad was watching closely did he see the sweat start popping out on Guthrie's brow.

When Guthrie did Blink 182's "All the Small Things" as their finale, Tad turned to the woman behind the bar and said, "You wouldn't have an ice pack ready for him, would you?"

She grimaced. "Yeah, actually he asked me for one when they got here and started to warm up. I may talk to the crowd and have them give him a break tonight for the second set. Roberta and the kids can do those classical versions of pop songs and let him sing." She grimaced. "Oops. He just got blood on my stage."

Tad winced. "Does he have any more gauze for backstage or—"

She pulled out a first aid kit. "You a friend of the band's?"

"Of Guthrie's," he told her. "But the night is young."

She laughed a little—same bartender as always, she had the sort of face made for chewing gum and cracking wise.

She wasn't doing either right now, though. "I'm Sarah. Guthrie's been playing here since he still played with his dad and his uncle Jock. You... you be kind to our boy there, 'kay?"

Tad nodded soberly. "It's the only kind of friend I aim to be." He winked at her, but her expression didn't change, and he understood suddenly what she was talking about.

He wasn't fooling *anybody*, or at least not Sarah the bartender. But she also knew better than to say it loud and clear in a room like this.

"I promise," he said softly, and her intense expression lightened up a little as the song wrapped up.

"Good," she said. "Go meet them in the back room. There's a sink, and maybe you can wrap his hand a little better. I think he changed the bandage himself this morning."

Tad's heart throbbed hard in his chest. He had some Band-Aids on his knees and his elbow, and a bruise on his cheek. Chris's wife, Laura, had dressed all of those that morning, replacing the EMT's work. Like a perfect mom, she'd bustled into the living room and told him to rise and shine. She'd started coffee, and if he wanted to shower, she had a change of clothes for him to wear to his apartment.

She'd taken off the clumsy gauze bandages and replaced everything with the more formfitting Band-Aids, and suddenly Tad wanted a Laura for *Guthrie*, who seemed to have needed one that morning far more than Tad or Chris.

Tad made his way through the crowd easily—he was no stranger to crowds, or shouldering his way through people who were expecting the biggest or the loudest to be the strongest. He met the band as they came off the stage with a nod.

"Good job, guys. Mind if I steal Guthrie for a minute to dress his hand?"

"Ooh," said the violinist. From texting with Guthrie, Tad knew she was Roberta, but he didn't know Neal from Owen yet. "So can you convince him that doing his own bandaging was *not* a good idea?"

"Nobody else in the house to do it," Guthrie muttered, and this close, Tad could see his face was white with pain and slick with sweat.

"God, Guthrie, you should have said something," Tad muttered.

"I saw the news, you know," Guthrie said. "Weren't you involved in, like, a *shootout* until fuck-you in the morning?"

Tad almost stopped walking. "You knew about that?" he asked.

"You didn't text," Guthrie mumbled, practically stumbling the last few steps to the backstage area. "I... I mean there's ghosting and there's being in the middle of a conversation and not replying. I had nothing but time while I was waiting in the hospital."

"What he's conveniently forgetting," said the rather short young man—that was Neal who played the keyboard, he remembered now—taking Guthrie's other side and guiding him to a big trunk near a small backstage sink, "is that he was so busy checking his phone after the gig last night, he let the mugger sneak up on him."

Guthrie grunted and leaned his head back against the wall behind him. "Yeah, he got the jump on me. I swung my guitar case late, and the guy had a knife. We'd made good tips too," he mumbled. "That sucked to lose."

Tad grunted. "Sorry about that," he said softly. "Now give me your hand."

Guthrie sat up uncomfortably and held it out, his face fixed stoically. "Nice bruise under your eye," he muttered.

"Look," Tad said, setting Guthrie's hand gently on his knee and starting with the haphazardly wrapped bandage, "I spent an uncomfortable day huddled under a patio while my lieutenant failed to negotiate a truce and SWAT waited for a good shot. Today I did paperwork, which, truth to tell, felt longer, more painful, and worse. This is different." He got to the skin under the bandage and grimaced. "For one thing, I haven't ripped out a single stitch."

"Aw shit, Guthrie," Roberta muttered. "Okay, that's it. I'm calling it—"

"I need the tips!" Guthrie burst out, and then glowered like he wished he hadn't said that. Tad recalled him saying that his bandmates all had better, more highly paid gigs than this one. His day job covered rent, but groceries and gas came from his performance money.

"Well, you can do vocals," Neal said. "The rest of us screech like a barn owl. Owen can do bass line on all the songs, and if you give us ten minutes, we can put together a set that's not so Guthrie intensive, okay?"

"There goes 'Devil Went Down to Georgia,'" Guthrie muttered.

"Yeah, well, we can do 'The Boxer' instead," Roberta told him pertly. "I'll do the guitar intro. I've been practicing, and I know you know the lyrics."

Guthrie sighed, and like having a thing *to* do as opposed to something he *couldn't* do calmed him down, he closed his eyes and let Tad settle into wiping the blood off his busted stitches, applying antiseptic, and rewrapping the hand.

"Here," Roberta murmured, squeezing Guthrie's shoulder. "Me and the guys will fuck off and get you some more painkillers."

"Ibuprofen only," Guthrie said. "No Vicodin or anything tricky like that. I can't play as well."

"Of course." She pulled a few lank strands of hair off his forehead, and gave Tad a guarded smile. "We'll be back."

The rest of the band disappeared, leaving Tad and Guthrie in the sudden silence, the bar noises and conversation surrounding the black curtain of the backstage area like a muffling blanket.

"This is so embarrassing," Guthrie muttered into the quiet, reclaiming his hand but keeping his eyes closed and his head tilted back.

"Why? Because you got hurt?"

He watched Guthrie's Adam's apple bob. "I just... if I saw you again, I wanted to, you know, not be stupid."

His unbandaged hand lay in his lap, and Tad, taking a careful look around, tugged it into his own lap and laced their fingers. Guitar calluses, ropy veins in the back, even crooked fingers, probably from hard work, made the hand rough and capable. Not soft at all. Tad had to stroke the tender part between thumb and forefinger so he'd know Guthrie could feel it.

"You're not stupid."

Guthrie opened one eye. "Say that with more convict—"

Tad had to stand slightly to kiss him. It wasn't a hard kiss, wasn't meant to tangle them both up or invoke passion or make them yearn.

Some of Guthrie's sass and irritation seemed to leak out of his body, and he opened his mouth and kissed back, sighing softly when Tad drew away and sat back down.

"I've wanted to see you for the past two weeks," he said. "Your texts have been the bright spot of a very tough year. I'm sorry you're hurt, but I'm not here because you needed me. I'm here because I needed to see you."

Guthrie's smile barely twisted his full lips. "I'm damned glad you're here," he admitted, and Tad figured that was as good as it was going to get.

Wasn't bad, really.

At that moment, Roberta stuck her head into the curtained area, paused like she was taking in their situation, and then said, "Okay. We've got a set list that won't tax Guthrie's hand too hard, but we need to have a consult about composition before we start. Tad, it's great to meet you. Go away. Tell Sarah at the bar I'll spring for your dinner—"

"You'll what?" Guthrie said indignantly.

"Shut up, Guthrie. I'm damned glad to meet your new—" Slight hesitation. "—friend. He came at a good time. Tad, go eat. Guthrie, we need you."

Guthrie sat up, and Tad could almost see each vertebra straighten until his shoulders went back. "See you after the set," he said to Tad with a mostly composed smile. Tad nodded and stood, brushing Guthrie's shoulder with his fingers before he left.

STAY

ROBERTA HAD given Guthrie a ride to the gig, although she lived about a half hour away. He could see her relief when Tad told her he'd be taking Guthrie home after the gig.

"Where's your truck?" Tad asked, following Guthrie's directions to 380 South.

"The apartment building," Guthrie said. "Neal and Owen took care of the truck after they dropped me off at the ER. They had work the next day, and when you're a studio musician, you can't really take sick days."

"No, I hear you. You all looked tired tonight," Tad said. "You gonna tell me what happened?"

Guthrie groaned. "Do I have to?" The second set hadn't gone badly. He'd forgotten how lovely the interplay of keyboard, cello, and violin could be when the three of them were trying to sound like a guitar riff. And the penultimate song—"The Boxer"—had brought down the house. They'd followed it up with "The Devil Went Down to Georgia," which had been a mistake. Their band was already a player short for that one—one of the reasons it was their signature song was because Guthrie could do a very basic drum set with the pedals while playing the guitar with his hands and doing the vocals. The crowd loved it; they watched avidly every week to see if he could do it again.

Well, this week he wasn't going to, obviously, so he played the drums while Neal tried to make up the guitar part on the cello. He was close, but there were moments missing from the song, and everybody knew it well enough to hear.

They still got pity tips, though, and Guthrie had taken his share gratefully, as well as some warm soup from Sarah because his molars were still loose. Underneath about three days beard growth was a swollen jaw that was going to take another week to go down.

Talking about it all would probably just make him feel worse.

"Yeah," Tad said dryly. "You have to. I'm… I gotta tell you, I'm feeling the urge to go out and arrest somebody. Please tell me they got the guy."

"Everybody knows who he is," Guthrie told him. "He's the son of one of the big fancy landowners in Bodega Bay. Not one of the guys who *leases* the big properties, but the guy who owns them all and keeps one for himself. His kid's got a problem, needs money to sustain his problem, and knocks over the unwary. We all know what he looks like, what he sounds like, and we know the cops won't do jack or shit about it, okay?" Guthrie's voice rose querulously, and he tried to rein it in. He'd seen the kid skulking in the back of the bar. So had Roberta, Neal, and Owen. They'd all walked out together, along with Sarah's husband, the bouncer. Red had been getting the others in their cars while Guthrie walked toward his truck, which was parked a little farther out, and the kid had rushed him. Guthrie defended himself, as usual, but the kid had a knife. Guthrie caught the blade across the knuckles, dropped his guitar, and then actually *grabbed the knife*, because he was dumber than a box of hammers. He kicked the kid in the kneecap, and the kid had dropped the knife, thrown a few desperate punches that made contact, grabbed Guthrie's tip bag, and run.

By the time Red got there, Guthrie had been climbing to his feet, battered, bleeding, and furious—and down the night's take. Red had helped him up, called the guys to come take care of Guthrie's truck, and taken him to the ER.

Where Guthrie had scrolled his phone endlessly, checking for violence in Sacramento.

Guthrie told Tad part of the story—not the part about the phone, or about the cops saying, "We'll look into it," when both Red and Guthrie had told them the kid's name—as Tad followed his directions to the guest parking of a very average little apartment complex in the not-quite-prime section of San Rafael.

Tad stared at the place and took a deep breath.

"Sorry," Guthrie said, feeling low-rent. "It's not great—"

Tad shook his head. "Not that." He gave Guthrie a lopsided smile. "Would you believe this building looks like the place Chris and I were getting shot at?"

Guthrie let out a fractured laugh. "Oh man. You should let me out here and say goodbye. This does *not* bode well."

Tad chuckled and shook his head. "Any homicidal day traders in there with a bucketload of coke and a death wish?"

Guthrie thought about it seriously. "Nope. There's a family in there that owns a restaurant that plays Mariachi music really loud at six in the morning on Sundays, but that only lasts about half an hour. You get up, you go pee, you check your messages, and 'bout the time you want to go scream at them in your underwear, they're all loaded up to the restaurant and ready to start their day."

"Seriously?"

Guthrie shrugged. "Yeah. Place ain't upscale, but it's not a single wide in a swamp either."

"I'll take it. Hope your couch is comfy."

Guthrie nodded. "Newest piece of furniture in the place." His first couch had been a hand-me-down with springs that would disembowel an occupant the hard way. The couch had been the only thing he'd really bought with his Fiddler and the Crabs money. He'd mostly used the proceeds to invest in his education.

Guthrie had a sudden thought of Tad on the couch while Guthrie curled up in his queen-sized and slept, and the thought made him lonely. He wasn't feeling particularly sexual—or even up to sex—but that kiss…. It hadn't seemed to want anything from him but basic animal warmth.

With a grunt, he opened the door to Tad's SUV, and Tad grabbed his backpack and Guthrie's guitar and followed with nothing more than a warning glare.

"What?" Guthrie grumbled, making his way into the heart of the place. "What was that look for?"

"I was glaring at you before you could say, 'Don't worry, I got it, it's mine!'"

Guthrie opened his mouth and then realized that was *exactly* what he'd been thinking about saying and laughed at himself. "Yeah, ya got me there." It was past nine o'clock at night, and many of the units were dark as folks either watched television in their bedrooms or were already asleep in preparation for an early morning. Some of the units were still lit, though. Some of them had what sounded like a family—kids arguing over what was on television, adults settling things down. Sometimes there was yelling, but it wasn't a rule. This place was more likely to have young people hosting friends for pizza and videos or games than a fight of some sort.

He smiled a little as they passed the three-bedroom unit that housed probably ten people, all of them related. Mexican, he was pretty sure, because they ran a taqueria nearby. They were the ones who played the music, and most days they were more the fun kind of neighbor than the obnoxious kind. He was pretty sure the whole apartment complex tolerated the early Sunday music because a worn, once-pretty middle-aged woman brought by leftover Mexican pastries about once a month.

"Not a bad place," Tad said as Guthrie let him into his ground-floor apartment.

"There's some nice folks here," Guthrie conceded as they walked through the door. He gestured toward the corner where a dinette table would usually sit. Guthrie kept his music equipment there instead, and he had Tad set the guitar down there. "They watch out for each other's kids. We keep a weather eye on the sixteen-year-old in the one-bedroom who's pregnant and only has a social worker visit. I bring her food from the Washoe sometimes, and I know I'm not the only one. Sweet kid." As he spoke he wandered around the little place, turning on the lights in the living room and the kitchen, which was only separated by a counter.

"I could ask my sister to make her a blanket," Tad said, sounding pleased. "She's always looking for another victim, erm, recipient of her work."

Guthrie laughed softly. "Knitting or crochet?"

"Crochet. She, uh...." His voice trailed off, and then he gave a resolute little nod over the kitchen counter. "She picked it up in rehab. I guess yarn is her new drug. I mean, better than meth, and she goes through it slower, so I do what I can."

Guthrie was aware Tad was peering at him from under nearly colorless lashes, as though this was some sort of test.

"Rehab's hard," he said. "I know folks who'd rather drink themselves to death than try to quit the sauce, and meth's a nasty drug. So good for her. There's a yarn store by my house. Tell me what kind and how much and I'll get it for her."

Tad grimaced. "Can't you let me do a good thing too?" he asked.

Guthrie's cheeks heated, and he felt like he'd been caught out somehow. "Yeah. Sure. Baby colors I guess. Let me know what I—"

"So help me, Guthrie, do not try to pay for it. If April wants to make it, that's a big deal. Jesus, you're stubborn."

Guthrie let out a sigh. "I don't want to fight about it anyways," he said. "Fine. Jaya would be happy for a handmade baby blanket. I think she got kicked out of the house. She's trying—getting her GED, working in a retail store—but you can tell the idea of a baby on her own is scary."

"See, helping people can be a group project," Tad said. His voice, which had grown a bit stony, softened. "And I don't want to fight about it either. Were you going to get something in there or not?"

Guthrie smiled a little. "I was gonna ask you if you wanted a beer."

"Wouldn't mind one," Tad said, glancing around the place.

With the exception of the music equipment corner, which housed a keyboard, music books on shelves, and Guthrie's drum set out of the cases, the rest of the apartment wasn't bad in Guthrie's opinion. Couch was leather and mostly new, with some store-bought throws on it and some pillows. TV was in the right spot, and Guthrie had some streaming services for the comedown after a gig. He had a shelf of books and some nice lamps that lit the place up and some prints on the wall—concert prints, mostly. Folks he'd seen live. One or two posters his dad had made up when they were Fiddler and the Crabs.

"Got some snacks too," Guthrie said. "Sarah usually gives us more than soup."

"You looked in pain and out of it," Tad said, coming to rifle through the fridge. "What you got to eat?"

Actually it wasn't bad. Some of those grocery-store soups, a fresh loaf of bread, some prime cold cuts, some salads-in-a-bag. Eggs and cheese. Living like a bachelor was one thing, but living like a pathetic bachelor was something Guthrie worked very hard not to do. No fridge full of old takeout, no living room decorated with pizza boxes and beer cans. Guthrie may have wanted a little more spare time—he'd *really* love a pet—but he had to live here, and he didn't want it to suck.

"Here," Tad said, pulling out stuff. "You go change or shower or whatever you like to do after a gig, and I'll make us something."

Guthrie opened his mouth to protest, and Tad held up his hand.

"For fucks sake, Guthrie, let me take care of you a little."

Guthrie swallowed, and suddenly the night hit him full force. His hand hurt like *fire*, and his jaw and neck and shoulders felt like he'd been in a car wreck. This once, he wasn't pulling himself together on his own—a thing he'd had to do even with the last two boyfriends he'd tried to have—and maybe he should take advantage of it while it lasted.

"Sure," he said, swallowing. "Thank you."

Tad sighed and set the eggs and cheese on the counter, along with a tomato and some ham. "C'mere," he murmured, and to Guthrie's surprise, he pulled Guthrie close—close enough for their chests to touch—and rubbed his nose gently along the unswollen side of Guthrie's jaw.

"You don't need to be so prickly around me," Tad murmured, doing nothing more than breathing him in. "I swear, I'm not going to go in for the kill. I'm not going to steal your lunch money or beat you up more or make fun of you for having a shitty night. We don't know each other well yet, but I promise I just want to fix you something to eat and make sure you get some sleep, okay?"

"Okay," Guthrie mumbled, and for a moment he leaned his head against Tad's shoulder. "Thanks."

"You're welcome. Now go change. Food'll be hot when you're done."

Guthrie grabbed a plastic bag on his way out to keep his stitches dry and took advantage of Tad's presence—of his care—to take a shower. He'd been smelling his own pain sweat all night and was about done with that.

He grabbed some flannel pajama bottoms and a T-shirt when he emerged from the bathroom. He felt cleaner, but the full weight of his exhaustion had hit him in the shower, and after dressing, it was all he could do to stagger down the short hall to the living room and sprawl on the couch.

He glanced up as Tad brought him a bowl, bottom wrapped securely in a clean dishtowel.

"Ketchup or no ketchup?" he asked.

"Definitely ketchup," Guthrie told him, and Tad pulled the squeeze bottle out of his back pocket and squeezed until Guthrie told him to stop.

He disappeared into the kitchen again and came out with his own bowl and two bottles of... water?

"I thought it was going to be beer," Guthrie mumbled through a mouthful of eggs. Delicious eggs. Hot, scrambled with the tomatoes, cheese, and ham, he'd never had anything so wonderful as these damned eggs.

"You need to take a painkiller," Tad murmured. "No beer."

"Mm fine." Guthrie was on his next mouthful of eggs, suddenly wondering what he'd eaten that day besides soup.

The answer was a resounding *nothing*, and when he set his empty bowl down on the coffee table, he was almost tearful he felt so much better.

"Painkiller's there," Tad gestured with his fork as he polished off his own eggs. "I found it in the cupboard. New prescription, so I'm assuming you haven't had anything more than Advil since you left for the gig."

"You're assuming right." Now that he didn't have to play, Guthrie had no problem knocking back the Vicodin. "Thanks."

"You're welcome," Tad told him, setting his own bowl down. He grabbed the remote control from the coffee table, leaned back, and patted his chest. "Now come here and lay your head on me while I watch some television."

Guthrie stared at him for a moment and then did what he asked. "This is it?" he mumbled, the comforting, glorious strength under his cheek feeling like a reward for things he hadn't known he'd done.

"Snuggling on the couch? Absolutely. Buddy, I don't know if you've seen yourself, but you're cooked and done."

"So cooked and done," Guthrie mumbled. "But this is nice. I'm sorry, though. I had… hopes. You know. We texted for two weeks. Does that count as a date?"

"Looking to get laid?" Tad asked dryly. He found an old sitcom, something innocuous that Guthrie enjoyed too, and let the television sit there, sound on low.

"I don't know," he confessed. "What are the rules here?"

"Mm…." Tad kissed the crown of his head. "The rules are that if you want us to move to that level, you tell me and see where I am."

"Oh God. So grown up. You're making a lot of assumptions there, buddy."

"I am," Tad admitted. "But that's not the one that has you worried."

"You gonna tell me what has me worried?" Guthrie asked, wondering how transparent he really was.

"You're worried that you're going to trust me and I'm going to let you down," Tad murmured. "No, don't say anything. Don't deny it. You may not know this, but I *am* a trained detective."

Guthrie snorted slightly. "So I've heard."

"Yeah, well, I'm not infallible. I've trusted a couple of people who, in hindsight, didn't deserve it. But I can see someone who's been snakebit bad. Was it the guy? The guy you sing the song to?"

"I didn't sing it tonight," Guthrie told him virtuously. He'd taken it off the set list the minute he'd seen Tad in the audience.

"You didn't find something to replace it," Tad teased. "But that was it? The guy?"

"No," Guthrie replied, forced into honesty. "No. That guy—he told the truth. He never took advantage. Was true to the guy he loved. Wasn't his fault I couldn't let go."

"Mm." Tad slouched a little more in the couch, and Guthrie wondered about his day. There was some driving between Sacramento and the Washoe. He probably hadn't gotten much sleep the night before either.

"Not gonna ask?" Guthrie didn't want the conversation to end, though.

"I'm gonna tell you mine," Tad said, like he'd decided something.

"All your super mature, really healthy past relationships?" Yeah, Guthrie was bitter.

"Yup. Listen and be jealous. Ready?"

"Sure."

"So about three years ago I was living with a guy. Lawyer. Uptight, sort of adorable. Worked for the DA's office. Gave to charities, bitched bitterly about a guy he saw as his hated rival, but truthfully I think Sam had a crush on him that he didn't want to cop to. Anyway, was gonna be marriage. I was sure. Then my mom got sick, and I had to spend a lot of weekends down in Bodega Bay, and he didn't want to come with me because they were his weekends too, which, you know. Fair. But she died, and I was starting to get worried about April, my little sister, and he told me to get over it. And by the time I got my shit together and went down to Bodega Bay myself to find my little sister, she was living on the streets and so strung out she still has the scars on her face from when she was picking scabs."

"Oh God," Guthrie mumbled. "That's so sad. You said she went to rehab. You got her there?"

"Yeah, but… but I went a little off the rails to get her there. I damned near kidnapped her and locked her in a shitty motel and weaned her off the damned meth. I… I got lice from her lice and fungal infections from her ringworm, and I had to shave her head, and we both bathed in permethrin for a week to get rid of the other shit, and…." He shuddered. "I told Sam it was rough, told him not to visit, and told him that once I got April into rehab and… and willing to *try* to get it done, I'd be back."

"I'm so sorry," Guthrie said, meaning it.

"I'm sorry for grossing you out," Tad muttered.

"I had to pick my daddy out of his own vomit three nights a week for most of my childhood," Guthrie told him, surprised it came out of his mouth. "I… I get it."

"Addiction is an awful goddamned thing," Tad said, and Guthrie could feel the passion of that statement welling up from his chest.

"Amen." Guthrie didn't have anything to add, but he did want Tad to finish the story.

"So I finally get April in rehab and to a place where I can go off my leave and go back to my work—and the promotion my partner, Chris, kept open for me because he's a good goddamned guy—and I get home and… Sam's gone. Hasn't lived there for two weeks. Responded to my texts. Paid the next month's rent. Left a note saying he hoped I was well, but he couldn't live with somebody who was so codependent on his family, and he needed to move on."

Guthrie was suddenly much more awake. "What. An. *Asshole.*"

Tad gave sort of a broken laugh. "Yeah. I was pissed at him for a while. But you know, in the long run, he was probably doing us a favor. I… I grew up with a single mother. She taught me and April to stick like glue. She taught us that sometimes all you have in your life was one or two people you could count on and never to take them for granted. I wanted a guy who would be one of those people. Sam didn't want that. He wanted easy. I wasn't. So there you go. That's the scariest thing about me."

Guthrie breathed quietly a few times, trying to get a handle on what Tad was saying.

"I would be afraid," he said. "I wouldn't want to let that person down. I… my unrequited guy? He and his husband are like that. They *stuck*. They stuck through shit that would make your heart drop out of your shorts. In fact some of the same shit you went through, but it was a family member. The whole time I was watching them dealing with that shit, I was like, 'That's hard. That's so hard. But God, I'd like to be the person you could count on during that.' So I get it. But I ain't never had that. At least not with a guy."

"What makes you afraid you can't?" Tad asked.

Guthrie was so tired his words slurred. He wasn't sure if what he was saying was going to make sense, but Tad had been honest. Brutally honest. Guthrie needed to be that same thing.

"My dad was a sonovabitch, but I loved him," he mumbled. "Pulled him out of his puke. Got him to gigs. Me and my uncle Jock both played to cover his shit. Honky-tonk guitar player, couldn't hold a job, me and Jock working to keep him fed, keep his lights turned on since I was fourteen."

"Mm." Tad nuzzled his temple, and Guthrie closed his eyes, hating how much he loved that. "That's what got you running?"

"I was twenty-two when I fell in love. For real. Fiddler came in and played the shit out of his violin, and the entire band changed, just to let him play. And... and we played together and ate together and split tips together and... and beat up muggers in the parking lot together. He taught me how to keep my hands safe. Unless the fucker had a knife," he corrected. "But not my heart. And I realized all them girls I was with, I was fooling myself. Those boys I was blowing—they were who I really wanted, and I only seemed to want the ones who thought I was weak for wanting them. But Fiddler... he went off. To make money. Be famous. Went to Italy. Stayed with us to make one CD that made me enough to finish my degree. Get real jobs so I could play at night and have a place to live. But I was heartbroken. And I...."

Oh, he couldn't finish. It was so stupid. Every gay boy knew where this was going.

"You told your dad," Tad murmured.

"Yeah."

"And all that devotion...?"

"Meant less than shit."

"Ah."

They were quiet for a moment, so quiet Guthrie almost fell asleep, and then Tad was urging him up.

"Where'm I goin'?" he asked, the painkiller obviously doing its job.

"Getting you into bed."

"And you're staying on the couch?" Guthrie asked, his eyes burning. Yup. He'd confessed everything, and Tad didn't want him. Couldn't blame the guy. Stand-up guy. And Guthrie was... what'd he call it? Snakebit. Best description Guthrie could think of, right there.

"Only if you tell me to leave," Tad murmured. He paused to pick up the dishes on the coffee table and turn off the light with his elbow. The light from the kitchen guided them down, and after he'd set the dishes in the sink and turned off *that* light, the night-light in the bathroom would get them to the bedroom.

"I've got extra toothbrushes," Guthrie said, feeling charitable.

"I brought my own," Tad told him, taking his elbow. "Here. Let me get you into bed. I'll be there in a minute, in my pjs."

"Then what?" Guthrie asked, suspicious.

"Then I hold you, and we fall asleep, and when you wake up in the morning, you think to yourself, 'I could do more of this.' Then we make plans for that too."

"Why would you want more of me?" Guthrie asked, feeling plaintive. They were in the dark now, the ambient light from the bathroom giving him the faintest outline of Tad in the darkness.

"Because you're a guy who would take care of his dad and then get hurt so badly he can barely talk about it and still love his dad. That's a guy who'll be there through the hard shit."

Guthrie's eyes were burning, brimming over. "I'm tired," he almost whined. "And stoned. Don't do this shit to me."

Tad chuckled and guided him to his bed, pulled back the covers and laid him down on the pillows, where he was glad his hair had mostly dried from the shower, because San Rafael got cold at night, even in the summer. Tad kissed Guthrie's forehead and said, "I'll be back in a minute."

Guthrie doubted. He thought, *Yeah, this would be a great time for him to disappear on me, and I wouldn't blame him one bit.*

He almost fell asleep on that thought before the bed depressed on the other side, and then warm hands circled his waist and strong arms hauled him back against the unyielding line of Tad Hawkins's chest, stomach, and thighs.

"I'm so mad we're not having sex," Guthrie confessed, and Tad chuckled again, this time almost directly in his ear.

"Hang in there, Guthrie. It'll be worth the wait when we do."

Guthrie fell asleep with the feeling of Tad's lips grazing the back of his neck… and the promise. When. He'd said when.

HE WOKE in the morning to find Tad gone—but his backpack still on the chair by the bed. Closing his eyes, he heard the shower going, and he smelled coffee brewing in the kitchen and… ooh. Fried potatoes?

He let his eyes adjust to the light seeping between the slats in the blinds and wished—for the umpteenth time—for a cat. They were supposed to be independent, right? A big bowl of food, one of those self-watering jugs—the cat could get by, right?

But it felt like a cheat. How lonely would it be in this apartment by itself, waiting for a human to come by to entertain it.

Maybe a cat and some fish. But that felt wrong, like he was buying cannon fodder. Maybe another cat? He would have to ponder that. He was just tired of coming home to a lonely apartment all the time. He couldn't imagine, after Tad was finished with… with whatever this was, having to come back to the apartment knowing there wasn't going to be someone else for a while. Definitely a cat.

"Whatcha thinking about?" Tad asked, and Guthrie focused on him as he came in from the bathroom, a towel wrapped around his waist as he dried his hair with another one.

"Getting a cat," Guthrie mumbled. "But I'm too busy for a cat. Did you make breakfast?"

"Yeah. It should still be warm. I've got to leave in half an hour so I can hit visiting hours with my sister. I'm taking her to the yarn store and the beach today."

Guthrie blinked. "Busy guy," he mumbled, absurdly disappointed.

"Yeah, well…." Tad made little scooching motions, so Guthrie rolled over to make room for him. Tad sank onto the mattress and, natural as anything in the world, started rubbing Guthrie's bicep. The touch, simple as it was, made Guthrie shudder, like he needed it, and he realized there was a mostly naked man on his bed and *still* they weren't going to do anything.

"Well, what?" he asked, rolling slightly so he was on his back. Tad changed the stroke to the wrist of his other arm, the one with the bandaged hand.

"Well, Chris texted. Our workshop on Monday was postponed, so I've got the morning off. I was, uhm, thinking—since I don't have to run out in the asscrack of dawn, maybe I could come back tonight, get you from the Washoe, and, uhm, take you home again."

Guthrie smiled at him shyly. "I might not be a wreck tonight."

Tad leaned down into his space and kissed the corner of his mouth gently. "You get some rest, take it easy, ask Roberta if she can give you a ride to the bar. If you're a wreck, I still get to sit on your couch and hold you."

Guthrie moaned a little and then wanted to take it back because he had morning breath, but it didn't matter. Tad Hawkins fixed his minty-fresh mouth over Guthrie's and kissed him, a sort of gently powerful kiss that rolled Guthrie over and over and over until his morning breath didn't matter and his fear didn't matter and all he had was Tad Hawkins, mostly naked, his bare skin under the palm of Guthrie's good hand, his mouth… *everywhere*. Guthrie's neck, his collarbone, his chest….

"If you suck my nipple, I'll come and never forgive you," he croaked, and Tad pulled away, chuckling gruffly.

"Feel better tonight," he said. Then he took Guthrie's good hand and placed it gingerly over the towel at his waist, and Guthrie groaned. His erection was a solid, earthy reminder that Tad Hawkins was every bit as human as Guthrie, and that he seemed to want Guthrie like Guthrie wanted him.

"Yes, boss," Guthrie panted. "Anything you say. Oh my God, seriously?" He pushed, on instinct, and Tad arched against him, his head thrown back like this—just this—was worth everything Guthrie had put him through the night before.

"Gotta stop," Tad panted, pulling Guthrie's hand away and then, disconcertingly, kissing his knuckles. "I want you so bad. But I want to take some time, okay? I… I gotta get dressed, have some breakfast with you, and go see my sister. You're my reward for being a good and virtuous boy, okay?"

Guthrie glared at him, his entire *body* reeling in the frustration of denial. "Son, I don't know where you think I'm fit for anyone 'good and virtuous,' but I've got—"

Tad's mouth cut him off again, this time overpowering, until he sagged against the mattress, his entire body limp with desire.

If he takes you this way, it'll be face-to-face.

The fear of that was the one thing that got Guthrie to back away. "Don't you got responsibilities, virtue boy?"

Tad panted a moment and then visibly pulled himself together. "You're a tease," he announced, throwing himself off the bed like Guthrie was lava. "And I hate being teased so much I'll be back tonight to collect." With a prissy little movement, he tucked the slipping towel in tight enough to stay put. He paused to give Guthrie a sultry wink before collecting his backpack from the chair and shoring himself up with another breath.

"I," he said with dignity, "am going to go get dressed in the bathroom so you don't get any ideas."

Guthrie groaned as he walked away, but he kept his eyes glued on his best towel, just in case the damned thing slipped.

No such luck.

With a grunt he rolled over and pushed himself out of bed. Now that Tad was gone, with his smooth skin and the freckles on his chest (yeah, Guthrie had noticed) and the washboard abs and heavy bicep muscles (because God, every touch got better) and kisses that melted Guthrie's *soul* into the bed and through the springs into the earth far below, every muscle in his body hurt.

He stood up, his legs wobbling for a bit, and teetered to his drawer for a ratty sweatshirt for warmth. This close to the ocean, mornings were chilly even in the summer, and besides the knife wound, his jaw felt stiff, and so did his neck and his stomach muscles—probably from clenching—and his thighs, probably from the same thing.

Urgh. Tad was right. He should probably text Roberta for that ride and spend the rest of the morning in bed. An hour or two to practice the night's lineup and then work.

And then... would Tad really be there?

"You going to put that on?"

Guthrie glanced up and saw Tad had set some sort of land-speed changing record as he emerged wearing one of those flannel plaid button-up hoodies over his T-shirt and a nice tight pair of jeans. "Oh my God, do you ever slow down?"

"Obviously," Tad told him wryly, "or we would have gotten laid by now. Do you need help with that?"

Guthrie stared dumbly at the sweatshirt in his hand and was unsurprised to find himself gently manhandled as Tad took the sweatshirt and helped him slip it on over his T-shirt, his injured hand, his stiff shoulder, and his frozen neck.

When he was done, Tad wrapped his arms around Guthrie's shoulders, pulling him tight, back to front, as Tad nuzzled the back of his neck. Then he spoke in Guthrie's ear.

"Now I know you'll be tempted to get all up in your feelings about how we're going too fast or too slow, or why would I want to come back or whatever. Don't. I want to come back. If I can't make it, I'll text. If I don't text, call the CHP because it means I went off a cliff or something, but otherwise, I'll be there, at the Washoe, unless you tell me you'll be somewhere else, okay?"

Guthrie nodded and leaned his cheek against Tad's. "I really want tonight with you," he confessed.

"Me too," Tad murmured. "Now you go brush your teeth and I'll plate up the food, okay?"

"Sure. Thanks."

In response Tad kissed his cheek, and Guthrie closed his eyes, just for a moment. Then Tad let him go, and it was time to start their day.

AFTER A satisfying breakfast, including spicy fried potatoes with some ham tossed in and a side of sliced apples that Guthrie was still impressed with, Tad tucked his backpack in the corner—a sort of reminder, Guthrie was sure, that he intended to return—and pulled Guthrie forward, hand on the back of his head, and kissed him, openmouthed, until Guthrie clung to his denim jacket and all but begged for mercy.

"Text me," Tad murmured, rubbing noses. "If you're not playing tonight, let me know and I'll come right here. Otherwise, I'll be at the Washoe, watching."

Guthrie felt that shy smile blooming, the one that only seemed to come out with this man. "You like watching me sing?"

"Yeah," Tad murmured. "Someday, maybe you'll sing something special for me."

"Maybe."

Tad chuckled, gave him one more hard kiss on the mouth, and left.

Guthrie sighed, shut the door after him, and wandered through the living room and kitchen, not surprised to find Tad had picked up their breakfast and put the dishes in the dishwasher and the leftovers in a nice little lunch package in the refrigerator.

Guthrie had a thought about that night, and he pulled his laptop up to the coffee table and sat down for a moment to order some groceries delivered.

He ordered ground beef and fresh produce, some milk, some more fruit, some ice cream, and some burritos—because everybody needed frozen burritos—just in case. A few other essentials he was low on, but mostly enough for a hamburger bar, including some tater tots because he liked those better than fries. He thought that if he chopped the produce and browned the grilled onions and mushrooms before he left for the gig, dinner could be pretty quick and, well, something. Not pulled out of thin air but planned. Like a real date and everything.

He set the delivery for early afternoon and yawned, suddenly exhausted. Then he texted Roberta about picking him up, if she could, telling her Tad would get him from the bar.

You feeling better? she texted.

Taking some painkillers and going back to bed for an hour, but yeah, he replied. *Think we can do a zoom jam before we all have to leave for the gig? I've got a song I want to work up.*

What do you want to replace on the list?

The Linda Ronstadt one. At least temporarily. So it wouldn't hurt Tad when he was there.

What do you want instead?

He told her, and waited, antsy, for her reply.

Ooh. Good choice. He'll love it.

I have no idea what you're talking about, he replied, trying to pretend it was true.

You do too. It's sweet. It's a good way for him to know how you feel.

He scowled. *How could he possibly know how I feel? I've known him about a minute, and most of it's been on text.*

Go to bed, Guthrie. You're being cantankerous. When you wake up maybe you'll remember what love songs are for.

He wanted to tell her to fuck off, but that would be rude. He sighed and closed his eyes—and almost fell asleep on his couch. *Fine. Text me at one if I don't poke you by then.*

Zoom jam at 2?

Yeah—but I've got to shower and dress. Thanks, Berta.

Love you, guitar man. Sleep tight.

ALL I WANT

"So," Tad said, hauling two giant plastic bags filled with yarn to his SUV, "you need all of this to make a baby blanket?"

"No," April said serenely. "There's the baby blanket, and then a blanket for the mom. Remember our mom? How tired she was? I just think it would be nice if this poor girl—"

"Jaya," Tad said, remembering the name.

"Yes," April continued, hopping in the car and letting Tad stow the yarn. "It would be nice if she had her own blanket. It's good Guthrie's neighbors are looking out for her. I like doing good things for strangers. There's none of that awkward emotional commitment, but you know you've put something good out in the world."

Tad blinked. "Isn't that... I dunno. Like teaching or volunteer work?"

"Did you hear me?" she asked. "I said there was no awkward emotional connections. My God, Tad, I'm a recovering junkie. How many spoons do you think I have?"

Tad shook his head. April had tried explaining "spoon theory" to him—the idea that she only had X amount of energy in her for making human connections, but he always got lost at the place where she got more spoons from being alone.

In the end, he sort of figured that if she said she didn't have the emotional reserves, he should respect that and not ask her what her fuel was. He had a suspicion it came in yardage of wool/acrylic worsted, and he'd never been good at math.

"Well, if you have enough spoons for Guthrie's neighbor, I think that would be nice," he said. "And I'm grateful."

"If you want to be grateful," April said, "tell me more about this Guthrie person that you're so excited to watch sing."

Tad tried to fight a blush. "No excitement," he lied. "We've known each other for five minutes, and there's been texting." And some really *good* kisses. And sort of a promise that there'd be more kisses that night. And maybe more than that.

"Does he seem like a solid guy?" she asked as he started the car up and headed for the beach. "Stop for some sodas and sandwiches, okay?"

He glanced at her happily. "I'll go to that deli you like."

"You're a good egg, big brother," she said with a quiet smile.

He slid a glance at her, saw her auburn hair pulled back in a ponytail, and her eyes—a sort of restless gray-green—were less troubled than he'd seen them in quite a while. Suddenly he wanted him and Guthrie to work out for *April* as much as he wanted it to work out for *him*. Then he thought of Guthrie, practically fainting to finish his gig, the commitment he'd made to his band, to the bar, all of it, driving him to play beyond pain.

Tad wanted him. So badly. He wanted them to work for *Guthrie*. He knew better than to try to judge a performer by their performance, but there was something so sublimely lonely about Guthrie, singing heartbreak songs for a rowdy crowd who, nevertheless, sank into his heartbreak and embraced it as their own.

"So," April said, breaking the silence, "we've established you're a good egg—now *talk*, egg, *talk*."

"He's a musician," Tad said with a shrug. "And he's skittish. He… he says he was in love once, and the guy was in love with someone else but was still really kind. Guthrie's got nothing bad to say about the guy, but you can tell. He's *terrified* about caring for someone else who isn't going to love him back."

"Yikes," April said. "That sounds… dangerous. Like he could hurt *you*."

Tad grunted. "The thought has occurred to me," he admitted.

"But you're going to see him anyway."

She couldn't help it. She didn't have the memory of Guthrie sprawled against his chest, so tired he could barely talk but still pouring out his heart. "I went to watch him perform three times before he even noticed me," he admitted. "I mean… *three times*."

"Was the person as good as the performer?" she asked.

"Better," he admitted, remembering Guthrie's calm way of taking care of the mugger, his irritation and lack of self-pity when he'd failed to ward off a second attack. "He's got this strength in his heart. And, you know, good egg. Like, I think he *really wants* a cat, but he doesn't want the cat to be in an empty apartment, and he's got a day job and gigs and rehearsal and stuff, so he hasn't gotten one."

"That's a good guy," April said decisively. "He knows how many spoons he has, and he doesn't promise spoons when he can't deliver."

"So yeah," Tad said. "I'm going to go watch him play tonight."

"And when are you going home?" April asked, raising her eyebrows.

He shrugged. "Maybe tonight."

"And…?"

"Maybe tomorrow," he admitted, his cheeks heating.

"Take care of your heart, big brother," she murmured. Then, "Ooh—let's get some ice cream before we stop at the deli!"

So they did that too.

Doran Beach was one of their favorite places. They brought a kite and flew it for about an hour before, thighs and arms aching, feet cold from wading in the surf, they retreated to the car in time for Tad to take her home.

He helped her into her room with her giant bags of yarn, and she gave him a hug before he left.

"Thanks for the visit," she said, her voice going rough.

Some of her well-being slipped away, and he was aware, again, of how lonely she was here.

"I'll always visit you," he said. "Are you sure you don't want to move up to Sacramento with me?"

In the past, he'd never been able to finish the sentence without a violent brush-off, but now she chewed her lip.

"I… I saw an old friend of mine," she admitted, surprising him badly. "She… she looked awful. Was wandering the street, half-naked. She didn't recognize me. And… I wanted to go help her, but I was suddenly so afraid. If I helped her, I might *become* her again. Tad, I don't want to be that person anymore. But here…."

She had no choices.

"I've got a guest room," he said softly. "You can get a job in a… I don't know. Craft store. I can't promise you won't see temptation, but…."

"But it won't know me by name," she said with a short laugh. "Let me think about it. Talk to some people. Maybe there's a halfway house in Sacramento I can move into, okay? I-I do better when I see you, Taddy. I wish I could be less needy, but…." Her voice wobbled, and he hugged her again.

"Hey, hey," he soothed, his eyes burning. "Baby, you need me all you want. You ask me for help. I am *made* to help you, okay? Tell me what you need, when you want to move, I'll see what I can do from my end. Deal?"

She pulled back and smiled at him, her cheeks shiny with tears but her smile gentle. "Deal," she rasped. Then she sniffed. "If *you* got a cat, and *I* lived nearby, I could *visit* your cat. That would be fun, right?"

"I'd love that," he said, seeing it so clearly it was all he could do not to stop and pick up a kitten on his way to the Washoe bar and grill. "Just like I'd love it if we lived close. I mean, I'd still be late, and I'd still work some weekends, but—"

"But I could wander over to your apartment when I was alone and feeling sad," she said. "And play with your cat."

"And play with my cat." And raid his DVDs and use his streaming service and play games and cards and go with him to farmers markets and… and be his *sister* and know that someone was in her life to make life not so lonely.

"Good. We'll do our homework and see what we can manage," she said. "Now go. You don't want to be late!"

One more hug. So much hope. And then he left.

HE GOT to the Washoe as the band was setting up, Guthrie sitting on a bench by the bar, sulking.

"They won't let you set up?" Tad asked, sauntering in, hands in his pockets, and Guthrie glared at him.

"No. No they won't."

"Won't let him play guitar," Neal said, walking out of the little back room with a stand for his keyboard.

"He can play the drums," Roberta said, poking her head from behind the kit. "But I get to set them up. It's fun, by the way. It's like giant Tetris!"

"I'm just mad," Guthrie muttered. "I *like* playing. And we've only got three more weeks here before Sarah kicks us to the curb."

"They switch up bands in the summer, Guthrie," Roberta said with patience. "They did it last summer too. You *like* Tickety-Boo."

Guthrie blew out a breath. "It's true," he admitted to Tad. "I do like Tickety-Boo—they're a good summer band. And we've got another gig down closer to the city we play, but these guys all have a theater run from mid-June to September." He scowled. "It's not like I'm gonna miss them or anything!"

"Yeah, Guthrie, we're not gonna miss you *at all*," Owen muttered, rolling his eyes as he stood up and set his cello by the stand. Then looking right and left, he said, "And I may be able to get us a one-night-a-week gig in July. Don't nobody count on it, but that way we can work up our winter season playlist."

"Cool," Neal said, and Roberta grinned.

Guthrie, on the other hand, *lit up* inside, and Tad suddenly realized what this band meant to him.

He'd said it, of course. The classical musicians all had paying jobs—they had plays, they had orchestras, they taught classes. Music was their livelihood.

Music was Guthrie's lifeblood, even Tad could figure that out. But it didn't pay his bills.

Abruptly Tad was hit by the sadness of that. Guthrie was good. Everything Tad knew about music told him Guthrie was an *amazing* performer. But paying your bills in the arts was never a sure thing. The kids with the education, with the contacts, they were going to make it. The honky-tonk bar guitarist, he was going to live for each performance and eat somewhere else.

As the band finished setting up and Guthrie swaggered up to the stage for sound checks before the crowd started, Tad thought achingly of how much of his heart Guthrie seemed to pour into each performance.

All of it.

And how much music seemed to be giving back.

The answer was "Not enough to live on."

Did Guthrie have enough room in his heart for Tad with all that music in there?

As Guthrie signaled for them to start keying up their first number, Tad heard the wild, plaintive tones of Guthrie's voice, the voice and the soul that had captivated him from the first, and brother, did he hope so.

Tad watched their first set thirstily, living for every note. When their penultimate tune came up, their torch song, Guthrie spoke into the mic.

"Now usually we do 'Long Long Time' for you all, but I thought we'd change it up. Don't worry—if you hate this song, we'll go back."

There were some disappointed "Aww" noises, but then Owen started on the keyboard with a familiar riff, and Tad's heart stuttered in his chest.

As the beginning notes of the old Journey tune started, he had to fight not to close his eyes. The music was sweet—heart-wrenchingly sweet—but the look on Guthrie's face as he closed his eyes and sang of faithful love while living a musician's life? Tad could see everything written there: The struggle to balance music and love, the hardships of a certain kind of life, and finally, the promise. The promise to stand by a lover in spite of all the pain and all the obstacles that the world could put in the way. Faithfully.

The last notes of the song died away, and there was a moment of absolutely awed hush in the bar before the crowd erupted, the cheering so long, so hard, that "Devil Went Down to Georgia" didn't see the light of day until the second set.

"SHOWER...," GUTHRIE begged as Tad pulled up to his apartment complex around ten that night. "And then I'll make you dinner."

Guthrie had begged off dinner, saying his hand ached and he was still a little tired from the day before. Roberta and the others had nodded and expressed their sympathy, but Tad had seen the young violinist catch Guthrie's eyes as they were leaving and mouth, "Sure!" with a roll of the eyes.

Yeah, Guthrie may have been able to pull off the "still tired" thing, but Tad was fooling *nobody*.

He'd had a simmering ache in his nether parts from the first moment Guthrie had stepped onto the stage.

He was so beautiful. Not when detailed like a laundry list; his nose was a bit Roman, his jaw a bit angular. Tad suspected those things helped his voice resonate. But as a whole, when he was pouring his heart into a song—or sitting at the table with his friends, listening to their banter—his face was so appealing. So... beautiful. It was Tad's only word. He wasn't a poet. He just knew something about Guthrie Woodson yanked so hard at his heart, he'd be stupid to resist it. If he were being pulled off a cliff, it was better to fall and land hard than to teeter on the edge, afraid of pain.

"I'll fix dinner," Tad told him. "What'd you have in mind?"

Guthrie gave him a grateful smile. "Burger bar. Uhm, the patties are already cooked. Heat them on the skillet, add cheese if you want some, heat the tater tots in the oven, and nuke the grilled onions and mushrooms. Set out the fixins and, you know." He gave a proud smile. "Burger bar!"

Tad gaped at him, delighted, and Guthrie disappeared, probably to take the gauze bandage off his hand and wash up.

Sure enough, when Tad checked the fridge, he saw all the ingredients, and as he began to assemble and heat everything, it occurred to him how much work Guthrie had done for this. He... he'd prepared for this. He'd hoped.

Tad reached to the top of the fridge and found fresh buns, the artisan kind, and his heart gave a little ping. He'd ordered *groceries* for this.

This wasn't a one-night-stand kind of thing. This was a beginning. And quite a nice one, he concluded as he warmed the mushrooms and onions.

He threw the cheese slices on the burgers after he flipped them, and Guthrie emerged from the shower right as he pulled them off and put them on their own plate.

"This is clever," Tad said, smiling at him. Guthrie's wet hair had been combed back from his face, and he looked young and vulnerable. Also his ears stuck out, ever so slightly, which Tad found sort of endearing.

Guthrie gave him a shining smile. "I... see, when I was a kid, Uncle Jock used to nuke potatoes and then go through the fridge. Everything was fair game—leftovers, lunchmeat. We'd put anything on that potato, and as long as there was cheese to go on top, it was a good thing. I... I mean, I'm a grown-up now, but I do like a refrigerator puzzle, like Uncle Jock used to call it. Tonight's burger toppings can be tomorrow's salad, right?"

"Right," Tad said happily, and then he sighed. "Although I need to be gone by nine. I report to work after lunch."

"I'm out of here at eight," Guthrie said regretfully. "You don't have to leave when I do—maybe we can wake up and have coffee together." Then as Tad pulled the tater tots out of the oven, he began to assemble two burgers, each one on a plate. "Ketchup? Mustard?"

"Yes to both," Tad said. "And all the veggies. And dill pickles."

"That's my boy," Guthrie approved. "Onions and mushrooms?"

"Totally. Those are genius, by the way. I may never eat a plain burger again."

Watching Guthrie preen was alone worth the drive down from Sacramento. "See? Not a complete disaster. Just...." He sighed.

"A guy without a lot of time," Tad said, understanding it. "It's okay. You're worth the trip, Guthrie. Do you have hot sauce?"

"For the tots?"

"You read my mind."

They ate dinner on the couch, talking desultorily about their days. Guthrie had a whole stack of stories—odd, everyday things—that he seemed to have been collecting during the past week.

"Okay," he said, setting his plate down with the burger mostly eaten and about half the tots left. "So I'm driving to work Friday morning, and there's this guy on a bicycle—a *bicycle*, mind you—coming from the direction of the hardware store. He was steering with one hand on a *very* busy road, and balanced on the nut-crusher bar by the seat, partly between his thighs as he pedaled and partly with his hand, was a—I shit you not— *six-foot topiary*. You know, one of those carved tree things? Like, it was obscene! Like a giant peen with a corkscrew base! And the bike was sort of wobbly, but he just kept plugging away, and the nearest cross street was a mile away. I think he made it. I mean, I didn't *see* any police lights or read about any accidents, but can you imagine? I mean... why?"

Tad was full-out belly laughing by now. "I've got nothing," he said. "But I wish you'd gotten a picture."

"I was gonna," Guthrie told him, completely sincere. "But about the time I had my phone out, the light changed to green, and, you know. You're in a car, you're behind the wheel, you sort of need to drive."

Tad chuckled some more and set his own plate down before sinking into the couch sideways, the better to peek at Guthrie.

Guthrie turned toward him and smiled self-consciously. "This is nice," he murmured.

"The eating? The talking? The fact that this is a real date?"

Tad watched as a faint blotchy pink marked Guthrie's neck. He'd shaved—no stubble tonight—and Tad wanted to capture that lush mouth with his own. But they were still a little full, and the conversation was nice, so he didn't mind stretching the moment out.

"All of it," Guthrie acknowledged. "So, uhm, my last 'real date' was about a year ago. I've uhm, tested since. How about you?"

"Same," Tad told him, then grimaced.

"What's up?" Guthrie was good at that, picking up on expression, nuance, mood. Maybe it was being a musician—or maybe it was being lonely—but he was highly attuned to his fellow humans.

"So I told you about Sam," he said grimly.

"Douchebag," Guthrie said.

"No, just, you know. Not… not solid. But anyway, Sam left, and I was vulnerable, and I got hit on by Jesse. Who was a *real* douchebag."

Guthrie reached to the table and grabbed his glass of ice water to take a sip. "You will explain?"

Tad nodded and hoped he could make Guthrie laugh about this story, because he didn't want to sound self-pitying. "Okay, so Jesse is a firefighter, and he's in the closet. Now I get it. I don't advertise. My partner, Chris, just came out as really liberal, so I came out as gay, and his wife doctored my boo-boos on Saturday, and it's official: I'm family."

Guthrie gave an appreciative smile. "My boss got mad because I admitted to playing with Seth Arnold, who married his husband. I mean, forget *me* being gay—knowing a gay *musician*, of all things, marked me for death, so your guy at work has gotta be a good thing, right?"

Tad nodded again. "Yeah. It is. And Chris is the best. But you know—you *know*—you don't always have that option, and I didn't know what Jesse's department was like, so if he's in the closet, that's his business. I want someone to watch movies with, so that's it. And we flirt a little and exchange numbers, and then last summer one of the detectives in homicide gets knifed going to his friend's business office after lunch. It was kind of a wrong place/wrong time and kind of wrong friends—or at least friends who were trouble-magnets, but it wasn't their fault. So we're all standing up for the guy on our off-shifts, right? That's our *job*—to show our brothers and sisters we've got their backs. And on, like, the day after he gets stabbed, I see Jesse come in, and I think he's going to come sit with those of us waiting to make sure the cop's okay, but he looks *furtive*. Like he doesn't want to be recognized. A few minutes later, the hurt cop's friends come in, go right back to the hospital room to visit Sean—they know the doctors—and Jesse goes hauling ass down the corridor, running away like he stole something. Ten minutes later, Sean's friends are on the way back, and I hear one of them say, 'Broke up with him *in the hospital*?' and holy shit. I mean… *holy shit*."

"What an asshole!" Guthrie muttered, appalled.

"Yeah, but it gets better. See, the guy in the hospital—he's *very* out. His whole crew is out. It's our own rainbow corner of Sac Law and Order, and yeah, I'm a little jealous. But that night Jesse shows up at my place with a fifth of Jack and a bag of DVDs that I later find out were *Sean's*, the guy he broke up with. And Jesse's like, 'C'mon, Tad—just a night. Doesn't have to mean anything!' and I realize that I have been saved from a fate worse than bad sex."

"Wow," Guthrie said, laughing like he was supposed to.

"It was *amazing* what a douche this guy was."

Guthrie took another sip of water and licked his lips, which wasn't supposed to be inviting, but suddenly it was. "Did he... I dunno. Get his... you know. Comeuppance?"

Tad grinned. "Like in *The Mummy*?"

Guthrie nodded and quoted, "Nasty little fellows such as yourself always get their comeuppance."

"Always?" Tad teased.

"Always," Guthrie confirmed, and they shared a chuckle. Guthrie rested his cheek on his bandaged hand, and Tad wanted to touch his face... and his chest... and run his hands over Guthrie's biceps and....

"Well, finish the story!" Guthrie said. "Did he get his comeuppance?"

Tad chuckled. "Yeah, actually! So fast forward six weeks later. Our injured guy has been nursed back to health by a *porn model*, of all things, and it's apparently true love."

Guthrie blinked. "Seriously? Like... like *porn*?"

"So hot," Tad confirmed. He'd been at the scene for this and had seen the kid in person—muscle, swagger, attitude, and a face that would melt the staunchest knees. "Anyway, Sean shows up at a crime scene with his porn kid because his friends are involved with stopping the crime, and Jesse shows up and starts hitting on Sean. And suddenly, the porn kid, Sean's partner, and one of the trouble-magnet friends are all standing in front of Sean, yelling at Jesse about showing up at Sean's house with... guess."

Without missing a beat, Guthrie said, "A fifth of jack and DVDs?"

"*Yes!*" Tad burst out. "And the porn kid has got nothing to lose. Sean's out and proud, the porn kid gives *zero* fucks, and he's *pissed*, and suddenly Jesse is outed in front of his entire department—not just as gay, which I gather they wouldn't have cared about, but as, you know, *a douchebag*, which apparently made him *very* unpopular. It was *beautiful*.

I mean, it was only luck I got called into that scene with Chris, but it was *so worth it*. I would have worked the scene for free."

Guthrie chuckled some more, and then, to Tad's joy, reached out and ran the fingers of his good hand down the outside of his arm. Tad shivered and gazed into Guthrie's eyes.

"So," Guthrie murmured. "No damage to the heart?"

"Nope," Tad said. "And only a little to the pride."

"And we're both negative?"

Tad felt a smile come on that was not entirely sweet. "Yup."

"You, uh, want to—"

Tad leaned across the couch and took Guthrie's mouth, hard, yearning, showing with lips and teeth and tongue the end to all the self-restraint Tad had been using during the entire meal to not ravish Guthrie the minute he'd come out of the shower.

Guthrie moaned and allowed himself to be borne back against the couch, cupping Tad's face and kissing him back. "Do you," he panted between kisses, "have any idea—ah!" Tad found the hem of his T-shirt and shoved his hands under. "How close I came to begging?"

Tad ran his lips across Guthrie's neck, along his jaw, nipped his ear. "You went to so much trouble," he breathed. "I wanted you to feel appreciated."

"I'm really damned ready for you to appreciate me. Oh damn!"

Tad got tired of playing with Guthrie's chest under the T-shirt and tugged it up, while Guthrie raised his torso off the couch so Tad could drag it over his head.

"Your wish, my command," Tad told him, and then… oh wow. Tiny sand-colored nipples with really pointy peaks. Tad pulled one into his mouth and was rewarded with Guthrie's greedy little cries and his fingers threading through Tad's hair. Tad moved to the other nipple and suckled some more, and this time Guthrie groaned unabashedly and bucked his hips off the couch in blatant invitation.

"My bed," Guthrie muttered. "Please?"

Tad groaned but conceded, rolling off the couch and offering a hand to help Guthrie up.

"I'll get the dishes tomorrow," Guthrie mumbled as Tad paused to turn off the lights and lock the door.

Tad had no problem with that, but he *did* have a problem with Guthrie's bare chest, his *bare skin*, glinting in the moonlight shooting through the blinds.

He couldn't stop touching it.

He herded Guthrie down the hall with mini-touches—a stroke down his back, a cup of his neck and gentle kiss on his shoulder, and Guthrie had to put his hand out to steady himself on the wall by the bathroom.

"We are *not* having sex on the floor," he muttered, and Tad backed him up against the wall and kissed him shamelessly until Guthrie ground his groin—covered in soft flannel and knit briefs—up against the placket of Tad's jeans.

Tad's hands went to his fly, and Guthrie slipped away from him into the bedroom. By the time Tad got there and yanked off his jeans and T-shirt, Guthrie was already naked. He'd stripped the covers down and was leaning against the sheets in the dark, his face buried in a pillow, the line of his body vulnerable and supplicating as he offered himself up to Tad's possession.

Tad drew near and kissed his shoulder, pressing his lips against the tenderness of Guthrie's throat.

"Not face-to-face?" he murmured, a little disappointed.

"I might embarrass myself," Guthrie said, and while Tad could tell he was trying to be light, he could also sense a thread of discomfort, of true embarrassment, in his words, and he kissed down Guthrie's spine, pausing to lave the beginning cleft that led to the canyon.

"Not possible," Tad murmured, placing a precise bite on Guthrie's pale backside.

Guthrie moaned and bucked up against the mattress, and then thrust a hand behind him with a small bottle of lube.

"You are in a damned hurry," Tad told him, pushing gently on his hip and setting the lube down. "Turn around so I can kiss you some more."

Guthrie complied reluctantly, but Tad stood and took his mouth, maneuvering them both so Guthrie was on his back on the sheets and Tad's body covered his. Guthrie's arms twined around his neck, and Tad kept kissing him, stroking his hand down Guthrie's chest, his hips, his thighs. Guthrie sensed the teasing and spread his legs, thrusting his groin up rhythmically as Tad moved his head down that long, stringy stomach to ground zero.

"I want to play!" Tad protested, and he rose up and began kissing his way down again. Guthrie's hands kneaded at his shoulders, at his biceps, threaded his hair. Tad stopped at his nipples again, this time suckling until Guthrie let out a strangled little sob.

"I will *come*," he threatened.

"Go ahead," Tad taunted, moving down his stomach, licking a line along his ribs. He made the touch hard enough not to tickle, and Guthrie's whine of arousal was enough to turn Tad's key. "Come. And I'll taste it and lick you and play with you some more."

"Sadist," Guthrie grunted. He spread his legs then, so obviously needy Tad couldn't deny him. He went directly for Guthrie's engorged cock, tasting it first, running his tongue around the head, teasing the slit and shuddering.

Sweet. He didn't know why this surprised him. It was the thing inside Guthrie that went straight to the core.

Tad needed more of it. Tad needed it *all*.

He lowered his head, took Guthrie's cock to the back of his throat, and swallowed. Guthrie gasped, his torso coming off the bed for a moment, stomach muscles straining, before he fell back against the sheets, fingers tangling in Tad's hair.

"Aw, please," he begged, but Tad wasn't having any of it. He slurped back along Guthrie's length and released him regretfully.

"All of it," he rasped. "God, Guthrie, you taste so good."

He went down again, using his fist to pump while he worked the head with his mouth, needing Guthrie's cock in the back of his throat so badly he would have sobbed for it.

Guthrie reacted like an open nerve. He clutched at Tad's shoulders, gave a soft cry, vulnerable and raw, and came.

Tad swallowed it, shuddering when a second spurt hit the back of his tongue, his lips a little raw from sheltering the shaft from his teeth. He felt his own climax trying to sneak through but pulled back, gasping, shaking from the effort of holding back, and pushed up along the bed, surprised when Guthrie tried to roll over underneath him.

"What the—"

"Please?" Guthrie begged, and Tad frowned, wanting to know why it was so important they did this act—this incredibly intimate thing—without being face-to-face.

But also not wanting to scare Guthrie away by being a controlling bastard. When two people were naked and alone, trust was a precious commodity, and Guthrie couldn't trust Tad if he didn't know Tad would do what Guthrie asked.

"Okay," Tad whispered, pushing back to allow Guthrie room to pull his knees up to his chest, presenting his backside for use. *Is this the only way you think you can have sex?* He carefully, gently kissed the back of Guthrie's neck, down his spine, and to his cleft again, glad he remembered where he'd set the lube.

Tad wanted more *time*, dammit, but he was starting to shake even more, his body primed and wanting. He squirted a dollop of lube onto his fingers and delicately rubbed at Guthrie's rim. Guthrie shuddered, and buried his face in the pillow to moan.

Was that it? Did he not want Tad to hear his noises?

Tad penetrated him slowly, measuring Guthrie's every breath as he shuddered again and thrust back against Tad's fingers until they disappeared inside Guthrie's body.

Two fingers now, scissored outward to stretch, and Guthrie turned his head to the side and whispered, "Please? Now?"

His voice was choked, warbly, but he was begging, and Tad needed to keep the promises their bodies had made to each other. He slicked himself up and positioned himself at Guthrie's entrance, taking in the sight of him, clenched and quaking, facedown against the clean china-blue sheets. He was beautiful, but so self-protective. When Tad took a breath and slowly thrust into him, Guthrie's gasp, the hopeful way he thrust back, the rhythmic feel to his shudders all triggered something in Tad, something prehistoric and caveman.

It was *Tad's* job to take care of this man. *Tad's* job to gentle him, to care for him.

Tad's job to drive him wild.

Tad gave his own wordless cry and fell into the rhythm sex demanded, thrusting into Guthrie's body and retreating, his cock gripped by Guthrie's hot chamber, his need so acute he wasn't sure he could stop.

"Yes?" he whispered. He couldn't see Guthrie's face—*needed* to hear the word before he unleashed the want driving him forward.

"Please!"

That's all he needed. He thrust again, again, again, hard, pulling back by a hair to keep from hurting, until Guthrie gave a guttural moan Tad felt in his *cock*, where they were joined, and begged, "Harder."

Tad couldn't hold on anymore. The want, the need, the *yearning* he'd felt for Guthrie, for his body, for his soul—all of it unleashed, and Tad fucked him hard and fucked him raw and drove himself into Guthrie's body with all his strength.

"More," Guthrie gasped, his voice still wobbly, still broken, but Tad listened to his word and kept going, kept fucking, until Guthrie's little gasps, his fractured moans, could barely be heard above the slap of his thighs against Guthrie's ass.

Suddenly Guthrie stiffened, head thrown back, body frozen, his asshole locked so tightly around Tad's cock that it felt like an angry fist.

The mewl that bullied its way through Guthrie's throat almost broke Tad then, but the shudders that rocked Guthrie's body as he came *destroyed* him entirely. He gave his own cry and poured himself into this new lover, his sweat stinging his eyes as it spattered onto Guthrie's backside, his hands shaking and cold as he tried to soften the heat of their bodies smacking together.

He tried to pull back his breathing, tried to talk, to say the usual things, when he realized Guthrie's breaths were sobbing—but it was more than just his breath.

It was him.

Guthrie was *sobbing* into the pillow, and Tad was confused. And horrified.

Guthrie fell forward, taking Tad with him, and Tad leaned over his shoulder, the two of them still joined. "Are you okay?" he asked. Oh God, had he *hurt* this man? In sex? The thought made him ill.

"Fine," Guthrie said, wiping his face on the pillow. Tears leaked steadily from the corner of his eye and down his nose on the side Tad could see. "I'm... don't mind me. I-I do this. When it's good. It was so good. *So* good."

He took another breath, and it came out shakily, and Tad slid to the side, reaching down to pull the comforter over their bodies.

"Do what?" he asked, invading Guthrie's space. "What—you're *crying*! Oh my God, Guthrie, what did I do?"

Guthrie shook his head and tried to turn his head to the other side, but Tad stopped him with a short, briny kiss of comfort.

"Don't turn away!" he begged. "Wha-what's the matter?"

Guthrie let out one of those laughing sobs people gave when they were overwhelmed with emotion and gasped, trying to pull it back enough to talk.

"I…. God, this is so embarrassing," Guthrie said, taking a deep breath. "I uhm… when sex is good, when I've *really* connected with someone… this happens. I just… I thought it would be a few tears is all. I-I've never just…." He shuddered again and worked hard to breathe through whatever was wracking his body, and Tad stopped trying to make him talk.

He pulled Guthrie close, his face into Tad's neck, and whispered into the now-dry strands of coarse satin hair that covered his face. "It's okay," he said, hoping he got it. "You don't have to hide this from me. It's all right. You can… you can cry. It's not a sin."

Guthrie gave a suspicious-sounding snort, and his heaving shoulders relaxed some as he began to calm down. "Sure it's not," he muttered, sounding irritated.

"Shh…." Tad held him tight, quietly, peppering his face and hair with tiny kisses. "You're safe here with me. It's safe. You can cry. Make fuckfaces. Monkey sounds—it's all good." He smiled, hoping the humor would make the moment not quite so big, not quite so overwhelming for the man in his arms.

"Fuckfaces?" Guthrie asked, his voice a little more level, his body relaxing in Tad's arms.

"You know," Tad told him, peeking through Guthrie's fall of hair and making sure he could see him cross his eyes and thrust his jaw out while he moaned in simulated ecstasy. "Fuckfaces."

Guthrie's broken giggles warmed him, and he let some of the tension, some of the fear of doing anything wrong bleed out. "You do *not* look like that," Guthrie told him tartly.

"How would you know?" Tad made another face, this one with fish lips and squinty eyes. "For all you know, this is what I do when I come."

"Ha, ha."

"No, seriously. I was holding back. I also trumpet like an elephant out my dick. It's mortifying."

Guthrie buried his face against Tad's neck and laughed harder. "You're such an asshole!" he complained good-naturedly.

"Yes, I have one," Tad told him. "And if you let me see your fuckfaces, you might get to see it someday."

Guthrie sighed, some of the giggles ebbing away. With a wiggle he slid far enough back to look Tad in the eye. "I've never... I mean, for obvious reasons, I don't top."

"Is there an extra penis I didn't see that would make that uncomfortable?" Tad asked suspiciously.

Guthrie was enough himself now to roll his eyes. "No, idiot. Just... what kind of top would I be if I'm sobbing through sex. That'll be fun for you." He thrust his hips. "Come for me," he mimicked, making his voice warble with pretend sobs. "Please... wah, wah, wah... please, baby... waaaahhh." He rolled his eyes again and snapped out of it. "That's attractive."

Tad sobered too. "Except it wouldn't be like that, would it?" he asked softly, rubbing his thumb across Guthrie's cheekbone. "Because you'd trust me. And if you let tears fall, and they didn't have to force their way out, you'd simply cry and keep making love. And I'd be happy, because... because that thing you said? About them happening when you were feeling a connection?" He bit his lip. "That's... that's about the best thing I've ever heard. That means you care about me when we're doing this. Guthrie, that's hope!"

"Oh my God," Guthrie complained, palming his eyes to wipe away the last of the tears. "Could you *be* any more of a Dudley Do-Right?"

"I don't know," Tad said, working on the "making Guthrie laugh" angle. "Does the guy in the white hat ever get laid? Because I'm feeling pretty good right now. Pretty satisfied. Does Dudley Do-Right get himself a prime piece of musician ass? Because, uhm, you know...." He pointed to himself and nodded. "Lookit me. I'm a stud. Don't know if you can *be* Dudley Do-Right and a stud. Don't think it's a thing."

Guthrie *did* laugh, and Tad felt like he'd won the lottery. "You are being a goofy asshole on purpose," he said, "but"—his voice fell—"you talked me off my ledge. I was seriously thinking about hiding in the bathtub all night, and that wouldn't be comfortable."

Tad smiled at him tenderly and moved in to kiss him with gentleness and warmth, like grown-ups. Carefully, he wiped the leftover tears from under Guthrie's eyes, the ones caught in the long blond lashes, and kissed him again, pulling back when Guthrie went boneless in his arms.

"I'm serious," he said. "You don't ever have to hide this part of you from me. I-I mean, I knew what we were doing was special. Was *important*. But this—this means you felt it too. I don't mind if you cry in bed, Guthrie, unless I'm *hurting you*, and you don't tell me because you think I'll stop."

Guthrie sighed and nodded. "I… it's going to take me a little, I think," he said, obviously choosing his words. "I ain't never trusted anyone to see that."

Tad nodded. "Well, I'll be honored if you do," he murmured.

"Mm…." Like an exhausted child, Guthrie yawned; his day had obviously caught up with him. "As long as I don't feel obligated to sleep in the bathroom, it's fine. Do you want a washcloth?"

Tad stopped him with a hand on his chest. "I'll get it," he murmured, kissing Guthrie on the cheek. "Stay here."

He understood the need to take a breath, to get some space. He'd bottomed before, knew the shakiness of the thighs, that need for safety, the need to hide for a moment, to master the vulnerability that came from opening your body for someone like that.

And he knew he needed a moment to recover *himself*. Because Guthrie's tears, his embarrassment, the depth of his *trust*—that Tad wouldn't mock those things, hold them against him…. Tad was suddenly reminded, in a real, painful way, that sex could be so important. Sometimes it was easy, fun, a naked handshake that needed cleanup afterward.

But with Guthrie, it had probably only been like that with women, because Guthrie needed that connection to make it good.

He'd said it that first night. He knew what love was now. He wouldn't settle for anything not worthwhile.

Tad had better make this worthwhile.

With a shaky breath, he ran some warm water on a washcloth, wrung it out, and grabbed a hand towel for drying before going back into the bedroom, shivering a little and scrambling under the covers. Guthrie went to take the washcloth from him, but Tad shook his head and wordlessly peeled the covers back and went about washing him off, then drying him, giving a little kiss on his bottom before sitting up and taking care of himself. He folded the towels neatly and set them on the end table before pulling the covers up over their shoulders and turning to face Guthrie in the darkness.

"You want dessert?" Guthrie asked suddenly, just as they were settled. "I got ice cream."

Tad chuckled and shook his head, snuggling closer. "Keep it for next time I'm here," he said softly. "Not next weekend—Chris and I are on the roster. But the weekend after that we should be off." Chris's daughter graduated on Tuesday of that week and left for a senior trip two days later. Chris had been excited about a weekend trip for himself and Laura to sort of celebrate Robin's successful launching for the last month.

"That brings us to early June," Guthrie murmured. "My weekends free up a little over the summer." He gave a tentative smile. "I could, uhm, visit you."

"I'd love that," Tad said. "I want any time I can get with you."

Guthrie gave a shy smile. "Wouldn't mind," he said.

Tad traced a finger over the shell of his ear, enjoying the quiet, the sound of his breathing, the warmth of their bodies under the covers. "We'll find a way," he promised. "I… sometimes my weekends get overrun. My hours aren't always regular. But I'll always be trying, okay? Don't ever think I won't be trying to get back to you."

SLEEP TOOK them over soon after that, and Guthrie's alarm rang at seven, which felt obscene. Guthrie showered first and Tad took second, making coffee and starting eggs while he waited.

When Tad got out of the shower and dressed in jeans with a sport coat, he shivered.

"You forget how cold it gets," he said, taking the cup of coffee from Guthrie gratefully. "I mean, compared to Sacramento. Once you pass Vallejo and those hills…." He shuddered.

"I don't mind the cold," Guthrie said. "The damp gets into the instruments, though." He paused with his own coffee, apparently waiting for the toast to pop.

Tad had noticed a small dehumidifier in the corner of the room with the drum set and the two guitars, so he guessed Guthrie felt that keenly. Then he noticed Guthrie standing in his chilly kitchen in his clean blue polyester shirt with the logo of the Gene Calhoun Auto Dealership on the pocket. He was shivering too, and Tad had a sudden moment of absolutely not wanting to leave.

With a grunt of frustration, he set his coffee down and went to his backpack, where he'd stowed everything he'd been wearing the night before. He came back with his red plaid flannel shirt jacket. It had knit sleeves and a knit hood, and it was the perfect amount of warmth for summer west of Vallejo.

"Here," he said, shaking it open. "Put your coffee down and put this on."

"I've got my own jackets," Guthrie grumbled, but he did what Tad said. Tad's chest was broader—he did like to work out—and the lightweight jacket was an XL, while Guthrie, under his shirt, was probably an L, but a slender one.

"Here," Tad said, doing a couple of buttons. He paused, their proximity achingly close when he was planning to leave for two weeks. "Just… you know. Think of me. Like this." Then he kissed him, the taste of coffee mingling, the taste of Guthrie lingering. Gah! He didn't want to go.

"So, if I keep this, you promise to come back for it?" Guthrie asked, when they came up for air.

"I really love this… shirt," Tad murmured.

"So that's a yes," Guthrie said. "I like that. I'll keep it safe for you."

Tad closed his eyes and pulled up Guthrie's hand, which sported a new, clean bandage. He kept his nails scrupulously trimmed, Tad noticed, which made his calluses even more apparent. These hands knew hard living.

He kissed Guthrie's knuckles and then gazed into Guthrie's eyes again. "You keep *you* safe for me. The jacket needs someone to keep warm, okay?"

Guthrie's "snakebit" smile appeared, the one that said he *really* liked what Tad was saying but wasn't used to thinking of promises and hope like they were a thing.

"I'll do my best," he said.

Tad kissed him again, and this time it was Guthrie's watch, beeping an alarm, that split them apart.

"Shit!" Guthrie cried, breaking away to grab a small lunch cooler sitting on the counter and his keys, which were in a bowl near the same place. "You got me all kiss-stupid! I gotta go!"

"One more!" Tad demanded, and Guthrie ran up to him and kissed him, hard and fast and dirty, before turning to launch himself out the door.

"Lock up and turn out the lights!" he begged as he cleared the threshold. "And text me!"

"I'll text you!" Tad cried, and then the door thunked shut, leaving Tad alone in Guthrie's pleasant little apartment.

Tad looked around, liking everything about the place except the fact that Guthrie was no longer in it.

Mournfully, he reflected that he would do anything—*anything*—to find a way for them to do this more often.

All the time.

Every goddamned day.

HELP ME I THINK I'M FALLING

"YEAH," GUTHRIE said into his earbuds as he stepped out of his truck toward work. The wind was *really* kicking it in today, which made him glad for Tad's plaid hoodie, but even more warming was the conversation. "I'd be happy to have Kelly's sister come stay with me for a bit."

Kelly's youngest sister, Agnes, *really* loved theater. She would be a junior in high school, but she'd gotten a part in a play in San Francisco: four nights a week, with rehearsals starting the next week.

"Lulu's going to come with her," Seth said, like Guthrie hadn't heard that part. "I know your place is small, man. It's just their mom will only let us help so much, and Kelly's doing finances. We're buying a house here in Connecticut and one in Sacramento for my dad and Kelly's mom and the girls. It's just a *lot* right now, but you know." His voice went soft. "It's Agnes."

Yeah, yeah. Guthrie knew about *all* of Kelly's family. The twins, Lulu and Lily; Agnes, the baby; even Kelly's late brother, who had cut a big damage path and left two special needs children in his wake.

Seth had been responsible for this family—or Seth and his *father* had taken responsibility for this family, Kelly and his mom included, when Seth was barely nineteen. That was how they'd met. Seth had needed money for Kelly's family, so he'd walked his gay Black ass into a honky-tonk bar because Guthrie's dad had put out an ad for a fiddler.

Guthrie had chafed for his friend then. Yeah, sure, he'd been in love with Seth, but God—hadn't Seth wanted more for himself than a bunch of old man's problems? It hadn't been until Seth had left for Italy that Guthrie had realized those old man's problems were the promise of Seth's life. That family he was helping to support was the best, most brilliant part of his friend's heart.

Agnes, the baby, was a lot like her big brother. Squirrel-bright eyes, wicked sense of humor, round, cherubic face. And apparently she was talented on the stage in the same way Seth was talented with music, and because this was Seth and Kelly's family, they were doing everything they could to give her the dream.

In this case, it was to sublet an apartment *outside* the city, but San Rafael was still kind of pricey. So Seth had called Guthrie, asking for a favor, and Guthrie had just lost his summer gig. Yeah, The Crabs would be playing at Scorpio for the next month and a half, but after that, the kids all had something bigger, more important, lined up. Money was going to be an issue, and Guthrie could sleep on the couch, drum up more gigs, and have a couple of roommates he really did love, and Lulu could take Agnes into the city four days a week and take an online summer course in physics, because Kelly's sisters were that damned smart.

Guthrie would gladly give up his bed and sleep on his couch for two months—not only for the help with the rent, but because Kelly's sisters were every bit as delightful as Kelly.

Besides. It was Seth.

"Yeah," Guthrie said now, pausing before he went inside because he knew his boss would give him shit if he didn't. "I know. It's Agnes. But honestly, Seth, the timing's great, and I got no problem with company."

"But, uhm, what about if *you* have company," Seth asked. Over the sound of the wind and the distance between phones, Guthrie heard him hiss, "See? I *did* ask him," and Guthrie masked a smile as he realized Kelly was prying into his love life.

"If I do have company," Guthrie said, pretending he hadn't heard, "then company is coming over Saturday night. You said the girls would be up in Sacramento then, right?"

"Wait," Seth said, his voice suddenly excited. "You got company?"

Guthrie shook his head, because the vote was still out on that one. "Well, sort of," he said, clutching Tad's shirt closer. "I *had* company two weeks ago, and I was supposed to have company this week, but company bailed."

He tried not to let his disappointment be too obvious. He'd expected Tad to ghost him. He'd been waiting for it. Instead, he'd gotten a text when Tad had gotten back to Sacramento and started work again, and… and it was like they hadn't stopped texting. Like the weekend—the awful parts and the amazing parts—were just an extension of… of… *knowing Tad*. He still sent Guthrie texts during the day. Guthrie still replied on his break. And at night? Oh damn. At night, once a night, unless Tad was working, Tad would call. They'd chat briefly—fifteen, twenty minutes, usually after ten at night when Tad knew Guthrie would be home—but it was so damned homey. Tad's voice on the other end of the phone so… so *normal*. Like they really *were* in each other's lives and not an anomaly. Guthrie had started to warm to the idea that Tad would… might be… just may become sort of an actual person in his life.

Which was why the night before had been so disheartening. Tad had been planning to come see their last performance at the Washoe on Thursday night. Yeah, sure, The Crabs had the other gig at the Scorpio— at least until mid-July—but their last night was usually a thing. And *Tad* had seemed to pick up on this, because he'd gotten permission to get his sister out of her halfway house. He was going to take her to the Washoe, then she was going to sleep on Guthrie's couch, and Tad would take her home while Guthrie had been at work on Friday so he and Tad could spend the entire weekend together.

There would be another trip to Bodega Bay on Sunday, hopefully, and… and it would be like they were *real*. Guthrie Arlo Woodson was in a real relationship, something with hope at the end.

And then Tad had called him up the night before as Guthrie was leaving work.

"Baby," he'd said, and Guthrie's eyebrows had gone up as he'd gotten into his truck.

"What's wrong?"

And instead of denying it, Tad had said, "Look—we're about to go out of cell service, so if the call shorts out, don't panic. But Chris's old mentor called up this afternoon and asked for SAC PD's help on a raid. He's up in a little tiny town in Tahoe National Forest, and he's not sure he can trust everybody up there with him. I…. Guthrie, Chris is my partner and—"

"And you need to go with him," Guthrie said. "I get it. You got his back, he's got yours. Don't sweat it." He was trying to sound grown up and mature, but some of his hurt must have seeped out.

"You know," Tad murmured, "I was really looking forward to this weekend. I should be back tomorrow, and I can be by your apartment when you get home from work. How's that sound?"

Guthrie swallowed. "It sounds like you need to concentrate on doing your job and staying safe," he said firmly. "I'd love to see you this weekend, but the safe part—that's gotta be your priority."

"Thanks, Guth—"

And true to his word, the call had dropped.

So Guthrie wasn't sure what to tell Seth now. "Listen," he said softly. "The girls'll be leaving on Friday night and coming home on Sunday night, and if my company gets the weekend off, that's his sweet spot right there."

"Where does company live," Seth asked, "that he can't come by other days?"

Guthrie sighed. "Company lives in Sacramento," he admitted. "Yeah, I know. It's a long way off for company, I get it."

"It's a hard way to have company," Seth said quietly. "Is he good to you?"

And by dropping the pretense of "company," Seth made it real.

"He's a detective in Sacramento," Guthrie said. "And he's been... *great* so far. But you know. Guys with old-man problems. I can't seem to stay away."

Seth snorted. "Maybe that's because old-man problems mean they're invested in bigger things. Family things?"

Guthrie thought of Tad's sister. "Yeah. Those things."

"It's *almost* like you want a guy with a big family, because you deserve a big family of your own," Seth said, then he ruined the snark by saying, "Did I do that right?" to Kelly, who was obviously still listening.

"You did that fine. Now give me the phone." And suddenly Guthrie was having another conversation.

"You can do long distance," Kelly said bluntly. "And you can do old-man problems. And you can do all the things if he treats you good. Does he treat you good?"

"Y'all, we've had a month of texts and a really good weekend," Guthrie said, laughing and exasperated at once. "He's been a prince."

"And he's your only prince for a really long time," Kelly said. "And the only prince you've ever told us about. So this is important, and it's going to *be* important and—what does he do for a living?"

"Law enforcement," Guthrie told him, cringing a little. Law enforcement would have blown right over Seth's head, but Kelly's family was *not* a fan.

"Great. You had better fucking fix your truck, *mijo*, or he'll be ticketing you for driving while poor."

Guthrie shook his head. "So far, he hasn't said a peep about the truck. I... I think he does bigger things. Investigations and stuff." He was tucked into a corner of the front of the dealership—the opposite end from where the smokers went to get their fix, but this side was in the wind. He was grateful for Tad's hoodie but still cold, and he had about three minutes before he'd be officially late. But God, he was glad to talk to Seth and Kelly. Roberta was sweet, but she hadn't had a big relationship yet. He wasn't sure if she'd ever had her heart broken—and Neal and Owen weren't in the market.

Seth and Kelly knew life wasn't fair. They knew shit got hard. He trusted them with this.

Kelly grunted. "That's not so bad. You think he's serious?"

"Hasn't missed a text in a month," Guthrie said with an inward shrug. The fuck would he know from serious? Something in his stomach vibrated. "Until today. He called yesterday to say he wouldn't make it to see me play, and then his phone went offline. I... I guess he's still up in the mountains with shitty service."

He'd been planning to be back that evening. Wouldn't he at least be in Sacramento by now?

With a start, Guthrie realized he trusted Tad would get in touch if he could.

If he could.

Oh God. Would anybody know to tell Guthrie about Tad Hawkins if he got hurt?

"Well I hope he gets back early," Kelly said. "You sound worried."

"It's... well, it's not like him not to communicate," Guthrie said, the uneasiness making him shift even more as he stood. With a sigh, he resolved to finish the conversation. "Which is neither here nor there for you guys. Yes, I'd be happy to have Agnes and Lulu stay at my place over the summer. They can have the bed, the couch is plenty comfy. Now I gotta get to—"

"Wait!" Seth said. He'd obviously grabbed the phone from Kelly. "One more thing. The end of August. We're coming to town to see Agnes's play, but there's more. I've got a recording gig for you."

"Me the band, or me *me*?" Guthrie asked, surprised.

"You *you*," Seth said. "I want to do a pop album, and you and me do good work. I'll be texting you songs you can work up on drums or guitar. Your choice, you get dibs, and if you want to do vocals, tell me. I want Vince on trumpet, Amara on winds, and you wherever you want. I've got some other people I want to play with, but you, Vince, and Amara get first dibs. I'll have contracts drawn up so everybody gets paid just for showing up at the practice and recording sessions, but...." His voice dropped wistfully. "I like playing with the people I love," he said. "And it's my vacation, and my agent got backing from a label and some streaming services, and that's what I want to do."

Guthrie smiled, his eyes burning unexpectedly. Seth *never* asked for things for himself. It figured that of all the things in the world his talent and his good heart could bring him, this would be the thing he asked for.

"I can't think of anything I'd rather do," he said, his heart in every word.

"Good. It'll be good money, Guthrie. I mean, I know that's not what you care about, but it'll be enough to maybe let you quit your day job. Enough to let you find more gigs and make your living doing what you love. I'd... I'd really like to see you happy."

"You're the greatest, Seth. I love you madly. Tell Kelly I love him too. Give Agnes and Lulu my info so we can get together on them moving in, okay?"

"Will do. Hope your 'company' is okay. Kelly's right—you sound worried."

Guthrie *was* worried, but that was a whole different subject. "I'll keep you informed," he said, not sure if he would. Seth had just promised to make Guthrie's dreams come true out of nothing more than friendship. Guthrie wouldn't bother his friend with his love life unless he had to. "But right now, I gotta run."

"Later, man."

"Later."

And with that he shoved his phone in his pocket and walked into the blissful warmth of the dealership, hoping Eugene Calhoun wasn't around to give him crap, because he sort of wanted to share his excitement with Martin. The last month or so had proven that Martin could be a much nicer guy when he was talking about music, and with a few HR lessons, Guthrie could get him to *not* be a complete dick about women.

But as Guthrie walked in the door, Martin gave him a quick dart of the eyes toward the back where employees were required to clock in. Calhoun was known to get in front of people, monopolize their time, and then dock their pay if they were so much as two minutes late, for spite, and Guthrie figured that was what was going on now.

Guthrie nodded and said loudly, "Hey, Martin, do me a favor and go to the maintenance bay. Tell Tracy about the computer glitch we had yesterday."

Martin slid out from behind the counter one way, winking, waiting for Calhoun to follow him as he complained loudly about how people *broke* the computers because they were stupid, particularly females because they didn't understand the machines. As Calhoun aimed his irritation at Martin's back, Guthrie slid around the corner and through the back from the other direction, making it to the time clock and out into the front before Calhoun could figure out he'd been had.

Martin was moving slowly. They'd practiced this maneuver before, mostly for Martin, who took the bus and couldn't always get there ten minutes early, but sometimes for the other employees because Calhoun was a prick and no amount of health and dental was worth the harassment. He was still there while Guthrie slid right into his seat, booted up his computer, and said, "Wait, Martin, I'm sorry. The glitch has cleared up. My bad."

Martin barely let a smile quirk at his lips as he said, "No worries. Here, I'll show you how far I got on the invoices, okay? I picked up from where you left off yesterday."

Calhoun was left speechless, no openings for discussion, no place to vent his spleen, so he stalked off to micromanage the sales force, and Martin and Guthrie both breathed a sigh of relief.

"Thanks," Guthrie murmured.

"Insufferable prick," Martin returned under his breath. They worked quietly for a few moments until they heard the squeak of the old man's office door and the rustle of his blinds. This meant Calhoun had retreated for his morning nip of scotch with some coffee, and they had some peace for the next two or so hours. Martin gave an exaggerated sigh.

"That was close—geez, the price you pay for being three minutes early instead of fifteen minutes early."

Guthrie chuckled, his stomach still rumbling uneasily, and he pulled out his phone, surreptitiously checking for a text from Tad, but there was nothing there.

"Yeah, I caught a call from a friend just as I was getting out of the truck."

"Bad news?" Martin asked, and Guthrie shook his head, remembering that it was, in fact, *good* news.

"No. Not at all. My friend's little sisters are going to stay with me for the summer. The youngest one is doing a play in the city for a junior theater company. It's a big deal. Her sister's going to escort her to the city and work on an online course with some visits at CSUSF. They're great kids, and, you know, my friends. So it's nice I get a chance to help out."

"Oh!" Martin grinned, the newly nicer part of him obviously lighting up. "So is this like… your, uhm…." He glanced up, like toward the music that was humming out of the speakers, and Guthrie nodded and gave him a wink.

"Sure is. In fact…." Guthrie glanced around surreptitiously. "He might…." He hated to doubt Seth like this, but he also didn't like to hope too much. Dreams were great, but sometimes plans fell through. "He's trying to get a recording session in place. Sort of classics meets pop music sort of thing. Wants me on vocals and drums and guitar if I want. Says his agent's got backers, and they just have to free up some studio space in the city for the end of August. I mean, even if it's nothing, it'll be a chance to meet up with my friends again, right?"

"And play?" Martin asked, mouth open a little in wonder. He'd confessed to signing up for guitar lessons at a local community outreach and had shyly admitted he loved practicing.

"Yeah," Guthrie said, the dream of that flooding him with endorphins. "And play."

"Righteous," Martin said softly. "Put in for vacation *right now* so the old man can't complain."

Guthrie grimaced. "I gotta wait until Seth gets back to me with dates—"

Martin shook his head. "Two weeks off, the last two weeks of August, dude. And if your friend can't come through, book your own session, even if it's in somebody's garage."

Guthrie stared at him, a little surprised. "Buddy, I am a honky-tonk guitarist and a backup musician—"

Martin shook his head even harder. "I was at Scorpio last week, Guthrie. I know you didn't see me because your crowd was *insane*, but your band is good, and you can work solo any time. I'm telling you this because…." He glanced behind his shoulder, as though expecting to see Eugene Calhoun there, breathing down their necks. "You are too good for this, brother," he said.

"Honest money's honest money," Guthrie told him soberly.

"I'm telling you, your music's honest. I'll put in for the vacation for you right now, and you approve it. I want...." He sighed. "I want somebody I know to have something good."

Guthrie frowned. In the last month he'd discovered Martin lived with his mother, who, as far as Guthrie could tell, was sort of controlling and overprotective, and he would probably be forever hurt that his father didn't want a relationship with him. Guthrie couldn't articulate how lucky the poor guy was that he did not. But Guthrie had never pried, and he wasn't sure how to pry now. Martin gave his head a violent shake and said, "Please. For me. Let me think of you getting your break and feeling good about it, okay?"

"Yeah," Guthrie said, helpless in the face of that much despair. "Okay."

His computer beeped in a few moments with the paperwork for Guthrie's own vacation—Martin hadn't lied. He'd put it in himself.

Guthrie okayed him and made sure the automatic email was sent. He realized that he'd committed to something—a promise of some sort to make his life better, to see his dream through, no matter what the cost.

But he'd tasted hope two weeks before. He'd had hope show up on his phone a few times a day since. And hope had gone to a cold, dark place the night before, leaving Guthrie on the stage with a band that probably wasn't going to make it till the end of summer, because those kids had whole different careers than he did. Guthrie had poured his *soul* into "Long Long Time" the night before, because he couldn't play "Faithfully" when Tad wasn't in the audience, and the other song he'd worked up, the one that was supposed to be a surprise, had felt like a lie.

Suddenly he *needed* that hope, that last gasp of summer, that need to drive his life forward instead of to tread water and wait for something more.

The day continued—Friday was often a reasonably busy day, particularly after graduation. A lot of wealthy parents were there with dazed, excited, and yes, sometimes entitled children shopping for a graduation present that would help them launch into promising lives.

Enough of that sort had come through the doors, chattering animatedly, that when at about one o'clock, a wraith-thin young woman in worn jeans and a faded hoodie came through the door, Guthrie glanced at her twice to check her out. She had auburn hair and green eyes, both of which seemed suspiciously familiar, and haunted elfin features.

With Guthrie's second glance he read SAC PD across the chest of the hoodie, which flapped around her ninety-pound frame, and stood.

"Do we need security?" Martin asked, and Guthrie shook his head.

"No," he murmured. "I think she's a friend's sister. I… if Calhoun shows up, tell him I took early lunch, and see if you can get Tracy back here to help you out."

"No worries," Martin said, picking up the phone, and then, as they both saw the girl—who had an *enormous* bag over her shoulder, like a cross between a duffel bag and actual luggage—wipe the back of her hand across her eyes, he added, "She looks desperate."

"Yeah," Guthrie said. He didn't have to check his phone, see the screen with zero notifications, to guess why.

"April?" he said, drawing near, and she gave a hunted glance around the unusually crowded foyer. "Sweetheart, are you Tad's sister?"

She swallowed hard and nodded, rabbit-like, and he extended his hand, but not to shake.

"Darlin', come with me. There's a quiet spot around back—let's go there to talk."

Her eyes watered over, and he thought about that blank screen, about Tad. Oh God. Oh *God*. Tad!

He pulled her into the coffee nook, which was a sort of recessed hole in the break room that more people had bitched about than God could count.

"Here, darlin'," he said, putting his back to the wall so she wouldn't feel trapped. "We gotta listen for my boss, though, 'cause if he sees you here, he'll have kittens. He's a shitty human being, and I'd like to spare you that."

"Tad," she rasped without preamble and then pulled out her phone, her fingers shaking as she spoke. "He was gonna come pick me up. We were gonna watch you play." She gave a half smile. "I was looking forward to it. We both love music."

He gave an encouraging smile. "I was disappointed not to meet you," he told her truthfully. "He called me on the way out of town—"

She nodded hard enough for it to be an actual sentence. "Me too. He had to bail on me so he could get you before service quit."

Guthrie grunted. "And it did," he told her, hoping for a smile, but she only turned paler. Finally she had her cell phone out, and she was busy punching buttons.

"Did he tell you where he was going?" she rasped.

"Just somewhere in the Sierras," he said. "Tahoe National Forest?"

"Colton," she said, fingers busy. She was jumpy—*twitchy*—and he had a thought.

"Darlin', how did you get here?"

She gave him a gaze of stark fear. "The bus. He... he didn't get in touch with me this morning, and then... then I looked up his name, and Colton, in case.... God, in case something... and I'm his contact person, but...." She shoved the phone at him. "But he's not dead. He's alive. But he's in trouble. And God, I need to be there. I *need* to be there. And... and he talks so much about you. I thought you could help me. Can you help me? Mister—*Guthrie*—I know you don't know me, but will you help me get to my brother?"

"Shh...," he soothed, and he took the phone in one hand but kept a gentle hold of her fingers in the other. She twined their hands together almost violently, and he started a soft massage over her knuckles with his thumb. "Here, darlin'," he murmured, opening his arm. "You tuck into there, and I won't take no liberties, I swear. But give me a minute to read this so I know what we're getting ourselves into, okay?"

It shouldn't have worked. She was rabbity as hell. But apparently the fact that Tad trusted him made her desperate enough to send her into the shelter of his arm. She huddled there, barely letting him touch her but in the center of his body heat, while he read the police blotter section of the Sacramento paper.

He tried to keep his breathing steady so he didn't freak her out.

> *SAC PD Detective one of four people stranded in an old strip-mining canyon in Colton, California. Search and rescue officials are looking for solutions to get to the four men who fell into the canyon during an investigation into the shooting of Sheriff Eamon Mills of Colton County. In addition to Detective Tad Hawkins, Undersheriff Aaron George, High School Principal L. Larkin, and missing local man Curtis MacDonald are all stuck in what was once a strip mine but is now a geographical hazard.*

Guthrie's breath caught as he continued to read the story, which gave precious few details about how the men had gotten stranded and was pretty vague on why it was so hard to get them out. His mind did manage to focus on the part about the gravel and loose shale being so prevalent in the small canyon that a helicopter rescue was absolutely not an option, because the small rocks would turn deadly in the copter's rotor wash, and then… oh God. They had a picture. It was an aerial shot, taken at distance, of two men climbing up an impossibly steep incline using a thin rope and a pulley system utilizing the wheels of an upside-down vehicle in the bottom of the canyon. The men didn't appear familiar, but… but this was pure MacGyver shit here, and Tad was part of it.

And Guthrie and April were five hours, at the very least, away.

His arm tightened around April's shoulders, and he heard himself say, "You got clothes in that bag, darlin'?"

"And my yarn," she practically whispered. He remembered that, remembered Tad's complete indulgence in her and her hobby, which was keeping her sane during a really shitty time.

"Well, you let me know if you need more of either," he warned. "Let me tell my coworker I've got to jet the hell out of here, and then we'll stop by my apartment so I can pack my own bag and my own woobie. You good with that?"

"Then we go find Tad?"

He nodded, his hands sweating with the need to move. "Stop for gas, get some food, and get the hell out of Dodge, angel—it's a plan."

"Thank you," she wept and practically melted into his shoulder. "Thank you. He's… you know… he's *Tad*—"

"Oh, honey, we're not leaving your brother in a pickle like that without letting him know we've got his back, right?"

"Right," she said. Then, "Uhm… I ran away from my halfway house. Is there any way you could call them? Let them know I'm not on a bender? I…. They yell."

"Sure," he said. "I can definitely do that. But we gotta get a move on, yeah? It'll take us six hours plus in Friday traffic, I don't care what Google tells us."

She swallowed against his shoulder and pulled away just as the door to the foyer opened, and who but Eugene Calhoun himself opened the door to the break room and shouted, "Why the hell are all these people milling around out here? That damned girl can't handle all this. She's useless!"

"Tracy's good at people, sir," Guthrie replied, ducking out of the coffee cubby and putting April behind him. "I told you to staff more today, and you blew me off. And it's too bad because I've got a family emergency, and I've got to go."

"You've got to *what*?" Calhoun was an almost gaunt man with bulging eyes and a red, bulbous nose from too much scotch with his coffee. As he came unglued, not only did his *eyes* bulge, but his nose seemed to throb along with the vein in his head.

"It's in our contract, sir," Guthrie said. "Everybody gets two emergencies a year without question. You approved it yourself." Guthrie had written it into the contracts and then waited until Calhoun was tired from a good day grifting, erm, selling, and *really* mellow from half a bottle of scotch in a pot of coffee. "I've been here two years, haven't taken one of those once. This is mine. Her brother's a policeman, and he's in mess, and he needs his little sister, and I'm the one making that work."

He turned to April and gestured with his chin to stay behind him as he swung around Calhoun to keep her at his shoulder. Calhoun had been known to reach out and grab a girl's wrist with hard, pointy witch's fingers, and Guthrie was *not* letting that happen here.

Calhoun did it with Guthrie's wrist instead, his fingers digging into the nerve, and Guthrie gasped. "You walk out of here, Woodson, and you won't have a job when you get back."

Guthrie snorted. "Sir, if you fire me, I get bennies for a full six months and car maintenance for three. Do you think you're the only game in town? This place was a disaster two years ago—you couldn't keep customers because your staff was running around like headless chickens and thumbless monkeys. You got a good staff now, and I keep this place running like a Swiss watch. You want to jeopardize that because you can't honor a contract you signed yourself, you go ahead."

"Some piece of ass wanders in here and asks you for help and you bail on me? Nail her in the bathroom if you need to, but do *not* leave me in the lurch!"

And it hit Guthrie—he'd covered his ass in all the ways he'd had, but he still might lose his job because Calhoun knew, like all good tyrants, that even if they'd put their names down, that didn't mean the little guy had the wherewithal to make them keep their word.

Guthrie peered behind him at April's pinched face, at the bravery it must have taken to get her on a bus to come here—Tad must have mentioned the place, that could have been the only way she'd known—to come *here* and look for Guthrie's help.

Guthrie wasn't rich, and he wasn't powerful, but by all that was fuckin' holy, he knew how to keep his word.

"You do what you gotta," Guthrie said. "My plaid flannel hoodie's in the lobby. I gotta go."

Later, he reflected that he might have bailed. He'd had to fight his way through a throng of people to get that hoodie, but it was Tad's, and Guthrie couldn't bear to part with it. As Tracy leaned forward and competently dealt with the person at the counter in front of her, he tugged it off the chair and turned to Martin.

"I've got to go," he murmured. "Calhoun might not let me come back, so if this is it, man, it's been good working with you."

Martin turned stricken eyes to him. "Aw man—no!"

Guthrie paused and realized that he might not miss the job, but Tracy, Martin, the other employees—they were all right. He glanced over his shoulder, saw April hovering in the doorway, and gave her a little wave. His wrist ached and his heart ached and his worry for Tad made his *stomach* ache, but he had a moment to give Martin a squeeze on his shoulder and a wink.

"Keep practicing, amigo. You deserve something good too." Then he brushed Tracy's shoulder with his knuckles and said, "You're doing good, sweetheart. Don't let nobody here give you shit, and *don't* let Calhoun touch you anywhere you don't want to, you hear?"

She turned to him, her dark brows drawn tight under a mane of fuzzy yellow hair. "Guthrie?"

"Take care of yourselves," he said. "If I can, I'll be back Monday."

But he wasn't counting on it. He slid his hands into the hoodie, checked his jeans for his wallet, phone, and keys, then turned to April and vamoosed.

He opened the truck door for April and gave her a hand up, because the giant beater wasn't short and April *was*.

"Did you…," she asked hesitantly as he started the thing up. "Did you just… just quit your job?"

"That's up to Calhoun," Guthrie muttered, putting the thing into gear and backing out. "I'm within my contract rights, which I know because I rewrote everybody's contract and the work handbook. But the problem with getting a drunk monkey to sign something that helps everybody is that in the end he's still a drunk monkey, and his best talent is flinging shit."

"You quit your job," she said in wonder. "Oh my God. Tad *finally* finds a guy worth his time and he falls down a fucking *well*?"

Guthrie sputtered a little laughter as he took the freeway onramp and headed for his apartment. "I don't think he fell down that canyon on purpose," he said, his lips twitching.

"I think it's typical," she sniffed. "Most other officers, they're worried about getting shot. *Tad*, on the other hand, ends up sliding down a mountain with MacGyver."

"Yeah," Guthrie muttered. "The hell *was* that? If I wasn't worried as shit, I'd be intrigued, you know?"

"Too smart for me," April said decisively. "I can barely put one foot in front of the other, most days."

Guthrie grunted. "I've had those days," he said. "Not like you, but the world gets damned hard."

"Tad makes it better," she said disconsolately, leaning her head against the window.

He heard all over again Tad's concern for his sister, his worry that she wasn't doing well in her current place, his hope that she could move to room with him.

"Let's get you to him," he said. "We'll get you to him, we'll move you into his apartment—"

"And we can get a cat," she said, like she was holding on to that. "We can get a cat, and maybe a big dog, the kind that likes cats. And I can get a job—something small. Volunteering at a library, or…. God, I'm a junkie, but I do love working with kids. Nobody'll want me with their kids, but I swear I wouldn't use—"

"Darlin'," Guthrie soothed, realizing that *this* was what April had needed all morning, and the one person who could have given it to her was the one they were both freaking out over. "You need to focus on the cat. Focus on pizza on Fridays and movies and trips to the park. Focus on listening to music and listening to your brother talk about his day. Keep these things in mind. *These* are the things you'll want after we get him back safe. Your brother, he's as solid as they come. Once we get this sorted, you know he'll be there for you, right?"

"What about you?" she whispered.

"I love cats," he said. "I could visit, be there maybe for some pizza Fridays, take some of those weekend jaunts. I'm not jealous about family. You were there first, right?"

She nodded, and while her tears seemed to fall more freely, she also seemed to be calmer. "We could get two cats," she said. "One for you, one for me."

Guthrie smiled as he took the turn that would lead to his apartment. "What about your brother?"

And suddenly she was sharp as a tack, neither freaked out nor helpless. "Oh honey, any fool can see you're like me. We'll be his damned cats. He can feed us and pet us and give us a place to sleep, and we'll let him know he's the best thing in our lives."

Suddenly *he* was the one with his eyes burning, and he had to take a deep, deep breath to keep from losing it now. Traffic on the 380 had been heinous. He estimated six hours at the minimum to get to Colton, if you counted pit stops and gas. Frankly, he didn't see April being able to sit in the truck for the whole four- or five-hour trip, so he needed to count pit stops and gas.

"Well, sadly," Guthrie said, pulling into his spot, "I have no cat. But I do have some bottles of water, some blankets and sleeping bags, and a knapsack so I can throw in a change of clothes. You want to come in and hit the head?"

She followed him into his apartment, pausing to look at the drum kit, which was set up, as well as his laptop, ready to record or transmit so he and the band could jam together. She saw the bookshelf with the Michael Connelly, the John Grisham, the James Patterson, and his copies of *Rolling Stone* and *Entertainment Weekly*.

"Can I grab some books and zines?" she asked. "I brought my yarn, but sometimes your hands get tired and you need to fuzz out."

"Knock yourself out," Guthrie told her. "Grab at least three."

"Three?" She looked at him curiously.

"One for me, one for your brother, one for you. Then we can switch off when we're done."

She didn't laugh, and she picked *five* books, so he figured she must be a fast reader.

He ran around and grabbed stuff. His sleeping bags, extra heavy-duty blankets, and, thinking mostly about April, a pillow so she could lean her head against it while he was driving. She watched him with incurious eyes, and he nodded to her to start picking stuff up.

"There's a lockbox in the back we can stow most of it in," he said. "Including my baby."

And with that, he picked up his smallest, oldest acoustic guitar in a battered black case. The leather was so worn it was flaking in places, and the edges were starting to crack, but the instrument inside held a tune in the worst situations—including playing by the sea or in the wind. It wasn't his best, and he usually performed with the electric, but the acoustic was... well, it was his crocheting, and like April, he needed something to give him comfort.

He had no idea what was waiting for them. He needed his fucking guitar. He'd been planning to order groceries sometime that day, so his cupboard was mostly bare, but he did manage a box of crackers and some chips and, oh hey, a couple of bottled sodas, which he threw into his lunch cooler.

"We'll get more at the gas station on the way out of town," he told her.

"You believe in being prepared," she muttered, taking the cooler and loading up on the other stuff.

"Yeah, well, we got caught out enough as a kid that I learned if I didn't want to go hungry, I had to pack my own damned granola bars."

In fact, this entire situation was enough to send his brain swimming back to his childhood, his dad and Uncle Jock wrapped in their jackets in the truck bed while Guthrie curled up across the bench seat, his stomach growling because they'd gotten a gig and needed to drive halfway across the state at the drop of a hat. And God forbid, Elmore Butch Woodson remember anything besides his licks. His son would have to suck it up and eat when they found a microwaved burrito or something because Guthrie's father had no use for foresight or planning.

"Our mom," she said, pausing, as though this memory was slow to surface, "she... she would put breakfast bars in our pockets on our way out the door. If we didn't like the taste, she'd put *Pop-Tarts* in our pockets, even though she thought they were a... what'd she call 'em? A 'nutritional abomination.'"

Guthrie smiled as he loaded everything in his arms, not forgetting the guitar. "I like that. I'll have to remember that."

"She was the best," April said bitterly.

"Tad misses her too," Guthrie said, nodding at her. "Let's go, hon. We're burning daylight."

She paused at the doorway and glanced around, gnawing her lip. "You work hard," she said, "at making a home."

"Won't be mine for long if I lose my job," he confessed nakedly. "C'mon, let's hit the gas station before people start getting out of work."

THE TRUCK was a good twenty-five years old, a Chevy Colorado that he tried to keep maintained but that was probably due for a complete overhaul. The bushings were going, and the belts—he'd been planning to take it in to the maintenance department because he had the employee maintenance package taken from his check and he might as well use it, but there was no time for that now.

Still, he'd hooked up a decent sound system in it, and he could hear his music even when it wasn't played at top volume. He put up a "road trip" list he'd compiled and—after the stop at the gas station, where he had April get them a shit-ton of nuts and candy bars to add to the grub he'd already packed—the music helped him get up the hill without killing anybody, even when he hit the giant fucking construction mess at the I-80 split near West Sac.

By the time he followed his flickering GPS to Colton, a little town in the Tahoe National Forest, he and April were tired, cranky, hungry for real food... and scared out of their minds.

April had slept a lot, arms crossed in front of her, one of his blankets wrapped around her shoulders, the cooler on the floorboards by her feet and her giant flowered bag next to her on the seat. He had the feeling she'd done that on purpose, surrounded herself with things to make everything not so big and scary.

Smart, he thought, realizing how hard this must be on somebody who was hypersensitive for whatever reason. Everything from the engine noise to the jouncing of the cab, which Guthrie took for granted, was probably scraping on a nerve filed down to a nub by now.

"So," April murmured, glancing around, "what now?"

Guthrie turned the radio down, where he'd been humming along to "Sympathy for the Devil," wondering how it was that the Stones never seemed to age. Old Mick was looking fairly corpselike, it was true, but the *music*, man, that was devil-at-the-crossroads stuff right there.

"Let me ask where the sheriff's office is," he said, eyeballing the gas station right off the main thoroughfare through town. "Everybody knows where to support their local sheriff."

TWO HOURS later, the sunlight that had been filtering through the tall pines as they'd pulled off the road had completely disappeared, and Guthrie thought if he got sent on one more wild-goose chase, he'd grab the next local he saw by the throat and shake them until dead.

The sheriff's office had been full to the brim with cops, none of whom knew what was going on. When Guthrie had approached the desk, a distracted-looking middle-aged man in a uniform with W. Coolidge on the name tag had shrugged.

"I don't know what's going on," he muttered. "The Sacramento people have taken over everything. Ask them."

"I will," Guthrie snapped. "Where the fuck are they?"

"The one hotel in town," Coolidge snapped back. "But don't get pissy with *those* people 'cause the SWAT team is up here and they'll shoot you into sushi if you so much as ask a question."

Guthrie raised an eyebrow. "Have they shot *you* into sushi yet?" he asked carefully.

"No, sir, but they are *not* sharing information, and search and rescue has got a giant banana up its ass." A mean smile twisted his lips. "Or at least that's what I hear."

Guthrie wasn't even going to fuckin' ask. "Great. Do you know where Chris Castro is? He's one of the two detectives that came up."

"Oh, who the fuck knows," W. Coolidge shot back. "I'm going to say the hotel, and if I'm wrong, sue me."

Guthrie blinked and said, "Okay then, son, the hotel it's going to be. And I cannot thank you enough for not being any fucking help at all."

And with that he whirled on his heel and went out to the truck, where April was huddled with the flannel blanket that she'd been hugging for the entire trip.

"So?" she asked.

"So," Guthrie said, gnawing on his lower lip, "Their sheriff got shot last night, and their undersheriff fell down the same goddamned hole Tad did. Right now you've got a lot of tired assholes wandering around in circles going, 'Have you heard anything yet?'"

"That's not promising," April muttered. "Where to next?"

"The hotel. I guess there's only one, and I saw it a mile back." He started the rattling truck and put it into gear, heading for their next destination.

A next destination that looked like a kicked hornets' nest.

The hotel itself was a very basic place: a two-story row of rooms with rickety stairs on each side of the strip. There were three big SUVs parked in front and an honest to God tactical van, with people geared up—masks, armor, the whole nine yards—running up and down the stairs shouting orders and directions to each other in the quiet dark of the mountains.

April made a muffled "*Meep!*" and slunk down practically on the floor, throwing the flannel blanket over her head and whimpering to herself.

Guthrie didn't blame her.

He slid out of the truck and started reading people's chests and backs, praying he'd see the thing he needed most.

And there it was.

SAC PD DET

Big letters across the front, like the giant shirt April had worn, probably hoping to prove Tad was her brother.

The man wearing it was fortyish and attractive—black hair, pale copper skin, large brown eyes. Guthrie took a risk.

"Chris!" he called. "Detective Chris Castro?"

The man paused by the door to one of the SUVs and turned toward Guthrie, surprised.

"And you are…?"

"Unimportant. But the lady in the truck is April Hawkins."

Castro's eyes went large and concerned. "Tad's *sister*? What in the hell is she doing here?"

"You went out of contact last night, and suddenly her brother's name is splashed across the news along with this little one-horse burg. She's *terrified*, and she's sort of a mess, and I told her we'd come and see what was going on." Guthrie held on to the tone of his voice—this was Chris, Tad's partner, and Tad spoke highly of him, but dammit, it had been a *long* goddamned day.

"You're the snakebit guitarist," Castro said, seemingly excited at having put the puzzle together. "Man, Tad's going to be happy to hear from you."

Guthrie grimaced. "I would love to oblige you, but nobody will give us a straight answer as to *where he is*. The guy at the police station said something about how the whole damned world had fallen down to the bottom of Daffodil Canyon, and seriously? That's the most coherent thing I've heard since one o'clock this afternoon."

Castro grimaced. "Look, I've been out to the canyon for half the day, and I came back because nobody had any ideas how to get them out. I understand a team of scientists and the search and rescue folks have teamed up, so this might end soon. The canyon is a pain in the ass to get to, and it's dangerous, and I understand it's *swarming* with people right now, so maybe you should go to the hospital and wait there. They've been out in the sun all day, and while I've heard they had some supplies, there were also some injuries. Odds are, *everybody* is going to be sent there to be checked out."

Guthrie nodded. "Okay, then." He took a deep breath. "So, the hospital…."

Was about half a mile away, and Castro gave *very* succinct directions.

Guthrie parked close to the front and glanced around the parking lot unhappily. It wasn't that the lot wasn't lighted, it was that the darkness here was so *absolute*, it seemed to devour the light from every other source.

"Do you want to stay or come with me?" he asked wearily.

"I gotta pee," she replied, and he slid out of the cab, feeling muscles and joints creak and a howling void in his stomach. He stopped and reached inside, grabbed a bag of nuts, and started shoving them in his mouth, offering some to April as they walked inside.

He was so tired he honestly thought about sitting in the bank of chairs in front of the ER and zonking out.

He walked up to the night nurse, who was monitoring her computer with absolute dedication, and said, "Heya. I… our friend—her brother— was in the news because he fell down a *canyon*, and I asked the sheriff's office and the SAC PD people, and nobody knows where to find him, but I was told to come ask you—and—"

At that moment, there was a gasp and the hurried pad of feet in tennis shoes. Guthrie and April turned to see a coltish young woman with masses of red hair and bright blue eyes practically sprint to the front counter.

"Annie?" she asked, and the woman nodded.

"Maureen George? I know your father."

The redhead nodded back. "You guys have supplies for us, right? Because I understand somebody was shot and there's somebody who's in withdrawals and Larx has a concussion and—"

Annie, the nurse, nodded and held out her hands. "Hold on, sweetheart. We've got somebody running a cooler up here with everything they need. Do we know about the gunshot?"

Maureen shook her head. "It sounded like they were more worried about infection than blood loss, but you know, they're in the bottom of Daffodil Canyon and—"

She might have said something else then, but suddenly Guthrie's entire world telescoped, and at the end of the telescope was a small word, swimming in an ocean of blood.

"Wait wait wait wait wait wait wait," he shouted, and then, gripping the counter so hard he felt like his knuckles must be white, he said, "Did you say *shot*? 'Cause our *friend* is at the bottom of that canyon and… and we thought he was coming here, and nobody can tell us shit, and *where in the hell is Tad Hawkins*!"

Maureen's eyes got big, and then she blinked. "Hey," she said. "Do you have the pickup truck I saw driving up?"

"Yes," Guthrie said, hearing his own voice wobble.

"Listen, we need something that can haul shit. We're going back down to the canyon with a care package for the people stuck there. Would you… would you want to come with us?"

Guthrie stared at her. "Who's us?"

Maureen laughed a little. "That's another story, and you don't look like you'd care. But if you and your friend—"

"I'm Guthrie, and this is April," he said, realizing she was about to do something really generous, and she didn't even know their names.

"Nice to meet you. So, if don't mind waiting for the medical supplies—"

"And here they are!" Annie said happily, taking the soft-shelled cooler from a young Black man who was already running back to wherever he'd sprung from. "Thanks, Jed. Here you go, Maureen." She gave Guthrie and April a sympathetic look. "I'd follow Maureen if I were you. Her father is the undersheriff, and he's stuck down in the canyon too. If they're sending down care packages, there's got to be somebody at the rescue site who can give you an explanation, okay?"

Guthrie nodded and turned to April. "Did you still need to pee?"

"It just crawled back up," she said, her eyes huge. "One more place? Guthrie, I'm *hungry*."

"We're stopping for burgers. The guys in the canyon are *also* starving." Maureen George was so perky Guthrie almost wanted to smack her.

Guthrie took a deep breath instead. Yes, it had been a *longassed* day. Yes, this was one more destination in the scavenger hunt that had become their search for Tad. But this nice girl seemed to have a line on the rescue operation, and if nothing else, she knew where to find *food*.

He was weary to every molecule of his being. His joints ached. His head was pounding. His stomach churned. And here they were, one more chase. One more destination. One more motherfucking lead.

"Lead the way," he said.

"Awesome." This Maureen George person seemed to be made out of puppy dog tails because she was perky like it was morning and she was coffee.

"Here," Guthrie told her, reaching his hand for the pack. "Let me take that. Least I could do."

GUTHRIE *THOUGHT* he was tired, but ten minutes later he had to admit the very pregnant woman now sitting shotgun in the pickup seemed to have him beat.

When they'd gotten out to the vehicles, it had seemed logical to split up; Guthrie and his very convenient pickup truck were going to get sleeping bags and warm clothes for the people stranded in the canyon, and the people Maureen had come with were going to get burgers. They'd all meet at someone's house (Guthrie was a little fuzzy on *whose* house) and plan from there. April was exhausted and, he was pretty sure, about done with his fucking noisy, bouncy pickup truck, so he'd suggested she ride with Maureen, because compared to the last eight hours, a minivan seemed the height of comfort.

Maureen had surprised him then by picking up on April's mood. The young man behind the wheel had a crooked nose and a crooked jaw… and wide, fathomless brown eyes that had taken in April's pinched, on-the-edge-of-the-cliff features with one sweep and had nodded her to the back seat, with a sort of mute promise to stay off her last nerve.

And that left Guthrie with Olivia Larkin-McDaniels, his guide through the darkened land of no streetlights, no city lights, and a whole lot of stars.

And also an amazing font of information about what in the hell had happened to Tad.

When she was done giving her snarky, *pithy* explanation, Guthrie wanted to shake her and yell, "Are you *fucking* kidding me?" but he couldn't. Besides the fact that this whole situation was *not* her fault, two people she loved were down in the canyon with Tad, and she and Maureen, and even the quiet Berto, were all working really hard to hold on to their shit.

Tad and Chris had been called up to help the Sheriff of Colton County, Eamon Mills. Thursday morning, after the local high school had graduated and a freaked-out parent had realized his son wasn't at the ceremony. Sheriff Mills—with the help of Olivia's father, the principal of the high school—had tracked the kid to a local meth house that backed up against Daffodil Canyon. Maureen's father—the Undersheriff of Colton County—hadn't been able to help in the search, because he and Olivia's father were hosting a giant to-do for the graduating class.

Guthrie had grown up in a small town. He knew high school graduation was a big fucking deal. To have a party hosted by the undersheriff and the principal wasn't something either one of those people could walk away from. But Sheriff Mills hadn't trusted all his men, either, so he'd called in Tad's partner and more backup.

Which hadn't stopped him from getting shot. Eamon Mills was apparently out of surgery and expected to make a full recovery, but in the meantime, the undersheriff had gone to the scene of the shooting along with Tad and some of the borrows from SAC PD to investigate further. Somebody had shot at them, and Tad and Undersheriff George had gone sliding down into the canyon, or "the giant fucking gravel pit" as Olivia referred to it, bitterness in her voice. The place was an ecological disaster. The surface was loose shale and scree, and while trees grew upright, that was because they had taproots that punched through the granite, so the canyon was pretty inhospitable.

So inhospitable that when Olivia's father had gone driving down on a service road to see if he could reach Tad and Undersheriff George, the road had collapsed under his car wheels, and *he'd* gone sliding down to a lower level than the other two people trapped in the pit in the first place.

Getting them out was next to impossible. Like the news blog had reported, a helicopter would shoot up the gravel and loose rock in the rotor wash, and that was too dangerous to risk. The lip of the "canyon" was crumbling; any rope or rescue harness lowered to the injured had the potential to bring half the canyon walls tumbling down on their heads. And there were injuries all around. Maureen's dad had a still-bleeding cut on his leg. Larx—Olivia's dad—had a massive concussion. And Tad apparently had a bullet in his ass.

Oh, and the kid they'd been looking for was under a tree, although whether that was voluntary or the tree had *fallen* on him, Olivia didn't know.

All of that—*all* of it—and Guthrie's big takeaway still seemed to be "Wait, so your dad and Maureen's dad are together?"

They were a couple. The whole town knew. He'd asked her if that was just... *okay*, and her response?

"It's had its moments."

And that was all. But Olivia and Maureen weren't only upset about their respective *fathers*, they were upset about their *parents*, as a team, and as Guthrie piloted the pickup truck through the darkness to Olivia's *fathers'* house, he had to swallow against a lump in his throat.

Sure. Apparently, some people got shitty about it—Guthrie knew all about that on a gut level. But just like in Seth and Kelly's family, some people had family rooting for them.

In this case, all their teenaged children—and Guthrie couldn't keep up with who was who—as well as Mr. Larkin's coworkers and the entire sheriff's department had put their brains together for a way to help search and rescue get everybody out of a pit designed to trap people at the bottom.

On the one hand, it boggled the mind. It defied emotion. Guthrie *could not* wrap his brain around it.

On the other, Tad—the man who had made love to him and cared for him and shown up at his shows and made him laugh and… and given him *hope*—was injured at the bottom of a black hole, looking up at the stars, not knowing that Guthrie and April had come all this way to see about getting him out.

Guthrie had to give his boy hope.

Livvy, as Maureen had called Olivia, directed Guthrie to a neat little house at the end of a long drive. It was surrounded by forest, but it had a lawn and planted flowers that were fragrant even in the cool dark of the woods. There was a second story, probably for bedrooms, but the bottom half was ranch style, and as Livvy detailed all the things wrong with the place—the absolutely impractical fireplace, the old kitchen, the carpeted stairs—all he could hear from her was how much she loved it here, even though she and her husband lived with Berto and his brother a couple of miles away.

This was the house she'd grown up in. *This* house was where she knew she'd be safe. The other house was what she was building into a home. He hadn't known the girl an hour, but this much he knew.

And this house had three cats and an enormous blond dog that full-out body hugged her when they walked in the door.

"Nice," Guthrie said, squatting down to pet an enormous ginger tom who had slipped in with the other cats after Livvy was done making out with the dog and let him out to pee.

"You have a cat?" she asked.

He grunted and changed his attention to a tiny calico.

"No." The little darling let him smooth back her whiskers, and he remembered his and Tad's conversation about cats and wanted to cry. "I got a day job, and I take gigs and sleep on people's couches and shit. It's… it's no damned good for having a cat."

"Or a boyfriend," she said, voice quiet, and he had to give her points for observation.

"Or a boyfriend," he agreed.

"But you came," she said.

"I did," he said, mostly to the third cat, a pudgy torti who demanded his attention. "He was supposed to show up to my gig last night, but he called to say he couldn't make it. This morning his sister showed up at my work just… freaked the fuck out. Said something about a shooting, and she couldn't get her brother on the phone and…. And I walked out on the best day job I ever had. Told them I'd be out for a few days, and we drove up here."

Boy, cats were great. Didn't demand emotional commitment, didn't care that you were baring your soul—or that you'd probably just lost your job.

"Surprised yourself?" she asked, sounding like she'd been there.

"Yeah." Oh fuck. The day was crashing down on him. "I-I didn't think I was there yet. Didn't think I'd *ever* be there. And suddenly...."

"Seeing his face was the one thing that was going to keep your world from turning black," she said, voice laden with compassion, and he glanced up at her.

"Yeah," he said again. "I...." He stood, not ready for this conversation. "Tell me what to get out of the garage. I can throw it in the back of the truck and we can make them comfy for the night."

"Fair," she said with a sigh. She was exhausted—any fool could see that. But what she said next made him love her with all his heart. "I'll go through their drawers for some old clothes. How big's your guy? Larx is mid-sized, Aaron's a little bigger."

He didn't even think about it. The plaid flannel hoodie that had kept him sane—*Tad's* shirt that he'd hugged around his body all day— slid off his shoulders, the shock of the cool night almost painful. Tad would know this shirt. He'd know Guthrie was there.

"Put this in the basket," he said. It was time to get cooking.

She kept him on his toes, showed him where the sleeping bags were, told him what to grab while she was packing. It was as cool in the mountains as it had been in San Rafael, without the constant ocean wind. Everybody who'd gone down into the canyon had been wearing short sleeves and cargo shorts or khakis, and a lot of that had been bled on. Or, Olivia told him, baffled, somehow completely lost.

"My father was reportedly wearing half a shirt," she said as she came out to the garage with a flat of water and a case of Gatorade, which she set on the work counter while she took a breath. "I... I have no idea why that is. Why would you be at the bottom of a gravel pit where the earth itself wants to kill you with only half a shirt? I... I'm boggled."

"He was wearing a whole shirt on the news-blog footage," Guthrie said. He'd gathered it had been her father in the picture, wearing the makeshift harness. She said that's how they all knew he was concussed;

apparently he was a runner and insanely fit, and he'd be running up the side of the canyon wall if something hadn't been wrong with him.

"I *know*!" she said, throwing her hands in the air, all exasperation. "I have the pictures on my *phone*. And now in spite of all the worry, I want to know. What in the hell did he do with the bright yellow *Star Wars* T-shirt I gave him for his birthday?"

Guthrie chuckled then, liking her very much. "Go do what you're doing," he told her. "Unless there's anything you all can't bear to part with, I'll finish up here."

"You could burn the garage down," she told him rashly, "as long as my dad and Aaron get home. You… you have to see them together. Like a team. They're teaching Elton and me what it means to parent, and they're *doing it to us* while we get ready to have our own squid." Her hand rubbed her stomach absentmindedly. "Ugh. I've got to hurry. I need to eat and take my meds and…."

"Blood pressure?" he asked, suddenly ready to chivvy the girl to the cozy living room *immediately*. She was at the tail end of her pregnancy. *So much* could be going on right now.

"I'm on the edge of all the things," she admitted glumly. "Blood pressure is *creeping up*, blood sugar is *getting a little high*—but no. It's bipolar meds. If I don't take them before I go to bed, tomorrow's going to be a house of horrors—all of it in my own brain."

"April needs them too," he said softly, remembering what April had told him about sneaking two days' worth of meds from the halfway house so she could get away. "She… she tried to self-medicate with street drugs, but…."

Olivia sucked in a breath. "Oh, that's rough. That's a hard thing to kick, then. My shrinks told me that, super concerned that I not try it. The things it does to brain chemistry are *bad*."

Guthrie nodded, liking this woman, this family, more with every moment he was in their home, and then to his horror, he saw she was picking up cases of water and Gatorade again. "Oh my God, woman, go put your feet up *and put that down!*"

She glared at him. "I'm—"

"Doing *my* job, darlin'. I've got nothing to offer here but a strong back and my fuckin' truck! Now go sit down, med up, and rest. Food's coming." He toned his voice down for a minute. "You don't do anybody favors by hurting yourself right now. Go rest."

"If you insist," she said, trying to sound snotty.

"I do." He winked at her, and she smiled, and he got back to work.

He finished with the bedding and the eggcrate—not only enough for the people in the canyon, but enough for some of the people on top of the canyon who were trying to assemble an apparatus that would pull the fallen up without tumbling the canyon edge down on their heads.

FINALLY—*FINALLY*—HE WAS headed back to Daffodil Canyon, just him and Maureen George. By the time Maureen had shown up with the food, Livvy had been too tired to move, and so had April. With that perfect empathy Livvy had shown him, she'd honed in on the fact that April was absolutely at the end of her rope. When he and Maureen had left them, April was scrolling through the aerial photos on Livvy's phone, cuddling with the giant blond dog, who had found his date for the night.

Now their destination was up the road, unspooling from darkness under their headlights and the rattle of the pickup. As Maureen directed him to some place called (har, har!) Dropoff Drive, he asked why the gravel pit was called Daffodil Canyon. *He* was imagining wildflowers or pioneers planting bulbs or some such bullshit.

"Fucking yellow pollen," Maureen said, shaking her head. "This time of year the air is thick with it. You'll find it in your clothes, your hair. It collects there on top of the rocks like a blanket sometimes. God, Larx—"

"Livvy's dad?" He still couldn't figure out why they'd call him that, and he wanted to know. He was *impressed* with these people, by their sense of community. Nobody was making the pregnant girl go until she dropped because she was the one who could organize shit—and Maureen seemed to regard her as a true sister, in spite of the fact that their dads had hooked up the year before.

"Yeah," Maureen was saying now. "Larx was the science teacher before this year when he took over as principal. He was… well, sort of the greatest. Took the biology classes to the river to take soil samples and, you know, to do all the outdoor active things that make science not boring words on a page. Built trebuchets with the physics students, made ice cream in chemistry. I hear he hired a geology teacher *special* because this area is unique and he wanted to explore that, and then he got the guy a job part-time at Truckee Junior College when he couldn't give him a full-time job at the high school."

"Wow," Guthrie said. "Dedication."

"Paid off!" Maureen laughed. "The guy is part of the team of people—Larx and Aaron's people—who put together this little search and rescue deal you'll see in a few. He's kept the damned search and rescue department from dragging the mountain down on our guys' heads about sixty-dozen times today, so, you know. Us grown-ups are buying that guy some *scotch* when this is over."

Guthrie chuckled. "Put me in for some of that," he said. "Who else is up there?"

"Larx's best friend, Yoshi Nakamoto," Maureen said promptly. "Who mostly just herds fish, because he's Larx's vice principal and he's good at it. My little brother, Larx's foster kid, Livvy's little sister, who will *feel* like ten people because she's exhaustingly optimistic, Berto's little brother who's like a spun top, Livvy's husband, Elton, who is damned cute but don't tell her I said that, and the other physics teacher that Larx recently hired, presumably because Larx is finally going to admit he's a human being and stick to being a principal instead of trying to do it all."

"Wow." Guthrie crossed his eyes. "The more I hear about this guy—"

"You've got no idea," Maureen said, shaking her head. "My little brother overheard the battles he had with the administration over being principal—they had to *blackmail* him with somebody both hated *and* incompetent before he'd take the job, and then he negotiated terms. In the end, he had to give up the track team to get Yoshi in as VP, and he kept the AP class in order to get veto power over hiring. It was small-town politics at its finest, done by a guy who spent his formative years telling politicians and bureaucrats to kiss his scrawny ass." She sighed. "It's a good thing my dad's marrying him, or I might have fallen in love with him as an adult, and that would have been both fruitless and embarrassing."

It took him a minute. "I take it you harbored a crush?" he asked delicately.

"Shh," she said, holding her finger up to her lips. "He made ninth grade bearable. Don't tell my dad—that'd be weird. Besides"—she shrugged—"it was a kid thing. What my dad and him are doing, that's grown-up actual love and relationship. A crush in the ninth grade is really nothing."

"Didn't feel that way in ninth grade," Guthrie said, trying to remember who *he'd* been crushing on. An image of Bruce Springsteen from his 1980's album covers floated behind his eyes, and then Billy Joe Armstrong and Brandon Flowers. Ooh... and Fitz from Fitz and the Tantrums. Nice!

He shook himself. "Sorry. All I've got is a spank bank of celebrities, and since I'm never gonna play with "Born to Run" era Springsteen, I think I'm safe from your situation."

She laughed hard, appreciating. "Young Bruce was *nice*," she said. "But young Steve Perry was *the shit*."

He pointed briefly to his own profile. "I got the nose but not the inclination," he said with regret, and this time she had to cover her mouth with her hands.

When she was done laughing, a melancholy quiet settled over the rattling old truck, and Maureen spoke into the silence. "You're nice. Can I be your friend as well as Livvy?"

Guthrie blinked. "Why, uhm, can't I be both?" Were they at friends-for-life now? He thought about Olivia, freaking out about her shirtless father in the middle of a survival wasteland, and recognized the act of will she'd used to pull herself out of her spiral by her bootstraps and shoulder on into the void.

It was sort of the same thing that had gotten him, after three tries, to a place where he *finally* knew where Tad was. Maybe he and Olivia *were* friends for life.

"Olivia was always so intense in school," Maureen said softly. "I... I wouldn't steal a friend from her for anything because she's a lot more guarded about that sort of thing. Not prickly, definitely not mean, but very much finding her way to her own heart with hard work. She relaxed around you in a way I've only seen with her family—or with Elton. I-I guess I'm a die-hard meddler. I want her to have all the friends." She gave a snort. "She and Christie are pretty much my favorite sisters, right?"

He blinked. "You've got another sister?"

Maureen shook her head in disgust. "Tiffany. She's pretty awful. Last Christmas Dad locked her out of his and Larx's house until she could come over and not be a twat, and she spent the entire time on the phone with the grandparents, trying to get away from their awful den of gay iniquity."

His heart ached for her. The only reason his father had kept talking to him when he'd come out was that Guthrie and Seth were friends, and

Seth was gay, and by that time, Fiddler and the Crabs was making some money. The minute Seth had left for Italy and it was just Guthrie, he'd ceased to exist for Butch Woodson. If it hadn't been for Guthrie's uncle Jock, nobody in the family would have kept contact with him *period*.

"Family can hurt sometimes," he said, his throat dry. He'd hated talking about this with Tad. It had felt so… so *sordid*. So shameful, compared to the warmth and dedication Tad and April had to each other. In light of what these people had, his relationship with his father felt like a dirty secret, something he didn't want to contaminate their little circle of kindness.

"Mm…," Maureen said. Then, through the trees, they could both see the ambient light of emergency klieg lights erected high up—not higher than the ginormous pine trees that surrounded them but midway—probably using the trees as mounts. "And here's a place where it doesn't. Here, turn right and you'll see the spot we're heading for. It's, uh, kind of hard to miss."

Hard to miss was right.

In the middle of that darkness, the lights—which *were* secured to a tree and powered by a generator somewhere far back—hovered like a UFO, and the mass of people looked like something out of *Close Encounters*. Except on closer examination, nobody was wearing a white Tyvek suit. In fact, Guthrie saw a bunch of shivering people in T-shirts, board shorts, and in one case, a Pusheen button-down.

"Pull up to the shoulder there," Maureen said, "but *don't* go beyond the yellow tape."

Guthrie frowned, seeing nothing beyond the yellow tape but more road. "What's the yellow tape for?"

Maureen darted him a quick glance. "About twenty yards beyond the tape is the service track that Larx rolled down. According to Mandeep—he's the geology teacher—the granite shelf that supports this hillside ends about ten feet beyond the yellow line. Everything else is on decomposed granite, scree, and tree roots, and too much weight can pull it down. It's part of the reason we haven't been able to get them, right? It runs all along this side of the canyon's perimeter. So the yellow line is a guideline—nothing heavy goes beyond it."

Guthrie frowned. "But if cell service is shit, and you can't go beyond the yellow line, how do you talk to the guys in the canyon."

Maureen shuddered and pointed to a weird apparatus hanging from a faraway tree. "That," she said. "We borrowed it from the theater department. Christiana—Livvy's little sister—hung out over the edge of the canyon and hollered."

Guthrie thought of that, and while not particularly afraid of heights, he still felt the bottom drop out of his stomach. "Great."

"Livvy was pissed. She would have done it, but, you know…."

"Preggers," Guthrie said, and Maureen nodded. He put the car in park, clutched the sweatshirt Olivia had given to him in lieu of Tad's shirt, and took a breath. "Let's go deliver some care, right?"

"Right," Maureen said. She flung the door open, slid out of the pickup truck, and sent out the siren song to all teenagers everywhere. "Food, people! I've got food, blankets, medical supplies. Everybody get their asses over here and help!"

Suddenly Guthrie was besieged. Four teenagers practically *teleported* to the truck, hands out. Not for the food, although Guthrie wouldn't have blamed them, but for the supplies to be handed down to the guys in the canyon.

He was surprised by a kid a few inches taller than he was, with blue eyes and dark blond hair, appearing at his elbow, saying, "Here, give me the medical bag and the eggcrate. We can use the eggcrate to wrap the med bag and make sure it gets down there intact."

Guthrie went to do that, and the kid said, "And by the way, tell Livvy she owes me a Powerwolf sweatshirt, 'cause, you know, that one still has life in it."

Guthrie grinned at him and looked down at the sweatshirt Livvy had pulled out for him, which had a bright neon zombie horse on the back and the band's logo on the front. "You can have it back when this is over," he said. "I promise, I had no idea I was trespassing."

"Kirby," Maureen huffed out in frustration, "you know she only did that so she'd have something to get you for Christmas. We were at a loss this year."

Kirby grinned. "Great," he said. "Keep it. There are some Rare Americans concert tickets I'm dying to get my hands on for February. Kellen, I'll get you to that concert if it's the last thing I do."

"I owe you a car trip with CW's greatest hits," said the shorter, stockier young man with the black hair. "Just so you know."

"Ugh," said the girl who could only be Christiana, Olivia's little sister. "You can both leave me out of your caveman bonding rituals. I'm listening to Taylor Swift and Beyoncé, and you all can bite me."

"I like me some Taylor," said the tiny fourteen- fifteen-year-old? dodging in to take some of the load. Guthrie, trying to remember Maureen's description of people, thought this must be the little brother of the guy in the minivan.

"Or Beyoncé or Rihanna," Kellen was saying. "But the country western guys will melt my panties, and sometimes I'm down for that."

Kirby burst into low dirty laughter, and Christiana rolled her eyes. While they were talking, they were also unloading the truck, and by the time Guthrie turned to take the bear-proof ice chest Olivia had packed, everybody had something, and the only thing left was the eggcrate and sleeping bags he'd saved for the back of the truck.

And his guitar, of course, which was in the lockbox.

He ventured with the youngsters to a sort of giant erector-set construction site and tried to put together what he was seeing.

"The edge of the canyon and everything about twenty yards back from it is unstable," Maureen said as they set everything down and motioned for the workmen and a few guys who looked like teachers or search and rescue workers to come get food. "They're building a sort of treadmill using PVC pipe and three rows of paracord. There's the EMT basket—" She pointed to a coffin-shaped metal basket that looked like what helicopters dangled when they were lifting victims into the cockpit to whisk them to safety. "—and it's hooked up to a winch on a flatbed that's parked way back on solid ground. The idea is we can drop the basket down and it will slide to them, then pull it up—" Now she pointed to pulleys suspended by trees high above the canyon's edge. "—and pull the basket back on top of the treadmill until it's on solid ground and we can let them out and have EMTs ready to check them over."

Guthrie studied the elaborate system of pulleys and physics and some really ingenious thinking and swallowed. "This must have taken half the day to set up," he said.

Maureen nodded. "We started in the hospital, waiting to see how Eamon—the sheriff—was doing after surgery, when the teenagers started spitballing, and then Yoshi showed up, and he called in the physics teacher and the geologist and...." She chuckled. "And Olivia used some sort of emotional blackmail to get the search and rescue guys to forego the red tape and get their asses out here. By the time we had the setup for Christiana to talk to the guys, it was dark, and...." She sighed. "We need more light. We need to be able to see cracks or shifts in the soil, to watch for scree or rockfalls, and to know where the guys are *exactly*. Right now they're under the trees, leaning against an enormous dead tree that ended up stuck horizontally against the younger trunks. We can't see much of them, even with the lights shining down, because of the shadows. It sucks—I mean, *believe me* it sucks. Christi's dad has a concussion so bad he can't holler, and that's not right, trust me. And you know, my dad is law enforcement. He'd be bleeding out his eyeballs and say, 'It's fine, honey. See to everybody else, okay?' So we know your worry and your impatience, trust me. But...."

"But you all already pulled off a miracle," Guthrie said softly, looking again at all that work in a hurry. "So we'd better not push it."

She smiled at him. "No, we'd better not. Now I know you wolfed down a burger at Larx and Aaron's place. Do you need any more food? Livvy packed a whole bag of apples...." She said it like she was luring him in, and he smiled, grateful.

"An apple would be much appreciated," he said, glancing around again. As he did, he took in a dilapidated, tattered old house that might have once been the epicenter of activity, but it sat, deserted and alone, falling in on itself toward the road. He realized that the football-stadium-sized area of industry he saw now had once been the place's backyard. There were vehicles—SUVs, sedans, battered cars, and teacher-mobiles—parked on the street in front of the house, and he saw a couple of guys sitting in their cars, eating. Search and rescue had brought vans, and that's where the guys in uniform were. The teenagers were putting together the care package in the center of the work area, shoving cheeseburgers and fries in their mouths as they worked. A small Asian man wearing the bright Pusheen button-down shirt and khaki shorts was helping them, also eating his burger one-handed.

Maureen dug into the bear-proof chest for the apples, showing Guthrie how the latch worked, and Guthrie thanked her and took his apple to go help with the organization process.

"Okay," the Pusheen guy said, "I think if we shove the eggcrate down on top of everything and wrap the straps over *it*, nothing should fall out of the basket during the initial drop." He glanced at another man with sepia-toned skin and a fall of rich black hair. "Mandeep, are you *sure* the edge isn't going to crumble when it touches down on the side of the canyon?"

"No, Yoshi, I'm not," Mandeep said shortly. "Remember, we pulled this whole thing out of our *asses* about eight hours ago." He sighed and stared out toward the gaping darkness that Guthrie knew instinctively was the canyon itself. "But it *should* hold. And we need to get them out."

Yoshi nodded. "Buddy, nobody's going to blame you if this doesn't work—but we *are* going to double-check with you, because you're the smartest one here." Yoshi shoved the last bite of food in his mouth and spoke while chewing. "I'm an Engrith teather, rmmbr?"

Mandeep rolled his eyes. "Yeah, Yoshi. Just an English teacher. My God—if you ever get to be principal without Larx, we're all going to have to run for the hills, because you are an absolute dictator." He shook his head, and another man—younger, wearing a denim jacket and sporting a couple days' worth of scruff—ran over from giving some of the search and rescue guys burgers. He was digging his *own* burger out of a bag, and he paused by the rest of them to eat it.

"Everybody fed?" Maureen asked.

"Everybody but the dads," the young man said. He glanced worriedly at Maureen. "How's Livvy? She settled?"

"Last we saw her," she said, indicating Guthrie with her chin, "she was on the recliner, talking Tad Hawkins's sister down from the ledge. Poor thing." Maureen shook her head. "She was beat. I gather these guys had been through the wringer to get here."

Guthrie grimaced. "This was *not* April's comfort zone," he admitted. "But she had to see her brother."

"Are you her boyfriend?" Elton asked as he wiped his hand off on the ass of his jeans. He extended it with a self-conscious smile. "Elton McDaniels—Livvy's husband."

"Guthrie Woodson," Guthrie said, shaking. "And, uhm—"

"Wrong sibling," Maureen said dryly.

Elton laughed. "Sorry about the assumption," he said. "But I'm glad you both are here." He sobered. "From what I understand, Tad is doing okay…." His voice trailed off like "okay" wasn't the word. "They asked for antibiotics, saline, and bandages—and ibuprofen. We've got a witness that says Tad took a shot in the upper thigh. It was from a distance, so blood loss isn't the problem, but infection…."

Guthrie nodded, feeling numb. "So you guys swing up there and talk to them?"

Elton shook his head. "We're not doing that again—we got eyes on them, but barely, considering the light. We're lowering the care package, and Yoshi's going to use the megaphone to talk to them, and then…."

He shrugged, the hamburger in his hand still held up to his mouth but forgotten. "Then we hunker down for the night. I'm going to run and get Livvy—and probably April, if that's okay—early in the morning so she can be there when we go to pull them out. You're welcome to settle down here with us."

"I've got the pickup truck," Guthrie said, feeling like he should contribute something. "It should sleep three in the back. There's eggcrate and sleeping bags, so anybody who needs to stretch out—"

"I'll take it!" Kirby said, straightening. "Kel?"

"I'll sleep in the cab," Kellen said, shivering. "All the stars overhead? Creepy."

"I'll take the pickup," Elton said, yawning. "That way I'll see the sunrise start to hit the canyon, and I can go get Livvy. She's going to be losing her mind."

THE LOWERING of the care package was almost a disaster. The thing went up in the air, over the edge, and then was lowered to the ground—to be met by a chorus of yelps and "The actual *fuck*s!" from their rescuees in the canyon. Apparently, they'd set up the basket's path to be directly over where the four men were holed up against the tree, and that sent debris onto their heads in an unwelcome hail.

Yoshi apologized quickly, and then, with a speed that amazed Guthrie, the entire operation was just… moved. The PVC and paracord contraption was picked up in sections and reassembled fifty feet to the south, the truck with the winch was moved to accommodate the new location, and he was one of the group of people who hoisted the rescue basket and hot-stepped it to where the S and R guys were reassembling the pulley system.

"Wow," he said, a little dazed as, less than half an hour after the first try, they sent the basket down again. Somebody had a searchlight in the trees driven by remote that they used to track the progress of Larx and Aaron, Guthrie was told, as they ventured across the inhospitable incline to drag the supplies back to their small base camp on the other end of the tree.

"Did he still have his half shirt on?" Guthrie asked.

"No," Elton told him, semihysterical laughter in his voice. "Apparently, by the time they got to the basket, there was *no* shirt. No shirt at all."

A surprised smile tilted at Guthrie's lips as the camp—reassured that the supplies had been retrieved and the rescuees were making the best of a very uncomfortable night—began to power down. They left the lights on for another hour as everybody found a vehicle and some blankets or sleeping bags. Guthrie was particularly touched by Christiana and Maureen, reclining in the seats of what Guthrie took to be a Chevy Impala that was *just* for the teenagers to drive. The girls were turned toward each other, each with a fleece blanket pulled to her chin, clutching each other's hands as the generator-driven lights were shut off, a few at a time.

Sisters, he thought, and the thought was followed by another: that he'd never really known his mother, or a sister—or even an aunt—but that he'd been lucky in his choice of friends, because he seemed to be surrounded by them.

Guthrie was watching the last of the lights go off when he felt the pull, the absolute *need*, to tell Tad about that. About loving women. Not as lovers but as humans, because they had a unique energy and for no other reason. Strong women, fragile women, melancholy women, extroverts, Guthrie adored them all.

But not as much as he… adored Tad.

Way to chicken out.

And suddenly he needed to say the real thing too. But he couldn't because Tad was way down on the side of a canyon, being tended to by, all accounts said, two of the best father figures a boy could have, while Guthrie had nothing to do but gnaw his nails and worry.

Or there was the other thing he had that soothed his nerves.

As Elton and Kirby were setting out the eggcrate and sleeping bags for what promised to be a cramped but cozy night in the bed of the truck, Guthrie reached into the lockbox and pulled out his guitar case. Ignoring the other men's surprise, he made himself comfy on the tailgate and cradled his baby, tuning it with his brain on autopilot, his emotions swelling up, blocking rational thought and turning on his fear, his grief, and, oh God, God *damn* you Tad Hawkins, the hope that he couldn't seem to shake.

Suddenly he knew which songs he wanted to play.

The beginning chords of an old Coldplay tune thrummed through the air, and he opened his mouth and began to sing.

I WILL WAIT

TAD'S ASS hurt—ached with poison fire—and there *was* no good way to joke about his ass hurting, because a gunshot was *never foreplay*, dammit, *ever*.

His day had put the *gawd* in gawdawful.

One minute, he and Undersheriff Aaron George had been peering over the edge of the canyon, following a blood trail from somebody who had escaped from the drug raid that had been conducted the night before. The raid had been a disaster. Tad and Chris had been doing their parts, riding behind SWAT, when suddenly shots had rung out in the ungodly darkness, and Chris's friend and old mentor had fallen. The resulting mess would go down in the history of goatfucks, and not only had they lost track of the kid they were looking for in the first place, but there had been nobody to step up to the plate of this small town to tell them what came next.

He and Chris had been milling about the hospital, ready to call the California Bureau of Investigation in pure frustration, when Aaron strode in, his partner, Larx, at his heels.

Watching Aaron order about the other men in the department, organize watch for Eamon, his boss and friend, direct a *very* competent investigation, *including* targeting one of his own men partially responsible for the mess, and ask respectfully for SAC PD resources—because with Eamon shot, shit had gotten suddenly big—had been fucking a-ma-zing. Chris and Tad had jumped at the idea of working with the man, getting shit done was the best of drugs in their line of work, and doing it without bullshit or ego was like an aphrodisiac.

Still, he and Aaron had been tired bordering on *exhausted* when they'd come to check out the original scene of the raid that morning. Aaron hadn't been called in till 3:00 a.m., and nobody had gotten any sleep. And there they'd been, poking around at the base of a tree, when the slug had landed in Tad's ass, followed by the thunder of the gun almost immediately.

The "almost" was important, Tad had thought as the day had slogged on. The "almost" meant the shooter had been far enough away to not just *explode* Tad's entire leg into flesh-and-bone shrapnel. A basic shotgun didn't have *that* great a range, and this wasn't a hunting rifle or a sniper rifle. After the bottom had dropped out of their world, Tad and Aaron had gone sliding down the side of the canyon in the world's worst sled ride, and they'd come to rest against this old, practically petrified tree, lying horizontal to the canyon's incline. The back of Tad's upper thigh had felt like a nuclear explosion, particularly after Aaron's first try to clean it out with half a bottle of water and his ripped-up khaki shirt. But it hadn't been fatal, as much as Tad might have yearned for a long, soft nap after they'd established *that*.

But they had a companion already trying the dirt-nap thing. The kid they'd been searching for had taken the same route they had—off the cliff and under the trees. Except he'd gone one better and was currently hiding under the *really big* tree, near the base where the root system elevated part of the bole just enough for him to have wriggled in. Tad wasn't sure—and didn't have the mental energy—to figure out why the kid had done that, and he *really* didn't know the triggers to get the kid out. He'd managed to coax April out from under a figurative tree by using… well, he hated to think about that time, and he wasn't going to now.

He was saving all his energy for what they had to do.

And it was a *lot*.

They'd barely gotten themselves situated against the tree when Aaron's partner, Larx, had driven down the service track, probably looking for a way to help them all get to safety. When Larx's SUV had been forced off the track (more shooting—God, so much shooting— that Aaron and Tad had fended off with their service weapons), Tad had needed to brace against a leaner part of the tree, shielding himself behind its bulk while he used the trunk to steady his shaking hand as he fired.

The firefight stopped, and Tad didn't know how to feel about that because it stopped when he and Aaron hit their targets. Some officers worked their entire careers without drawing their pieces, and he and Aaron George had not only pulled their weapons but had wounded— possibly killed—suspects, but Tad had no idea how to process that. He couldn't even put a face to the person he'd wounded. He'd fired at the gun in the trees.

He didn't have time to process it anyway. The SUV had tumbled down the hill, and Aaron needed to venture down to the lower part of the canyon to help Larx get back up. For an interminable, *broiling* afternoon, Tad sat, back against the tree, trying to establish contact, any contact, with the mostly unresponsive kid suffering withdrawals in the shadows, with no luck.

He could no longer fight off those horrible days with April. He remembered her handcuffed to a shitty bedframe in a No-Tell Motel where he'd washed her and shaved her licey hair and sedated her through the worst of her withdrawals. Kidnapping. It had been kidnapping. He knew it. He should have been arrested—he should have been *imprisoned*—and April had hated him, bitterly. She'd screamed at him until her throat bled. She'd begged him. She'd kicked, she'd bitten, she'd cursed.

In the end, she'd simply lain there, broken, her body wasted from the drugs, an IV trickling nutrients into her arm, as Tad spoke to her, softly, telling her every moment he could remember of her and their mother and their childhood. Every good thing he could summon, every hope he'd had for her, every beautiful thing he'd seen in his sister, whom he'd die for.

On the fifth day, she'd vomited water.

Then she'd asked for food.

After a few saltines, she'd fallen asleep, and he'd sat in a corner of that shitty room and sobbed. The next day, of her own free will, she'd requested rehab, and he'd needed two days in a clean motel, treating himself for all the things he'd picked up from her—scabies, lice, fungal infections—while he'd eaten and slept.

And grieved, because the things he'd done to haul his little sister from hell weren't things he could just wipe off his soul with some medicated lotion.

And now, his ass on fire, his body shaking with fever and aching fiercely in every joint, he could only whisper to the kid under the tree, not knowing the things that would help *him* find his way home and in no shape at all to find out.

He'd been dozing, the smell of the kid's vomit and filth trapping him in that memory with April, when he heard Aaron calling to him. Aaron and Larx had managed to get halfway up the incline with supplies, which was, as far as Tad could tell, a miracle. They had a plan to get up to his level, the supplies with them, but Tad needed to step up. The pulley system they'd arranged and built out of paracord and a prayer had been ingenious, but in the end it depended on raw muscle and Tad being able to catch the rope they were flinging up the hill so they could set it up again. By the time they'd levered the supplies up to where Tad and his despondent friend under the tree were camped, and then helped Larx—who was *not* okay after rolling down the cliff in the SUV—get up the incline, Tad was done. Absolutely done. He was sure he couldn't do another thing but go fetal and moan until somebody magically teleported him to a place with morphine and sterile gloves.

He'd had to settle for the supply drop instead.

When all was said and done, his wound had been more thoroughly cleaned, antiseptics and antibiotics had been *generously* applied, and his ass had been wrapped in the cleanest gauze to be found in the middle of a gravel pit anywhere. And he had clean sweats—oh thank God, thank *anyone* who had donated the sweats to him. Aaron had assured Tad they were *his*, a little too long but they fit nicely in the thighs, and they were warm and not stained with blood and sweat.

And then Larx had reached into the clothing duffel and pulled out....

Tad shivered now, pulling the flannel hoodie closer, burying his face into the collar, smelling Guthrie's shampoo, his soap, even a little sweat in the lining.

He knew there was an explanation somewhere, and he wanted to hear it. Wanted to hear how Guthrie had found him, had known he was there. Tad wanted to touch his hand, tell him how grateful he was.

Wanted to kiss him, see his face in the sun.

But all of that was subsumed under the amazing truth that the hoodie represented.

He's here. He's here. He's here.

No matter how skittish his new lover was, no matter how shy, Guthrie had shown up when showing up was impossible, and Tad could have *cried* with how much that meant.

But there were other things to tend to first.

Food was pressed into his hands, and he realized how much protein bars and Gatorade had *not* done the trick since ten that morning. The burger wasn't hot anymore, but it wasn't congealed either, and it tasted like manna from heaven as he gulped it down. Even the fries were delicious at this point, and Larx gave him an apple to go with everything in the end.

"Eat the apple," he said. "It'll keep you regular."

Larx was funny. Aaron was steadfast, but Larx was funny. They were both in their late forties and so… so *dad* he couldn't even fathom a word for their *dadness*. Aaron, blond and broad, had been the muscle behind the pulley system, but Larx, smaller, leaner, with dark hair and eyes, had been the one to think it up. Both of them had tended to his wound, and they both had what Tad could only think of as the "dad touch." Absolutely nonsexual but firm. Kind. Practical.

The kind of practical, Tad had learned, that sacrificed part of his shirt to cover a nest of sleeping rattlesnakes found near the landing place for the supply basket to make sure the snakes *remained* sleeping and wouldn't notice all the human activity near their lair.

Tad was going to take Larx's word for it that the snakes would stay put—but he'd noticed Larx and Aaron shoving their bloodied clothes and a closed bag of trash into a space under the tree between their camp and the snakes' camp, so he decided the faith was well placed.

And now, after Aaron and Larx had cleaned up their camp and offered their poor psychotic addict under the tree a blanket and some food—and a sedative, which they'd administered in the hopes of getting him to calm down and get some sleep and maybe gather the wherewithal to come out from under the tree—they were settling down on a mat of spongy eggcrate with the tree at their back.

Aaron held Larx against his chest, and Larx held Tad, all of them gathered under a layer of sleeping bags and blankets. Now that Tad had gotten some painkillers and some food and was no longer shivering in his bloodstained black jeans, he found there was something immensely comforting about being held by two strong fathers who had already proven they were letting nobody go on their watch.

He could also count all the ways his body hurt—not just his ass, but *everywhere*. He and Aaron had fallen down a cliff, for sweet fuck's sake. There were going to be bruises, bangs, and scrapes. And he'd *really* needed somewhere soft to lie during that interminable afternoon.

The comfort of his new friends against his back and the spongy eggcrate under his ass was wonderful, but above their heads the stars stretched wide and impersonal, and he felt small and insignificant and oddly alone.

Larx and Aaron were so obviously in love. Their teamwork had shone through every interaction, every plan, every idea. Apparently, an entire troop of teenagers and a brain trust of *very* underpaid teachers were putting together a miracle for them on the plateau above their heads, but Tad was… incidental in all of that. All he had to comfort him, really, was that shirt wrapped around his shoulders and the smell of Guthrie against his skin.

The ambient lights from the construction above flickered off, and the sense (if not the sound) of profound industry faded, leaving their little encampment in almost absolute darkness.

The stars glared, malevolent in their icy indifference, and Tad was shivering with fever, willing Larx to hold him closer before he disappeared.

And that's when they heard it.

A guitar, played in the silence of the canyon, and a clear, strong voice singing a lonely song. A song about waiting for your lover until the world ended.

"Til Kingdom Come."

Guthrie had mentioned it a few times as a possibility to replace the both revered and reviled Linda Ronstadt song that had so enthralled Tad at the beginning. Tad loved it. The simplicity of a lover who would wait for his love forever if need be, asking humbly for the same promise in return spoke to Tad. Weren't they all, in the end, waiting for love?

And love—that was all it could be called—was soaring out over this lonely, inhospitable canyon, carried through the dark by Guthrie's voice, by his music, and by, Tad was absolutely sure, the purity of Guthrie Arlo Woodson's heart.

Guthrie sang "I Will Wait" next and let the final chords of the song—a sort of clanging guitar masterpiece, hang in the air above the canyon like the final smoke of a fireworks display, and at first Tad thought it was a misfire. He should have ended with a lullaby. And then Guthrie pulled out Death Cab for Cutie's "I Will Follow You Into the Dark," and he breathed out a sigh of contentment.

The next song was soothing, an invitation to sleep, but he still heard that almost cacophonous finale and the lover's belted promise, again, to wait.

And he realized that Guthrie wasn't going anywhere, not tonight. As darkness washed over him and he tried to sink below the shivering fever and the pain of his wound, he heard himself humming.

I will follow you into the dark….

He knew in his heart that for the man who would bring him kindness, bring him comfort, through all the madness the day had entailed, he would make the promise and keep it, even if he had to wait the rest of his days.

THE NIGHT passed in a blur of fever, of pain, of Larx's quiet comfort. At one point he'd awakened with a throat full of broken glass, thinking April was under the tree and he couldn't get her out. Then he dreamed that Guthrie was there with her, falling down the canyon, falling farther, faster, like Larx had done as Tad and Aaron had watched helplessly. He woke up crying Guthrie's name.

"It's okay, son," Larx said softly. "He's here."

And Tad could *smell* him on his shirt, against his skin, and for a moment, he calmed down.

The morning dawned bright and chill, and Tad knew he didn't have long left. He'd spent the night wrapped warm and tight in what was essentially a summer night in the mountains, and he'd been sweating and shivering with cold and fever so badly he'd barely registered the body heat of the two men trying to keep him safe. They'd put him in the rescue basket, tucked him in tight, and *hauled* him to where the coupling links were to hook the basket up again.

Larx gently covered his face with a cloth and told him to close his eyes—the end of the ride was scary.

Tad was so out of it, he only recalled a feeling of weightlessness, of rising instead of falling. For a while he heard the rasp of the bottom of the basket on gravel, and then felt a slither as it hit plastic of some kind, and then—oh God, he was *flying*, like on an amusement park ride, hauled up and dangling in the air before being tugged backward and gliding along the ground.

Was he dead? This was like the dead guy in *Gladiator*, he thought muzzily, but if he was dead, shouldn't his body *hurt less*?

Finally the basket came to a rest, and someone uncovered his face. There were EMTs unpacking him from the eggcrate and the sleeping bags used to make him secure under the straps of the basket, and then he was on a backboard.

And then a stretcher.

Somebody said, "Let them through. They know Detective Hawkins."

Chris? That was Chris's voice, but that was *not* Chris's rough hand in his grimy one, and definitely not Chris's sweet, sweet voice in his ear. The face over his was in shadow, thanks to the strong morning sun through the trees and a fall of greasy blond hair, but Tad knew him now, knew his smell, knew his *feel*.

"How you doin', son?"

"Guthrie," Tad croaked. "God. You're here."

"I'm not the only one," Guthrie told him, placing a soft kiss on his forehead. "C'mere, darlin'. He needs to see your face."

And there was April. Oh God, that eternity of a night when he'd dreamed of her in withdrawals, trapped in his worst memory of both her and himself, and she was here. She was *here*, clean in all the ways, weeping softly as she held his hand.

"April," he breathed.

"Oh, big brother," she sobbed, "you have *no* idea how glad we are to see you."

He smiled, and he would have told her the feeling was mutual, but the EMTs had enough, and he was lifted into the back of the bus, and the world became a white blur of antiseptic after that.

Bridge over Troubled Waters

"It was part of Ms. Hawkins's agreement with the halfway house that—"

"I get it," Guthrie snarled. "She broke the rules. She broke the rules, and apparently going to see her brother during an emergency means she needs to be flogged. That's great. I'll take the lashes, okay? She needed to come here and be with him—"

"We have no verification of an emergency—"

"Turn on the fuckin' news, darlin'. It's fuckin' everywhere!"

There was a pause. "I'm at my computer now. What should I be looking for?"

"Local Sheriff rescued in Colton County."

"That? But there wasn't a...."

Oh good. The bitchy robot woman on the other end of the phone could fuckin' read. Wasn't that a fuckin' blessing? Guthrie scowled at the phone in his hand and glanced around the hospital corridor to see how many people were running for the hills.

To his surprise, there was only a very limp Olivia, emerging from one of the hospital rooms to sink into one of the gawdawful chrome-and-vinyl torture masterpieces the hospital called "chairs" propped up against the wall. She gave him a weak smile and a wave, and Guthrie returned it, on the verge of saying something when the voice on the other end spoke up.

"Even so," she said, "this doesn't give a complete stranger any right to involve himself in April Hawkins's transportation—"

"Lady, she came to me and begged. You may be a stone-cold bitch, but I am not. If you could maybe pull the ice tray out of your ass, you could see these are special circumstances and let the poor kid come home and leave her alone about it. This is her brother, and I haven't known the two of them long, but I can tell you that's a big furry deal to them, so maybe you need to defrost a bit and make like a Disney princess and fuckin' let it go."

Across from him, Olivia snorted into her hand and then motioned for him to keep going. He gave her a droll arch of the eyebrows and waited to see what Robot Ice-Princess had to say.

"If you can assure me Ms. Hawkins can be here today—"

"We. Are. In. Colton. And neither of us has slept. Do me a favor— you're on your computer right now. See how long it'll take me to drive from Colton, California, to Bodega Bay, in traffic."

There was a pause, and she said, "Six hours."

"Yes, ma'am, and that's without stopping for food or using the bathroom. I made that drive in traffic yesterday, and then I stayed up most of the night waiting for them to drag April's brother out from the canyon. Did you find the footage? 'Cause you should. It was horrifying. And now April still doesn't know if her brother's going to be okay. I might— *might*—bring her home tomorrow, depending on what the doctors say. I'll call you to let you know."

"You can't just keep her—"

"I can and I will. You people are fuckin' exhausting. Jesus."

He hit End Call and stared at the phone, hoping he hadn't caused April too much trouble but not sure if he could do anything about it if he had. With a groan, he leaned back against the wall and searched around for another chair like Olivia's to sink into and saw only the one in the bench next to her.

"Go ahead," she said, patting it. "Aaron's in there resting. We're still waiting for Larx to come out of all his tests and stuff." She shuddered. "Apparently, his concussion is worse than we thought. They're—" She swallowed hard. "—worried. They might have to, you know. Drill."

"Bwah," Guthrie said with feeling. He got the concept; drill through the skull to relieve pressure, but that didn't change the fact that they were punching a *hole* through someone's *head*.

"Right?" Olivia's voice rose a little with suppressed worry, and he patted her knee.

"It'll be all right," he said gruffly. Tad was still in surgery, and April was down in the cafeteria, getting them some food. He wasn't particularly hungry, but the halfway house had been hounding her so relentlessly that he'd set her phone to forward their calls to his and then answered.

The woman on the other end hadn't just been "unfriendly," she'd been downright rude. No amount of explaining that this had been a bona fide emergency could convince her that April hadn't violated the terms of

her living arrangement willy-nilly, and Guthrie remembered Tad's worry
about his sister in Bodega Bay. He was willing to place a good weight
of her fragility on her hatred of her halfway house, but God, who was he
to say?

He hadn't wanted April to hear him dealing with the people,
because he wasn't sure of his temper, and he'd been right. How was she
supposed to respect these folks when Guthrie was about ready to run
them over with his truck?

"Who were you talking to?" Livvy asked. "You sounded pissed."

"April's halfway-house people." Guthrie growled again. "She…
she literally hopped on two busses to come find me, because she was
worried, and they're all freaked out and threatening to kick her out
because she didn't tell anybody. I asked the lady if she would have let
April go if she *had*, and she said she was required by law to tell the
police if April threatened to leave town, and there were no exceptions."
He shook his head. "And part of me gets it—but part of me is, like, the
girl isn't high, she hasn't been looking for drugs over the last two days,
she's been looking for her brother! And I feel like maybe there should be
a happy medium between letting folks in this living sitch run around and
do all the drugs again, and the Spanish fucking Inquisition!"

Olivia let out a short laugh. "You're a good friend, Guthrie. Is she
really holding up?"

He nodded, surprised at this. Tad had been *so* worried. "She just…
I mean, I'm not gonna lie. I'm hoping she can sleep on your folks' couch
again, because she was so happy to spend the night hugging that big doofy
dog. Your house, the kindness, even the kids made her laugh. But before
that she'd held it together until the very end. You've got no idea. The
hospital was our third stop, and the amount of folks not fucking knowing
what was going on was astro-fucking-nomical. I mean… *damn*."

"I do know what you mean," she said. "That's what was going
on in the hospital when the plan sort of came together. I got through to
search and rescue, and we started asking ourselves, 'But what can they
do?' and it occurred to some of us that they couldn't do *anything*. The
dads and Eamon are such a force of direction for the town. I think people
really got to see what life would be like without them. Which, you know,
is sort of good, because it means they'll start setting up fail-safes so shit
doesn't fall apart again."

"Well, they got themselves out of a terrible situation, and they got supplies up to Tad and that other kid. I mean, it's a whole town of gen-u-wine heroes, you know?"

Livvy snorted. "You think what you did for Tad and his sister doesn't qualify?" she asked.

He stared at her. "No. It's… anybody would have—"

She cocked her head. "Not just anybody, Guthrie. Somebody who cared." She paused and then spoke into the silence before he could. "How's your job?"

He gave an exaggerated sigh and flopped back against the wall. "They asked me if I could come in today, and I said no. I'm waiting to be fired by text."

"Mm. That's too bad, honey. I'm sorry. It shouldn't be that way. You and April—you did a big thing. It's not right people keep trying to punish you for it."

"No," he said, considering, "but for us, I think the doing the good thing is the reward." He thought of Tad's expression as Guthrie had bent down to kiss his sweaty forehead. He'd looked so relieved, so happy. Guthrie had helped do that. "Tad's okay. It's all either of us wanted."

He felt some of his weariness start to catch up to him, and his eyes fell to half-mast in the ensuing silence. He'd gotten a few hours of rest in the cramped back of the truck, but his busy mind, full of the what-ifs of Tad's rescue, hadn't made for much real sleep. In the quiet hum of the hospital corridor, Olivia laced their fingers together and laid her head on his shoulder, falling into a doze. Guthrie used her head to rest his cheek and did the same thing.

He had no idea how long he'd been like that when April sank to the other side of him on the bench of chairs, smelling faintly of sandwiches, and he felt her small hand in his and then her head on his shoulder.

That's where they were, three people who had been strangers until the day before, clinging to each other like a pile of kittens, when a nurse came to address them from the corridor.

"Livvy, honey, your dad's asleep, but you can go sit with him while he comes to. Aaron's company is gone, and the doctor's with *him* now, so maybe wait half an hour or so. Mr. Woodson?"

"Yes'm," Guthrie mumbled, trying to clear the grit from his eyes.

"Mr. Hawkins is in a recovery room. He's asking for both you and Miss Hawkins, but the room is a little crowded...." She trailed off delicately.

He turned to April, understanding. "Go talk to him, honey," he ordered softly.

"But Guthrie," she said, her voice shaking. "You did so much—"

He gave her a kiss on her crown, protective of her as he wasn't of the other women in his life. Roberta was awkward, but she was strong. She had to be to work as a musician; her skin was thick and her work ethic was stunning and she just... *moved mountains* to be where she needed. All the family from Seth and Kelly's life were strong. Hell, Guthrie had shown up here and run into Maureen and Olivia, who were very different, but damn, could those women move their own damned mountains.

April couldn't. April needed a champion, someone who could move mountains for her. Her brother was out of commission for the moment, so that meant it was Guthrie's turn to step up.

And that meant giving up being the first one Tad saw when he woke up.

"Sweetheart," he said gruffly, "I'm going to have to take you home tomorrow, and it's going to suck bad enough. You go spend as much time as you can with him, okay?"

"Okay," she whispered, then looked up at the nurse. "Can Guthrie go in when I'm done?"

"Sure, hon, but if he's asleep, you need to let him rest."

"'Course," she muttered. "But Guthrie gets some time. It's only right. Oh!" She turned to the small table next to the bench of chairs. "Guthrie, here's your sandwich!" And with that she thrust a sub— hopefully Italian something or other—into his hands, the paper crinkling slightly.

"You two are good for each other," the nurse said softly. "That's important in in-laws, right?"

Was this what having an in-law was like? The thought tickled Guthrie as much as it scared him, but he didn't say either of those things to April as she stood and followed the nurse to Tad's room in recovery. Olivia was still struggling to stand up when Guthrie stood to give her a hand.

"Thanks," she muttered grudgingly. "God, I swear, when I'm not forever pregnant, I'm... well, a little less klutzy."

"I believe you. Where you headed?"

"To the cafeteria," she said, sounding determined. "That smells wonderful."

He winked. "Sit back down, darlin', and I'll share it with you." He had no intention of eating any of it. Olivia sat down, probably more because she was tired than for any other reason, and he unwrapped the thing and gave her half, watching as she attacked it with a ferocity he personally only reserved for a nice rare steak.

She finished the first half, and he handed her the second. She was halfway done before it occurred to her that this wasn't "sharing."

"Aw, man—Guthrie, I just ate your lunch!"

He glanced both ways down the hall, like he was telling a really big secret. "I've got news for you...."

She took another bite and grinned as she swallowed. "You, uh, didn't really want the sandwich?"

"Nope," he told her. His eyes tracked to the room where April had been led, and he tried to tamp down on his yearning to see Tad. Stupid cop. Seriously, one month of hope and this guy gets shot and falls off a cliff? Guthrie sure could pick 'em. If Tad Hawkins hadn't been the single most decent, kindest, funniest guy who'd ever set out to woo Guthrie with a stealth campaign of texts and phone calls, he would have been out of there so fast....

He'd have a permanent dent in this blessedly uncomfortable seat.

God, the thought of leaving the guy now? In any form? Ripped Guthrie's heart right out of his chest.

"You'll see him soon," Olivia soothed, like she could see right through him.

"Man, what am I supposed to say?" he asked. "Hey, missed that third date?"

She snorted. "Maybe ask him how the weather is in the bottom of the canyon. Larx likes to have students record temperature fluctuations depending on topography. He'd be fascinated."

Guthrie blinked, remembering all those super-intelligent people talking as they gathered to rescue their friends. "Your family is something special, do you know that?"

Olivia grinned again and wiped her mouth with an offered napkin. "Blame Larx. I mean, Aaron too, because Larx wouldn't love him if he couldn't keep up, but my dad... man, I can't wait for you to meet him."

Guthrie's face heated. "I, uhm…I don't know much about good dads. I mean, the other kind, yeah, but the good kind, not so much. Maybe I'll just be your friend and hear about him."

She cocked her head and wiped her hand on the napkin before resting it on his knee. "Honey, you don't have to know about good dads. You sort of show up and they feed you and hug you and get busy in your life. You and Tad don't stand a chance. It's too bad you don't live up here. There would be family dinners and running into each other in town, and…." She trailed off with a happy sigh, and it hit Guthrie that she was talking about *him*. She wanted to see *him*.

"I'd think you've got enough company," he said, thinking about her and her husband's living arrangement with the two brothers.

She shrugged. "Berto and Jaime are like family. And of course my family is right around the corner. There's just something to be said about a friend. I mean, I think Mau-Mau could fit the bill, but, you know, she's got a life down in SoCal, and she's going for her teaching credential. I, you know, want you up here for my own selfish reasons, 'cause I'm a selfish biotch."

Guthrie chuckled and, unbidden, came the vision of the sky the night before. No ambient light, just the stars, strewn across the velvet black sky. He'd grown up in a town this size, a town in which the high school graduation was such a big deal two of the town's most prominent citizens would be there to make sure the kids were safe and celebrated in a big way.

Or would have been if, say, anybody had cared.

Sand Cut, California was a tiny town that had been formed during the construction of a tunnel through the hills surrounding the Monterey Peninsula, leaving a small population of settlers who'd spent a decade supporting the work. Guthrie had been on the road enough to know that there were small towns and small towns, but Sand Cut was one of the smallest, and most of that was in the residents' minds. When Fiddler and the Crabs broke up, Guthrie had stayed in San Rafael because it was near the city, near the music, near the hope of better things to come, but his dad and Uncle Jock had gone back to the small house he'd grown up in back in Sand Cut.

That moment of melancholy freedom under the stars in Colton had felt like it was galaxies away from the small town Guthrie had known.

Like here in the mountains there was a hope the washed-out town by a sand dune had forgotten.

"I like it here," he said into the sudden silence. "I don't think you're selfish. I think you need someone who gets you to make this place home."

She patted his knee. "Which is a great conclusion, but now we need to get you and Tad *here*."

He chuckled again at the absurdity of it. "Darlin', I'll be lucky if my truck'll take me back to Bodega Bay."

She teared up suddenly, probably a result of hormones and exhaustion. "I'd rather you were staying here," she said and leaned her head on his shoulder, like April had.

He let her. Sometimes it was nice to be needed, in any small way.

APRIL EMERGED about twenty minutes later, looking drained and disoriented. "He's asking for you," she rasped. "But you may have to wait a couple of minutes while the nurses tend to him."

Olivia stretched her hand out to April as Guthrie got up.

"Come sit with me," Olivia said softly. "Elton's coming in a little bit to check on me. If Guthrie's not done, Elton can take you back to the house and you can sleep some more. You know, Dozer needs some love, right?"

April brightened at the mention of the family's giant blond retriever mix. "I might have to fight Jaime for his attention," she said, and Guthrie recalled the smaller, younger boy who'd been at the rescue site.

Olivia chuckled. "Well, Jaime likes a good belly rub too," she said. She sobered. "This winter, when Jaime and Berto were having a really rough time, I'm pretty sure Dozer saved Jaime's life. Jaime played with that dog until he *broke* him. Dozer couldn't move anymore he was so tired. And Jaime couldn't play with him anymore, so he just… curled up with the dog on a pillow and slept. Sweetest thing in the world. So yeah. They're bonded. But I think Dozer's got a big heart—he'll curl up with you too."

"Is that okay, Guthrie?" April asked, so needy for it, for the warm family, for the happy dog, for the chance to rest somewhere *not* her halfway house, that Guthrie would have stood guard at the threshold with a weapon to make sure she got that time.

"We don't pack up until tomorrow," he told her. "You go chill and rest, and if you can get a ride here this afternoon, I'll take you back there tonight." He glanced at Olivia apologetically. "I'm imposing," he said, absolutely appalled. "If April can sleep on the couch, I can sleep in the truck again—"

Olivia gaped at him. "Over my dead pregnant body!" she gasped. "No. Just... no. The icky boys can share a room like they do over Christmas, and you can have Kellan's bed. Don't worry, don't object— it's done. I said so, and since both the dads are in the hospital, I'm in charge." She gave him a smug glance. "You can't tell me no—it'll make me appear weak in front of that herd of teenagers. You need to have my back, boo."

He smiled a little, grateful. "Fair," he murmured. Then he kissed April gently on the forehead. "Get some rest, sweetheart. I'll watch after him."

"Thanks, Guthrie," she said. "I know you will."

And with that he ventured down the hall and into the darkened room.

FOOLS RUSH IN

APRIL SEEMED tired but sound.

"You came all the way up here?" Tad asked, his head sort of deliciously swimmy from the pain meds and exhaustion but his emotions in full operation.

"Guthrie's truck," April said, stroking his hand. "Tad, you gotta know… he just…. I walked into his work, and he just took me aside and said, 'Yup. We gotta go.' I mean… I know you think he's a little bit gunshy, but… but he fought for you. You…." She kissed his knuckles. "You gotta know."

"Thanks, honey," he said, closing his eyes. He wanted to dwell on that, bathe in it, let Guthrie's kindness seep into his pores. He'd do that later; he had to. Right now he had to worry about April because the getting on the bus thing, the coming up to Colton—that was some unprecedented self-actualization on her part, and he had to make sure that was okay. "How's your place? Are they okay with it?"

April made a suspicious sound, almost a laugh. "No," she said, hiding her mouth behind her hand. "They are not. But Guthrie's been talking to them. Callie Leonard hasn't ever had to deal with a Guthrie before."

Tad swallowed. "Baby, I… I hate that you have to go back there. I want you in Sacramento. I'll… I'll be laid up for a good eight weeks after this. Maybe you could, I don't know. If we're rooming together and I'm not gone all the time at first, maybe that's a good way to start? What do you think?"

April nodded like this had already occurred to her. "We'll get two cats, one for me and one for Guthrie," she said calmly. "We'll eat pizza on Friday nights and have movies, and Guthrie will come and go, but we'll make sure there's a home."

Tad stared at her. "You and Guthrie have, uhm, bonded?"

Her thumb stilled in its massage of his battered knuckles, which was a relief. He hadn't wanted to tell her that all his skin hurt. "He's good, Taddy Bear. He's… he's good. There's—" She rubbed her chest.

"—something there. I can almost see it. It's like an aura of sadness, but even if it's there, he's still good."

Tad nodded, relieved. Two days and a thousand years ago, he'd planned to have the two of them meet, and he'd been happy and excited and hopeful. What he'd wanted to happen—that the new person in his life and one of the main people in his life—would meet and get along, had happened in a much deeper way than he'd expected, and he was grateful. So grateful.

He'd fallen silent, almost sinking to sleep again, when he registered April's question.

"Wha'?"

"Tad, did you really mean it? That I can come live with you soon?"

He nodded. "Let me get out of the hospital first," he murmured. "I'll call them and start making arrangements once I get back to Sac."

He heard another suspicious noise and really looked at her. "Baby?"

"I'm just so glad," she said, voice choked. "I... I know why I stayed in Bodega Bay at first." It was where they'd grown up. She loved the ocean. She hadn't wanted to leave. "But I'm bigger than the place we were born. I-I... the bipolar made me afraid. Of everything different. But I was on my meds—I brought them, Taddy Bear. And the truck ride sucked, and the getting here sucked, and the being scared for you *sucked*, and if I can get through all that without wanting to use, just to be with my brother who'd do anything for me, I think of what I'd do in the same town as you, and I think I'll be okay."

"Aw, baby," he murmured. "We'll do that, then. I promise."

She gave a tremulous smile and pulled out the bag she'd brought. To his immense relief she released his hand and reached for a bright pink blanket, almost done. "I should be able to have this finished before me and Guthrie leave tomorrow," she said earnestly, her hands starting their deft watch over the developing fabric. "And I've got some more yarn in here. I'm going to make hats for *everybody*."

Tad's smile took up most of his face and most of his energy. "You mean the Larkins and the Georges?"

"And the Benitezes and the McDanielses," she said, and he laughed.

"See, you know everybody's names," he said. "All I know is that Aaron and Larx are heroes and their kids saved us all."

She regarded him levelly. "Oh, they are," she said soberly. "And they did. You've got no idea. Guthrie and I were on our last fucking nerve when we finally hooked up with Aaron's daughter. It was *amazing*. I've never…." She bit her lip. "Mom was so good, Tad. She worked so hard to keep us together, to keep us happy. I wish she'd had people in her life like this. I…. Olivia, Larx's daughter? She's bipolar too. We talked last night, and she… she's such a grown-up about her meds and her baby and her husband and… she's given me some faith, you know? That I can be normal. I can stay off the bad shit and keep doing the good. Whatever you gotta do to stay tight with these people, do that, okay?"

Tad gave a small laugh and confessed something to her that he hadn't even confessed to Chris, who had actually been the first in to debrief him. "Aaron kept threatening to poach me from SAC PD," he said. "I don't want to do that to Chris, but I think you're right. I think we should let ourselves have some friends."

"And you should let yourself have a boyfriend," April said softly. "You never told me the whole truth about why Sam left—"

"Because he was a douchebag," Tad said quickly. He still didn't want her to know the details. He'd told her the embarrassing story of Jesse because he knew it would make her laugh, but Sam had simply claimed he wanted something different.

"Because of me," April said without heat. "I'm not stupid. You disappeared from Sac for two months, and when you went back, you didn't have a boyfriend anymore. I… at the time it registered, but I couldn't…."

"It's okay," he told her softly. "He wasn't husband material. I should have figured that out when… when Mom passed. I need someone who sticks."

"Guthrie wants to stick," she said, and he grimaced.

"Yeah, but like you said…." He was bruised and sore, but he could still make a weak rubbing motion around his heart.

"Yeah," she repeated. "But maybe he needs a guy who will stick right back."

He shrugged then, his eyes closing. She leaned over and kissed his cheek. "I'll stay here a minute," she said, "then send Guthrie in."

"Thanks," he mumbled. And he meant all of it: the coming to see him, the reassurance, the effort to be with people. It was all important. That she'd do that for him was worth being ghosted by Sam, was worth taking a risk on the far more ephemeral-appearing Guthrie. April, his little sister, was *here*, when he'd thought he was all alone in the world.

And she'd brought the man Tad had been trying not to obsess over. Who had stood up.

Who had *really* stood up.

The enormity of what Guthrie had done for him, for April, was still settling in. Who… who *did* that? Who left a job they needed to follow a woman as unstable as April had undoubtedly appeared into the wild blue yonder after a man he'd slept with *once*.

Apparently, Guthrie.

Tad had been hopeful before, but this went beyond hope. This was perilously close to the human connection of a lone sweet voice reaching through his heart, through a velvet black void.

This emotion, this attachment, this *need* couldn't be taken back. It couldn't be countered. It was like getting shot and falling off a cliff. One minute you were standing there, taking in the lay of the land, and the next the bottom dropped out of your world, and God knew when the pain would hit, but you knew it had to be coming.

And he couldn't help it. He fell anyway.

Not on his ass this time; that would be too easy. He knew exactly where the pain would be when he hit bottom. Wasn't a thing he could do to stop it.

As his eyes fluttered shut and he succumbed to exhaustion and the painkillers and the things his body was doing to heal, he suddenly realized why Sam had left. Tad had never really loved Sam. He couldn't have. *This* was what falling in love was like. *This* was the fear it wouldn't ever be returned.

This, in all its fear and its adrenaline and its glory, was why Guthrie was so terrified.

Tad got it now, and he could only pray that Guthrie was there with him like he'd been the night before. He wasn't sure he could survive this fall if there was nobody out there to save him from the cold dark void.

He wasn't sure how long he was out, shivering in his sleep. He knew the nurses came in and checked on him, but their touch was impersonal, and he could ignore it. But suddenly there was a quiet around him, and a comforting smell. Someone put something warm around his shoulders and… gah! It smelled like Guthrie. Tad used the hand not hooked up to all the tubes and shit to burrow under it, shifting even more to his side than he had been in an effort to be comfortable.

He saw a vague figure standing across the room.

"Move closer," he slurred. "Sit."

"If you like," Guthrie told him, his twang leaching into Tad's bones and soothing some of their ache.

"Who hauls a freaked-out woman two hundred miles to sing to a man under a starry sky and hides in the back of the fuckin' room?" Tad mumbled, although the answer to that should be obvious.

Guthrie approached and sat down in the chair April had vacated, gazing at Tad with those mournful brown eyes. "You didn't ask for that," he said softly. "I didn't want you to feel obliged."

Jesus save him.

"Seriously?" Tad groused. "No, idiot, give me your hand. I've been dreaming about you for two weeks, and you're just going to sing to me and leave? God, you suck."

He heard Guthrie's amused chuff of air but, even better, felt the roughness of guitar-callused fingers as they twined with his.

"Well, I wasn't leaving until tomorrow," Guthrie told him, like it was a secret, "but I was planning to come back."

"What's tomorrow?" Tad asked, squeezing his fingers.

"April's home needs her back," Guthrie said. "And I was going to leave my keys at my own place so the girls I'm going to apartment share with can get them and move in whenever they want." He squeezed back. "And I may stop at a friend's apartment and get him some clothes and shit to make staying in the hospital easier."

Tad shuddered under the sweatshirt, which smelled like somebody else's fabric softener but Guthrie's skin. "I think your friend would *so* appreciate it," Tad mumbled. "God, so much. Some pajama pants and some T-shirts and some underwear. You have no idea. Eventually, I'll get out of this johnny, and I'd like to look good."

Guthrie used his other hand to brush the hair back from Tad's forehead, and Tad closed his eyes, savoring the tenderness.

"You look good already," Guthrie said softly. "You're alive. You're mending. You keep looking alive, I won't be able to resist you."

Tad chuckled. "But all bets are off if I'm dead?"

There was a sudden stillness, and for a moment Tad thought he'd gone too far. Then Guthrie took in a sharp breath and let it out.

"Probably. I can't stand a man who smells worse than I do. But right now, you've got a while to catch up."

Guthrie had driven all day yesterday, then slept in the back of his truck, and then picked up April and come to the hospital to wait for Tad's surgery. What Tad found to be comforting could probably be damned embarrassing for a man who was only comfortable on stage or in the quiet of his own home.

Tad relaxed, thinking he'd escaped scaring Guthrie with the morbid joke, when a suspicious sound broke the quiet.

After a startled moment, Tad focused on Guthrie's face and saw what Guthrie had probably been hiding while leaning against the wall, what he hadn't wanted Tad to see when he'd come to visit.

"Aw, Guthrie—"

Guthrie shook his head and tried to let go of Tad's hand, but Tad wasn't having it.

"Drop the side rail," he ordered. "I know you can figure it out."

The sound continued while Guthrie obeyed him, and Tad cursed hospital rooms and awkwardness and gun-shy lovers until the thing was down and Tad could order him to bring the chair closer.

Guthrie's tear-streaked face was finally close enough for Tad to cup his cheek.

"Baby," Tad breathed.

"I'm stupid, and you should ignore me," Guthrie told him, brows drawn down. "It's just, you know, been a day. And...."

"And you thought I was going to die," Tad said, getting it.

Guthrie shook his head. "It would figure, right? I finally find someone good? It felt like I'd doomed you." He gave a half laugh that sputtered tears, and Tad rubbed under Guthrie's eyes with his thumb.

"I didn't mean to joke about it," Tad whispered.

"No, you did. And it was funny." Guthrie nodded, so earnestly that Tad found himself smiling. "It's just... damn, son. It's good to see you."

"Good to see you too." And because Guthrie had cried first, had been vulnerable and in pain, Tad let some of his own fear show through. "I...." His voice caught. "I almost cried when I saw the hoodie, you know. And when you started to play? God, Guthrie. You saved my life just by letting me know you were there. You saved all of us. We... we had the *worst* fuckin' night. And suddenly there was this song, and it was so sweet. And the night didn't feel so big and black anymore, and home didn't feel so far away." He took a shuddery breath, aware his own dam had burst, his own tears were falling.

"There was nothing I could do," Guthrie whispered. "You were okay, and I was going to see you, and then... God, you dropped through a hole in the world?" He glared at Tad through the tears. "How could you drop through a hole in the world? That's not right!"

Tad laughed a little. "Well, I was lucky, you know—"

"Oh I know," Guthrie said, his eyes shifting wildly. "If you had to drop through a hole in the world, you ended up doing it with, what? Dad gods? Is that what you found? Dad gods of backcountry California?"

Tad laughed a little harder. "*Yes!*" he said, hysterical. "Oh my God, *yes*."

"Did you know there were aerial photos of the damned pulley system? How much paracord did that take, by the way? I need a minimum amount to fuckin' stock."

"You're killing me," Tad wheezed, still laughing. "And you'll have to ask Larx. I guess it was his idea. I... from what I can gather, Aaron slithered down the damned canyon to get him after the SUV rolled, and Larx was lying there, his brains practically leaking out his ears, telling Aaron how they were going to get the supplies and themselves up the hill. I mean—" He pulled in a shuddery breath and sobered. "—they kept me alive. They... they could have stayed down there and left me and the MacDonald kid to die, but they didn't. They came all the way back up for us." He dragged his fingers through the mess of Guthrie's long hair, thinking this man needed cozening. He needed a hot shower and some soup and some kindness, and Tad could literally not even sit on his own ass. "They did all that with the pulleys and shit to keep me and that poor kid under the tree alive. Guthrie, I swear, between you and them and Chris, who was apparently moving hell and earth to find the people who'd been shooting at us, it was, like, a day for heroes."

Guthrie grunted. "Don't forget the teachers and teenagers, buddy," his said, settling down a little. "I mean, you fell down a *magic* hole in the earth, that is for certain."

Tad settled too, remembering a moment when he and Larx and Aaron had been huddled on the hill. Larx's daughter, pretty as a pixie princess, had appeared over their heads, floating on a contraption straight from the high school stage.

"Magic humans," he said, echoing Larx. "We found magic humans."

"You did," Guthrie said softly. His eyes sobered. "Listen, if you get a chance to get April here? With these magic humans? You've got to do it, okay?"

And Tad felt the sting of rejection deep in his gut. "But you and me—"

Guthrie shook his head. "I didn't say that was the end of us," he muttered, and this time he soothed Tad with a touch to the face. "I'm saying you and me will be you and me. But you and your sister deserve all the magic humans you can get in your life. Do you understand?"

Tad nodded. "But right now, I'll be glad there's you and me. Are you glad, Guthrie? That there's an us?"

"You have no idea," he whispered. He pulled back and wiped his face on his shoulder before resting his chin on the bed again so they were face-to-face. "You... you give me a whole new faith."

Tad smiled, suddenly exhausted and drifty and floaty again. "Good," he slurred. "Keep believing."

And he fell asleep again.

WHEN HE woke up, he peered around blearily and saw Guthrie sitting cross-legged in the back corner of the room, eyes closed in sleep, the sweatshirt he'd put over Tad's shoulders back around his own.

"Don't get too excited," said a man's voice. "April's going to come in and say good night, and then Livvy and I are taking them *both* home."

Tad squeezed his eyes shut and then opened them again, trying to get a fix on the guy sitting in the chair. He wasn't big—midsized, slender, with a full two days' worth of brownish beard. He had hazel eyes and what was probably a round chin and full lips under the scruff. Cute, Tad thought muzzily, in a boyish sort of way, but those hazel eyes regarded him with steady patience, and Tad got the feeling this young man was underestimated a lot.

"'M sorry," he mumbled. "Who're you again?"

That drew a laugh. "Elton McDaniels. You might not know me, but does an electric-blue Kia ring a bell?"

Like it was in slow motion, Tad saw the unfortunate vehicle balancing precariously on two wheels before it went slooooooowwwwwllly over the edge of the service track in the canyon, pulling down the rest of the road with it.

"Larx was really sorry about that," Tad said, remembering Larx and Aaron's banter about how the thing had been stocked to the gills. "Are you his son-in-law?"

A faint smile. "I am. My wife seems to have taken a shine to your sister and your boyfriend. I wanted to let you know they're in good hands. I understand Guthrie has to take April home tomorrow, but they'll be visiting before they go."

Tad nodded. "I can't believe they're here," he whispered, the relief of their presence filling him all over again.

"Neither can we," Elton said with a small smile. "Do you know Guthrie badgered the sheriff's department, SAC PD, and the hospital before he found you?"

"April told me."

Elton shook his head. "Whole town about rolls up its sidewalks after eight. I should know." He shook himself. "Look, I just wanted you to know. After April comes in, you'll probably fall asleep again, and he won't be here until tomorrow. Don't worry. We're taking good care of him. Livvy says he needs to eat, and he *really* needs to sleep in a bed. You get better, and we'll make sure we don't scare him off."

Tad smiled and glanced at the figure in the corner again. Guthrie's arms were wrapped around his knees, his cheek resting against the wall, eyes closed.

"Thanks," he said softly, but Elton shook his head.

"Aaron and Larx'll be in to talk to you tomorrow. Truth is, you had Aaron's back out there. Whole family appreciates it. We, uhm...." He glanced around. "Look, I'm new here and the last person they need to hear from, but you gotta know. If Aaron offers you or your partner a job up here, he's not blowing smoke. Half his department just quit because one of the guys you took out was a member of the department who's been gunning for Aaron since he came out to date Larx. Yeah, saying. If at any time you'd like to throw your hat in for a low-paying, low ambition spot in this tiny little town, you'll be up to your eyeballs in casseroles and dinner invitations, because Larx and Aaron mean something here. So, you know. We'll take care of yours 'cause you took care of ours." He chuckled. "And before you think, 'Oh, I could never fit in here,' I need you to rethink what I just said and remember—until February I was a San Diego surfer with middling ambitions for Silicon Valley and a trust fund. This is a good place. We'd love more good people."

A rustling at the door caught Elton's attention, and he stood and smiled. "Come sit, April," he said softly. "He's awake. Livvy had me come so she could drive you home and I could take Guthrie's truck. God, you can hear that thing rattling all the way down to Tahoe, right?"

April shuddered. "He kept apologizing because it needed servicing. I didn't want to tell him it needed to be *shot.*"

"Don't shoot my truck," Guthrie mumbled from his spot in the corner of the room before his head fell forward onto his knees and he all but curled up on his side, right there on the hospital floor.

"Won't shoot your truck, sweetheart," Tad said, and it may have been wishful thinking, but he could *swear* Guthrie's huddled posture on the floor relaxed.

Then April took Elton's place, and she pulled out her yarn work, and he invested himself in her stories of three cats and a giant dog and girls who kept trying to see if she wanted old T-shirts. And how very much she *did* want their old T-shirts because they weren't black and they may have been hand-me-downs but they didn't smell like her rooming building, which reeked of old smoke and ammonia, but rather of fabric softener and girl things and memories of when April had thought she was like these girls.

Tad listened to her talk and dreamed a little of April talking to peers, to "girls" or young women like her, who didn't judge her for her addiction but celebrated her freedom from it.

And curled up in his heart was Guthrie, who didn't want him to shoot his truck.

MOVE ALONG

GUTHRIE'S LAST glimpse of Tad before he and April left Colton was hopeful. Their boy was awake, eating solids fitfully from a tray while lying to his side and trying to be brave about them leaving.

The fifth time April said, in a falsely chipper voice, "But Guthrie will be back in two days!" Guthrie broke a little.

"Listen," he muttered to Tad. "You're the one who wanted your own damned pants. Besides, Chris told me we could do a car thing and get your SUV from the precinct parking lot and to your apartment. Stop pouting like we're leaving on a cruise or something."

Tad slid him a little side-eye… and a smile. "If you *were* leaving on a cruise, I'd expect you to come back fat and happy. Which is my way of reminding you to eat."

Guthrie rolled his eyes. "Musicians are always hungry. Ain't you learned that yet?"

"Your band looked well fed," Tad replied tartly, and Guthrie grimaced.

"Well, my band has the rest of June and July to be my band," he said, hating to confess this. "We're doing gigs at Scorpio like we promised, but, you know, them kids—they move on. So I'm gonna be a little hungrier after that." He wanted to tell Tad about Seth's offer—in fact, it still blew his mind that he *hadn't*—but he remembered the kind of money that had come with his last go-round with Seth, and that had been *before* Italy and New York and all the prestige that went with Seth Arnold's name now. It seemed a little pie-in-the-sky for someone who'd just lost his band to weekly matinees of *Wicked* and *Hamilton*.

"Aw," Tad murmured. "I'm sorry to hear that. No more weekends at the Washoe?"

"If they're desperate, they let me hang around and do solo stuff," Guthrie replied, and that had always been surprisingly lucrative, even when all he did was play for a meal and tips.

"I'd drive to see you play." He gave Guthrie a luminous smile then, and Guthrie didn't know what to do with that. He was starting to see the downside to roaring into town with April two nights before: Suddenly *everybody* knew the lengths Guthrie would go to see this man, and Guthrie was afraid he couldn't live up to his own goddamned hype.

"Not worth the ticket," he said with a wink. "Don't worry, son, I'll play anything you want in person."

Tad bit his lip then. "I love to hear you play," he said, but there was something complicated on his face, like he wanted to say more.

Guthrie bent down and kissed his cheek. "Well, I'll bring the guitar when I visit. Back tomorrow, okay? I'll let April say her goodbyes."

April returned from the doorway she'd lingered in while they were speaking and said, "I saw Olivia down the hall, Guthrie, if you wanted to tell her goodbye."

He was looking forward to it—he did like the girl.

And this would get him gone before he confessed that he hadn't only lost the band—his boss had fired him by text because he hadn't felt like waiting until Monday to get 'er done. Martin had texted him immediately after, on the down-low, saying he'd kept Guthrie's health and bennies and his auto service for at least six months and that the boss was a total douchebag. Guthrie was grateful for the first and aware of the second, and, well, plumb out of a job. He still had some of his Fiddler and the Crabs money saved, but not much. He was counting on those gigs from Scorpio and the sublet apartment to get him through.

And none of this was something he wanted to burden Tad with. Because his boy—that's right, *Guthrie's* boy—had problems enough.

So he had one foot toward the door when Tad grabbed his hand.

"More," he said, and Guthrie turned to blink at him.

"More what?" he asked, honestly befuddled.

"Not the cheek, Guthrie. The lips. I brushed my teeth for this special this morning."

Guthrie smiled at him, charmed. "Alrighty, then," he said, and his face was hot and his neck was sweaty, but he didn't care.

He bent down and brushed his lips against Tad's, surprised when Tad captured the back of his head and dragged him down harder. God, the little shit was stuck in a hospital bed, and he was still dominating the kiss, and Guthrie…. Guthrie opened his mouth and let that sweetness guide him.

Tad finally released him with a satisfied grunt, and Guthrie had to remember where he was and what he was doing for a minute before he straightened.

"See you tomorrow," Tad said, pretty damned smug.

"Yeah, all right," Guthrie muttered. "You got my number. I'll be here."

Tad's grin spread ear to ear. "When you stop by my house," he said, "remember I like the soft knit pants and the socker slides under the bed. Feel free to look around." The thought of being given carte blanche to explore Tad's apartment made Guthrie practically stumble out the door, but he was pretty sure he was smiling too.

FIVE HOURS later, after he and April finally left Colton and made their way to Bodega Bay, Guthrie was no longer smiling.

April had gotten more and more withdrawn as they'd gotten closer to the ocean, although Guthrie had seen her eyes restlessly exploring the shore. She seemed to find peace in the waves and the bay itself, but when they ventured into town and then into the rusty older suburb back a ways from the ocean, he realized that, for all her quietness, her fragility, he'd been seeing April Hawkins at her most empowered.

There was a force here, sucking the quiet sarcasm, the sweet devotion to dogs, the determination to do that yarn thing, all of it, right out of the young woman, and Guthrie died a little on the inside. He remembered that fantasy of hope she and Tad had spun for each other, of her living with him, with pets, and Guthrie coming to see them, and he realized, scrutinizing the dilapidated building, with no lawn to speak of and crooked stairs, joists, and door frames, that she needed for that fantasy to be real.

"Darlin'," he said gently, "don't worry. I know it'll be a bit before he can drive, but y'all got me now. I'm your friend. I'll make sure you don't have to stay here without a friendly wave, okay?"

She gave him an uncertain smile. "Guthrie, you don't have to do that," she rasped.

He brushed the knuckles of the hand clutched tightly over her yarn bag. "Honey, I really do. You're a friend now."

She nodded, and they both swung out of the pickup truck and headed for the stairs to the office where Callie, the counselor who ran the place, crouched like a spider.

Guthrie did not like her at *all*. One look at her—in her suit and her pulled-back hair and her perfect nails and her business black pumps—told him this woman had never had trouble in her life. What on earth was this woman doing counseling addicts when everything about her screamed bureaucrat? He'd seen *professionals*, right enough—he had loved some of the professors at state college who'd helped him get his degree. But *this* sort of professional, the kind who wore starched shirts in a jeans sort of town, who stuck to the letter of the law instead of the heart of the human, these were the people who absolutely loved it when a little bit of bureaucracy fucked someone over.

"May I help you?" she asked as Guthrie pushed in through the squeaky, crooked screen door.

Perversely, he wanted to dick with her a little. "I know folks who could fix that for you for the price of a cup of coffee. You want me to hook you up?"

Her eyes went dead. "Our maintenance budget is thin at best. I'm afraid I don't have the cost of a cup of coffee to spare." She raked him up and down with those lifeless eyes. "Are you looking for a cup of coffee?"

"No, ma'am," he said, giving her a thin smile. "I am, in fact, here for April Hawkins. I want to make sure she doesn't get into too much trouble for going to see her brother. He's one of our boys in blue, you know, and he was injured in the line of duty. It sure did ease his heart that she made it to Colton to see him."

"Well, actually, sir—are you her brother?"

"No, ma'am, I am a friend of the family. You and I spoke on the phone yesterday, and I told you April would be arriving this afternoon."

"And I'm afraid that's too late," she said. "Your friend left the home without permission, and she didn't return when requested. She's been exited from the program, and as you know, programs like this are hard to come by. Her room and her spot have been filled. I've got our maintenance man, Griff, clearing out her room now." She gave a catlike smile. "He makes more than a cup of coffee."

Guthrie's breath caught at the absolute casualness of her cruelty, and then his vision went red and he didn't remember much after that until he and April were throwing her hastily boxed things into the back of his pickup and they were well on the road to San Rafael.

"DEAR GOD," April said for about the fiftieth time.

"I'm sorry about that," Guthrie said blankly, his mind swimming.

"I've never heard anybody talk to her that way," she said, and he grimaced.

"I was raised better than that," he apologized humbly, although it wasn't strictly true. As heaven was his witness, he didn't remember a word that came out of his mouth after Callie Leonard talked about a cup of coffee, but April had been right outside the door, and apparently she remembered *all* the words.

"You said you'd use her ass as a spear sharpener to hone the weapon you'd give God to thrust into her cold dead heart," April said, and there was a healthy dollop of unholy glee in her usually restrained tones. "I thought she was going to bleed out her eyeballs!"

"Honey, she was screwing you over in the worst way," Guthrie told her, still outraged. "Half the musicians I've known have been to rehab. Most of those places have a three-strikes policy, and this wasn't a strike. This wasn't even a foul. This was hardly a fucking swing."

"But… but you told her *off*," April said again. "My brother *hates* that woman. *Loathes* her. And he's been trying so hard to be sweet to her, and you… you… you're *amazing*."

Oh hell, this felt like a teachable moment right here. "Well, your brother's way is probably better," he said. For one thing, her brother could have gotten the lazy fucking maintenance man to give them a hand throwing her boxes in the back of the truck. "Right now, we've got to figure out what our plan is."

"Oh….," she said softly, and her entire body curled into itself, and he suddenly *knew* what the plan was.

"I mean, we're gonna move you into your brother's place," he said blithely. "That's a no-brainer. You guys were hoping to do that anyway."

Her spine straightened. "We can do that?" she asked. "Like, for real?"

"Well *yeah*, darlin'," he said, remembering to smile. "This was his plan the whole time, right? That spear-sharpener lady speeded things along a bit, that's all."

"Oh, Guthrie," she breathed. "You just became my second favorite brother."

He let out a weak chuckle. "Fair enough. But first we've got to stop by my apartment again, darlin'. I need to pack more clothes and *burn* that polo shirt I was wearing when you came and got me."

She let out a gurgle of laughter so young and carefree, he was pretty sure it was the reason Tad had gone to hell and back again for her. You couldn't turn down someone making that noise, not a chance.

THE APARTMENT manager had let Lulu and Agnes in, and they were there when he stopped by, and he was grateful because it meant he could explain the situation, and of course show them where he put the shampoo and towels. He'd felt badly at first. He'd seen himself as sort of their chaperone—their guide—in this new place, but he should have known by now that Kelly's sisters would be *extremely* self-sufficient.

"We did some moving around," Agnes said excitedly, practically jumping up and down. She was a tiny girl with a heart-shaped face and enormously expressive brown eyes, and watching her was a delight— but also exhausting, much like Livvy's sister. Where did these young women get their energy? They were *unstoppable*. "I hope it's okay," she continued, "but Lulu brought some portable drawers, so mine are here, and hers are there, and all of your stuff is in your place, and we put up flowered valances so, you know, people know this is a girl's room, if that's okay and all. Kelly said you were sort of awesome, although I know we only know you from our brother's wedding and all, but you're Seth's friend, and you know, Seth needs people to watch his back, so that's okay. Oh, who's this? I thought you were gay 'cause you were in love with Seth. Was Kelly full of shit or do you collect girls?"

"Oh my God, *Agnes*!" Lulu, her more restrained sister said in exasperation. "I could swear you were raised by humans. For God's sake, let the man speak!"

Guthrie turned to April, who was chewing her lower lip, overwhelmed. "This is my friend Tad's sister. She, uhm, sort of lost her apartment, and we're moving her into her brother's place."

But Agnes took in April's pale face and her timidity, and she wasn't stupid. "Is she a sister like Matty was our brother?" she asked suspiciously, and Guthrie grimaced. He'd heard stories of their brother Matty.

"Not quite," he said gently. "Some people reach for the rope to pull themselves up."

Agnes's troubled look lifted. "Oh good. I'm glad. I wouldn't wish that sort of pain on anybody." She gave April a brilliant smile. "Good luck and everything. Remember, if you've got a brother who's willing to do everything for you, you've got something special. 'Cause our brother, Kelly, is like that, and his husband, Seth, is just as good. So anyways, you remember that like he said, use the rope to pull yourself up, okay?"

Lulu grimaced. "I can't believe you're some sort of savant," she said grimly.

"It's on the stage," Agnes retorted. "I'm *obviously* dramatic."

April made a tiny grunt of laughter, and Guthrie took a breath. "So is it okay if we take a break here, make ourselves some sandwiches, and then we'll be on our way? We need to make Sacramento before it's dark so I can meet up with her brother's partner on the force. We're doing a car thing."

"Wait," Lulu said suspiciously. "Your brother's a cop?"

April said, "It was a disappointment to me too."

Guthrie choked back a snort, and Lulu relaxed a smidge. "What're you gonna do," she said philosophically. "It's not like they ask our opinion."

"I'm saying," April told her. "But, you know, at least his taste in men has improved."

Guthrie gave her a panicked look.

"What?" April asked. "They knew!"

"Your brother's at a weak moment right now," Guthrie muttered. "You don't want to pin him down 'cause I did a nice thing."

April snorted. "Men are weird. Go. Do what you gotta. I'm gonna sit on the couch and finish the blanket for your poor neighbor girl about to have the baby."

"Ooh," Agnes said, sinking down on the couch next to her. "Can I watch? I'll be quiet and shit. I just never seen anybody do it up close, and it's cool."

"Yeah, sure," April said, and Guthrie went into his room to repack his knapsack and throw his bright blue polo shirt away.

To his consternation, Lulu followed him.

"'Sup, darlin'?" he asked, his hands full of clothes.

"Explain to me again what you're doing?"

Guthrie blew out a breath. "Her brother got injured up near Truckee. She needed a ride home. Her halfway house kicked her out because she *dared* to visit her wounded brother without their permission, and now I'm taking her to *his* place and then taking him his pajamas."

Even to his own ears it was complicated.

"For a guy you're not sure loves you?"

"For his sister who needs a break," Guthrie said and then sighed, knowing all this would be relayed straight to her brother and then to Seth. "And for her brother who... who sort of made me hope right before he *literally* fell off a cliff."

"Oh!" Lulu said. "That was in the news!"

Guthrie laughed a little. "Yeah. That was in the news. Anyways—"

"What about work?" she asked, concerned, and he sighed.

"They fired me," he told her simply. "April showed up, freaked out about Tad, and I left to take her to him. My boss was an asshole. I'll be taking my laptop and sending out resumes I guess."

"Yeah, but to where, Guthrie? Sacramento or San Rafael?"

He grimaced. "Maybe I can get a temp job in Sac—I'll look for that until he's better."

"Agnes and I can take over rent here," she said. "I know you were going to charge us half, but you're not even going to be here, and not having to come up with first and last months or the money for the lease is huge."

"Naw, honey, I promised your brother—"

"Guthrie, you gave us your *bed* for three months. Seriously. It's fine. Lily and I were trying to get out of Sacramento anyway. Maybe after Agnes goes back, Lil and I can move in here and you can move in with your cop. It'll work out. Don't worry about it."

Guthrie grimaced. "Honey, if you and your brilliant sister are moving in, you can probably afford better than this place."

She snorted. "Do you think we grew up in a castle? God, Guthrie, don't you listen to *any* of Seth and Kelly's stories about home?"

He shook his head; he knew better. "It's too early to commit," he said with dignity.

"Well, is it too early to hope? C'mon, you've been single as long as Seth's known you."

He sent her a helpless look, and it was *her* turn to grimace. "Well, yeah. Kelly told us about that. But, you know, you've got to be over that by now?"

"I am!" he said, because he was. "But... but not having that sort of thing returned, that leaves a mark." And so help him, that's as honest as he'd been with anybody but Olivia, who had guessed it, so Kelly's sisters maybe really were super geniuses.

She sighed. "Yeah. Watching my brother when he and Seth had their breakup, I guess I can see that."

"What about you?" he asked curiously. "You ever had your heart broken?"

She shrugged. "It'll come," she said. "But first, I want to get a cat."

He stared at her. "What is it about cats? April and Tad want a cat, you guys want a cat—"

She raked him up and down with her eyes. "I think it comes with liking scrawny musicians," she said with a shrug. "You like scrawny musicians, you need a cat. There's probably a rule. Now go." She motioned with her hands. "Pack. Agnes and I brought groceries, so we can fix you better than sandwiches. I'll let you cook."

AN HOUR later, after a thoroughly enjoyable lunch of homemade carne asada burritos and fruit, Guthrie and April were finally on their way to Sacramento. Following his GPS, Guthrie made his way past midtown to an old, yet sound, apartment complex, and he parked his truck in one of the few spots along the road.

Guthrie eyed the place and decided that April didn't have *that* much stuff for the ground-floor apartment, and the two of them sat back and blew out a breath.

"It's cute," she said critically. "The trees around it make it less like inner city and more like a suburb. And Tad's been on his own a while. How bad could it be?"

He smiled slightly, tired from the drive but still taken by her optimism. "Let's go see," he said, and together they hopped out and grabbed their bags before making their way to his apartment number.

"It's nice," April said, peering inside. "I mean, it's not lived in, really, but he decorated, and there's a dining room table you can see the top of and everything. And two bedrooms. I mean, that's better than your place, right?"

"Yeah, well, given I didn't have any sisters of my own, you can't blame me for collecting them now," Guthrie said dryly, "but yeah. Not bad at all."

It was, in fact, homey. The walls were decorated with prints, the furniture was used but not battered, and there was warmth and color almost everywhere. Together, he and April checked out the guest bedroom, and he was encouraged to find the bed there and made, albeit in a spartan, utilitarian way. There was a mostly empty set of drawers and a closet used to hold Tad's dress blues and some tools on the top shelf. The room was a blank slate, Guthrie realized, and wondered if Tad hadn't been hoping for April to come live with him all along.

Together they schlepped all her boxes into the room, and April glanced around, an almost beatific contentment on her face.

"You going to be okay here?" he asked, checking his phone. Tad's partner had buzzed him, and Guthrie was going to have to leave.

"Could you bring back some takeout?" she asked. "I can be mostly unpacked by the time you get back."

Guthrie laughed a little. "Preferences? Anything else you need?"

She shook her head. "Naw—you choose. I've got everything I need right here."

Spontaneously he went in for a one-armed hug and got a full body press in response. "You look pretty happy here," he said softly.

"I... I feel free," she said back. "I've never wanted junk less in my life. I... I'm *wanted* here. How could I not see my brother wants me in his life?"

He clutched her tighter, a little bit afraid. He knew that often it was at their very highest that addicts would search out their greatest adversary to find a way to fall again, because they weren't comfortable happy. But she was so hopeful.

"You deserve a place where they want you," he said gruffly. "You gotta promise me you'll be here when I get back, though, okay?"

She pulled back and nodded soberly. "I'm not letting go now," she said, looking around again. "I finally have somewhere to hold on to."

He breathed out a sigh of relief, and his pocket buzzed again, and he had to do what Tad did and trust her while he went to take care of business.

NOT AFRAID

"YOU LEFT her at my place?" Tad asked, his eyes wide, and Guthrie's determined swallow was his answer.

"Man, they kicked her out," Guthrie said defensively. "They kicked her out, and you know what? Just the fact that she ain't—hasn't used while she lived there is probably a testament to how strong your sister really is. Tad, that place was awful. I mean... it was *awful*. I hated it—that woman was pure meanness. April.... God, you should have seen her. By the time I dropped Chris off at home after he brought the SUV over, she'd redone the bed and put up curtains and found boxes for her craft stuff. She's... she's *happy* there. And I promised I'd come up and get you, right?"

In the end, Tad stayed in the hospital for four days, which was some sort of record, even with a shot in the ass. When Guthrie returned, the caveat was that if he could stay fever free overnight, they would load him up on painkillers and he'd be free to return home and resume care with his regular physician. Tad would miss the people in Colton. Aaron had visited every day, and while Larx was still in a darkened, quiet room, Tad had been given ten minutes to visit to at least thank the guy for everything he and his kids had done.

And the kids had visited too. Maureen, Aaron's middle child, had gone back to her home in Southern California, but the entire "passel of teenagers" Guthrie had told him about had come to visit in various configurations, often with food *not* spawned in a hospital. Tad hadn't been allowed to be lonely, and he hadn't been allowed to fret over his sister or his gun-shy boyfriend (Were they there yet?) or any of the other things that would have ridden him.

Which was why on the afternoon Guthrie returned, the news that April had been kicked out of her halfway house because she'd come to make sure Tad was okay was something of a shock.

But freaking out was hard to do with Guthrie sitting right next to his bed, looking tired and worried and so, so good.

"Yeah," Tad said, taking a breath. "I shouldn't lose it. I'm sorry. She's just… I've been worrying over her for so long, I don't know if I'll ever stop."

Guthrie reached out nervously and took his hand, patted his knuckles with little strokes. "She's fragile," he said after a minute. "I can see that. But she thinks the world of you. You've got to know that. I… I just couldn't beg for her place back, T. I couldn't. It's… the girl deserves some pride, and that woman, that place—they'd suck all the pride out of a person." He gave a quick little smile. "I hooked her up to your Wi-Fi and told her to search for animal shelters, maybe find herself a cat or something. It… it made her light up. I hope that's okay."

Tad nodded and turned his palm over, seizing Guthrie's hand firmly and trying to ease his anxiousness. "That's real good," he said and then frowned. Something had hit him while Guthrie had been gone, something Guthrie hadn't mentioned once. "Hey, how's work dealing with your absence? Are you on leave or vacation or something?"

Guthrie glanced away, and Tad saw his Adam's apple work silently. "Something like that," he muttered, and Tad's dawning horror couldn't be contained.

"They *fired* you?" he asked, wishing he could sit up. But he still had stitches in his backside.

Guthrie shrugged, and his gaze met Tad's briefly before it flickered away. "Boss was an asshole. Who knew, right?"

"Oh, Guthrie," Tad said, absolutely distraught. "You… you *lost your job* for me?"

Another shrug, and this time his gaze lingered. "It was a shitty job," he said bluntly. "That asshole was mean about your sister, mean about music—how can anybody be mean about music? I swear to God he almost ripped out the sound system when he recognized a Seth Arnold number, because how dare they play gay shit over his stereo?" Guthrie shook his head. "Nope. I got my bennies for six months, and I can find something else. Something that doesn't feel like selling my soul to work. It'll be fine."

"But what about your rent?" Tad asked.

"That's no worries—at least not for a couple of months," Guthrie said confidently. "Kelly's little sisters are living there until the end of August. I mean, I get the couch if I need it—they know I'll be in and out. But I'll be doing the little gigs at Scorpio and going to Sac to check on you—"

"Stay with me," Tad blurted. "At least until… until you get your shit sorted. But… but we haven't had any time. Maybe this will give us some time. To, you know, be *together* together. I…. Guthrie, you've done all this for me. Can you stay with me a little and give me a chance?"

Oh God. Oh God, he'd said it. The thought had been bubbling over in the back of his brain that this man needed him as much as he needed Guthrie—it had been a ledge, a cliff that he'd been afraid to jump off, but he'd said it. He'd said, "Stay with me," and he'd meant it.

Guthrie gave him an almost embarrassed smile. "I could help for a while," he acknowledged, and for a moment Tad was hurt. He wanted to scream *I don't need your* help, *I need* you. And then it hit him—*really* hit him—who the man he'd fallen so hard, so fast for, truly was.

Proud.

Guthrie had a streak of pride in him. It had let him see what Tad had not: that April's halfway house had stripped her of her pride. But it also meant Guthrie—who was between jobs and used to going hungry to drive to gigs and ready to drop his life on a dime to help out a friend or an obviously distraught woman or complete strangers who seemed to be doing good works—*that* Guthrie needed to feel like he brought something to the table.

Something more than a guy who would do all that and was worth so much more than a rent check or a truck that may or may not continue to run.

"I could definitely use the help," Tad told him seriously. *Help getting you to fall in love with me enough to forsake your damned pride.*

Guthrie nodded, pleased with the idea. "I could do that," he said. "I could…."

Tad brought Guthrie's knuckles to his lips and kissed them gently. "Good," he murmured. "Because I want to see what it's like to have you in town." *In my house. In my bed. In my life.*

Guthrie rolled his eyes, but that didn't disguise the flush that blotched his neck. "There's a thousand other guys in the same town," he muttered.

"Maybe," Tad conceded. "But how many of them can make me cry with one damned song?"

The flush intensified, and Tad saw a smile start at the corner of his mouth. "I thought I wasn't playing that song anymore."

"Any song," Tad murmured. "Any song can make me cry."

"Stop," Guthrie mumbled. "You know my button, and you keep pushing."

"That's the idea," Tad told him. "But I'll leave you alone for now on one condition."

"Sure," Guthrie said, giving a sigh of obvious relief. "What do you want?"

"One thing. Anything. Tell me something personal about you. The name of the first boy you kissed. Where you grew up. Family pets. How you knew you liked music. Parents' names. Anything."

Guthrie shifted uncomfortably, and Tad knew without pushing even a little bit that he was regretting the bargain. Guthrie's eyes moved to the right as he probably sifted through facts, looking for the smallest, most innocuous thing he could say that would reveal as little as possible.

Tad decided to cut that off at the pass.

"My mother's name was Lucy Hawkins, and my father, Charlie, died when April was a baby. I don't remember him at all. She was a dental hygienist and raised us with a lot of laughter and a lot of vinyl albums. I was probably the only kid in my class who could sing Judy Collins, and believe me, that didn't make me a tiny bit *less* gay. Your turn."

Guthrie scowled. "God. Fine. I grew up in a tiny town by Monterey. My mom took off when I was three, and my dad and Uncle Jock did most of my raising. They were honky-tonk musicians, and they made me pick up a tambourine when I was seven, the drums a few years later. I picked up the guitar on my own, but they didn't let me play 'cause that was their jobs in the band. All the guitar work you see me do is my own practice. It's mine. I got ownership of that, so there you go."

Tad sucked in a breath at the almost angry recital, and suddenly so much about Guthrie became clear—including his pride. Forced to pick up an instrument when he was a little kid? Well, he would earn his own damned way forever after, wouldn't he? Wouldn't let him play the guitar because that was a man's job? Well Tad's boy was going to prove he was a man, dammit. He *was*.

Tad nodded, smoothed the back of Guthrie's knuckles again, and decided that was a start. He smiled slightly. "Know any Judy Collins?" he asked, feeling sleep creeping up on him.

Guthrie leaned forward and smoothed Tad's hair from his forehead. "Yeah," he said, voice gentler. Then he opened his mouth and sang "Both Sides Now," and the song—written by Joni Mitchell—was almost as heartbreaking as "Long, Long Time," but that was okay. Tad's eyes may have burned and his throat gone a little achy, but he fell asleep clutching Guthrie's hand and smiling, ever so slightly, to himself.

THE NEXT day, Aaron and Larx saw him off after he'd been released from the hospital. Larx's daughter, Olivia, begged them to stay another night, and Guthrie put her off with a wink and a smile, saying they had to go check on April, which was nothing but the truth. But when Guthrie fled the room to go pick up Tad's prescriptions, Tad called her over.

"You look worried," he said.

She shook her head, smiling at her father, who was still pale and pained, having just been released that morning himself. "Just... careful," she said softly. "You know Guthrie lost his job, right?"

"For what?" Larx asked, surprised.

"For leaving work to come check on Tad," Aaron filled him in.

Tad nodded. "He just told me," he said and then grimaced at Olivia. "I can't believe he told you."

"I kept wandering in on him when he was having uncomfortable conversations," she said dryly. "By the way, you should have heard your boy defend your sister to the awful woman who runs her halfway house."

"Ran," Tad said dryly. "That's why we have to go check on her. April's living with me now, because Guthrie didn't have the heart to send her back there." He smiled fondly. "April is probably much better off for it, so it's not a bad thing."

"I'm just saying," Aaron told him. "If you want to come work for me, we've got a couple of good venues up in Truckee where he could play. There's cafes and roadhouses, and it's all very artsy, and if he's looking for something bigger, there's always Tahoe."

"I'd go listen to him," Larx said wistfully. "After that serenade the night we were in the canyon, I could listen to him play for a week."

Tad grinned at him. Apparently, praising Guthrie's playing was a way into Tad's list of friends, which had grown considerably since he and Aaron had fallen into a canyon together.

"I could listen to him play for*ever*," he said pointedly, and then he lost some of his bravado. "I just need to get him to take the gig."

Olivia nodded. "Be... patient," she said after a moment. "Just...." And like April had, she made that indeterminate gesture around her chest.

Tad wasn't stupid; he knew they were trying to warn him without warning him.

"Too late to be careful," he said softly. "I'll have to be patient instead."

The others nodded, and Guthrie walked in, small brown bag of antibiotics and painkillers borne proudly aloft. "And with this, my lady and gentlemen, Detective Hawkins and I can be on our way."

THE FIRST week back was uncomfortable and woozy and exhausting, and Tad didn't remember much of it besides Guthrie or April bringing him his medication and changing his bandages, a thing that he hated having them do but that they didn't seem to mind much, either of them. There was a lot of falling asleep in front of the television while sitting on a donut pillow specially placed so he didn't put pressure on his wound, coupled with playing with his tablet while he lay on his side in his own bed. Everything hurt, he could barely go to the bathroom by himself, and it felt like all of his energy went into *not* ripping the faces off the two people who were running around taking care of his apartment and taking him to the doctor visits and generally babysitting his stupid wounded ass without whining about it, so he tried not to whine either.

Tad freely admitted he would have had a hell of a time without April and Guthrie, a thing made *very* apparent when Guthrie left to play his two-day gig with his band.

It wasn't until he left that Tad realized that a) Guthrie had been sleeping on the couch since he'd gotten back, and b) he didn't know whose couch Guthrie was sleeping on *now*.

Suddenly he wasn't toodling around on his tablet anymore; he was talking to the guy who'd been pretty much unpaid labor in his home with absolutely zero emotional returns.

I'm sorry—you left while I was napping. I forgot to ask who you're staying with.

My old apartment—I get the couch, the girls get the room. They're fun roommates. Apparently, their brother taught them how to cook, because I'd get fat here if I lived here all week.

Tad smiled faintly, knowing it wasn't true. Not much could make Guthrie fat. Too much restless energy in his body—even when he wasn't taking care of Tad, he was always flicking his wrists, like he was drumming a set or fingering imaginary fretwork or frowning over lyrics only in his head. Tad had never realized how consuming music could be for a musician until he'd zoned off into space for an hour next to Guthrie and realized the man had spent the hour drumming his favorite Led Zeppelin songs while mouthing the lyrics, and doing it with so much passion, his hair was drenched in sweat.

Why are there girls in your apartment again?

Because Seth and Kelly are buying their parents a house on the West Coast while also buying one for themselves and the kids on the east coast, and Seth's stretched a little thin. He's world-class, but that doesn't mean made of money.

Tad had heard a *lot* about Seth and Kelly since he and Guthrie had started dating. He knew Seth had played with Guthrie's band with his father and knew he was famous as a pop-culture violinist, but for the first time Tad got a pang of jealousy when he saw the name in print.

Yes, but why you?

Because we got each other's backs, Guthrie replied, and Tad could *hear* him saying it. Such a simple thing, but knowing there was more behind it.

Explain that, he insisted.

Well, like we've gotten mugged together often enough to know how to fight back-to-back.

Tad saw that and actually shuddered, remembering the last time Guthrie had gotten mugged. Oh God. It had sucked badly enough *then*, but *now* Tad was having a retroactive panic attack.

Is he a good fighter?

He fights with his legs to protect his hands. I once watched him dislocate three knees in one fight. It was pretty impressive.

Tad found he was grinding his teeth. *Bully for him*, he typed and then regretted sending it. He was being an ass.

Go ahead, Guthrie replied. *Ask me.*

Tad caught his breath, and suddenly he couldn't do this in text anymore, and he hated that he didn't think to have this conversation until Guthrie was down in San Rafael.

He hit call without a second thought.

Guthrie's face appeared, and he seemed to be sitting on his couch, his phone resting on his bent knees. As the image came into focus, he was covering his mouth as he let out a giant yawn, and Tad recalled his day and the fact that he'd just driven three hours to get his equipment, then another hour to get to the venue. Then he'd performed two sets, eaten with his band, and gotten his equipment back to the apartment.

Tired. Tad was having this stupid shitty conversation with him, and Guthrie was weary to the bone.

"I'm sorry," Tad said. "You look like it was a rough night. We can have this conversation another day."

Guthrie blinked hard, like he was trying to wake up, and shook his head. "No worries," he said through another yawn. "It wasn't supposed to be a secret. Yeah, Seth was the one."

"The world-class violinist," Tad said bitterly. He'd actually heard Seth Arnold's music. It was *really* good, and Tad hated that he liked it so much.

"That's the guy. Went to his wedding in January. You don't got anything to worry about, Tad."

"You were in love with him," Tad said softly. "And you're apparently still a part of his life."

Guthrie blew out a breath. "Yeah, and he's planning a recording session that can keep me in the black for another couple of years while I find a job I don't hate, maybe near you, and put together a band now that this one's going away. And he's a friend. His husband's a friend. We used to all gather together in his tiny little dorm room and watch movies on his laptop, him and Kelly, his friend Amara, her husband Vince. It was, you know, like you probably did in college. Taught me lots, I guess, about *having* friends that I didn't get in high school."

"Why not?" Tad asked. "Why no friends in high school?"

Guthrie grunted. "'Cause my daddy and Uncle Jock had me on the road most weekends and lot of weeknights to boot," he said. "I barely fuckin' graduated that place, but boy, I knew the name of every bartender between Monterey and San Francisco."

Tad frowned, not sure what to say to that. "Sounds lonely," he said.

And there it was—that Guthrie shrug. The one that said *Why are we worried about this when I've got other things to fuss over?*

"I didn't think of it like that then," he said. "I was making music. I liked that. Felt grown-up. Important. And Daddy and Jock got drunk most nights. Didn't care who I spent my time with."

"Ah," Tad said. "Lots of boys?"

Guthrie shook his head. "Not at first," he murmured. "Little of both. Then a few more boys. Then the girls started to feel like a lie. Then we hired Seth and...." He sighed. "He's different. His head's up in the clouds most days. But he... he played Christmas music one night. We didn't have a Christmas set worked up, but the crowd was feeling sentimental, and he stepped up and just... played old hymns, and every note was so pure. It made me feel like I had to be a better musician to be on the stage with that much talent, so I got better." That shrug again. "Look, man. We've all got a past, right? You got a guy you lived with that you realized you didn't really love. I got a guy I loved that I kissed once so I'd know what it would feel like when I found that again. I know we haven't kissed a *lot*, Tad, but I'll tell you something. That one kiss with Seth was worth all your fretting, because I know what a real kiss is. I know that's the sort of kisses I have with you. Is *that* what you wanted to know?"

"Yeah," Tad said, ashamed and moved and sleepy all at the same time. "That and why we can't have these conversations when we're in the same room."

Guthrie's expression went soft. "Baby, you are still healing. You're falling asleep over your tablet as it is. Put the tablet down, get some sleep, and I'll be at your place the day after tomorrow."

It felt like forever. "April needs to go yarn shopping," Tad mumbled. "She wants you to take her. Is that okay?" He'd been so involved in his own pain he hadn't even seen how Guthrie and April had been getting along.

"'Course it is," Guthrie said, smiling a little. "She sure is a wonder with that, right?"

"I love how you value her," Tad said, not even sure if he was saying it right. "My sister. I... you make her feel important."

"She is," Guthrie said and then yawned, then grimaced. "Baby, can we start this conversation tomorrow night? I love that you were thinking about me, but I'm beat."

"Why don't you sleep in bed with me?" Tad asked baldly, and Guthrie's eyes shot open.

"Because you're hurt and you don't need me thrashing around in there now," he said, but it sounded like he was floundering, and he must have looked left six times since he'd started speaking.

"That's a lie," Tad said on his own yawn. "You want to make sure I'm of sound mind and body before I pull you back into my bed."

"Oh God. Tomorrow night. We'll have this conversation tomorrow night."

"No," Tad said, scowling. "We don't need to have this conversation again because when you come back, you're sleeping in my bed. With me. It's where you belong."

"When you're not wounded," Guthrie said stubbornly.

"No, no, that's not how the rule goes."

"Oh God. It is *so* past your bedtime."

"I'm not screwing around, Guthrie. I get I've been out of it, and I've been tired and grumpy and drugged, but I finally remembered what I really wanted you here for, and changing the bandages on my ass *is not it*. Promise me."

"I promise nothing," Guthrie said with dignity. "It's not a carte blanche thing—it's an individual invitation thing. You've got to invite me, every time."

"That's bullshit," Tad said, meaning it.

"Well you don't get to make all the rules," Guthrie replied, looking mulish. "You may have had long-term relationships, but I've had relationships that have to be negotiated by the hour. I don't take an invitation to someone's bed as a lifetime achievement without a ring on it, and even then I think you should have re-ups on that sort of agreement. Like boosters for the flu. A renegotiation to fight off bitterness and self-sabotage. So no. You are going to have to invite me on a case-by-case basis, and that's how things'll stand. Now go to bed."

"We're not done here."

"Tad, you're beat—even *I* can see your eyeballs swimming."

"I'm not calling this the end."

"Well, can you just call it good night?" he begged in exasperation.

"Fine. Good night, Guthrie. I miss you. See you tomorrow. Have a good set."

"Night, Tad. I miss you too. Get some sleep, baby. You need to heal so you're not so bossy."

Tad snorted, and Guthrie ended the call, and Tad wondered if there was a nice way to assure Guthrie that it wasn't the tiredness that made him bossy, it was the being right and knowing Guthrie was wrong.

THE DIFFICULT KIND

GUTHRIE LOADED up his drum kit and made sure it was secure in the bottom of the bed before turning to Owen, Neil, and Roberta for their obligatory "You okay, bro?" hug.

They were, in fact, *very* okay—they'd made lots of tips, gotten lots of buzz, and had even been recognized by groupies who'd followed them from the Washoe. Scorpio, which was *much* trendier, was a fun club to play, but Guthrie was itching to go ho—

Back to Sacramento. Where Tad and April waited, and he could talk to Tad in person instead of having their worst, most painful conversations over the screen.

"You heading to the apartment?" Roberta asked, all of them glancing around to make sure they were alone and in the lights.

Guthrie had been planning to say yes, of course, but what came out of his mouth was, "I'm still pretty wired. I think I'll head up to Sac, you know?"

The others nodded, seemingly unsurprised, and as he watched carefully as they all got in their vehicles and started up, he thought, *Why not?*

Well, lots of reasons. Who knew how long his buzz of excitement would last, for one thing, and Tad wasn't expecting him until tomorrow for another. The girls weren't exactly expecting him either, but....

He pulled out his phone and texted Agnes. *Hey, angel—you guys in for the night?*

Yeah, Guthrie. Why? You need us to cook dinner?

What a sweetheart. *No, sweet pea. You guys settle in. If it's okay, I'll head on up to Sac from here. I'm good for it."*

Sure. We'll miss you but stay safe.

And with that, she signed off, and Guthrie was good to go.

He didn't text Tad, though. Something about the spur of the moment thing, the decision to just up and fly free—he liked that. He didn't feel obligated. Nobody expected him, so if the truck broke down or he was forced to pull off at a rest stop and nap in the back, he wouldn't be putting them out. He could just… drive up. Hopefully make Tad happy, but not be beholden to anybody.

He didn't want to look into that feeling at any depth. The simultaneous desire to be near Tad, near his cozy little apartment, his gruff, fragile sister, his kindness—and bossiness—and insistence on making Guthrie a part of his family, coupled with his… his what?

What was he afraid of?

For the first time in a long time he heard his father's voice in his head.

People like us don't get no happy ever after, son. People like you got nothing to do but burn in hell.

Ugh. God, he'd spent years trying to flush that conversation. Longer than that trying to flush his entire childhood. The music he could keep, but everything else—the being on the road, the being subject to his father's moods, the loneliness—that shit he wanted to pretend hadn't happened. Until Tad had started probing over the phone the night before.

So was that it? Guthrie was keeping his distance from Tad because he was afraid his father was right?

Wow. For a grown-assed man, that was a really childish jump in logic, wasn't it?

Still, after a stop for coffee and a moment of choosing his Spotify playlist designed to keep him awake, he shook off his internal analysis and concentrated on getting to his destination. It didn't matter what the destination was to *him*, only that he got there in one piece, right?

Still, his mind wandered, fretting around words, around music, and at one point, he hit pause on the playlist and started singing his own stuff out loud. He'd composed music before—he knew the process—and had even performed a couple of his songs at gigs, depending on the band's preferences, but he'd never felt a real… *drive* to do so. Until now.

An hour and a half later he pulled into Tad's apartment complex and found a parking spot right in front of Tad's building, which was something of a miracle. Instead of getting out immediately, he pulled out his phone and started making notes, writing down his lyrics with chord progressions and such, wanting to keep that song in his head, because for that ride home, that song had been *him*, all the things in his heart that he never let out, and it felt like this was a way to do it.

He wasn't sure when he set his phone down, satisfied, and leaned his head against the side window, but that's where he was when a sharp rap on the glass woke him up.

"Guthrie!"

He startled, arms going wide out like a baby's as he tried to orient himself to time and place.

"Wha? April?"

"Jesus, Guthrie, what're you doing out here?"

"Was gonna come in in a sec," he told her, because that *had* been the plan.

"But what are you *doing* here?" she asked. "You weren't supposed to be here until tomorrow. Tad called you and got no answer, so he checked your location."

Guthrie grunted. "Didn't know he could do that," he said, still disoriented. "Good to know. Yeah, I decided to come up tonight instead. Shut off the engine, took a breath… guess I fell asleep."

She let out a helpless little laugh. "Well, come inside. My brother's losing his mind!"

"Let me get my gear."

"I'll get your guitar," she said, "and you get everything else. Did you bring any clothes?"

He had, oddly enough, brought his knapsack out of habit. "Knapsack's next to the guitar," he told her and got out, leaving her to it.

She went into the house first, carrying the guitar case and the knapsack, and he followed with the two cases and equipment bag of the drum set in his arms. April set everything down in a corner of the little-used dining room and then took his stuff from him in time for Tad to launch himself into Guthrie's arms.

"Where *were* you?" he asked, and Guthrie found himself being held so hard it should have hurt, but didn't.

"No worries," he murmured, burying his face into Tad's neck and closing his eyes. Tad had a *smell*, a good one, beyond shampoo and body wash and such, and Guthrie had been missing it. It was like a food or something, the way his stomach recognized it, wanted more.

"But you weren't at the apartment. You didn't answer your phone."

Guthrie grimaced. "Old truck," he explained. "Put the phone on mute when I'm in traffic. Sorry. I just—"

"He fell asleep in the cab," April said dryly. "Tad, back away from the Guthrie, I think he needs to eat."

Guthrie shook his head. "Naw, we ate at the—" His gurgling stomach put lie to the idea that the chef's salad he'd had was enough.

"Grilled cheese sandwich," April said decisively. "Go sit on the couch. Make cow eyes with my brother. Explain to *him* why you fell asleep in the truck. It'll be riveting, I'm sure."

Tad pulled back far enough for Guthrie to see the purely adolescent irritation in his face. It was the look a big brother gave his irritating little sister when she was butting in and unwelcome. Before Guthrie could laugh, Tad took a deep breath and turned toward Guthrie.

"She's a pain in the ass—and I should know—but she's got a good plan. Come *on*."

Tad grabbed his hand like kids on the playground and dragged Guthrie to the couch on legs that seemed almost steady now. He paused for a moment, making sure his donut pillow was in the right place, and then settled delicately, his game leg extended, before gesturing imperiously for Guthrie to take his place on the other side of the couch, facing him.

"You know," Guthrie said, yawning, "I'm going to fall asleep right here, clothes and all."

"You will not," Tad ordered. "Because April's going to feed you, and then I'm going to take you to bed."

"That's forward," Guthrie poked. "And presumptuous. I can always go back to sleep in the cab."

"You will not!" Tad's cheeks were getting pink. "Now come on—talk to me. What were you doing?"

"I think we've established I was sleeping," Guthrie said dryly, and then held out his hand. "It's no big deal. I... I wanted to be here and not in San Rafael is all, so I drove here instead. I took a few minutes after I parked to make some notes on something in my head, and then I fell asleep." He relented on all his snarkasm. "I didn't mean to worry you. I just honestly didn't know anybody was expecting me when I got here."

Tad gave him a glare of pure exasperation. "We were," he said. "*I* was. Guthrie, you're important to us."

Guthrie felt an uncertain smile flicker on his cheeks. "You, uh, know I'm basically a freeloader. Won't you at least let me pay rent?"

"No," April said from the kitchen. "I pay rent 'cause I get the spare room. You don't pay rent because now that you've made a big deal out of it, Tad and I won't let you."

Guthrie gave her a droll look over his shoulder. "You're gonna hurt my pride," he said, and there was a kernel of truth in that, and Tad must have heard it too.

"It's not pride," he said primly. "It's vanity. And control. You don't want to be in anyone's debt because you don't trust that they won't hold it over you. So tough. We won't hold it over you. You'll have to trust us."

Guthrie was going to argue, but at that moment April came around the corner with a perfectly grilled cheese sandwich. Guthrie stared at her, surprised.

"That was damned quick," he muttered.

"I did this thing," she confessed, "where I used mayo on the crust and then got the pan really hot and threw water on it and put a cover over it before I flipped it really quick. It makes the edges crispy and the inside gooey. It's *amazing*."

Guthrie stared at her, bemused, and Tad chuckled.

"We watched cooking shows for the last two days," Tad said, grinning at his sister with pride. "She made blankets, and we watched cooking shows, and I'm finally awake enough to contribute to the conversation. I was practically human."

"And I'm almost done with Guthrie's blanket," she said proudly.

"My blanket?" Guthrie asked through a heavenly, crispy, and gooey bite of grilled cheese sandwich. Mayo on the outside—who knew?

"Yeah," April said. She gave a nod toward her big laundry basket by the recliner, where a handsome fawn, sage, and lavender blanket sat. It was made in strips, each strip with a textured design on the surface, and Guthrie's heart went a little wobbly.

"I saw you working on that, sweetheart," he said, reaching out to touch it. "Is that for me?"

"Yeah," she said, giving a proud smile. "If I can make a blanket good enough for you, maybe I can *finally* make a blanket good enough for my brother to replace that crap one." There were two blankets on the back of the couch now, and Guthrie knew one was from his mother. The other, a basic back-and-forth stitch in a variegated blue, had been one of April's earlier efforts.

"I like that blanket," Tad said mildly.

"I'm better at it now," April retorted. "You need a better blanket."

"Well now I'm torn," Guthrie said, catching Tad's eyes. "'Cause that's more than good enough for me, but nothing's good enough for your brother."

She bent to kiss his cheek. "And that's why you get a blanket," she said with satisfaction. "I'm going to make you another sandwich." With that she took the little plate but left him the napkin.

"I absolutely can't eat another sandwich," he said quietly to Tad, who laughed.

"April, how about you put a hold on that. Let him finish, okay?"

"He's skinny," she said, her lower jaw shoving out mulishly. "And he was *asleep in the car* outside the apartment. I don't trust him to take care of himself. He needs to eat."

Guthrie opened his mouth to tell her he was a grown man, but Tad beat him to it. Sort of.

"I'm sure he does, but we'll have to get him on a feeding schedule and feed him a little bit more every day, okay?"

"I don't believe this," Guthrie muttered, and Tad sent him a mulish look of his own that told Guthrie he wasn't over the sleeping-in-the-cab-of-the-truck thing. Guthrie yawned then and wiped his face and his fingers with the napkin.

"Go crawl into bed," Tad murmured. "I'll be there in a sec. Don't argue, okay?"

Guthrie might have if he hadn't been so tired. As it was, after brushing his teeth, stripping to his briefs, and climbing into bed, he was barely conscious when Tad came in, turned off the light, and slid in next to him. With a murmur he backed into Tad's broad chest and welcomed the arm around his waist by covering Tad's fingers with his own and lacing them together.

"I like you here," Tad murmured.

"Wait until I do something cool," Guthrie said back.

"You're here. That's cool."

Guthrie was asleep before he could even laugh at that.

SOMETIME IN the night, they reversed positions, with Guthrie careful not to bump up against Tad's backside but Tad practically snuggling him off the bed in an effort to get closer. Toward the morning, Guthrie got up to use the bathroom, and when he came back, Tad had changed position, so it was Guthrie's turn to be little spoon again, and he liked that. Liked Tad's possessive arm around his middle, liked the way Tad splayed his hand on the soft skin of Guthrie's bare stomach, liked the way he—hello!

"That's not my stomach," Guthrie mumbled as Tad's fingers dipped below his waistband.

"Nope," Tad murmured. "Want me to stop?"

Oh! His fingers brushed against Guthrie's cock, still full from his morning wood, and it was like a magic touch. His entire *body* melted against the bed, against Tad, and without volition he lowered his hand and trapped Tad's fingers exactly where they were.

"No," he hissed, beyond pride in that one touch. Tad's smell had haunted him as they'd slept. It had permeated his senses, sunk into his skin. *Tad* was there, warm and strong and *touching him*, and now the touch was *on purpose*, and Guthrie couldn't resist, not in the name of pride, not in the name of reason, not even in the name of privacy.

He glanced toward the bedroom door and saw that, unlike during the night when it had been partially open, it was closed all the way, something Tad must have done when he'd gotten up to pee.

"This was premeditated," he mumbled, arching into Tad's grip, and Tad chuckled grimly.

"You're skittish," he said, stroking with a firm touch. "Need to keep you from running. Sorry."

"That didn't—" Guthrie gasped as Tad skated his thumb across the head. "—sound—oh God, Tad, I'm not going to last—sincere!" he managed, and Tad grunted and let go of his cock to pull down his shorts.

Guthrie was suddenly bare in the warmth of the summer morning, and Tad was scooching around the bed to take his cock into his mouth.

"Oh God," Guthrie moaned softly when Tad's lips closed over him, and that quick, all that was left was the heat and the home inside. Then Tad added the pressure of his fist and swirls with his tongue, and Guthrie threw one arm over his face and then used the other to massage the back of Tad's head through his now-shaggy hair.

Tad chuckled and kept up with the blowjob, and Guthrie arched into his mouth, the hand in Tad's hair shaking, his body overwhelmed by simple touch. All those hours on the road and his skin felt shaken to a windsock, and suddenly he was being *touched*, and *sexually*, and it all came crashing into him, how sensitive his skin was, how much he craved the attention, and Tad was giving it, and he was *flying, and*—

The hand covering his face moved to his mouth as he came, biting his palm, shaking so hard he wasn't sure what to do with his limbs next. His other hand came up from the back of Tad's head so he could cover his whole face and let loose with the damned tears that seemed to curse his time in bed, particularly with this amazing man who bossed him around for his own good and made sure he ate and worried about him when he didn't know where Guthrie was.

Tad backed away, and Guthrie caught a peek between his fingers of the exasperating man grinning in satisfaction.

"Hey," Tad murmured, his tenderness Guthrie's undoing. "C'mon, look at me." He nudged Guthrie's hand down, and Guthrie saw his mouth, swollen and rimed with glossy come, and he groaned.

Tad moved his other hand and took his mouth, letting Guthrie taste himself, letting him get lost in the kiss, in the sex of it all. Guthrie opened his legs, wishing Tad was naked and realizing that he *was*. Guthrie ground up against his hard cock, wanting more even though he was still soft from his orgasm and not likely to get hard in the next few minutes.

Tad let go of the kiss long enough to reach under the pillow behind Guthrie's head.

"I want to fuck you," he murmured. "You may have to buck your hips a little, but I think we can do it."

Guthrie whimpered, suddenly needing to be taken. "You're better?" he managed to rasp.

"God, I hope so," Tad muttered, pulling the lube out from under the pillow. "I stroked myself last night, thinking about you. I wanted you so bad."

"Ooh," Guthrie breathed. "I had no idea."

There was a moment of fumbling and then Tad's fingers breached him, not roughly but with intent, and Guthrie bore down on them, accepting their stretching and the gentle ache that came with it. He shook, overwhelmed again, and without meaning to, raised his hips to give Tad better access.

"God, you're so needy," Tad whispered, but not like it was a bad thing. "I've needed to be needed like this my whole life."

And then he was there, at Guthrie's entrance, and oh… oh God. Oh damn. Guthrie shuddered, and he felt the damned tears again, and Tad took him over, invaded him, made him whole. He tried to raise his hand to cover his eyes as Tad took up a gentle rhythm inside him, but Tad stopped him, took his hand, laced their fingers together, and nuzzled his cheek.

"No hiding," he whispered. "It's fine. Whatever you feel, as long as you want this, it's fine."

Guthrie let out a whimper and arched his back, torn between wanting to hide and just *wanting*. Tad took him at his blatant invitation and thrust in again, keeping their hands laced as he balanced his weight on his good knee and used his abs and good thigh muscles to fuck.

Guthrie watched, helpless, through blurred, stinging eyes as Tad tilted his head back and smiled, obviously enjoying himself. The sight made *him* smile, made him catch his breath, made him raise his hips and wrap his legs around Tad's, inviting him deeper, begging him to go harder, wanting more.

Tad complied, a look of such open joy on his face as he thrust that Guthrie's eyes stung even more, spilling over. He was finally forced to close them, simply feeling, allowing the dark pleasure to overtake him, detonating him from the center out until he convulsed around Tad's cock, his body swept into another orgasm he hadn't even known was coming.

Tad gave a gasp of his own, almost a laugh, as Guthrie shuddered, and then Tad was rutting, coming inside him, burying his face against Guthrie's neck and collapsing against him, still coming even though the position forced him out of Guthrie's ass.

For a few moments they simply clung to each other, their orgasms stuttering to completion, and then Tad gave a little sound of discomfort, released Guthrie's hand, and rolled to the side. Guthrie tried to turn away then, so he could bury his face in the pillow and let the shame wash over him, but Tad grunted and pulled him so his head rested on Tad's shoulder and he had nowhere to hide.

"It was good?" Tad was still breathing hard, and he had the smuggest smile on his face. "Tell me it was good. My ass is gonna hurt for a week after that. *Tell* me it was good."

Guthrie couldn't help the smile and little sputter of stupid, useless sex tears that came with that. "You know it was good. Whoever taught you the sex things, gotta give 'em props."

"Taught me?" Tad harumphed. "Nobody *taught* me anything. All of that was good old-fashioned *study*. I read every gay romance book known to man in my late teens." He paused. "Not as many as there should have been. Anyway, you learn a few things."

"Such as?" Guthrie prompted, mostly to hear him talk. God, it was easy, lying here with him. Guthrie's fears subsided, and he tried to keep his eyes open so Tad would keep saying shit.

Tad turned his head, then, and with a throat-tightening tenderness, pulled the long strands of Guthrie's hair out of his eyes. "Like you gotta make love to the person in your bed, not the ghosts that follow him," he said softly. "And you gotta listen to them, to their noises, to their expressions, to see what's going on. Don't turn away from me, Guthrie. Not when it's you and me. Okay?"

Guthrie swallowed, eyes still burning. "Do you *know* how embarrassing this is?" he asked.

Tad kissed his temple. "Maybe if you let some of your heart show sometimes when you're *not* in bed with me, it won't all be backed up when you are," he said. "You ever think that? You're so guarded, but you're one of the best people I know."

Guthrie shook his head. "One good deed doesn't make me a good guy," he said, and unbidden came his childhood, growing up with two rednecks who made fun of anyone not straight, White, and moderately poor. Those years of struggle, of trying to figure out who he was, hadn't come without hurting feelings, without being the douchebag who'd take a girl to bed because his father was getting suspicious and then try to let her down gently because he just wasn't feeling it. Until Seth had walked through the door, Black, with blond hair and green eyes, his head in the clouds, his clothes ill-fitting and falling apart—hell, even his sneakers had been unlaced—Guthrie hadn't known how small his world had been. No matter the years of heartbreak that had followed, of stupid, hopeless yearning, Guthrie would always have Seth to thank for showing him that the world was as big and as small as the kid in your own backyard that you might not have seen for the blinders put on you by family.

"Tell me," Tad murmured. "Why aren't you a good guy?"

"I don't know," Guthrie mumbled, not wanting to talk about himself. "Tell me why you *are*?"

Tad grimaced. "I'm not such a good guy," he said, and Guthrie turned to stare at him.

"Oh I doubt that. Why not?"

"Fine. My turn. Because April didn't go into rehab voluntarily—not at first. I mean…." He puffed out a breath. "Man, how good a guy can I be if I handcuffed my sister to a bed and gave her sedatives until the meth shakes were gone, and then kept her there and cleaned her up? I mean… I had to shave her head, Guthrie. And then I had to shave my *own* because lice don't go away. I had to treat her for fungal infections and… and bed bugs and pressure sores and the whole time she was begging me for one more goddamned hit."

Under Guthrie's head, Tad's shoulder was shaking, and Guthrie could hear the pain in his voice.

"I'm sorry," he said, feeling this with all his heart. "My dad's a real bastard when he drinks. Sometimes the only way I could cope with it was to be a real bastard back. There's no… no magic pill to help us deal with people when they become someone else. It's like Dr. Jekyll was a real nice guy but Mr. Hyde would kill you. Sometimes the only way to deal to deal with Mr. Hyde was to become… you know. The nine-hundred-pound gorilla Mr. Hyde's afraid of."

Again, that quiet, kind brush of lips at Guthrie's temple.

"What kind of gorilla were you?" he asked, voice a little broken. "I was the kind that screamed in my sister's face and slapped her, *hard*, when she bit me. I… she had a bruise across her cheek, and my bite got infected because her teeth were *awful* before we got the caps on and…." He shuddered. "I had to spend a week in a hotel dosing myself with lice remedies and antifungals and antibiotics before I felt clean enough to come home. And the whole time I was caring for that fucking wound I was like, 'Good! It's infected! It should be, because I'm a shitty person and I deserve it.'"

This time it was Guthrie offering comfort. "Oh baby," he rasped, turning his head to kiss Tad's chest. "No. That's not true. That's not… you were trying to save her life. It looks like you've done that, but it was hard work. That was *blood* work right there. I-I didn't make the same sacrifice you did. I couldn't. Right before Seth left, I came out. And as long as Seth was there, my daddy smiled at Seth and was okay and a little standoffish, and I thought, *It's okay—he'll still be my dad, and me and Uncle Jock and my daddy can keep on going, but I'll be looking for love in a different place is all*, and that was okay. But the minute Seth was on the plane to Italy, and there was no hope that… that *brilliant* shining boy and his amazing talent was going to bless my daddy with any more goddamned money, he kicked me out of the band. Told me to get my faggoty ass the fuck out of his sight. After all he did for me. Uncle Jock just… just stood by and watched and…." He shook his head. "Last text

I got from Jock was a year ago. Apparently, Daddy crawled into a bottle and stayed there, and Jock wanted me to come back and pull him out."

"No," Tad said, his voice cracking. "No, you don't owe him—"

Guthrie shook his head. "It ain't that simple. It's never that simple. 'Course I said no, but how much of that was righteousness and how much of that was spite? How much of that was a little kid going, 'Apologize first, you big poo-poo head!'"

Tad let out a snort, the laughter through tears kind. "And how much of that was a hurt little kid?" he asked softly.

"Yeah," Guthrie admitted sadly. It was still early, he thought as he turned on his side into Tad's warm body, and he'd been damned tired the night before. "But see? Being a good man—sometimes it's harder than just rescuing kittens from trees. Sometimes you don't know who's worse, Mr. Hyde or—"

"The nine-hundred-pound gorilla," Tad filled in. "I hear you. But you're not—"

Guthrie shook his head, tired suddenly. "There's more," he mumbled. "There's always more. Can we not have any more confession today? I don't get a man in my bed often. And you're the best one so far. Can I enjoy this, please?"

"Yeah," Tad whispered, adjusting his position so Guthrie was still tucked against his chest, but he was a little more on his good side and less on his back. "And if I'm the best one so far, I want to be the best one period. No other guys for Guthrie. Just me."

Guthrie gave a humorless chuckle. "Like there's another man in the world I'd look in the face. Ever."

And then, before the meaning of that could sink in or grow huge, he fell asleep so he could dream that this place, where people made him grilled cheese sandwiches and blankets, where lovers told him he was okay and good, wishing it could stay forever, never change, be his as long as he lived.

But Guthrie knew better. Dreams like that weren't real. That's why he sang about perfect love and perfect pain. He knew there was no such thing.

GIVE FAITH A FIGHTING CHANCE

TAD STARTED walking outside the next week, painfully, with a cane, Guthrie or April—or sometimes both—by his side. The first time, he barely managed to make it around the apartment complex. By the time Guthrie had to leave for his gig, Tad could go around the block.

The next time Guthrie left, he could go a half a mile, which should have made his recovery go faster but somehow didn't.

He *hated* when Guthrie left. There was something so practiced about the way he packed up his equipment, threw his clothes in a knapsack, and went. True, he'd been bringing more clothes from his apartment in San Rafael, but Tad was starting to realize he didn't have that much to begin with. When Tad's wound had healed enough for him to go swimming in the apartment pool, Guthrie had needed to go buy a pair of board shorts to join him. In spite of the fact that it was rapidly approaching *July* in a city that lived at over 100 degrees in the summer, Tad had yet to see him wear more than one pair of shorts. When that pair was dirty, he wore jeans without complaint, and Tad thought he got most of his ventilation through his T-shirts, which were *not* in good shape. His performance clothes—new jeans, two pairs, and three slick, studded-up country and western shirts—were sharp, though, and he had a decent pair of boots to go with them.

Tad and April had started buying the odd T-shirt or pair of socks or underwear whenever they ordered something for themselves. Tad was expecting two pairs of cargo shorts to arrive this time so Guthrie could enjoy the summer and not suffer through it.

At eight in the morning, before the heat got too intense, he and April had just started walking along the outer apartment sidewalk when he saw a familiar police-issue SUV pull up and park where Guthrie usually did. Tad might have resented that if he hadn't been so happy to see who was inside.

"Chris!" he said, taking slow steps to greet his partner. "How's the department treating you?"

"Not bad," Chris Castro admitted, "but right now I still have hero stink on me. I need you to come back so that doesn't go away."

Tad grimaced. "Four more weeks, minimum," he said. "And then mostly desk duty, I assume, until I can do the physical stuff again."

Chris nodded. "I hear you. Mind if I walk with you? It's going to be hot as balls today. Might as well get my steps in."

Tad grunted. "Hot as balls" was a pretty accurate description of Sacramento in July—although the breeze off the river seemed to help things in the evening. He found himself missing the ocean, or even the mountains of Colton, where there was at least shade.

"Yeah," he said. "I'm an AC baby after my swim. Can't take the heat when I'm hurt."

Chris gave a laugh. "Well, your complexion pretty much makes you a walking heat blister anyway. It's going to be a boring summer for both of us, buddy, but, uhm…."

Tad's gaze sharpened. "Uhm what? You're not ditching me, are you?" He paused, and April grunted next to him. She hated the heat as much as he did and wanted to move to the swimming portion of their morning.

"No." Chris shook his head. "But, uhm, you remember Aaron George?"

"The guy who saved my life several times in Colton?" Tad asked dryly. "*That* Aaron George?"

"And his soon to be husband…."

"Larx." Tad smiled just saying the name. "Yeah—I got an invitation to their wedding. Did everybody else?"

"Oh yeah. Me, Janine, Mary Lee—everybody who came to help with that situation got an invite. There's already talk about who's going in which vehicles, and people are making hotel reservations. The whole nine yards. You going?"

Tad tried to tamp down his smile and couldn't. "Well, yeah. Guthrie's playing at the wedding. George's daughter asked him in particular." Guthrie had refused the fee; Tad had caught that part of the conversation, and his heart twisted for the weight of Guthrie's pride.

Chris nodded. "Yeah. Well, Aaron called to chase down how many of us were attending, and then… well, I know he'd done this for *you* before you even got rescued, but this was the first time he'd done it for me."

"Offered you a job?" Tad asked. He wasn't particularly surprised. Aaron had joked about "poaching" Tad before they even fell down the damned canyon.

"Offered *us* a job," Chris said seriously. "As a package. Has already tapped a real estate agent to get us a break so the wife and I can move into a house, and there's probably one up there for you. He's got a project for you until you're ready for the field, and he's working on getting funding for it, and it's right up your alley." Chris smiled at Tad's sister, his voice going gentle. "He'd like to hire you too, Miss April. No pressure. If you don't feel up to it, you don't have to."

"What's the job?" April asked.

"He wants to start an addiction treatment center in Colton. It would be small, because the place is small, and the model would be based on the CPS model, in which all branches of law enforcement and health care are tapped depending on the recipient's needs. That kid that got stranded in the canyon with you?"

Tad nodded, remembering Curtis MacDonald with a hazy intensity. Poor kid—his life had been a *mess*, and much of it hadn't been his doing. And then someone he'd trusted had offered him a taste of "candy," and Curtis had learned what a real mess was.

"Yeah," he said softly. "How is that kid?"

"He's in a sixty-day rehab program, and Aaron's getting him funded for an extra thirty days because the kid doesn't have a support system. He's in Auburn, which is about an hour's drive from Colton, and Colton's the only place the kid knows. So Aaron wants a small halfway house, a rehab center, something to meet the needs of the population and to educate people on addiction. Tad, you'd be doing setup at the beginning. April, you'd be a consultant and then maybe a resident or a counselor—or even a dishwasher. Aaron wasn't picky. He said sometimes helping people is the best therapy, and he wanted to offer you the chance to do that."

"Oh," April said, and she put her hand to her mouth. "Wow. Tad, did you hear that?"

Tad nodded, thinking about how nice it would be to live in a small town again, and how April seemed really excited about the prospect.

And the downside hit them at the same time.

"What about—" she started.

"Guthrie," he finished, both of them looking guilty.

"Would he be willing to move up with you?" Chris asked, glancing from one to the other.

"Maybe," Tad said, shaking his head. "But he needs time, Chris. He's still doing gigs down in the Bay Area. How soon does George want us up there?"

"First week of September," Chris said. "And to be honest, we need to give our notice before the end of July. I talked to the captain, and she understood. It's a great opportunity. My wife would love it up there, the kids are all moved out of the house, and, you know...."

"It's smaller," Tad said. "Same problems, but...." He'd seen the way things worked there. Law enforcement, education, health care—there was a strong network of people wanting to do some good. It was why he'd wanted to work in Bodega Bay, but better, because the good ole boy network wouldn't be working against him. He peered at April and saw both hope and unhappiness radiating from her eyes.

She loved Guthrie too.

"We'll talk to him," Tad said, clearing his throat. If he turned his face toward the sun and closed his eyes, he could see Guthrie as they'd last made love, tears leaking like they did, but a look of openness on his face, of acceptance, that Tad *only* saw there in the aftermath of touching together. Oddly enough, Guthrie had rolled into Tad when they were done, and as though they'd been in the middle of the conversation and had never stopped, asked if, when he got back this time, he and April could go pick out a cat for April. Tad had been excited. It was... was a promise of sorts, that Guthrie would be around to play with said cat. Tad wanted to be part of that. Unbidden, hope fluttered that his musician, who disappeared every so often and turned up at odd hours of the night unwashed or unfed, looking like something the cat dragged *in*, might actually be around for a while.

"Yeah?" April asked, and he smiled at her.

"Yeah," he said. "Colton's two hours away. It's not the ends of the earth."

They were rounding the corner for the end of the block, and Chris grunted. "Yeah. My wife started talking about getting a dog. A big dog. And a little bit of property. In twenty years I never knew she had a giant crush on golden retrievers and pit bulls, but apparently they are the *things* that have been *missing* from her *life*."

Tad and April laughed, and for a little bit, they talked about other things. Chris's children—how his youngest was enjoying her summer in

Santa Cruz, where she was working a part-time job before school started, and how Laura was excited about the wedding and wanted to talk to Janine and, yes, April, to see what they were wearing. Although April didn't say much besides, "Shopping would be nice," Tad could feel a longing in her for normalcy, for companionship in small doses. After all, Guthrie had turned out to be a good friend, right? Maybe she could find other friends outside the halfway house. Maybe she could remember what real life felt like without the drugs. Small doses of reality; he was all for it.

By the time the walk was done, Tad was more than ready for his time in the pool, and Chris had to get back to work. He was paired up with a veteran of the force since Tad was on leave, someone Chris said, sourly, "Actually retired years ago, but he's been collecting a paycheck ever since." They gave a bro hug before Chris climbed back into his SUV, and he said, "Talk to your guy, okay? I... this move, up into the mountains, this sounds like dream-job shit to me, and you and me saw all the *bad* shit about it when it almost killed you. I sure would like to check it out."

Tad nodded. The place had put a bullet in his ass, but he'd also started to yearn for the scent of pine dust and the quiet in the black dark of the night.

"Will do," he said. "I... hopefully any place I hang my hat's home, right?"

Chris's expression softened. "That's how it works for me and Laura," he said. "It should work that way for everyone else."

Tad nodded and started the slow walk toward his apartment. He was never so grateful for picking a downstairs unit as he had been since he'd gotten shot, and suddenly he wasn't sure if he was going to make it to the pool today.

"What's wrong?" April asked softly.

"I... what if he's not ready?" Tad asked. "I mean, I *think* he's happy with us, but...." He remembered the things Guthrie had said about how he'd grown up, about becoming the nine-hundred-pound gorilla to defeat Mr. Hyde. Was this what Guthrie was afraid of? How could Tad defeat a ghost like that, particularly when it still lived in some nameless town down south?

April blew out a breath. "He-he doesn't seem to have roots," she said after a moment. "If he does, they're hidden. Maybe we ask him and we'll see what we're dealing with." She leaned her head briefly on his shoulder.

"Don't worry for me, big brother. I've got you. I'm gonna get a cat. As long as the cat can move with us up the hill, I'll be okay. What about you?"

Tad made a hurt sound. "I'll live," he said sadly, "but it won't be much fun."

"Yeah—well, if this falls out badly, it'll be worse for him," she said. "But I don't know how to fix that."

By caring for Guthrie as best they could, Tad guessed. But sometimes, not even that could do the trick.

THEY EXPECTED Guthrie the next night, but when he didn't show up, they weren't too concerned. Tad called Agnes to see if he was sleeping there, and her answer was *not* reassuring.

"No, he said he was going to try to go to your place tonight, but supposedly something went down at Scorpio, and we can't get any information. I don't know where he is, and Lulu isn't home yet, and I'm worried!"

Tad's breath caught, and he checked Guthrie's phone to see if the tracker still worked. It said between San Rafael and San Francisco, but that was where the damned club was. Dialing Chris's number took no thought at all, in spite of the lateness of the hour.

"It's midnight, Tad. The hell."

"My Guthrie sense is tingling—and no, not in a good way. He didn't show up, and he's usually here by now, and his other apartment says he was planning on coming here tonight. The roads are clear, there's no accidents—"

"Hold your horses," Chris muttered. "I'm texting dispatch right now. Give me the address of the club."

Tad did and waited breathlessly for the answer.

"Okay," Chris said, coming off hold a few minutes later, "so don't panic."

"Nothing in the history of ever that started that way was good," Tad said, panicking.

"He's fine, but there was a mugging. I guess he took a knife to the shoulder. I got hold of an officer down there who said he'd lost his phone in the scuffle. My guy's going to look for it so he can call you."

"Oh Jesus." Tad felt sick. "God, Chris, I can't even go pick him up."

Tad *might* have been able to sit for the hour and a half it took to get there at this time of night, but the way back would have been ex*cruciating*, and he wouldn't have been able to drive.

"Yeah." Chris sighed, and it sounded like he was moving. "Laura, honey," he murmured. "Want to help me do a thing?"

"Chris?" Two months ago, Tad had been afraid to trust this man with his dating history. Apparently, they really *were* partners now, the kind who had each other's backs.

"Do you have a code word or something?" Chris muttered. "Like, 'This guy's a cop, he doesn't bite'?"

"Did you bite him up in Colton?" Tad asked.

"I wasn't real gentle," Chris admitted. "But I was worried about you."

"Well, fine. Tell him I'm worried about *him*, and maybe you should drive the truck back because that thing's a monster and I think the suspension's going."

"And the bushings," April muttered, "and the chassis and the brakes…."

"Great," Chris said. "I'll have Laura say a rosary for me. It's worked so far. If he calls, tell him to watch out for us. We'll be there before he's discharged."

Tad felt tears in his throat. "Thanks, man."

"Can we go to Colton now, partner? Please?"

Tad laughed a little, and the tears started to break free. "Yeah. I'll talk him into it. You'll see."

"Blackmail. It's a way of life. Talk more soon." Chris ended the call, and Tad sank onto the couch, missing his donut pillow by a mile and wincing.

"He's okay," April said softly.

"No," Tad told her. "He's in the hospital. Again. Because he got mugged. Again. And he's probably thinking nobody's coming for him—hell, for all I know, he'd planned to sleep in the hospital and *walk* to the gig to find his phone. God*dammit*, April—at least when we have a cat, we can keep it in the house!"

She sank down next to him and put her head on his shoulder. "Tadpole?"

"Yeah?"

"Guthrie's more complicated than a cat."

He sighed. "I know."

"You've got a partner who has your back," she said.

"I know."

"Have a little faith."

Another sigh. "Fine."

THE PHONE was apparently smashed beyond repair. Chris gave him a call at 4:00 a.m. to say Guthrie was being released in the morning. Chris was catching some shuteye on a spare bed, because LEO had its privileges, and they'd drive up after Guthrie got his pain meds.

"How is he?" Tad asked anxiously, trying to clear the sleep from his eyes.

"Surprised to see me," Chris admitted. "Loopy as fuck. He was going to turn down the ride home until my pretty wife pointed out she would have driven me down here for no reason at all at fuck-you in the morning. He seems to melt around women, Tad. Are you sure he's gay?"

Tad thought about what Guthrie had told him about his childhood. "I'm sure his mother wasn't in the picture and his dad was an asshole," he said, because that was the extent of Tad's knowledge.

"Ah," Chris said with a yawn. His voice dropped seriously then. "He's *really* high and trying not to admit he's shook, Tad. I've seen some tough cookies before, but this is special. His big worry was his band. He was the last person into his car, and he wanted to make sure none of the others got jumped too. This happen often?"

Tad grunted. "Three times since I've known him?" he answered. "I think maybe he's having a run of luck, but people know musicians get tipped cash. And he's had to live hand-to-mouth before, so he doesn't just roll over and pay up."

Chris blew out a breath. "Okay. So maybe you talk your boy into coming up to Colton with you, and you can escort him home from any gigs. What do you say? I'm *not* going to be okay with him on his own now that I know he's bait."

Tad fought back a hysterical laugh. "Your mouth, God's ears. Can you arrange that for me? Please? That would be great."

"I'll see what I can do," Chris murmured and then yawned again.

"Catch some sleep. You're beat," Tad told him. "Chris, I can't thank you enough."

"Coffee and a breakfast burrito," Chris told him. "The kind from the place in your neighborhood that Laura calls cholesterol in a blanket. I want that. I want it bad."

"Call me when you leave, it'll be hot and ready when you get here," Tad told him loyally.

"Good man. Night, kid."

"Night."

Tad signed off and collapsed against his own pillows. April was lying next to him, on top of the comforter but under her own blanket because she wanted news when he got some.

"What did you promise him?" she asked.

Tad gave her the order, and she hummed while making a reminder in her own phone. "Tell me when he calls and I'll go out a half hour before he's supposed to get here," she said. "Mind if I sleep here, big brother? No designs on your virtue, I swear."

He grunted. Their mother had been the best, but she'd also been overworked and always tired. He and April used to climb into each other's beds as kids whenever they had nightmares or something was bothering them at school. April had been the first person he'd told about his crush on a boy in the seventh grade, and knowing that she didn't actually care had given him heart. And boy, had she not cared. She fell asleep in mid telling, and when he woke her up hissing, "April, did you hear me? I'm *gay*!" her reply had been, "So. I'm still getting beat up in the bathroom. We all have our problems."

He'd beaten up her bullies the next day, and she hadn't said a word about him being gay to anybody until *he'd* been ready to come out.

"No," he mumbled now. "Thanks for...." And it hit him. "April?"

"Yeah?"

"I really needed you tonight. I've needed you this whole last month."

She gave a little gasp. "So?"

But he knew she knew why this was important. "I've needed you. And you've been here. Honey, you've *really* been here. Think about it. I know recovery is always a process. I know there's going to be hard times ahead. Just... remember. You can be here for me. You *are* that strong. You *are* that person. So even if you need help, that's okay. You give some you get some, okay?"

He felt her back up to him so they were touching through the blankets, but not ickily close. "You're a good brother. Go to sleep, Tadpole. We'll take care of each other. I get it now."

And he did.

NOT AFRAID

TAD'S PARTNER was a nice man. He must have been since Guthrie actually felt a gush of relief when he saw Chris Castro's Hollywood-handsome face peering into his ER cubicle. He was holding Guthrie's trashed phone.

"Guthrie?" Castro said. "You remember me?"

"Yeah," Guthrie mumbled, and then to his chagrin, a beautiful woman with dark hair, dark eyes, and a heart-shaped Latina face peeked in under Castro's arm as he held open the curtain. "My band?" he asked, but then he was interrupted.

"You're Tad's young man," she said, like she knew for sure. "You must be. You're so handsome. No wonder he's smitten."

Guthrie stared at her in horror. "Oh God," he said.

"I'm Laura Castro," she told him, swooping right in toward his bed. "And you and me have to know each other better. LEO spouses need to stick together, you know?"

Guthrie blinked. Spouses? "Oh God," he said again.

"Laura," Castro murmured, his voice pained. "The boy's in shock. Maybe give him some breathing room."

"Tad was sorry he couldn't come," Laura said, ignoring him completely. "But he didn't want you to be alone. Chris got a friend to drive your truck over. Your equipment's all safe. I know musicians—my brother used to play in a band when he was in college. That equipment is your *life*, you know?"

Guthrie nodded, because he *did* know. "Thank you," he managed, which was a change from "Oh God."

"So Laura's going to take the SUV home, and I'll drive you back to Sacramento when they let you out," Castro said. "Any idea when that might be?"

Guthrie shook his head, suddenly tired to his bones. "No." He glanced at his shoulder, which was bandaged and aching under the haze of painkillers. "I had to give my statement," he said, feeling dumb. "I couldn't identify shit. Was just trying to make sure Roberta and Neal and Owen were safe.

They're safe, right? How was I supposed to know what he looked like? Who checks for birthmarks when they've got a knife on you? Seriously. Another scumbag with a knife. Oh good!" Guthrie chuckled. "A scumbag with a *concussion*," he said, satisfaction in his bones. "My guitar case is *reinforced*. They told me that asshole didn't know his own name."

Castro let out a chuff of air. "Well done. But what about *you*?"

Guthrie tried to shrug, hurt his shoulder, and grimaced. "I'll figure it out," he declared, although he was staring dolefully at his phone in Chris's hand. "But I *do* have my tips, so maybe I could call a cab and go to my apartment in San Rafael. Wait. I could *drive* now. 'Cause you brought my *truck*."

Castro gave him a level look. "And you are *high as a kite*, and you're driving *nowhere* tonight."

Guthrie sulked. "He's waiting for me," he told Castro plaintively. "Waiting. For *me*. I've got to get back to him. You know that, right? I'll figure out a way. You don't need to worry."

"Aw," Laura said, smoothing Guthrie's hair back from his forehead. "No wonder you were so overwhelmed. You're *wasted*. What did they give you?"

"A teeny tiny bit of fentanyl with a Vicodin chaser," said a voice over Chris's shoulder, and Guthrie looked up to see the seasoned ER veteran who'd treated him coming to check the chart on his bed. "He kept saying he couldn't afford a hospital stay, so we didn't want to knock him out completely."

"My department will pick it up," Castro said, pulling a card from his pocket. "Bill them."

"Thanks," she said. "Give it to the nurse when she comes to check you out in the morning." She gave Guthrie a frustrated glance. "He needs to take it easy. The knife wound is the big thing, but I guess there was quite a scuffle before the other guy broke out the knife."

"Had to make sure they got away," Guthrie said soberly to the pretty woman with her lovely heart in her lovely face.

"They did," the doctor confirmed. "They're the ones who called the cops, because you refused to go until they were safe." She turned to Chris. "Your boy paid the price. There's bruises and contusions. He's going to feel like he got hit by a truck when the pain meds wear off."

"Whee!" Guthrie sang, because he really *was* sailing.

"Do we have some meds for that?" Chris asked, and Guthrie decided he *liked* Tad's work wife. He was a *great* guy.

She ripped off a prescription. "I thought you'd never ask. Will he have help for the next week?"

"Yeah. His boyfriend's healing from his own wound. They can lean on each other when they go to the head," Castro said dryly.

"Well, that's special." She gave Guthrie a stern glare. "I've treated you before," she said. "You've got a healed scar on your hand from two months ago. Is there any way you could avoid darkened parking lots when you're carrying loads of cash?"

"I'm not sure," Guthrie replied, feeling like this was an important question. "Is there any way to get the cash without carrying it to my car?"

She sighed. "Maybe have your boyfriend walk you out next time."

"Lives in Sacramento," Guthrie told her mournfully. "Because I don't get good things. You gonna let me out now, Doc?"

She gave him a level glance. "Mm… I'm going to wait to see how your wound is draining, and we're going to see where your pain level is after the good stuff wears off." She glanced apologetically at Chris and Laura. "I realize that's an inconvenience, but I like to keep an eye on this one."

"No, no, that's fine," Chris said sourly. "It's in the public good to keep kittens out of traffic."

"Right?" she said, and Guthrie scowled.

"You see that?" he confided to Laura. "They're conspiring against me. That's *heinous*."

"It's a protector thing," she said, patting his good hand. "They like to make sure the rest of us are okay."

"You can go," he told her. "I'll find my way home." *Which* home was sort of muddy. All he could picture was Tad's broad face, freckling a little from the sun and the ginger complexion, lighting up when he walked through the door. It did that all the *time*, he marveled, comfortable in the drug haze. Tad's face. Lit up. When Guthrie said something funny. When he took April to the yarn store. When he came home. When he offered to go walking with Tad. When they were in the pool. Always that *lighting up*, like Guthrie was the sun when he smiled. Why did it *do* that? And why couldn't Guthrie clear that face from his vision, even when he was in pain and embarrassed and stoned?

"Oh honey," said the woman over his bed. "I got out of my bed in the middle of the night to bring Chris down here to take care of you. I'll drive back, but there's no way I'm leaving you alone."

He swallowed. "That's very mom of you," he told her soberly. "I got women who want to be my sister and my friend and my roommate and my mom—how does that *happen*? Where were all you people when I was eight years old?"

Oh Jesus, had he actually said that?

"Honey," she murmured softly, her hand still stroking his hair back from his forehead. "We heard you crying, but we couldn't find you until now. Do you forgive us?"

His eyes grew hot because he was a whiny little piss-baby pussy, according to his father, but he nodded because he couldn't hurt this nice woman's feelings.

"Sure," he said, because it was easy with her offering comfort. "It's fine. But you don't have to get me home."

"We want to," she whispered. "I think the whole world should be offering to get you home."

He was falling asleep now, and he smiled a little, his eyes at half-mast. "That's a nice thought. I'm stupid, though. I hope I don't get lost."

Her breath caught, and he felt her kiss on the cheek as he dropped off. "Us too," she said. She smelled nice. Like women's things. That had been the only part of pretending to be straight that he'd enjoyed. Smells, like lavender and rosewater and vanilla. So pretty.

"Fresh linen," he murmured, the smell penetrating the hospital antiseptic and letting him relax. "With eucalyptus shampoo." Then he fell asleep.

TEN O'CLOCK the next day, he was in the passenger seat of his own truck while Tad's handsome partner drove him up I-80, looking both grim and bemused.

"Seriously," Guthrie said, head against the window. "If I said anything untoward to your missus, I'd like to apologize."

"No need," Chris said, humor in his voice. "Apparently, you're a complete gentleman even when you're stoned as fuck. She's going to file the papers for adoption any day now. It's fine."

Guthrie snorted and tried not to burst into tears. "I hate hospitals," he muttered. "Sleep like shit."

Chris must have heard something in his voice above the engine noise of the damned truck, though.

"Your pain meds wearing off?"

"No worries," Guthrie told him. If he was going to take a pain pill, he'd need to eat. If he was going to eat, they'd have to pull off the road. If they pulled off the road, that would add fifteen minutes to their time, and right now that time was what was separating him from Tad.

He did *not* want to stop to take a pain med.

But apparently dads didn't give a fuck what you wanted because Chris gave a grunt and crossed two lanes of traffic to take the next exit.

"Sweet or savory?" he asked as they headed for the outlet malls near Vacaville.

"What?"

"Never mind," Chris decided. "There's an IHOP. We'll get you chicken and waffles and you can have both."

"We can do drive-thru," Guthrie told him.

"No, we can't," Chris said. "I need at least two gallons of black coffee, and *you* need a meal. Don't argue. My kids all learned how not to argue from the very beginning, but I bet I can train you up."

"You telling me Tad doesn't argue with you?" Guthrie asked peevishly. "Because I've met the man, and he's bossy as fuck."

"Yeah, well, he's a grown-up. When you're grown you can argue." Chris pulled into the parking lot and surveyed the foyer. Apparently satisfied, he parked and chivvied Guthrie into the restaurant.

"Am too a grown-up," Guthrie muttered as Chris took a booth for the two of them. "And I want steak and eggs."

"That's fine," Chris conceded, pulling Guthrie's prescription bottles out of his pocket. "I'm just having coffee because Tad's sister is getting me my favorite burrito for when we arrive. Plus you seem like the type of man who will eat about half your steak and eggs, and I can finish that off to hold me over."

Guthrie gave him an unfriendly look. "Never underestimate how much a musician can eat," he said direly. "Restaurants go broke doing that."

"Fair," Chris told him. "I'll get biscuits and gravy. And then you can tell me why Tad's afraid to ask you to move to Colton."

Guthrie stared at him, so shocked that Chris had to order for the both of them, including coffee and a chocolate milkshake for Guthrie.

The server left, and Guthrie blinked, his brains still scrambled. "Why'd you order me a milkshake?" he asked.

"Because you looked like you needed one. Your brains back in your ears yet?"

"Yeah. I just… did that nice family really ask you both up there to work? Who does that?"

"Nice families, I guess," Chris said, a small smile playing on his lips. "You got to know them when you were up there?"

Guthrie nodded. "Olivia Larkin-McDaniels and I text," he admitted. "She's funny," he added with a small smile. She also read his song lyrics, which, somehow, he hadn't been able to bring himself to show to anybody else in his life—not Seth, not Kelly, not even Tad. The girl didn't just say, "Oh, that's great!" she said, "Maybe a different word here," or, "Are you trying to convey despair or yearning, 'cause they're very different, and I'm getting one instead of the other."

"So you can see the appeal of moving to Colton," Chris asked gently.

Guthrie nodded. "Yeah. I mean, of course. Same job, less stress, and it's gotta feel good, Aaron George wanting you both as a team. I'm… I'm surprised he hasn't told me."

"I don't think he expected a formal offer," Chris said with a shrug. "But Aaron came by the day before yesterday, and I went to Tad's yesterday morning." He stared directly at Guthrie. "Tad and April only had one reservation."

Guthrie swallowed. "We're new," he said defensively. He felt like he'd been saying it a lot since he'd met Tad, but the last three weeks hadn't felt *new*, they'd felt *good*, and he was still working that out in his brain. "My life is in flux. I'm losing my band. I lost my job—"

Chris frowned. "Lost your job?"

Guthrie swallowed. "That whole Colton thing," he muttered. "I walked out to take April up there. It's no big deal. I need to do the resume thing and—"

"Well, why not hitch your star to Tad?" Chris asked kindly. "There's worse things than ending up in a new town because of a love affair."

"Because I don't want to 'hitch my star' to him," Guthrie snapped defensively. "I want him to *love me*." He stopped then, so shocked he clapped his hand over his mouth. "I didn't say that," he mumbled from behind his own palm. "You didn't hear that. Can we go now?"

"No," Chris said, definitely bemused. "We can't go now because you still have to eat."

"I… I need to go," Guthrie said. He started to stand up and bumped his arm against the table, which blew a whole shot of pain up to his shoulder, sending him back to his seat. "*Dammit!*"

"Sit down," Chris said in that stern dad voice that made Guthrie wish for things that were obviously long past having. "Sit down, eat the food when it comes out, and stop panicking. Guthrie, there's no sin in hoping for love. You know that, right?"

"Can I just die?" he asked, covering his *whole* face with his good hand.

"No. I won't allow it, and Tad would never forgive me. Now see, I started this conversation thinking you weren't as serious about Tad as he was about you, and a little worried about that, but that's not my worry anymore."

"I'm so glad," Guthrie said, not moving his hand.

"My worry is now you. Why would you think Tad wouldn't love you?"

"I do not want to talk about this," Guthrie said plaintively.

"Tough. Take your hand off your face and look at me like a man, son. Talk to me."

Guthrie dropped his hand because it *was* childish, and he sighed. "Listen, you seem like a really nice guy, but I'm not great at baring my soul—"

"I'll say it again." Chris crossed his arms over his chest. "Tough."

Guthrie scowled at him. "There are things that Tad doesn't know about me because I haven't told him. I have been not a nice person in my past. Not a criminal, but an asshole."

"You mean because you were raised in a small town by rednecks and you were doing shit to survive?" Chris asked, and Guthrie stared at him in horror.

"Get out of my head!" he sputtered, and Chris rolled his eyes.

"Puh-leeze. I know you may not have heard this, but Tad and I are detectives. Which means we're pretty good at sussing out human behavior. Do you think you were the only teenager on the planet to scream out slurs because you were afraid your daddy would figure out you were exactly what he despised?"

"It's like I'm naked," Guthrie muttered, more to himself as he realized the horror would continue.

"Yeah, well, you know what you look like naked?"

"Aren't you straight?" Guthrie asked, but it was a weak attempt at evasion, and they both knew it.

"From a clinical point of view," Chris said, one corner of his mouth turning up. "You look no better or worse than a thousand other guys I've seen who are trying to live a good life with a shitty rule book. Give it up. Give up the guilt. Give up the fear that you'll suddenly be that guy again. You know why you and Tad don't feel new? You gave up the right to be new when you walked out on your job to take care of his sister after a month of knowing each other. You took that relationship through the fire, and it's still strong. Don't be afraid to ask him to love you. He's already there. Be afraid of passing up this opportunity, because from what I can see, son, you haven't had a lot of those in your life, and maybe that's why you don't see this one for what it is."

The server arrived then and deposited a magical meal of carbs, cholesterol, and red meat in front of Guthrie that made him suddenly faint with hunger, and an order of biscuits and gravy that made Chris sigh appreciatively.

"It's like vacation," he said softly, pulling his phone out to do something. "Yup. April's leaving in an hour to get my burrito, and my wife will never know."

"You are lying to that nice woman who drove you down to San Rafael last night?" he asked suspiciously. "Why should I believe you now?"

He scowled at Guthrie. "Because a good marriage is compromise. I've been living on quinoa and pomegranate juice for the last two months. I've earned this. Now shut up and eat your own delicious poison while I enjoy mine."

Guthrie was halfway through his steak and eggs—and starting to see that maybe Chris was right; he wouldn't be able to finish—when something occurred to him.

"Why two months? What happened two months ago?"

Chris stopped in mid chew and washed his bite of biscuits and gravy down with a sip of orange juice. "My wife woke up and said, 'Wait a minute. Our youngest child is graduating from high school, and you still have ten years to retirement. You had damned well better work at staying alive so we can go to Europe or I will never forgive you.' So we made a pact to take care of ourselves. Yeah, bullets, car wrecks, falling down canyons, yada yada yada, but dammit, cholesterol is not gonna get me."

Guthrie smiled a little. "She's a good woman. You're a smart man."

Chris nodded sagely. "I like to think so. And you and Tad could be just as good for each other. Give it some thought. Now give the rest of that steak and eggs to me and I can tuck April's burrito away for lunch later. Tomorrow I'll be right back on the wagon, and Laura will never know."

THE PAIN pill kicked in almost as soon as they left Vacaville, and Guthrie slept until Chris was pulling up in front of Tad's apartment. Tad and April spilled outside the door and to the sidewalk almost before the truck's engine stopped turning over, which was a good ten seconds after the key was removed.

April caught him in a hug first, gentle and careful of his injury, and then she gave him a peck on the cheek and went to help Chris with the gear in the back. That left him face-to-face with Tad, and he wasn't sure what he would have done, but Tad reached out a shaking hand and pulled the long strands of hair from his eyes.

"You always look so… so lost when you get here," Tad whispered. "Like you're afraid we won't want you."

Guthrie gave a nervous smile. "I'm always glad you do."

Tad nodded and leaned forward, pressing their foreheads together. "Baby, I wish you'd stop scaring me like this. The first time sucked, but this was worse."

Guthrie nodded. "Sorry," he rasped. "I'm—"

"No sorry," Tad said softly. "Just… can we move the rest of your stuff from San Rafael to here? Can you… can you call this home?"

Guthrie closed his eyes and remembered all the things Tad's partner had been trying to tell him. "But you might be moving soon," he said hesitantly.

Tad scowled at Chris, who was striding by cheerfully with Guthrie's drum-set cases in hand. Guthrie saw him smirk and got it. Tad couldn't be mad at the guy who'd brought Guthrie home.

"Then us—consider me and April home," Tad begged. "Can you do that? Even if it's only for a little while, okay?"

Guthrie nodded. "I'd rather it be for a bit," he said dolefully. "Until a wedding in Colton and a studio gig in late August, I'm sort of out of a job."

Tad brushed the bandages on his shoulder. "Good. Stay here. Heal with me. Let's make plans for something bigger. Okay?"

Guthrie nodded. "Okay. Sorry to worry you," he said, and this time Tad let it slide.

"I'm just so glad you're home."

THAT DAY and night he slept like the doctor had ordered him, exhausted and stoned, and the next morning he showered. Tad was down to one bandage on the back of his thigh—he could shower and swim at will. But Guthrie had a long, deep slice in the meat of his shoulder and down his collarbone. He needed a plastic bag to shower and then an hour of napping to recover. And the doctor hadn't been exaggerating about the bruises and contusions.

Guthrie woke up from his after-shower nap to find Tad sitting on the bed next to him, trailing shaking fingers along his bruised ribs, down the swelling of his hip joint, and over more bruises on his thighs. Guthrie reached for the blanket to cover up, but Tad stayed him.

"This was really brutal," he said, voice shaking. "I didn't look this bad after falling off a cliff and into a canyon. Why is this so bad?"

It was on the tip of Guthrie's tongue to say, "To make up for not being shot," but he managed to temper himself.

"I fought back," he confessed. "I… it was our last gig, Tad. That's the last money I'm going to see until the studio thing in August, unless I get a gig bussing tables up here. I just… I needed that money." There was more to it. The money from the first CD was running out, and the lease on the apartment in San Rafael was expiring at the end of August too. Lulu was hoping to keep the apartment—even after Agnes came back to Sacramento for her senior year in high school, Lulu wanted to finish out the program she'd started in the Bay Area, and her sister, Lily, wanted to move down there with her, because the two of them had never liked being separated for long. Guthrie's name needed to be on the lease, otherwise the landlord would hike the rent and the sisters wouldn't be able to afford it. That needed another deposit, and as it was, he didn't have it. The money he'd saved by taking a beating would pay for repairs to his truck and gas for the next month. His savings might take care of food.

"Then get a gig bussing tables!" Tad told him. "Or, you know, let me pay for groceries. April tells me you try to pay for it yourself when you guys go shopping. She's got my card. Let her go. Don't worry about rent here. C'mon, Guthrie, you could have *died*. I know my knife wounds—this is a lucky shot."

"Like that bullet in your ass?" Guthrie scowled, and Tad let loose a sigh.

"Fair. Just… look. Chris and I helped a guy who owns a restaurant about two blocks from here. Can I, maybe, get you a summer job waiting tables or tending bar, and you can do that for cash while we figure out what we're doing?"

"While you get ready to move?" Guthrie clarified, feeling the hurt.

"*We*, Guthrie. If it was only me and April, I'd tell you to fire off resumes. I'd let you move back to San Rafael to sleep on your own damned couch. I'm not stupid. You've got marketable skills, man. You can get a better job than that, I know it. But... but if *we* are going to move, this might be a better option. What do you say?"

"We?" Guthrie asked. His head was still swimmy from pain pills, and damn if he might not have to fall asleep after having this conversation while lying on his back, but even *he* knew that word was important.

Tad leaned forward and cupped his cheek. "How many times have we made love now?" he asked. "Have you counted?"

Guthrie closed his eyes and tried. The first time, he remembered. The first time after Tad got back—that one was clear too. But there'd been so much in the past three weeks. Honeymooning, in a way, and he knew Tad was celebrating his own healing body. But it was more than that. It was that sometimes "making love" was a quick one-off in each other's fists. Sometimes... sometimes it was what they'd done four nights ago, before he'd gone down to San Rafael, when Guthrie had showered that night after spending the day in the pool and Tad had come into the bathroom when he'd been toweling off. Guthrie had found himself bent over the sink, looking into his own eyes in the mirror, as Tad had settled onto the closed seat of the commode and parted his cheeks and... oh God. He was in pain and embarrassed and tired, but the thought of what Tad had been doing to him that night still made his cock try to swell in anticipation.

Did that count as once? Did what they'd done afterward, Guthrie bent over the bed like he'd been bent over the sink, Tad thrusting inside him with undisguised delight. Did that count as a separate time? The same time? What about when they'd been done and Tad had rinsed off and come to bed, and suddenly Guthrie had *needed* to taste him, had pulled his cock into the back of his mouth and stroked him to completion, swallowing every bit of come Tad had left?

Did that count as a third time or the same time because it was the same night?

There was no counting.

There was no adding up the times they'd orgasmed versus the times they'd touched versus the times they'd simply kissed in passing as they were walking across the apartment.

"No counting," Guthrie murmured, cheeks heating. "Just touching you counts."

Tad leaned forward and feathered his cheek with gentle lips. "Then it doesn't matter if it's been a long time or a short time," he said. "Sam and I had sex exactly twelve times before we moved in together. He kept a diary so he'd know when it was time to ask."

Guthrie stared at him in horror, and Tad laughed.

"Yeah. I know. It's awful. I can't believe I dated that guy. But it sounded so sensible. Common sense never let me down, right? But that guy wouldn't have walked out of a job to help my sister. That guy wouldn't have literally taken the shirt off his back to let me know I wasn't alone. *That* guy wouldn't have sung love songs into the starry night sky to give me hope. So maybe *that guy* isn't the guy I needed. Maybe you're the guy I need. Think about that. Maybe two months with you means a whole lot more than two years with anyone else. Let's find out."

Guthrie felt his mouth twitch even as his eyes drifted shut. "Okay," he mumbled, sleep overtaking him. "Okay."

He felt the bed shift as Tad stood up, and then to his surprise, felt the bed shift behind him. Tad had crawled back in, because on that side of the bed he could lie down facing Guthrie, one hand gingerly spanning his tender midriff.

Guthrie fell asleep feeling safe, and that had to count for something.

TWO MORE weeks. Two mellow, healing, sweet weeks during which taking walks with Tad or trips to the craft store with April, or getting a bonded pair of kittens from the SPCA were the highlights of his day.

He got to name one of the kittens—Lennon, because John Lennon, natch—and April called the other one McCartney, or Mac, or Arty, or Scooter-Pie, or Jesus-You-Fucking-Asshole, because McCartney had never met a drape or a blanket or a couch or a pair of jeans he didn't want to climb. After the end of the first week, they were Mac the Knife and Lenny Bruce, and somehow nobody in the apartment noticed the transition.

And in between those things, when Tad was on his computer trying to catch up with paperwork from home and April was deep in her audiobooks or music while she was crocheting, Guthrie would practice on his drum pads or soundlessly on his guitar, and more and more as he practiced, he found himself "twiddling." He'd completely orchestrated three whole songs, saving them on his computer, and he had lyrics written for four more. He'd learned music notation from Seth at first, and then had gone to school for music theory classes, and now he wrote the songs down and practiced the guitar and the percussion and even the instrumental parts on a keyboard, like Seth would. Like a professional. Like somebody who knew what the fuck they were doing.

After two weeks of healing, he was sitting on a dinette stool in the living room, guitar in his arms, pretending to strum and staring thoughtfully into thin air when Tad glanced up from his computer and took off his noise-dampening headphones.

"What?" he asked.

Guthrie gave him a quick grin, almost a death rictus he was so nervous. "It's noth—"

"Guthrie, you've been sitting there looking constipated for fifteen minutes. Just, you know, play it. It's fine. I'm listening."

Guthrie scowled at him, and without knowing he was going to do it, his fingers started working, and the guitar was in tune, and it played so sweetly Guthrie wanted to bless it with holy water for following him through the wars.

Then he started singing.

> *Driving through midnight*
> *Black ribbon of road*
> *Stretching before me, a future not told*
> *And all I have in me is an old love song*
> *I sang under stars so bright*
> *That song hurts me tonight.*
> *My heart's like thunder 'cause*
> *What if you don't*
> *Want to see me like I want you*
> *But two hundred miles sit between us*
> *And there's nothing for me to do*
> *But drive through midnight*
> *Black ribbon of road*
> *Singing before my eyes*
> *Driving through midnight*
> *I pray to those bright stars*
> *Nothing you said was lies*

Please want me like I want you
Love me like I love you.

He played the final notes of the song, lost in the music until the very end, and when he looked up, April had taken her earbuds out and both of them were staring at him.

"What?" he croaked, suddenly terrified.

"That was…," April started, wiping her eyes with her palms.

Then they heard it. A hiccup. A strangled breath. A sob.

Guthrie and April both stared at Tad as he tried to breathe through his tears, and April said, "Tad?"

"He said it," Tad gasped. "He said he loved me. I never thought he'd say it."

April stared at him and said, "April, peaceing out," as she grabbed her stuff and scrambled for her room. Guthrie set his guitar down in the case and came to crouch in front of Tad, taking his hands.

"What?" he asked, trying to understand.

Tad wiped his face on his shoulder and then did it again. "God, Guthrie—I've loved you since you fixed my damned flat tire. I never thought you'd love me back."

Guthrie kissed Tad's knuckles, saw brine on them, realized they were both crying. "Of course I love you," he said, partly in wonder because he'd said it, and partly in surprise because how did Tad not know? "Do you think I… I… all the things I've done for you—do you think I do them for anybody? Nobody's had the parts of me that you do. Not a single soul. You've got to know *that*, right?"

"No, you asshole," Tad hiccupped. "Because you don't *tell me*."

"Oh." Guthrie stood so he could pull Tad's face against his stomach. "Well, I love you. Now you know."

And Tad laughed and cried against him for way longer than Guthrie expected. When he'd finally calmed down, Guthrie heard the waiting silence and thought it would be a good time to ask.

"So you like the song, right?"

And that started Tad off again.

WHERE'S MY LOVE

TAD FINALLY had to excuse himself to clean up... and to catch his breath. God. In a thousand years, he never thought Guthrie would say it. It figured that he'd say it in song, right?

And what a song.

Tad had loved music all his life, and he'd never heard something that called to him so plaintively, had evoked all the things Tad felt about the man he wanted to make a future with.

It was like those other attempts at love didn't exist. All other love had to take a back seat to this thing he had with Guthrie because it dominated his heart, and Tad was subservient in all things to what had overwhelmed him as he'd listened.

It was a good thing Guthrie seemed to want the same things he did. There was no objection to April living with them. Guthrie didn't just tolerate her—he embraced her, seemingly glad to have a built-in family when he chose to throw his lot in with Tad. Guthrie had hesitantly given the go-ahead for Tad to put his notice in with Chris; if Aaron George put an offer in writing, they were both leaving SAC PD at the end of August and moving to Colton in early September. He'd even—again, hesitantly—confided in Tad that he had a gig at the end of August, in the studio with Seth Arnold and his friends, and that he was hoping the result would be enough money for Guthrie to establish himself as a solo artist and to maybe not have to find another band that would simply leave him for bigger and better things.

He'd be happy, he said, to play small venues, to cut big albums, to wait tables and bartend in between paying gigs, as long as he could, please God, be allowed by fate to play.

He'd said it that way too, and Tad had seen the desperation in his eyes, the need to keep making his living doing this thing he loved more than all the gold, and maybe even all the love, in the world.

Tad had prayed for it to happen as well, to make Guthrie happy, but until this moment, that song lancing the swollen, painful places in his soul, he hadn't realized what he was praying for.

He was praying for Guthrie's sweet voice to move people like he'd just moved Tad and April. He was praying for the money and the time and the talent to make songs like *that* one, that had opened Tad up and let all his fears and worries out into the cleansing air.

Guthrie *needed* to make music.

Tad understood now.

And Guthrie loved *him*. Tad got that too.

Guthrie had been planning to go with Tad to ask Tad's friend for work in a couple of days, but Tad wanted to tell him not to. Wanted to tell him to stay home and keep writing. Wanted to tell him to cut his *own* disc and see if he could get it to sell.

A song like that didn't belong in a tiny apartment in Midtown where nobody could hear it but Tad and April. That song belonged to the world. Tad felt like it was his job to help Guthrie get it there.

When he came back from the bathroom, he'd wiped his face, and his eyes were no longer swollen, and he felt like he could talk without sobbing anymore. Guthrie was back on his stool, playing a different tune softly, and Tad's thighs were still a little unsteady, so he sat and asked, "If I'm super nice to you, will you play me your other songs?"

Guthrie gave him a shy smile. "'Course. Hope it's okay—I set my computer up to tape so I can send them to Seth. He, uh, told me to send him anything I composed myself, 'cause he wants us all in on the album. Thought maybe he could choose from the songs I've got done."

For once Tad wasn't irritated to hear Seth Arnold's name. Guthrie wasn't playing for an old lover—he was playing for a bandmate, someone with powerful contacts who could maybe help Guthrie get work. And, Tad had to admit, for a friend who knew this side of Guthrie, the side that made music and poured his heart onto the stage better than Tad did, because Seth Arnold had made the same sacrifices and had the same river carving its way through his heart.

"Yeah," he said. "Tell me how he likes them." He managed a lopsided smile. "It could be I'm a little, uhm, biased. You know. About your songs."

Guthrie bit his lip. "I'll play that other one last, okay? So if you gotta cry, I can turn the recording off."

Tad regarded him fondly. "I was crying because you love me, Guthrie. Although the song was absolutely lovely."

Guthrie shrugged. "Just in case," he said, nodding with sober intent. And then he launched into another song about punching the clock for The Man that made Tad laugh because it ended with the speaker walking out.

> *Have fun finding your life, Mr. Man. Have fun finding*
> *   your money.*
> *Have fun finding your business plan, or the phone number*
> *   with your honey.*
> *Good luck with those insurance forms, good luck with*
> *   your contract history.*
> *I know once you've seen the back of me, your whole office*
> *   is a big fat mystery.*
> *I've got bigger hopes than this shithole, and someday*
> *   you'll know it's true*
> *I've always had a bigger soul, with more to do than you.*

Guthrie gave a cheeky grin at the end of that one, and then leaned forward to take a swig from the bottle of water on the table.

"You know where this one came from," he told Tad, and then launched into a song about hearing music through a cold black river of stars.

Tad shuddered, hearing the loneliness and isolation of that song, and then, in the guitar riff, he felt the hope.

"God," he whispered when Guthrie was done with it. "You... you captured that night so well."

Guthrie's next smile was a little self-deprecating, and then he hit a comic riff on the guitar, something plucky and country and western that reminded Tad of a song about squirrels, before he launched into the ballad of Lennon and McCartney.

Or Johnny Law and McMoron.

Or Imagine Using the Cat Box and Stop Climbing my Drapes Around.

Or Giving Cats up for Lent and Gonna Eat me Some Cat Stew.

The song went on, highlighting the joys of kitten ownership to date, and finally ended with a moment of contemplation.

> *But oh, look at them when they're sleeping,*

Oh, look at their little beans.
Look at their claws creeping
As they hunt our toes in their dreams....
Lenny get the mouse and Mac get the knife
Everyone in the house is now afraid for his life
Baby you should run 'cause they're back on the prowl
Mac and Lenny, Johnny Law, McMoron Mc Mouser,
The two damned cats have got us on the run again.

Tad laughed long and hard when he was done with that one, and so did April, who had crept back in when Guthrie started to play again. The apartment had grown really warm by then, so Tad insisted they leave for a swim before ordering takeout, and Guthrie sent the songs.

Tad's heart was so full—of admiration, of delight, of simple love—that he couldn't imagine not touching Guthrie when the lights went down.

It felt like that's what he was born for.

GUTHRIE GOT a text while they were getting takeout. He checked his phone, probably hoping for notice from Berta or the band. He talked a good game about knowing the band was breaking up, but he'd been so protective over those music students—Tad knew he had to miss them.

But it wasn't Berta or Kelly or Kelly's sister. Tad didn't have to look at the phone to see that. All he had to see was the set to Guthrie's jaw, the way his back stiffened, or hear the sound of his breathing, like he was working very, very hard not to let it get too fast or too angry.

"Who was that?" Tad asked softly, and Guthrie shook his head.

"Not important," he murmured back, and then it was time to get their order.

Back at the apartment, they watched a movie—something with lots of explosions, because April liked that kind of thing. Tad would remember that night: April's complete happiness as she sat in the recliner and did her yarn thing, and Guthrie, his head on a pillow in Tad's lap, because Tad could not stop fingering the coarse strands of his hair. Guthrie took care of his ponytail, used conditioner and oil on it so it didn't get dry, kept it trimmed. He was even just a bit vain about it. Tad had heard him ask the haircutting place for a little bit of layering on the bottom so it would flip. "Otherwise," he'd say, "it looks like I don't give a shit, but if it's got a little bit of shape, that makes it a *choice*."

Tad liked his choice. He'd never known he could be a sucker for a guy with longer hair until he'd spent hours just *fondling* it, while Guthrie trusted him to only use touch for good.

That's all Tad wanted to do, and apparently, that's all Lenny the cat wanted to do too, because the marmalade tom parked himself across Guthrie's hip and purred, while April sacrificed some yarn scraps to keep Mac the Knife from destroying everything she was doing.

It was such a good evening—such a *perfect* evening. Tad should have known.

But he was aware of nothing but Guthrie's body near his and how they were both nearly healed, nearly whole.

He was aware that Guthrie loved him, and that was a thing he *knew* in his bones now. Guthrie had written him a song, and said the words out loud in front of April, even, and then he'd said them intentionally without music, and held Tad as *he'd* fallen apart.

Every touch fired between them, and the ache in Tad's groin was *delicious*. He wanted to rush Guthrie to the bedroom, to take him *right then*, but instead he savored, enjoyed the rough satin of Guthrie's hair, April's grumbling at the kitten she adored, and Guthrie's hand on the inside of Tad's knee, burning against his bare skin since Tad was wearing sleep shorts, promising things Tad intended for him to keep.

The movie ended and everybody stood and stretched. Cats were given one last feeding, doors and windows were locked, lights were turned out, and they made their way to the bedroom, pausing for a moment to see where Lenny would sleep.

The cat hadn't moved from his droop on the couch, so Tad locked the door while Guthrie went to brush his teeth and relieve himself. When Tad got back from doing the same, Guthrie was texting furiously on his phone, his brows drawn together as he apparently told somebody to go to hell.

"What's up?" Tad asked, concerned.

Guthrie swallowed and shook his head, hitting Send on what seemed to be a blistering message. "Nothing for you to worry about," he said, and his smile, which started out a little forced, melted as he took in Tad, very deliberately taking his sleep shorts and briefs off and leaving them on his dresser for later use. "I am apparently overdressed."

Tad had to laugh as Guthrie, staying under the covers, started doing the undressing shimmy as he took off his own shorts and briefs on the bottom.

"The T-shirt too," Tad murmured, sliding into bed and turning off the light.

"You know, most guys don't care about the—"

Tad shut that up with a kiss. He didn't care about "most guys" or other men. All he cared about was touching *his* man. Guthrie must have wanted it too, because he didn't argue or push back.

Instead, he lifted himself up and pulled Tad down after him, losing them both fully in the kiss until Tad was gasping for air.

"Aren't you bossy," he gasped, aroused already while Guthrie wrapped his legs around Tad's hips.

"I'm *hungry*," Guthrie complained, and Tad knew he couldn't be talking about food because the man hardly ate.

Tad kissed his neck, his shoulder, then nibbled on his ear. "I'm hungry too," he purred. "When are you going to top?"

He actually heard Guthrie swallow, and he *knew* he felt Guthrie's erection soften.

"Never mind," he breathed, taking Guthrie's mouth again. "Not tonight. Tonight it's just us, and none of our demons, okay?"

"Yeah," Guthrie murmured, and allowed himself to be taken again, led away into the sexual haze that Tad had been creating for them both.

A part of Tad was fine with this—he'd always loved to top—but part of him was sorrowful. *You can trust me to guide you, Guthrie. You can trust yourself.* Later. They'd deal with it later. Right now, Tad felt a freedom in Guthrie's arms, a blessing, a knowledge that all their touches tonight would be the good kind; all of it would be right.

His two-finger breach into Guthrie's body elicited a groan that raised the hairs on the back of Tad's neck. Something huge and needy had opened up in his boy, something painful. It was Tad's job to fill those empty spaces. How could he forget?

He stretched Guthrie's entrance, aware of Guthrie's finely muscled trembling, and then slid inside him, unable to draw this out because Guthrie needed him so bad.

Guthrie gave a sigh of completion when they were merged, and his caresses on Tad's biceps, his flanks, his neck, never stopped. Tad felt worshipped and treasured.

And loved.

When Guthrie was writhing with the need to come, Tad rocked back on his thighs and stroked him, thrusting slowly in time to his strokes, just to watch Guthrie fall apart, arms flinging out, head tilted back, eyes squeezed shut, his orgasm rocking him into the stratosphere while it triggered Tad's like a rocket.

As Tad's vision went white and his breaths screamed in his ears, he recorded the tears steadily dripping from Guthrie's eyes, squeezed so tight there was no room for anything *but* the tears.

"Shh...," Tad whispered as his own climax rushed him. "Shh... baby... I gotcha. I love you. I gotcha."

"Love you too," Guthrie whispered, fingers digging into Tad's arms. "So much. You gotta know how much."

That frisson of fear that had brushed up against Tad's senses when he'd seen Guthrie texting so violently returned, and he took Guthrie's mouth with all the possessiveness in his soul. Guthrie returned the kiss, drinking him in like water, and as their bodies stilled in the apartment hush, Tad tried to tell his fears to quiet. These weren't the kisses of a man who didn't want to stay. This wasn't the body of a man who was halfway out the door.

They fell asleep, limbs tangled, Guthrie's head on Tad's shoulder, eyes still leaking the tears he knew Guthrie hated.

A man who hated his life, or was afraid of his lover, didn't sleep naked in his arms like this was the only home he'd ever know.

Which was why Tad was poleaxed, gobsmacked, destroyed, when he woke up and saw Guthrie, fully dressed in his jeans, hair ruthlessly pulled back from his face, tying his boots with white fingers as he sat on the edge of the bed.

His knapsack, the one Tad had grown to hate when Guthrie had been playing at Scorpio in those last weeks, was fully packed and sitting next to the bed.

And Tad knew the other shoe, the one he hadn't realized had been hovering over their heads, had finally dropped.

Awkward Teenage Blues

GUTHRIE'S HEART pretty much fell out of his body when the first text appeared on his phone.

This is Jock-o—how you doin' kid?

He'd stared at it in shock while he and Tad had been waiting in line at the sub shop. Jock? Texting him *now*? This was apparently his punishment for not changing his phone number out two years ago, when his father had made it known that Guthrie was nothing to him.

I thought I was dead to you. Can we go back to that?

That's not fair, Guthrie. Your dad made that decision, not me.

And you sure stood up against him, didn't you? I'm blocking you.

So Guthrie had.

But Jock wasn't stupid. Sure, his father had *treated* his little brother like he was stupid, but Robert Coltrane Woodson was, in fact, a pretty smart cookie. Unlike Butch, he might have gone to college if the family had believed in education.

Guthrie had managed to put the text and its implications out of his mind. That blissful moment on the couch with his head in Tad's lap made him feel safe and cherished and loved. That feeling sank into his bones, making him feel confident and joyous and so, so ready for Tad to come to bed and touch him with that amazing sensuality Guthrie had just discovered.

And then his phone had buzzed again.

Goddammit, I can only afford one burner so don't block me on this one!

Fuck. This was pretty tenacious for Jock. He was usually the first to quit. Guthrie remembered plenty of times when, "C'mon, Butch, the boy wasn't doing no harm," turned into "Never mind, never mind, he's your kid," before the first sentence even ended.

I'm broke too. I got nothing you need. Go away.

Guthrie had been pretty sure his dad and Jock would piss away their Fiddler and the Crabs money. Tad had said it—Guthrie had marketable skills. He'd spent that money on the ability to have a resume and some hope and a day job that would fill in the lean times. Suddenly the embarrassment of his dwindling bank account wasn't quite so acute.

C'mon, Guthrie. Don't be like that. Your dad is sick and I need help. I can't be the only one taking care of him.

Oh Jesus. *How sick?* Guthrie asked, hearing Tad moving around in the bathroom.

Ain't gonna see September.

Guthrie closed his eyes and swallowed. *Well he don't want to see me, so I'll have to live with that.* He pounded the text in, trying to keep his hand from shaking. *Jock, you two made it really fucking clear that I was not wanted and I was not family. Hurt like hell, but at least I can peace out of this. PEACE. FUCKING. OUT.*

And with that he muted his notifications and set the phone down on the bedstand. Tad had emerged from the bathroom, freshly scrubbed and sexy and oh so hopeful. Suddenly Guthrie needed him—*needed* him, needed the completeness of his touch, the wholeness he felt when Tad was inside him, and the glory of his skin.

As their bodies moved together, Guthrie felt the need overtake him, opening up and swallowing the moment whole. *Take me*, he begged in the silence of his own skull. *Take me and bless me from the inside out. I need you to make me the man I want to be.*

When their breathing had stilled, Guthrie rolled into Tad's arms and hid his face against Tad's shoulder, turning his back on the incriminating phone.

But even as he fell asleep, he knew the man he wanted to be hadn't seen the last of that text stream. The man he wanted to be had some unfinished business to tend to.

HE'D GOTTEN up to pee the next morning when his text notifications came back on, and his phone buzzed repeatedly while he did his business. When he came back, he took a breath and checked, the texts coming thick and fast as Jock detailed a four-hour trip from Sand Cut to Sacramento, including pit stops and engine noises, including the cheerful acknowledgment that hey, Jock had figured out how to track Guthrie's phone. That last one horrified him, even more so when he saw the last two texts in the stream.

Look, I'm here. I'll be waiting outside until you come talk.

If you've got coffee, that would be real fucking human.

Guthrie checked the timestamp on the last one and sighed. Two hours. Jock had probably fallen asleep in the front of his old truck—a Ford instead of a Chevy because God forbid Guthrie follow in his family's footsteps without a fight—with his arms folded and his head leaning against the windshield.

Thank God the temperature had dropped the night before because Jock and Butch hadn't been too pro on hygiene, and there was nothing like the hot cab of a pickup truck to really ripen the sweat on a middle-aged man who had a long association with alcohol.

With a sigh he slid on some clothes—including the new cargo shorts Tad and April had snuck into his drawer, like he wasn't going to notice that—and stepped into his flip-flops in the hallway. His hand was on the doorknob when he realized that there was only one pair of flip-flips left.

Why was April outside?

His heart almost jumped out of his rib cage when he saw her standing by Jock's truck, wearing one of Tad's oversized T-shirts over sleep shorts, her arms crossed in front of her and a scowl on her face as she chewed Jock a new one. Jock was parked in a neighbor's spot, Guthrie realized. Jimmy Collier worked the night shift and would be there any minute. She must have seen the truck and gone to clear it out. Jimmy had been a big help when they'd brought the kittens home.

"And I'm saying," April growled, "that you can park somewhere else while you wait for him to wake up. Like the delta. In the river. Or maybe the junkyard. Or Utah."

"Little missy," Jock replied, one of his best shit-eating, women-hating grins on his face, "I get that you're trying to stand up for your man—"

"I'm standing up for my neighbor, you asshole. I don't even know who you're here to bother, but I hope it's nobody I know. Now move!"

Guthrie made sure to clear his throat before putting his hands gently on her shoulders. "I'm afraid he's here for me, darlin'," he said softly. "Go on inside and try to make sure your brother doesn't hear this, okay?"

She turned troubled eyes to him. "Oh, Guthrie—oh no. This guy's your people?"

Guthrie swallowed. "Not anymore. But, you know, the past ain't always in the past. This is my uncle Jock, and he's here—"

"To take you back to your family," Jock said loudly. "You got responsibilities, Guthrie, like it or not. He may not be much of a daddy, but he *is* your daddy—"

"I'm pretty sure he told me I wasn't his son, Jock. You want me to come back now and walk him into the next world on your say-so?"

"Oh, Guthrie," April murmured, her soft gasp cutting into his anger and his hurt. "Oh no. You can't go. This… this is bad—"

Guthrie closed his eyes. "Please," he begged her. "Don't let your brother see me have this conversation, okay? Just please." He gave her a little nod back into the apartment and waited until he heard the door click before he turned back to Jock.

"Talk," he said grimly.

"You didn't have to send her away, son," Jock said, his salacious grin churning Guthrie's stomach. "She had the cutest set of titties. You live with that?"

Guthrie's hands started to sweat with the effort to not clock Jock in the saggy jaw.

And it *was* saggy. He could see the age in Jock's once-handsome face, the slackness that alcohol and a bad diet had given him, the lines and wrinkles that Guthrie hadn't seen two years ago because parents and parental figures didn't really age.

But Jock had.

And that, in the end, was what stayed Guthrie's hand.

"Jock, if I ever see you talking to that girl again, I'll break your jaw. Then I'll break your fingers. Then I'll go to work on you. If you touch her, I'll kill you. I'm not exaggerating. I've reinforced my guitar case to ward off muggers. Gave the last one a concussion. I will *beat your head in* if you attempt contact in any way. That girl does not need you."

Jock's eyes went wide in surprise, and he regarded Guthrie in shock.

"Boy, you can't possibly mean—"

"Every word of that." Guthrie shook his head. "These people you followed me to—they're good people. I've seen you grab too many asses, take too many liberties. When I was a kid I could think, 'Oh, that's just Jock, he don't mean nothin'.' But I'm grown now. Just being Jock don't get you a pass, not with someone who cares about me like that girl and her brother do. So if all you got is a weakshit pass on a girl I'll protect with my life, you can motor on your way."

Jock's jaw hardened. "She's sallow," he said with a sniff. "Probably on the junk anyway."

Guthrie turned as crisply as he could in flip-flips and was waylaid by Jock's honest plea.

"No, no—don't go. Guthrie, I wasn't shitting around about needing you. Man, it's your dad. Like I said, he's sick."

"What's gotten him?" Guthrie asked.

"Everything," Jock muttered, shaking his head. "Liver's shot, lungs are shot—if the cirrhosis don't get him, the cancer will. He's got a month, maybe, and he wants to go out at home. But home is... you know. Not like we stayed there much anyway. I gotta work on shit like plumbing and electricity so the place don't go up with us in it, and he needs everything, from a drink of water to a trip to the bathroom to piss. He's my brother, man, but I can't do it all!"

"Don't you get a nurse from the state?" Guthrie asked, scowling.

"Five days a week," Jock said, nodding. "And some of the folks around town regard your dad fondly. So we got some help. Backup's not twenty-four seven, but it will be if you come help me see it through."

Guthrie shook his head. "Why? Give me one good reason to see it through."

"We took you in when you was little!" Jock whined. "Me and your dad. It was us or foster care!"

"I was your kinfolk," Guthrie said flatly. "That was your job, and you did the minimum amount. Remember when I used to show up behind the diner to eat the scraps 'cause you and Dad would leave for a gig and forget to leave me food? The only reason you started taking me with you is cause Rick Cobb threatened to take me away, and we all know the money you got from the state in child credit was what kept you and Dad in beer."

Jock sighed and rubbed the back of his neck. "Yeah, me and your daddy, we gotta make our accounts square with the Lord, and believe me, he's gonna settle up soon. But you're gonna have to do your own settling up. You want leaving your old man to rot in his own shit to be on your ledger?"

Guthrie shook his head. "I wanted to be able to leave the two of you to your own bullshit and not have to worry about you again. *He threw me out*, remember? Realized you weren't going to get any more money off Fiddler, so suddenly I wasn't worth anything to either of you.

There I was thinking, 'Yeah, well, my family ain't perfect. They don't get me, but they're still my dad and uncle Jock, and Fiddler walks across the stage, and Dad tells me he don't want no faggots in his band, and I can't sleep under his roof if I'm gonna be that way. Message received, Jock. I don't have to be in his fuckin' band, and I don't wanna be under his goddamned roof, but you can't have it both fuckin' ways. I can't be trash when you don't need me and blood when you do."

Jock stared down at his shoes in something like shame. "Your dad shouldn't a done that, Guthrie. You…." He looked up miserably. "You heard me try to stand up to him, didn't you?"

Guthrie held out his hand and wobbled it back and forth. "You tried, sorta. He said, 'Shut the fuck up, Jock,' and you gave it up and went out to nail a waitress who kept trying to feed you Altoids 'cause your breath is fuckin' gross, and I don't know what happened after that 'cause I was fuckin *gone*. Remember *that*, Jock? 'Cause that was the last time I saw you, and I been happy about that!"

Ugh. His dad's twang was throbbing in his voice, and he hated it. He used to only hear the syllables, the music in it, and he'd thought having his dad's and Jock's Alabama music in his tones was a good thing. Then he heard the things they were saying in it, and he'd hated those things so much he'd hated his own voice. Going to school had helped him weed some of that out, and he'd since reconciled that the music was real and their words were *their* words and not his, but he hated that his grammar and his intonation and the whole fuckin' works went sliding down the hill the minute Jock showed back up in his life.

Jock glanced away. "I'm sorry about that, Guthrie. I… I shoulda stood up for you better. You're not wrong. But I'm begging you—*begging* you now. Don't leave me alone with this. When your dad is gone, I got a job at Walmart, which will help me keep the house since it's all paid up. But I gotta fix the house—them nurses won't come in if there's no place to take a piss, right? So I need your help. I'll do anything—"

"Jock, I got gigs," he said, and while his voice was hard, he knew in the pit of his stomach that it was the last argument of desperation. "I'm playing a wedding at the beginning of August and cutting a new album with Fiddler at the end. I would leave the devil himself puking blood to get to these two gigs. I'd steal cars and deck policemen to make it on time. I can't go down to Sand Cut in mid-July 'cause you won't let me back up—"

"I will," Jock said, relief flooding his voice. "I will. You know us, Guthrie. Gigs are sacred. You got gigs, and we'll let you work 'em. I won't hold you back from no gigs!"

Guthrie felt the sand slipping from underneath his feet. *This is what Tad must have felt right before he pitched off that cliff into Daffodil Canyon.* He took a deep breath and heard all his harsh words in the last ten minutes. *God. God, Tad can't see me be a nine-hundred-pound gorilla, not even to fend off Mr. Hyde. I'd rather die.*

"There's no 'letting me work them,'" Guthrie snapped. "If you try to stop me, I'll hurt you."

Jock swallowed and backed away. "Jesus, Guthrie, you got mean. Why you gotta be so mean? I used to feed you, remember? Keep ole Butch off your ass? You don't gotta be mean to me. We're gonna be the only two guys in the boat in the next month or so, you know?"

Guthrie shook his head. "You kicked me out of the family—and even if it was Dad who done it, you walked away and let him. And then you show up here and disrespect someone I care about—"

"I thought you were a faggot," Jock said, and his tone was curious even if the word was offensive. "Why you so protective over her?"

"'Cause the girl's like my sister."

"You fuckin' her brother?" Jock asked, and again, nothing but curiosity and that ever-foul mouth, but suddenly Guthrie had him by the throat through the window of the truck and was pushing him back against the torn upholstery.

"You talk to them, either of them, call them, pass them a note, tell them about how you think you know me from the good ole days, and I will shove your nose so far down your throat they'll need forceps and a tractor to pull it out," Guthrie threatened, his voice cold and faraway in his ringing ears. "As far as you and my father are concerned, these people don't exist. I don't want your bullshit in either of their lives."

Jock swallowed, and his eyes searched Guthrie's face, looking for mercy where Guthrie knew there was none to give.

"I'm sorry," he rasped, and Guthrie was so shocked he let go of Jock's collar and stepped back.

"Sorry?" For the first time since engaging in this conversation he felt confused, vulnerable—like the kid he'd been when Jock had been the one who remembered to feed him or buy him shoes that didn't have his toes finding holes to grow through.

"We… what I let your daddy do that made you hate me so much," Jock said, his eyes growing red-rimmed and sad. "'Cause… 'cause I cared for you when you were little. I thought… I thought I did an okay job. But I let Butch hurt you there at the end, and I'm sorry. But if I was ever good to you, if you ever had any fond memories of me, you'll come help me now, Guthrie. Please don't leave me alone with this. I-I couldn't have raised you alone back in the day or I woulda tried. I can't walk your daddy to the grave alone. I'm… I'm a weak man, and a bastard, and a shitty bass guitarist, and I'm not that bright, but at least I know that. Please help me. Please. Then I'll have the house, and your dad'll be gone, and you can be quit of us. You don't never need to visit again."

And now Guthrie was looking at his feet—down, down, down— as he tumbled into that canyon, the one you couldn't get out of. That's where he was going, down into hell, where you needed a backhoe and a pulley and a winch and a crowd of scientists to get you out, because nobody got out of Sand Cut alive without help.

He peered back up and sighed. "I gotta go pack, Jock. I gotta tell them I'll be back." He gave a little laugh. "They're moving, you know. End of August. By the time this is over, I'll have to go find them in the mountains. They'll think I forgot about them."

Jock shook his head, and made maybe his first step in earning Guthrie's forgiveness. "Naw, kid, they'll know you're comin' back. Any fool can see you're the type to stick."

Guthrie's face was tight, and he had to fight the tears because he didn't want to give them to Jock. Uncle Jock didn't get any tears, not right now.

Besides, Guthrie had to say goodbye to Tad first, and he'd need all his tears for that.

"WHERE YOU going?" Tad asked, rolling over in bed. Guthrie took a moment, letting the tension out of his face, his neck and shoulders, so he could brush Tad's lips with his thumb and memorize how he looked, ginger hair on end, green eyes bleary with sleep. He was tousled and grumpy and so, so dear, and Guthrie's heart gave a vicious twist.

"My…." He took a deep breath. "My daddy's sick," he said, trying to get through this. "And I'd let the old man die, but… but Jock, my uncle, needs help with him. So I gotta go, so I can help Jock. I…." His voice wobbled. "I'll be back, Tad. You trust that, right? That I'll come back? I wouldn't leave you. I-I'll come back home when it's done."

Tad's eyes were wide now as he scrambled to sitting. "But… but Guthrie, we might not even be living here when it's 'done,' as you say. Where are you going? Why can't I come with you and help? We could go do that while we're waiting for the transfer, and—"

Guthrie made a hurt sound. "No!" he said, almost shouting. "No." He lowered his voice. "You and April—you can't. April was trying to tell Jock to move his car, and I feel like I failed her just letting her get that close. You can't let these people touch your lives. You *really* can't see me with them. I'm… I'm rattlesnake mean. I got things I gotta do to survive talking to my daddy, Uncle Jock, hell, anybody in my old hometown. I… I can't let you see me be the nine-hundred-pound gorilla that rips apart Mr. Hyde. Do you understand that? I can't let this touch you. You and your sister—you're the good in my life. You're my home. You're worried about me not being able to find you in Colton? I could feel you pulling my heart in the dark. I found you when you were in the middle of the goddamned canyon. I'll find you again. But I need you to trust I'll do that, okay? I…." He squeezed his eyes shut. "Please. Please don't come see me be the bastard I'm about to become. Please—"

He squeezed his eyes shut, but it wasn't any use. He couldn't stop the tears during sex, when he was happy, and they let Tad see into his soul, and he couldn't stop them now, when he was angry and hurt and devastated.

"Please wait for me," he croaked, and Tad sat up in bed and wrapped his arms around Guthrie's shoulders, holding him so tight he couldn't breathe.

Good. He didn't want to breathe. He wanted to die, right here, where he was wanted and cared for and he didn't have to make stupid awful choices or become the man he'd feared the most in order to survive.

"Of course I'll wait for you," Tad whispered. "But… but you'll text. You'll visit—"

Guthrie shook his head, thinking about the working conditions Jock had outlined. "I'll text, but Sand Cut, California, is like Colton. It's a fuckin' technology black hole. Look for emails when texting fails, okay? I'll… I'll find time to talk." His voice broke. "I never used to like to talk, you know? But you and your sister, even Livvy—I'll miss talking."

Tad blew out a breath. "Don't forget how," he said. "And God, Guthrie, take more than that fucking knapsack. Take a suitcase. There's one in the closet. Please?"

Guthrie shook his head. "No," he said bleakly. "All my clothes are here, baby. The knapsack means I'm on the road. You need to keep being my home."

Tad's arms tightened around his shoulders. "Always," he promised. "But…. God, Guthrie. You don't talk much about your dad, but the stuff you've said… do you have to go?"

Guthrie swallowed, more and more of his childhood coming back to him. He'd thought that Jock had aged in the last two years, but it wasn't until just then that he'd realized how *young* Jock really was. He was younger than Larx and Aaron George. He must have been a teenager when Guthrie was a little kid. Guthrie's father was in his late fifties, but Jock—he must have been at Butch Woodson's mercy since *he* was a little kid. Unlike Guthrie, though, Jock never escaped.

Jock had done his best, Guthrie knew, remembering his anguished plea, his acknowledgment that he was a weak man but didn't know what else to do. Jock had been the one to remember breakfast bars and blankets—probably because Guthrie's dad had forgotten them for Jock. Jock had been the one running interventions whenever Guthrie managed to piss the old man off. Sitting here in this safe space, with his lover's arms around him, Guthrie had a clear memory of Jock showing Guthrie a rhythm with his finger on the sly so Butch wouldn't take his head off after the performance. Guthrie had been fourteen and pressed into service. Playing the drums right then had been like mowing the lawn.

"Baby," Guthrie said, taking a deep breath, "I gotta go back. For the same reasons I had to bring April up to the canyon that day. Or you had to take a risk and do some tough love for your baby sister. Because nobody gives us a blueprint or a checklist to be the kind of men we need to be, but sometimes we recognize it when we see it. I see it. If I'm gonna be the kind of man who deserves you, I'm gonna be the kind of man who goes and does this. Just…." He clasped Tad's hands where he'd laced his fingers around Guthrie's shoulders. "It's gonna be a bit. I'll find you in Colton if you gotta go while I'm still in Sand Cut, but please, baby, wait for me."

Tad sputtered some tears of his own and sang softly from Guthrie's impromptu concert that lonely dark night. "I will wait for you…," he sang.

Guthrie turned and took his mouth in a salty, painful kiss. He pulled back and said, "Good. 'Cause I'll come find you."

He took a deep, shuddery breath and stood, turning to cup Tad's cheek.

"Promise," he said, meaning it with all his soul. "I gotta go."

Because if he put it off, said he'd be in Sand Cut tomorrow, told Jock he'd get there eventually, he wouldn't. He'd stay here and pretend he was the good guy—*Tad's* good guy, and that was all that mattered. He knew that being Jock's good guy wasn't going to get him a job or a boyfriend or even the family he found he so desperately needed—but you didn't get to choose who you got to be the good guy for. You either were or you weren't. He'd promise to Tad, because he knew he'd keep it.

He wasn't sure he was strong enough to keep a promise to Jock if he didn't leave right the fuck now.

He took one more look behind him, though, and saw Tad wiping his eyes.

"Don't cry, baby," he murmured. "It's not long. A month? Two months at the most? I know you're the kind to stick. Have a little faith in me, right?"

Tad nodded. "Right," he rasped. "Drive safe." His eyes were red-rimmed, and he looked as shitty as Guthrie felt, but that was as good as it was going to get for the moment.

"'Course."

When he got to the front room, he found April had packed his laptop and his guitar in their cases, and had provided, against all imaginings, two of the household's travel mugs, both filled with coffee.

"Aw, darlin'—"

"I put your sleeping bag and pillow in the lockbox in the back of the truck," she said, clutching his cat to her chest. "And some egg crate and blankets. Don't stay anywhere you're not welcome, Guthrie. You taught me that."

"You heard," he rasped, suddenly afraid. He hadn't counted on them knowing he planned to sleep in his truck. God, he didn't want Tad to know how bad this was going to get.

"Every word. Open windows." She swallowed, her eyes growing red and shiny. "I won't tell him. But... but you're coming home, right? Even if home's in Colton?"

He held open his arms and she went, cat and all. He hugged them both gently. "I know you think Tad's your only family," he whispered, "but you're wrong. I'd come back just so you could be my sister. With your brother waiting here, you can't keep me away, you understand?"

She wiped her face on his shoulder and pulled back to kiss his cheek. "You're just like Tad," she said. "Take that as the compliment it is. Come home when you can. Don't look back."

"Will do, hon," he said. He was good at loading up—had the computer case and the knapsack over his shoulder, both the mugs in one hand and his guitar case in the other. Still clutching Lennon in her arms, April opened the door and nodded her head as he left.

Jock was still waiting in the parking lot for him, and Guthrie walked up and nodded brusquely.

"Grab one," he said. "And don't you say another word about the girl who made you coffee."

Jock smiled hopefully. "Think we can stop in Vacaville for food?" he asked.

"Don't see why not," Guthrie said. "I'll need gas by then anyway. How's your truck running?"

"Like shit. Exhaust leaks like you can't believe."

Awesome. "Then I'll go in front. Watch for me to pull off. First stop, Vacaville. Any particular place?"

Jock closed his eyes. "Think they got an IHOP?" he asked, and Guthrie almost laughed.

"I know it for sure," he said. He wanted to text Chris Castro and have him check in on Tad, but he knew the guy would already. He just hoped "check in on" didn't mean having Tad dump him at the first possible opportunity.

Guthrie had every intention of coming back.

FIVE HOURS later, his stomach still grumbling from the stop at IHOP when they got gas in Vacaville, Guthrie passed through the tunnel that marked the end of civilized internet and the beginning of the peculiar ecosystem that made up every small town.

The view before the tunnel seemed welcoming—eucalyptus trees, hills, bright sunshine and cool shade was a refreshing change from the Sacramento heat. And the smell… something about the air when you got twenty or so miles from the ocean. Guthrie could admit he missed salt and eucalyptus and the faint tang of fish on the breeze. Living on the edge of a storm was exciting; there were zero lies there.

But there was no rest there either.

The sky in Sand Cut was almost a perpetual fog or storm gray, with the truly sunny days or truly rainy days few and far between. As Guthrie had grown older, had toured some more of the state, he came to recognize the kind of emotional constipation of such a sky. There was no moving on for actual residents of Sand Cut. His father seemed to have known this too. When the band had been doing good, his dad and Jock had kept a trailer in San Rafael. Guthrie had gotten his own apartment—and a better one after they'd cut the Fiddler and the Crabs LP—but just because he'd still been in a band with his father and Jock hadn't meant he'd wanted to *be* like them.

Of course, once Seth had gone, graduated from college, took off for Italy and the destiny he'd earned with all that was good in his heart, Guthrie hadn't had any reason to visit Sand Cut, to see the crumbling house sitting on an acre of rusting vehicles, nettles, and spiders, or to sit on the hood of his truck, scenting the wind, trying to find proof of sea or farmland or city—because this small town between the tunnel and the sea was too far away from any of them for "out there" to be real.

But this was real, Guthrie thought, driving over the cracked pavement of the main drag to take a right after the drug store and before the liquor store. There was a fire station, a library, a grange, and stretches of property after that. And then, about a mile out of town, it appeared. Three acres of overgrown land. A stream sat on a corner of it, so the blackberry bushes had taken over a good quarter of the property without the house. As they'd grown, they'd devoured an entire Honda Civic and an old electric stove. Guthrie had hidden out by them when he was a boy, but all he could make of them now was the occasional glimpse of orange primer or crap green enamel.

The rest of the property was in the same state of disrepair and entropy, although Guthrie could see where Jock had started to make inroads in upkeep.

Jock was actually a better carpenter than bass player, and he was pretty good at things like keeping the nettles and growth tempered and the house painted, when he was given a little bit of money and some time. About half the place had been cleared out, and most of the junk that had lived on the lawn had been hauled away. A pile of clean new lumber sat by where a dilapidated carport had been torn down, and Guthrie could see most of the new structure in its place. Jock wasn't kidding about working on the place, and Guthrie's conscience gave a twinge at the thought of Jock out here alone, trying to take care of Guthrie's dad and make sure the one thing he'd have after Butch passed away wasn't going to crumble into dust.

Guthrie parked the truck in a bare spot under a small copse of cypress and oak trees, knowing he'd appreciate the cover when he was sleeping in the bed. It *did* rain every so often, even in the summer, and the trees might keep the fog from swallowing him whole.

He slid out and stretched, hearing his back crack and the muscles and joints taxed from the beating giving a sigh of complaint as he did so.

After about two minutes of side-of-the-road yoga, there came Jock's truck, smoking like a pack-a-day trucker, pulling into the yard and heading toward Guthrie's truck. There was another vehicle there, a small red Toyota, about ten years old, huddling in the same direction Guthrie and Jock had parked.

Jock emerged from the driver's side and gave his own painful stretch.

"Looks like Jolene's here," Butch said, smiling fondly. "Woman offered, but we had to be back before her shift started at the bar. I should go in and relieve her before I tell your daddy."

"Before?" Guthrie asked, although he knew.

"It's gonna be ugly, Guthrie," Jock said with a sigh. "Just... if you could maybe remember you're doing this for me and not your dad, the next few weeks might be easier."

Guthrie gave his own sigh and shooed Jock away. From inside the house, he heard the unmistakable bellow of Butch Woodson.

"You're lyin', you fuckin' whore. Jock would not come back here with my no-good son, 'cause the little faggot's no blood of mine!"

Guthrie took his last breath of free air and decided that maybe it was time he faced the ugly head-on.

Making Love on the Telephone

TAD GLARED at the phone in his hand and fought the temptation to chuck it across the room, through the sliding glass door to the patio, and through the window of his SUV.

The sunset's the only good thing here. Have one.

There was a picture with the text to show him that Guthrie had made it to Sand Cut—a place Tad hadn't even *heard* of before today—and he was doing okay.

Tad remembered the expression on Guthrie's face as he'd left and begged to fucking differ.

"What's it say?" April asked from her place on the recliner. Uncharacteristically, she didn't have yarn in her hand. Instead, she had a cat on each side of the chair, both of them asleep under her arms in an attempt, she said, to stop her from doing that weird thing with the string.

"It says he made it," Tad muttered. "It says the sunsets are nice."

April grunted. "It says the people are so fuckin' awful he doesn't want to talk about it."

Tad touched his nose. "Bingo." He heard her own unhappy sigh and gave her a suspicious glance. "What aren't you telling me?" He'd had doubts when she'd come into his room and cried that morning, making the sudden absence Guthrie had left exponentially worse. She'd been inconsolable, and he'd finally had to give her a sedative prescribed for heavy emotional swings to calm her down enough to sleep. They hadn't spoken much for the rest of the day—they'd gone for their walk, taken their swim, made lunch and dinner, and gone about their day in quiet, but he'd been trying to hold his anxiety back the whole time.

Guthrie had said so little about his childhood, but what he *had* said had left shivers down Tad's spine. Tad could talk about being a latchkey kid and being in charge of April all he wanted, but at the end, their mother came home, made them dinner, checked their homework, and sat with them on the couch as they watched television and talked about their day. She'd taken them places on the weekends, spoke warmly about their father, who had passed away when April was a baby, and made sure they had clothes that fit and somebody in their corner on their good days and their bad. When Tad had come out as a teenager, his mother had told him she'd always love him and then had hugged him when he'd gotten tearful and emotional because that's what you *did* when you shared your heart with a parent. She'd baked birthday cakes and cookies—and yelled sometimes because kids were a handful, but laughed a lot more and most importantly *cared*. She *cared* about the two of them. Losing her was hard because she'd left a hole in their hearts; it was as simple as that.

A simple, profound loss would leave a simple, profound hole.

Tad had no idea what the loss of Guthrie's father would do to him.

And Guthrie had just *left*, promising he'd return. Of *course* Tad believed him. There was nothing about Guthrie—not a thing—that said he'd wander off into the sunset. Besides the fact that Tad had his drum kit, which Tad knew was a big deal to him, even if his clothes weren't, there was Guthrie's innate sense of honor. Of decency. If he promised, he'd follow through unless the devil himself stepped in to stop him.

Tad just wished he knew who the devil was, in case Guthrie needed help.

"If it helps," April said after a silence that went on too long, "he... he wasn't going back to help his daddy. I mean, that's what he was going to be doing, but not who he was doing it for."

Tad blinked and frowned. "Who, then?"

"His uncle. Jock or Jocko or whatever." She let out a hurt sound. "Guthrie was going to say no. I was standing by the window, thinking, 'Do it, man—do it! Don't let guilt take you away from us!'"

"What'd Jock say?" Tad asked, as riveted now as April must have been then.

Her voice cracked a little. "He said he was sorry. He said he cared for Guthrie when Guthrie was little, and letting Guthrie's dad turn him away made him feel awful. And.... And that's what made Guthrie break. Sounded like Jock was the one who cared for Guthrie when he was a kid—worried about food and clothes and such. Guthrie couldn't... couldn't let him do it alone."

Tad's eyes burned. He wasn't sure which felt worse, that Guthrie had gone back to help a man who'd rejected Guthrie out of hand or that he'd gone back to help someone who'd failed him, but Guthrie seemed to have forgiven anyway.

"He's such a good man," Tad said, voice thick.

April turned a little in the recliner and actually looked at him for the first time since she'd awakened from her sedation-induced nap. "He's the best," she said. Her voice was steady, but her eyes were red-rimmed. "Took you long enough to find someone this good."

Tad snorted. "He's the only boyfriend you've even talked to," he said.

"Sam was such a douche," she muttered. "I mean… he kept checking his phone during Mom's funeral. I wanted to kick his teeth in."

Tad grunted. So much had been wrong with Sam that he'd forgotten their bitter fights about Tad's trips to Bodega Bay to help April take care of their mother. In the end, all they'd done was strengthen Tad's resolve to not let a man, any man, tell him what he could "get away with" doing or not doing.

Guthrie didn't need to tell anybody where his duty was. And he hadn't needed Tad's permission.

Of course Tad had given his blessing.

"What about you?" he asked, hating himself for it, but it was something that hadn't even come up in the last year. He knew what April had done on the streets to get high—he'd been a beat cop for five years before moving up to detective. He knew what drugs did to people, what they made them do. He knew that coming to terms with what she'd done versus the true person she was had been something the counselors at the halfway house had been supposed to help her deal with, but they'd been supposed to take care of her too, and that hadn't turned out well.

"What about me what?" she asked, but she looked away from him, face flushed.

"Are you… thinking about seeing someone?"

She shrugged. "I, uhm, have a friend. Someone I've been texting. He, uh… he's got some damage too. I met him in Colton."

Tad grunted. "And the great part of that is I was so out of it when you were in Colton, I'd have no idea who it would be."

She laughed softly. "Remember Olivia and Elton's housemates? Berto and Jaime?"

Tad blinked. "Barely," he apologized. "Jaime, yes. The kid was like pure energy. They should bottle him. But not his brother."

She shrugged. "*I* remember his brother."

Tad smiled. "Good," he said softly. "I, uh, like that it seems to be slow."

"We're texting," she said mildly, stroking the cats on either side of her. "He's got a gentle soul. Like Guthrie, sort of, but without that… that wandering star in his heart, I guess. You're stronger, big brother. You can handle the wandering star. I just want the gentle soul."

Tad's eyes burned some more. "Well, right now, we've got each other. And the cats." He stared at his phone again and saw that another text had popped up—this one, a sound file.

He hit Play and then turned the phone up so April could hear it. The opening chords of "Iris" filled the room, and Tad gave it up, leaned his head back against the couch and let the melancholy of the song fill him.

"And Guthrie's fuckin' music," April said when the final chords—played acoustically they practically tinkled to a delicate close—faded. Underneath them, Guthrie said something, and Tad fiddled with the phone to hear the last words again. Holding it up to his ear, he hit Play and heard Guthrie saying, "Love you. Don't forget it."

He sent back, "*I won't*," but whatever magic had carried the first text had died because the text didn't get delivered.

He closed his eyes and sighed. "It'll be enough," he said hopefully. "Until he gets back."

"Yeah." But she sounded resigned to the wait and not hopeful it would be over soon. He reflected sourly that sometimes April was very wise before he hit Play again. For tonight that was his song, and he wanted to hear it a few more times.

"HE'S WHERE?" Chris asked a week later, after taking a pull on his oat-milk decaf and sighing. "The oat milk is good—sort of sweet, and the dash of vanilla is nice—but decaf coffee is Satan's piss in a travel mug, and there is no way to put lipstick on that pig."

"I'll post that in *Java Review*, a totally made-up website I'm suggesting you create so we can stop dissecting your poor life choices in the car," Tad told him, cradling his own iced caramel frappe reverently. Most of the time he made his own iced coffee and nursed it throughout the day, but today he got to go into the office and do paperwork like a real boy, and the coffee was a celebration. It was also, oddly enough, the first time he'd been in a vehicle for any length of time since Guthrie had brought him home from the hospital, save doctor's visits, and he was so happy his trusty donut pillow was doing the job of shielding his ass from the bumps of the road that he wanted to cry.

"You're avoiding the question," Chris said. "Don't we have a wedding to go to in two weeks? Isn't he *playing* at that wedding?"

Tad grunted. "He'll make it," he said. "That was part of his negotiation. We haven't hashed out any plans for how we're going to do it, but his cell service is spotty as fuck. I checked with Olivia, though, and she said he's been emailing her for specifics and he's on point. All he needs is his suit from my closet."

"Why Olivia?" Chris asked, surprised.

"Apparently, they bonded the night I was in the canyon." Tad shrugged. "He attracts girls. It's his thing."

Chris sent him a puzzled glance. "Is it a gay thing or a Guthrie thing—I'm just curious. You seem to attract neither more nor less females than the average unavailable guy."

"It's definitely a Guthrie thing," Tad said, shaking his head in disgust. "Witness my own damned sister, who would rather trade me in for Guthrie as a big brother on any day of the week. Ask her. She won't even deny it."

Chris gave a cracked laugh. "That's cute. You're adorable. But you're dodging the question. What's going on with this otherwise perfect guy you pretty much moved into your apartment? Where is he?"

Tad let out a breath, suddenly done with this game too. "His father is dying," he said finally, his voice raw. "His uncle asked him to go back to his tiny hometown that he hates like poison and walk his father, whom he hates *worse* than poison, into the grave. Guthrie said yes because Guthrie doesn't let people down. He told me he'd make it to Colton. According to April, he told his uncle he'd make it if he had to leave Satan vomiting blood behind him, which is a...." He flailed.

"A particularly Guthrie way of stating things," Chris said, nodding appreciatively. "But it also doesn't say much for the *ease* with which he will leave."

"Yeah," Tad muttered in frustration. "That. That's... on my mind."

"You been texting him?" Chris asked, apparently forgetting for a minute that texting was not a thing.

"Trying," Tad said. He smiled a little. "He sends me audio files with songs on them. It's nice. I think he's found a... you know, place where the signal doesn't suck. I get pictures of the sunset or the wildlife from there. There's a stream nearby. Pretty spot, really." He didn't want to talk about the other things he'd noticed in the picture: Guthrie's obvious bed in the back of the truck, or the remnants of dinner he'd seen in a couple of pictures. Apple cores, orange peels, and McDonald's wrappers had been neatly gathered in the corner of the back of the truck, ready to toss away. Most disturbing of all, a baby monitor with a red light on to indicate it was being used had been stashed near the pillow. Guthrie was apparently on for nursing activity even if he was sleeping in his truck.

It was all Tad could do not to go pull him out by the ear.

Chris grunted. "Kid, do you think I'm stupid? I mean, we've worked together for nearly a year and a half now. I like to think you don't think I'm stupid."

"No, I don't think you're stupid," Tad told him, stung. In fact, Chris was possibly the best work wife a boy could have!

"Then why are you trying to gaslight me on how well your boy is doing?"

Oh. Tad swallowed. "'Cause Guthrie's pride is catching?" he said hesitantly. "I uhm… I don't want you to think badly of him, you know? So far, you've seen him—"

"Beating the system like a champion to try to find you in the middle of the wilderness," Chris reminded him.

"Well, yeah, but also—"

"Beat the fuck up after a mugging and telling my wife she should go home so he didn't inconvenience her too much. He'd be fine."

"I wasn't there for that," Tad said with dignity.

"And then there was a conversation we had at IHOP that he probably didn't tell you about," Chris told him. "When he told me that all he wanted was for you to love him."

Tad had to set his coffee down because his hands were suddenly shaking. "I'm sorry?"

"Yup. There I was, being all, 'How serious are you about my boy?' when he blurts out that all he wants is for you to love him. And suddenly I'm like, 'Oh no. Oh *no*! Tad, brother, you'd better not fuck this kid up!'"

"I would *not*!" Tad protested.

"I know that," Chris said. "But imagine how vulnerable he must seem to make me switch loyalties like that. And people are vulnerable when they're hurt. And according to you, your boy just went back to the gauntlet that hurt him in the first place. So I'm going to ask you again, this time knowing that I only have yours and Guthrie's best interests at heart, how do you think he's doing?"

Tad tried not to whimper. "I think he's sleeping in his truck with a baby monitor so he can make sure his dad's okay while the fucker still won't let him sleep in the house."

"Augh!" Chris was taking deep breaths, like he was trying to control himself.

"Too much honesty?" Tad asked, dripping with bitterness.

"Why is that kid allowed out on his own?" Chris asked, sounding cranky. "I don't care *how* old he is—he needs somebody making sure he eats and sleeps and does all the things. *Why haven't you dragged him back yet?*"

Tad grunted. "Because he said he had to do this so he could be as good a man as I am." Spears to the heart had nothing on Guthrie when he was paying a compliment.

Chris made a sound like somebody who'd walked into a post. "What an asshole," he muttered.

"I'm saying." Tad let out a breath. "So, talk to me. We're going in to do paperwork. I've been catching up on a lot of it at home. Any chance we'll catch a case? Or even be pulled in on the assist? I get I'm all computer work right now, limited desk duty, but I would *love* to play cop again."

Chris sighed. "I don't know. Me and Dunderhead have been running down a ring of thieves by tracing pawned merchandise, but Kryzynski and Christie have a murder that might lead directly to this same ring of assholes. Dunderhead"—which was Chris's charming name for Jim Draper, his interim partner, whom he detested—"doesn't want to work with them because it would mean he has to work, but I think offering you up to help them run down leads from the desk might help get *me* on that case. I'm just saying. I'm as excited about going back in the game as you probably are."

Tad gave a sigh of relief, glad to know he wouldn't be stuck on paperwork forever. "You know, there's no guarantee Colton will be much better," he said, because he was trying not to build the new job up in his head.

"It'll be different," Castro admitted, piloting the SUV to the police station on Richards. "I mean, there will be just as much boring time in the car, but the scenery will be better. We'll be dealing with the same ratio of shitheads, but we'll get to know the people better. Same problems will be there—domestic abuse, drugs, theft, murder—but we'll have a better chance of dealing with it because there's fewer people. And George, he's trying to set up things like rehab facilities and an abuse shelter, so instead of writing a referral to a social worker, we can *take* somebody to the abuse shelter and then track down the abuser and put him in jail and make sure the restraining order gets filed and he's prosecuted. I mean, people will still be dirtbags, but we'll have a bigger sponge per square mile to clean them up a little."

Tad grunted. "Wow—you've been thinking about this."

"I called George again last week. I was wondering if I'd built the job up too much in my head, so I asked him, you know. 'Hey, what's that like?' And he'd spent time down in Sac before he moved his kids up to the small town. He knows what *we* do versus what *he* does, and he was able to explain it really well."

Tad allowed himself to relax a little, even though he was still worried about Guthrie. Chris was putting some of his worries about uprooting his small family to rest. It wasn't that he hadn't enjoyed growing up in a small town, but he'd worried that what was good for April—and, he suspected, for Guthrie—wouldn't be the most exciting career trajectory for *him*. But knowing his new boss was somebody who had done city police work as well as small town law enforcement, and found the small town satisfying too, that soothed some worries he hadn't wanted to admit to.

"It's good to hear," Tad said. "I-I want the move for April, really. She puts a good face on it, but she's not comfortable living in the apartment complex, so close to so many people. And Guthrie...." He worried his lower lip. "I'm not sure what Guthrie wants. He seems to think of any place he settles down into as a hub, and he's a satellite, going off to gigs. I get that on the one hand, but on the other...."

"You want him to be home," Chris said softly.

"I want him to be *appreciated*," Tad said, with considerably more passion. "He's good, Chris. I know you haven't heard him play, but... but the songs he writes are *really* good, and his voice is just.... Do you remember the first time you heard Neil Young play 'The Damage Done'?"

Chris made a quiet sound of discomfort. "I cried," he whispered. "I... I was in my twenties, and someone at my college had just OD'd. I didn't even know the guy, but that song... the way it made everything human, even someone dying of drug abuse. It was a gut punch."

Tad nodded. That song had gotten him through that terrible, terrible time with April—he *refused* to let her promise, her person, be destroyed like the friend in the song.

"Guthrie's voice, his guitar playing, even his songs, they *do* that. Not just to me. I've seen the look in the eyes of the people he plays with. None of them play rock or pop or even country—they're *theater* musicians—but I swear they put their life on hold to play with Guthrie. I just… people should come to see *him*. He shouldn't have to uproot his life to get a chance to play out in the world."

Chris opened his mouth to say something, but while Tad had been talking he'd pulled up Guthrie's audio files—this one, "Iris." Turning his phone up to top volume, he turned off the radio and hit Play as Chris found a parking spot near the front of the building. Chris let the car idle as the first notes filled the air.

They listened to the song, and Tad closed his eyes and let the longing of unrequited love wash over him before the song ended and he reset his phone.

"Well," Chris muttered, "fuck you for that, because now I'm all verklempt, and I'm supposed to be a *man*, dammit, but you didn't have to screw us both up emotionally right before shift, you know."

"What do you mean?"

Chris shook his head. "I *have* heard him play, kid. I was there that night, eating the food that Aaron George's kids had rounded up and Guthrie helped distribute. I was looking at that miracle thing they built in the moonlight before it hauled you guys up in the morning, and saying all the prayers to all the saints, and he started to sing. You don't have to tell me he can make someone's heart stop and then drive them to hope all at the same time. I've *heard* it. And you're right. He deserves to have people come see *him*. But you know what he deserves more than that?"

Tad grimaced. "I know this one," he said.

"I know you do, but I want to hear you say it."

"A home," Tad said.

Chris tapped his nose. "Got it in one. Now let's go inside before the pavement starts melting our shoes. God, getting off the city streets at the end of July is enough of a reason to move."

AS BORING as desk duty was, it was still considerably more interesting than Tad's apartment at this point, and the day passed fairly quickly. Tad remembered to text April near lunchtime, asking for "proof of life" photos of the kittens, and she obliged. He asked her if she wanted to take his SUV to go anywhere, and she replied, *Going to the pool. Taking phone. Don't worry so much.*

She sent him a selfie of her out in the sun, and then another one an hour later of the TV at the end of her toes as she worked on her newest yarn project.

You're bored, he typed. *When we get to Colton, you need to get a job.*

Your sheriff guy has one for me. I want to do that. And then, to his surprise, she *emailed* him a file of ideas she'd put together for Aaron's proposed rehab center. Good shit. Things like fiber craft and woodcraft and mechanical skills to be taught to the recovering patients, as well as basic housekeeping and cooking skills, in which the patient contributed to their own upkeep and their own environment.

This is great, he texted. *I'll send it to Aaron. He'll be happy you're on board.*

There was a pause then, and she typed, *But not too many hours to start with. Is that okay, Tadpole? I feel like I won't be good if I'm ON too much. I don't want to disappoint him.*

Aw, man. His sister. He realized that the past five weeks, if nothing else, had given him a chance to see his sister come back to herself. Quieter. Not quite as confident. But still wry and funny. Still smart. But now more balanced—and more of an advocate for her own self-care.

You take care of yourself, and then you can take care of your job and other people. I think he'll be fine. I know *I* am more proud of you than I can say.

Blargh. So drippy. Go away and solve crime.

He sent her a bunch of heart emojis to make her laugh and left her alone. Before he went back to running financials on the target of Castro's investigation, though, he sent her file of suggestions—and suggestions for implementation on a budget—to Aaron George. Before the end of the day, he got a reply, along with some options for contacts, asking April if she'd like to start talking to people before she even moved to Colton. And a budget. And pictures of the facility he'd already scheduled the county to lease, starting in September.

Tad smiled and passed it on and felt the hope for his sister bubbling up so strongly in his stomach he almost couldn't breathe. Guthrie had been right; they *had* to move to Colton. This was a thing Tad could do to help his sister, to help their small family, to do good in the world.

Tad wished so badly for Guthrie to be coming with them he wanted to cry.

THE WEEK progressed, and Tad got back into the swing of things as best he could. He made sure to use the gym facilities at the station—working out, walking, rebuilding his wind and his speed and the muscle loss that came with an injury so he was tired when he got back home to the apartment, with less energy to worry. For her part, April seemed content. She'd begun emailing back and forth with the people in Colton, and from what Tad could see, she was already a vital part of their new approach to dealing with the substance-abuse problems in their small area. She continued her yarncraft, and she still liked to binge murder TV, but she also seemed to be particularly motivated to start their move.

And she was *really* excited about Larx and Aaron's wedding, which was approaching at the speed of light.

Tad was trying not to worry too much. Guthrie had been texting in the evening, like always, and he'd nailed down some dates and times, planning to come to Sacramento on the morning of August fifth so they could travel together to the small hotel in Colton and stay—in two rooms, Tad had insisted, one for April, one for them—until the morning of the seventh, when they'd return Guthrie to his truck and he'd travel back to Sand Cut to finish his grim duty.

At least Tad assumed it was grim. He had to assume because Guthrie told him nothing about it. His texts featured the little corner of the yard where his truck was parked, tapes of him practicing, and even two new songs he'd written. For all Tad knew, he spent his days raiding small towns along the coastline, pillaging and burning like a Viking, and then returned to his truck to eat kittens for dinner. Unlikely—Guthrie *adored* Lenny/Lennon/Leonard Bruce—but still. Tad wouldn't know if he was doing that because Guthrie wasn't talking, *was he*?

Tad's worry was about off the charts when, the morning of the fourth, at about 6:00 a.m., right before he'd planned to wake up, his phone buzzed in the charger. The ringtone was Guthrie's "I Will Wait for You," and Tad's stomach clenched as he answered because this couldn't be good.

He picked the phone up to hear an unfamiliar voice saying, "Detective Tad Hawkins of the Sacramento PD?"

"Yes, who is this?"

"This is Deputy Kenny Wilson from the Sand Cut branch of the Monterey County Sheriff's Department, and—"

"Oh God." Tad sat up so suddenly he pulled his thigh muscle and had to work not to yelp like an injured hound. "Is Guthrie okay? Was there an accident? Did he get mugged?"

"He's fine." There was a pause. "Mostly. There was a bar fight, and he would have held his own, but there were four of them. I had to stop it, so I put him in the local lockup for his own protection. This isn't an out-and-proud kind of place, Detective Hawkins. There's only so much I can do to keep your boy safe. I think maybe it's best you get him out of town for a few days until the dust settles. What say you?"

Tad blinked hard several times in a row and tried not to snarl at Guthrie through this nice small-town deputy who, it seemed, was really doing his best.

"I can be there in four hours," he said, glancing at the clock.

"Hmm... better make it five. We don't want you to get a ticket on the way. Don't worry, he's sleeping it off right now. By the time you get here, he'll have had his coffee, maybe some breakfast, and he won't be quite so cranky. Look forward to meeting you in person, Detective Hawkins. Gotta say, you're a step up from who I used to have to call."

With that, Deputy Wilson signed off, and Tad was left to frantically dial Chris's number to tell him he wouldn't be coming in that day.

"What're you going to be doing?" Chris asked suspiciously. "I might want in on that too."

"I'm driving to Sand Cut to bail my boyfriend out of jail," Tad replied sourly, not even able to *believe* this.

"Oh, I'm definitely in," Chris said happily. "I'll pack a bag, make some hotel reservations—two rooms. We can stay down by the sea. Laura and Robin are making a college visit this weekend and picking out dorm stuff and bonding and shit. Whooppeee! Two vacations in one month! I'm in!"

And with that, Chris ended the call, and Tad was left to bury his face in his hands.

How in the hell had this happened?

Seven Nation Army

IT STARTED pretty much the minute he walked into the father's house. They hadn't even gotten inside before a fortyish, exhausted blond woman ran out, wiping her face with the back of her hand. She waved at Jock to stay away and didn't give Guthrie a second look, just jumped into the red Toyota under the trees and roared away, leaving Jock swearing and Guthrie unhopeful about the state of Jock's love life.

Before the car was even off the property, Guthrie could hear his father. For a man dying of lung cancer, among other things, his voice still carried.

"Goddammit, Jock, I told you I don't want that little faggot in my house!"

Guthrie paused on the cracked walkway and gave his uncle a flat-eyed scowl. "Really?" he said.

Jock swallowed hard. "Let me talk to him," he said. "I told him I couldn't do this by myself. He's just making noise."

"I'll be here," Guthrie told him, standing on the stoop with his arms crossed. Jock opened the screen door, outlined in peeling white paint, and the miasma from inside rolled into the decayed yard.

Cigarette smoke—a lot of it still fresh—ammonia, and, oh God, shit and piss blew out in a choking cloud, mixed with a sort of rotting overtone, a death smell that Guthrie had only caught in whiffs and clouds in the depths of hospitals when someone wasn't going to make it.

He'd never thought of himself as particularly weak-stomached, but he had to fight against nausea as he stood there and listened to his uncle beg and plead for Butch to let his son in the door to help him die.

Finally, Jock surprised Guthrie by shouting, "Look, you old fucker, me and the kid are gonna work in the yard while you sit in here and stew in your own shit. Yeah, I can smell it. How long's it been since you crapped yourself? An hour? Well Jolene's gotta go to work, and I'm not going to change it without his help, so you either learn how to be a human fucking being or this is how you're gonna fuckin' die."

And with that Jock stomped out, slammed the door behind him, and took a deep breath of free air when he'd cleared the threshold.

"So," Guthrie said, not sure how to feel about this. "It's gonna be a short trip."

"Looks like," Jock said grimly. "But I sure would appreciate the help around the house while he rots in his own filth and dies."

Guthrie raised his eyebrows. "You think that's gonna happen?"

Jock shook his head, gesturing for Guthrie to follow him to the carport, which was one of the most modernized things on the three-acre lot. Jock was a decent handyman—the thing appeared sturdy, although the wood was still raw and needed staining and painting, and there were obviously parts that Jock intended to add on to.

"I'm working on the plumbing," Jock said frankly, indicating a couple of shovels and a pile of pipes in the corner. "I need to get that done in the next two hours or he really *will* die in his own filth. I don't need no help with it, but God, Guthrie, anything else you see that you want to do. I've got supplies for about everything—painting the carport, painting the house, painting the gutters. I've got trash pickup scheduled in two weeks, and I'd love some help hauling shit to that one spot in the front of the house. It's gonna cost me a couple of hundred dollars, and I want *everything* out there. I've got hip waders and long gloves for that, so maybe we could do that work in the morning. I figure…." He swallowed and looked sheepish. "I'm sorry. I asked you out here, and now I'm ordering you about like I'm no better than your daddy—"

Guthrie shook his head. "There's a difference between outlining a job, Jock, and ordering someone around. Tell me what you figured."

Jock gave him a brief, sad smile. "God, I missed you, kid." He swallowed again, like he didn't want to have that discussion now, and said, "See, what I thought was that we'd get up in the morning, I'd come out and work, you'd take care of your daddy's needs for an hour or so, and then you could come join me. We'd put a baby monitor in there and carry it around—I already bought one cheap—so if he needs anything he can call out. We work till noon or so, you go make lunch and help him, and then maybe spend a couple hours with me out here. Then nights, I got him, and you get some time off."

Guthrie thought that through. "But when's *your* time off?"

Jock snorted. "When I'm out here fixing the place up!" He shook his head. "God, it's all I wanted to do those years. We were touring

California, getting gigs, and all I could think of was, 'Maybe we'll make enough money to fix up the house. Make it a home.' But no. Butch just wanted more money so we could follow more gigs. But now I got some money saved from the album we cut—Butch didn't know about it and now he can't spend it—and I want...." He glanced around the neglected property and the dilapidated house. "I want it to be a home," he said, his eyes sad. "I don't got music like you and your daddy. I got a girl I like and a job waiting for me, and I want to be able to have her come over and not be embarrassed." He gave a weak smile. "I'll miss your daddy, Guthrie, but sort of like you, I guess, I'm ready to set all his meanness free from my heart, you know?"

Guthrie nodded. "Amen to that," he said. "I'll start with sandblasting the old paint off the house before I paint it and the carport. How's that? Do we have an air compressor?"

Jock's lower lip wobbled a little as he nodded and pointed to the equipment in the corner of the carport. "Thank you," he whispered. "God, Guthrie. Thank you."

Guthrie let out a sigh—and let out some of the anger he'd harbored toward Jock. "I missed you too."

The hopeful smile on Jock's face was both pitiful and beautiful, and Guthrie returned it. Together they started for the carport, ignoring Butch's vitriol as he shouted for Jock's attention from inside the house.

Jock pulled out his phone and set it for an hour. "I'll go back in and see if he's changed his tune," he said. "Jolene texted and said he hasn't been stewing that long. He may be sick, but your daddy's got his pride like any man."

"I wouldn't know anything about pride," Guthrie lied, and apparently Jock knew it too, because he rolled his eyes and together they went to work.

That first day it took Butch two hours to agree to let Guthrie tend to him, with Jock's help.

"You like looking at that?" Butch taunted as Guthrie wiped him down and rubbed ointment on his reddened skin. "Bet you love looking at your daddy's ass, you worthless fucking faggot."

Guthrie snorted. "Nobody loves looking at *your* ass, old man. Except the women you had to pay who were thrilled to see the back of you."

There was a shocked gasp. "Now that was just *mean!*" Butch said in surprise. "When'd you get so mean?"

"You kicked me out, fucknugget." Ooh, this was fun. "You got no pull on whether I'm mean or whether I'm nice or whether I think you're a father or a saggy pile of shit. I'm just here to help Jock." Guthrie talked a good game, and it was awesome being able to tell the old man exactly what he thought of him without fear of a crack across the face. But inside he was heartsick. His father's body—once a barrel-chested example of a middle-aged man who existed on beer and red meat—had wasted to baggy yellow skin on brittle bones. His stubbled face was so lined and loose that Guthrie figured a good shave would rip it off. And the whiskey voice he'd once used to belt across honky-tonks and charm women who were way too good for him was now a sour cigarette rasp.

It was one thing to hate your father, but it was another thing entirely to see him dying. To hear him curse you with almost his last breath? Well, that hurt.

Guthrie would fight back as best he could, but as he set about changing his first adult diaper, he had to wonder how much of his soul would be left when he got back to Tad.

THAT FIRST day set the tone. Jock may have been a half-assed bass player, but he actually had a good head on his shoulders when Butch wasn't ripping it off. His original schedule, with Guthrie supervising Butch's care between bouts of escaping into helping Jock with the house, gave Guthrie an outlet to release some of his frustration over dealing with his father.

And there was a great deal of that.

Guthrie hadn't realized his father kept a scorecard of grievances from Guthrie's childhood, but boy did he pull that out when so inclined.

For instance: "Remember that Christmas you threw a tantrum about being at a bar on Christmas Eve? The owner got so pissed he didn't pay us for the gig. No presents for you, you little shit, and you bitched about that too."

"No, old man, I don't remember it. Jock told me about it, though. I was four. Merry Christmas, you drunken bastard."

That one was fun. And Guthrie finally figured out where he got his cavalier regard for Christmas. Suddenly, *achingly*, he wondered if Tad did the holiday up right, with a tree and tinsel and Christmas songs and everything. He resolved to ask him… in person. Not on text, though, because dammit, that little stretch of property was like the goddamned nineteenth century.

But then there was: "Yeah, it's not like you didn't need some fucking medical care. You broke your arm when you were twelve, you fucking faggot. Remember that? Jock and I didn't have beer money for *months*."

"That's a lie, and we all know it," Guthrie told him. "You never paid that hospital bill, and Jock cut the cast off with a fucking Sawzall. I'm lucky to still be alive." He was also lucky the broken arm was all he'd gotten; what Butch hadn't mentioned was that he'd broken his arm running away from *Butch* and getting hit by a car. If the accident hadn't happened out of town, with an out-of-town hospital and law enforcement, Guthrie probably would have died because he'd had a concussion then, too, and he'd gotten to spend a week in the hospital recovering. Of course Butch had lucked out because Guthrie's bruises had been blamed on the car. The reason Jock had cut the cast off was that that'd been the first time Guthrie had fought back. Butch had cracked him across the face, and Guthrie had given him a black eye with the cast. Butch had been angry enough to kill him, and Jock had gotten Guthrie out of his sights. The good news was, after that, Guthrie had stopped taking the physical abuse. The rest of that shit was just par for the course.

Or maybe not.

"I can't fucking believe you let Fiddler go. If you were going to be a cocksucker, the least you could have done was sucked *his* cock and made him stay! That kid was our ticket to something *good*, and you let him walk off the stage and out of our lives!"

And that was enough. Absolutely enough.

"Seth Arnold was better than any of us deserved. None of us—not me, not Jock, not you—*none* of us deserved to have that boy in our lives. And he was in love with someone else. They're married now, Dad, and they're parents. *Good* parents, who are kind and gentle. Hell, they even *feed* their kids, and they're men enough to keep them clothed and to *provide* for them. And they don't hit, and they don't abuse, and they don't yell. So fucking *live with that*, motherfucker. Those people you hate so much, they're *better than you*, and they always will be."

Butch sucked in a breath at that—Guthrie was giving him a shower, forcing the old man to wash his own privates, shampooing his hair, the whole nine yards. For the most part, Butch huddled on the shower chair and spewed invective, but at Guthrie's words he sat up straight and spat, right in Guthrie's face.

Guthrie was wet from the waist up anyway—and wearing an old pair of Jock's gym shorts and flip-flips because he'd done this before and he knew the job could be messy. He turned the spray on himself, on his face, spitting and rinsing several times before wiping the water out of his eyes. Then he turned to glare at his father, who was cackling like a demented witch. Deliberately, making sure Butch could see him, he turned the hot water off, leaving what was coming out of the showerhead ice-fucking-cold.

Then he turned it on his father and, ignoring his shouts, bathed the old man's pits and privates, ignoring the discomfort of the cold water, ignoring his father's screams and curses. When he was sure the job was done, he stood and sprayed Butch in the face, turning the shower sideways for a moment to say, "You gonna behave, asshole?"

He had to repeat the action three times before Butch nodded his head, his furious expression made less threatening by his shivers. Guthrie turned the water off and gathered the towels, helped the old man dry off in icy silence. Guthrie got him back to bed, worn out, and set him up with the television while Guthrie made lunch. He brought back a warm mug of soup so Butch could maybe heat up his core temp a little, but before he handed it over, he turned off the television, making sure he had the old bastard's attention.

"Butch, I got you? You hearing me?"

His father nodded, scowling.

"Good. That's great. Now look. Jock asked me to come help him out, because frankly, you were killing him. I agreed, 'cause Jock was a bright spot in my life when I was a kid and I felt like he deserved that much. But frankly? You don't. You deserve to die in a ditch, far away from civilization, mewling like an animal where no man can hear you to help."

Butch stared at him, shocked. "You don't got no killer in you, boy."

Guthrie shrugged. He wouldn't lie—not to this man. "Nope. No, I don't. But you know what I do have? I have access to the medical system. *You* put Jock in this position. *You* told him you wanted to die at home. *You've* been such a pain in the ass we can't get a nurse to stay longer than a week. Jock hasn't had a chance to live alone, but I have. I moved out when I was eighteen, remember? Stayed with the band until Fiddler left, but I know what it's like to live in my own goddamned place, even if my own goddamned place is my own goddamned truck." When he'd turned eighteen, he'd started to talk privately to the bar owners, making sure he got his fair share. Turned out if he wasn't drinking his fair share away, it was enough to get him a used truck and an apartment.

"So? You gonna brag about living in your truck now?" Butch groused, but it was clear he knew where this was going.

"I'm living with a *family* now," Guthrie told him. "One you can't fucking touch, not with your meanness, not with your vitriol. *I* can get away. But I'm not leaving Jock with you here alone. Before I go, I will take you to the hospital and sign all the fucking papers, and I will surrender your care to the state, old man. I'll do it freely and gladly, and Jock won't have to feel one drop of guilt. You wanted to die here—I guess so you could feel the wind on your face from the window, see the sky, smell something besides your own piss. I get that. That's great. You want that to happen? You will be a goddamned human fucking *being* to me and to Jock, or the last thing you will see will be white walls, and the last thing you will hear is the beep beep beep of your heart failing, and you will never see sky again, and you damned sure won't hear any music. I'll make a point of it. You know how Jock plays the radio for you at night on that country western station? I'll tell them it makes you crazy. No music for you in your last days. No television. No remote control. Not another human who cares whether you live or die, just some underpaid orderlies hoping you won't clock out on their shift. This is it, Butch. This is your last stand. You've got the power to make your last days decent or a sterile hell, and it all comes down to this: Can you or can you not be a human fucking being?"

Butch glared at him, absolute hatred burning from his eyes. "I shoulda given you to the state," he said after deep consideration.

But coming from Butch, that was mild.

"Too late now. What's it gonna be? And you might want to make up your mind 'cause your broth is getting cold."

Butch shivered, and Guthrie noted that his lips were still a little blue. "Fine. We don't need to say too much to each other. Too late now to wish your mama woulda flushed you."

Guthrie had heard that before. "Same could be said of you. Here's your soup. I'm going outside to do anything but this. You need something, holler." And with that, he gave Butch the remote control on the television and set up the baby monitor and strode out.

When he got to the front yard—mown now, thanks to Jock's tireless efforts, and covered with a fine layer of paint dust, thanks to his own—he leaned forward and rested his hands on his thighs and breathed. Just breathed. In and out, shuddering the last of the rage and the hurt and the violence into the quiet around him.

Jock rounded the corner, hauling half a stove on a wheelbarrow, and stopped, seeing him there.

The panic on Jock's face was enough to tell Guthrie Jock's worst fear.

"You're not leaving me here, are you?" he asked, voice shaking with tears.

"No," Guthrie said. "But Jock, you gotta hear me out."

With that he stood and outlined the things he'd threatened Butch with, and while his big fear had been that Jock wouldn't back him up, he'd been gratified to see Jock's posture straighten, a little at a time.

"So we can do that?" Jock asked. "We can give him to the hospital?"

"Jock, we are barely legal with his care regimen as it is. If he fights us like a toddler every day, we can't meet it. If he wants to die on his own terms, he's going to have to stop being a fucker, and that's all there is to it."

Jock nodded, and to Guthrie's absolute shock, turned his head and wiped his cheek on his shoulder. "I-I didn't think I could do anything," he confessed brokenly. "I felt so *trapped*...." And his voice broke. He shook his head and held out his hands when Guthrie would have said something. "Hey," he said after a minute. "Could you... could you maybe come sit with me on the porch after he goes down to sleep? I know you been sitting in your truck, using the good internet, but... but I don't got no one to email. Could you, you know, like when you was a kid. Could you—for a little while—pretend to be my friend?"

Guthrie's eyes burned. "I wouldn't be pretending," he said heavily. "Sure. You come get me after he's asleep. We'll sit on the porch and talk as the sun goes down, how's that?"

"Thanks," Jock said, and Guthrie knew he was crying, but he kept hauling that damned stove to the trash pickup spot like nothing was happening.

Guthrie let him. He was about done with feelings for the moment. With a sigh and a conscious straightening of his back, he went to the carport for some paint. He'd finished prepping the outside of the house the day before. It was time to swap out the attachments on the air compressor and put some lipstick on this tiny two-bedroom, one-bathroom pig.

NONE OF this went into his email or text to Tad that night. April didn't hear a word of it. Olivia only got plans for her father's wedding and internet jokes. Kelly's sisters got kitten videos. Martin, from the auto dealership, shared a YouTube video of Eddie Vedder in concert that made Guthrie super happy, and he shared his favorite of Eminem.

And then he picked up his guitar and tooled around, fixing the last song he'd written, setting it in music notation on the laptop he kept charged in the kitchen, along with his phone.

At around eight o'clock, just as the last light of the sun was fading from the sky, he heard Jock's quiet "Guthrie? You want to come sit? I got us some cookies from the store when I went for groceries. That okay?"

Guthrie swallowed, throat thick. "Yeah, Jock. That's real good. I appreciate it. I'll be right there." He tucked his laptop away but grabbed his phone, in case Tad texted him back like he tended to do.

That night, he and Jock sat and talked. Jock caught him up on the gigs he and Butch had been playing before Butch got sick, and Jolene, the woman Jock dated on and off but whom he'd like to see more. And Jock listened, heard about Seth and Kelly's wedding, and while his language might have been pretty much the worst, Guthrie heard honest joy for Seth, their "Fiddler," and that put paid to a lot of resentment Guthrie had felt toward him about how shit had fallen out after Seth had left their band.

After a little bit of low-key begging, Jock promised to work on cleaning up his language, as long as Guthrie promised to come out and sit with him again the next night.

Guthrie could promise that.

His loneliness for Tad and April and their little home with their cats was like a black hole opening up under his sternum. It was starting to suck the color out of the sky and the scent of the ocean out of the wind and the sweetness out of the flowers and the sawtoothed grasses in a giant cosmic whooshing storm.

Jock's human companionship didn't fill it, but it did dull the roaring of its wind in his ears.

SO JOCK was a bright spot in an otherwise dismal time. The lack of cell coverage was no joke. Guthrie retreated to his truck every evening for an hour or two to use the internet—because he got signal there—contact his people, and decompress. After Jock finished with Butch at night, they'd retire to the porch to talk, to play; Jock still loved to play, even though he'd never be beyond a garage guitarist, and since those classically trained musicians like Roberta and Neal and Owen and Seth had taken pity on Guthrie's own flaws and foibles, Guthrie paid that forward by giving Jock some time to fill his soul.

At night, after Jock took his one last beer to bed, Guthrie returned to his truck. He kept the guitar locked in the moisture-proof case and the computer behind the seat in the cab. His phone was fully charged after some time in the kitchen, and it was Guthrie under the stars, tucked in his sleeping bag with the blankets April had sent.

One of the blankets was fleece, and very much appreciated in the damp, foggy nights so close to the ocean. The other blanket was crocheted, and that one Guthrie tucked into the sleeping bag as more of a talisman than anything else. It was warm—more as a couch throw than as defense against the fog—and pretty, but mostly it was home. It was Tad's sister, who loved him, and Tad himself, who also, it seemed, loved him. Guthrie read books on his phone sometimes, or texted Tad if he was awake.

Once Tad started working, Guthrie could sense him falling asleep earlier, and the thought made him smile. His boy was healing, getting stronger and more active, and Guthrie tried to imagine a life with the two of them. Yeah, there'd be some gigs, some local stuff, but this album with Seth had taken on a life of its own. Guthrie had sent Seth some of his songs, and Seth had demanded more. In return, Seth had sent back instrumentation that he and Amara and Vince had come up with to make the songs richer and more complete.

Except for the one about the ribbon of road.

What do you want to do with that one? Guthrie asked. Even he had to admit it was the best song of the bunch.

I want you to play the guitar and sing it, Seth sent back. *We may hire someone to do some quiet percussion. Vince has a lonely trumpet riff. The rest is you.*

Guthrie laughed a little. *No, seriously.* One of the hallmarks of this album had been Seth's deft hand at instrumentation, at making the classical instruments and the modern music blend into something amazing.

It's the best track on the album, Guthrie. None of us want to ruin it with too much. Trust me on this, okay?

Guthrie had stared at the text, shocked.

Guthrie?

I'm not sure what to say.

Say you'll be there the last week of August. You said you were taking care of your father, but your internet is shitty. Here's the address. Commit it to memory. The production company is fronting our hotel and food expenses. Make it if you have to crawl. It's going to be everybody's time to shine.

Guthrie had to smile at that. That was Seth. Loving music. Loving to make it with the people who loved it like he did.

Looking forward to seeing you all, he texted.

Maybe we can meet your policeman friend.

That was Seth too—not subtle. *He's moving to the mountains with his sister.*

Then Christmas. We're renting places in Monterey again. This time your plus one can be him.

And his sister?

Course. You know us. Sisters welcome.

Guthrie laughed softly to himself, and then Seth signed off and he was left alone, his only companions the indifferent stars seen through the drifting tulle of fog.

He'd gotten used to putting words and music down in the last month. Something about his time with Tad had made him more confident, broken the ice of the things he kept in his head but didn't say. The song flowed out of him like a river.

Two-dozen crappy memories of Christmas
No toys, no food, no lights
I want to see you at Christmas
But it's too far away tonight
Way off I might see happiness
Chocolate sugar mint high
Far away like the stars on a foggy night
I'll reach for you to make you mine
Last night I dreamed I saw heaven
In a cabin across a lake

All I had to do was swim the distance
To reach out my hand and take it
But I couldn't find the wind to keep going
The water was dragging me down
And my breath was getting shorter
I was going to drown
And when my head went under
When my eyes closed in despair
Your hand closed over mine
You pulled me into the air
We'll cling to each other on a lifeboat
With the cabin right there in our sights
We'll make it, I swear we will make it
If I just get to hold you tonight

Guthrie stared at the lyrics on his phone, his eyes burning, sobs trapped in his chest. This was dumb, he thought. So dumb. He was going to see Tad in a week. He'd taken his stand against his father, refused to take abuse, made his peace with Jock. He could last a week, right? And after that, there were only a few more hurdles between him and a whole new life, with everything he'd ever wanted in the package.

A whole new life. A little cabin of heaven. Tad.

He buried his face against his arm and cried.

BUT TAKING a stand against abuse wasn't the end of things. It never was.

Butch didn't spit anymore, and he didn't throw stuff or drop his cups on purpose or dump his plates, but how much of that was respect or fear, and how much of it was simply dwindling strength, Guthrie would never know.

But that didn't mean he didn't have some barbs left.

"Lookit you," Butch muttered one day as Guthrie bustled around the house, cleaning up. "You can't wait for me to die."

Guthrie took the earbud out, surprised. Butch was in his afternoon mode—he usually just stared at the television until he slept. Guthrie had seen the newish carpets that Jock had bought, waiting for the right time to install them. In fact from what Guthrie could see, Jock had been quietly hoarding all sorts of things—indoor paint, discount tile, used appliances he'd gotten that still had some life in them. Guthrie suspected that the moment Butch passed on, Jock would move in and fix the house into a decent home, the one Jock had always wanted but Butch had never been willing to settle down in.

It made Guthrie proud in a way. No, Jock had never lived out from under Butch's thumb, but he wasn't planning to get drunk and wallow or wander lost. Jock had apparently been imagining how to be his own man for quite some time and using the few life skills he had to make that happen.

But Guthrie had assumed Butch had missed all that.

"Well," he said now, to Butch's rude—if accurate—comment, "if you'd wanted us to be excited about your life, you shouldn't have been such a bastard."

Butch rolled his eyes. "You and Jock—always fucking whining about something. I was *trying* to keep us in gigs!"

"For what?" Guthrie asked. "To make music? 'Cause I assure you, Butch, you make better music when you're not falling asleep in your own puke and running away from creditors and the cops."

Butch grunted and then coughed, a deep wet one that spewed blood into the dingy handkerchief in his hand. "You act like you didn't love every fuckin' minute of it," he gloated.

Guthrie sighed, some of the fight draining out of him. "You got me there," he admitted. "When I was a kid, I thought that was livin'. Then I grew the fuck up and realized how much more there was to life than faking music."

"You mean *making* music!" Butch crowed. "Me and Jocko taught you and that faggoty fiddler a thing or two, didn't we!" Seth wouldn't have cared about the slur, and Guthrie had been protecting his sore spots, his hot and bare nerves, from Butch since he'd walked in the house. At this point, the only way to explain to the dying old pusbag how wrong he was would be to rip away the only self-delusions the old fucker used to keep breathing. Guthrie had needed to balance honor and compassion against cruelty and vengeance on the blade of a knife for the last two or three weeks, and when he'd been with Tad, he would have said he could fall on the side of icing, white feathers, and marshmallow fluff. But something had slipped in Guthrie these past weeks, the whispering conscience that would have kept him from saying the ultimate cruelty to a dying man.

"Oh get off it, old man," he snapped. "All you ever knew was a garage band's chord progression!"

"I was a music man!" Butch whined, and that meanness Guthrie had warned Tad about was suddenly the nine-hundred-pound gorilla of his nightmares.

"You were a *drunk*! And a shitty father and a liar and a thief—"

"We never got a break," Butch told him, and it sounded like a plea for Guthrie to understand, but Guthrie was beyond that. "One good break we had, you let him slip away. Couldn't even suck the right dick."

Roar! "Oh *bullshit*. You make a big deal out of Fiddler deserting us after we gave him his break. Dad, Fiddler was *our* break. We *lucked* into that kid wandering into the bar and trying out for us. He's not just good—he's a *prodigy*. Everything he touches turns to gold, and for a bare, precious moment, he gave us some of that shine. You drank yours away. Jock saved it so he could fix your shitty house when he got a chance. I put mine into my education because I knew I wasn't ever going to be no Fiddler." Guthrie's eyes burned, because Seth was still trying to give him a break, and he refused to tell his father about it. It was obscene enough that the old man tried to use his friend like a sledgehammer to take Guthrie out at the knees. "But before Fiddler came around," Guthrie continued, "you were no better than a teenager playing 'Smoke on the Water' on a shitty guitar. You couldn't hold a tune in a fucking bucket. You'd pawned your axe so often you forgot what it looked like and you were playing on a Walmart kid's special and it showed. The only reason bars were hiring you at the end was because you drank enough liquor to make up for the customers you drove off, and I know this because I played at some of those places after you'd left, and it was hard to get those people to trust me once they heard the name Woodson. Do you get me? Fiddler was always the sunshine, and you and me were always here, scrabbling in the dirt, but I ain't played in your shadow since I was seventeen, old man. You been playing in mine."

Oh, it poured out of him, and he knew it was pure meanness. He wanted to rail at things like living in the front of a truck when he was eight years old, or going without meals, or going without a bath for two weeks, until he showed up for a rare stint at school and had to put up with the kids making fun of his smell. He wanted to ask Butch why he couldn't have been a fucking parent, or why he had to be an asshole, or why he had to get pulled out of his own puddle of puke every night before they could go up on stage and earn at least a meal. But none of that would hurt his father—Guthrie knew that. So he went for the jugular, the truths that would really hurt, and he knew he'd won this round when a mewl like a rat getting its balls crushed issued from the old man's throat.

"You ungrateful little bastard!" Butch screamed, and that was the last coherent thing Guthrie could hear from him because he'd grabbed his keys and his phone and stalked out.

Jock was waiting for him by his truck with a fistful of twenties.

"The Alley Kat's still open," he said shortly. "This'll get you enough beers to cool off."

He had the baby monitor on his belt, and Guthrie could hear Butch sputtering, his voice weaker and weaker.

"I'm sorry, Jock," Guthrie mumbled, feeling a *powerful* need for a beer and a fuck or a fight or a chance to take a sledgehammer to a wall or something. He wasn't sure what he'd hoped for when he'd come down here—he'd told himself it was nothing. Told himself he was down here for Jock and no other reason, but *God* that was a lie, wasn't it? A moment—just a moment—of humanity from the man who'd raised him—it shouldn't have been a goddamned dream, should it? But Butch wasn't going to change. Was going to go to his grave without remorse for the shit he'd done to Guthrie. Hell, the shit he'd done to Jock. For all Guthrie knew, the shit he'd done to Guthrie's mother, who had taken off and left Guthrie in his care. Expecting a change of heart from Butch Woodson was like expecting to wake up one morning to be the next Elton John. It wasn't going to happen, and the only thing—the *only* thing—Guthrie could do was to wake up every morning and try to be the best *Guthrie* he could be.

He just needed a minute before he tried.

It was unfortunate that there were only two places in town to get a drink. One of them was the Cut, where the construction workers who maintained the tunnel hung out, and the other was the Alley Kat.

As Guthrie pulled his truck up to the Alley Kat—his bedding, computer, and guitar all hidden behind the seat or locked in the lockbox because he wasn't a fool—he scanned the parking lot and almost turned around to go back.

It was damned near full, and while there was no live music playing tonight, as there sometimes was, the juke box was loud, and the rednecks were hollering, and Guthrie was forced to wonder how many of the kids he'd sort of gone to school with had stayed here in Sand Cut, where there was no future and no forgiveness and no hope.

God. All he wanted was a fucking beer some place besides Butch's house. Was that really too much to ask?

The place hadn't changed that much from when Guthrie, Butch, and Jock had played it when he'd been a kid. Ralph Simpson at the bar looked the same—just skinnier, more grizzled, and yellower from nicotine. He wasn't allowed to smoke in the place, but he disappeared every half hour like clockwork to get his fix out back. The wood was still weathered and smoky, the smells coming from the kitchen were still full of grease that hadn't been changed in far too long, and the brass was still buried under a week's worth of fingerprints.

And Bud Light was still on tap.

Guthrie found himself the quietest corner he could, and without acknowledging Ralph's startled spark of recognition, pointed to the tap and held up a finger.

One to start.

He didn't want to talk.

He leaned his head against the wall for a moment and peered around the room more closely. It was almost the exact same crowd, he thought with a touch of sorrow, except the old drunks of his childhood had been replaced with the adults he'd known as children.

The head cheerleader had put on weight, had a couple of kids, and now dyed her hair *all* the way blond. The football quarterback had done the same, but he didn't have enough hair to dye. Guthrie accepted his beer from Ralph and took them in, noting that her mouth was turning down at the corners, and her husband, the football player, had lips that were flat and thin and grim.

He'd say trouble in paradise, but they'd both been cruel and shallow in high school and had probably made each other's lives cruel and shallow too. As he watched, a waitress—probably barely twenty-one herself—sashayed by the football player, and he patted her behind when his wife wasn't looking.

Classy.

Guthrie sighed and went back to his beer, trying to let the taste of something fresh from the tap wash out the words he'd hurled at Butch.

Nope. He was going to need another swallow.

He was on his second beer and starting to relax when it happened, which was a shame because he would have liked the excuse for being on his *sixth* beer and a little incapacitated. But no, it had to happen when he was on his second beer and still spoiling for a fight.

Dwight Climp strolled in, and with the sort of gaydar that could be found in a lot of repressed rednecks, his vision went straight to Guthrie, nursing his brew in the shadows and trying hard not to interact with a soul.

"Guthrie? Guthrie fucking Woodson?" Dwight called across the bar. "I thought we kicked your faggoty ass out of this town years ago!"

Maybe because it was Butch's favorite slur too, but Guthrie was reluctant to smile and sidle out. "No, sir, I left this flea-shit town all by myself."

"That didn't last long," Dwight scoffed, and Guthrie rolled his eyes.

"You're assuming I got nowhere to go when my business is through. Buddy, I am *spoiled* for choices. I got so many places I can live when I leave this shithole, I got people begging me to come drink *their* beer. Who wants you besides San Quentin?" Yeah, he'd heard that Dwight had done two years—not in the big house but in a local minimum security. It didn't matter, though. He'd scored a direct hit.

Dwight hissed and moved in closer, his eyes narrowed and rattlesnake mean. "You want to know the best thing about prison, you fucking fag?"

"The cuisine?" Guthrie asked, chuckling to himself. Yeah, he knew what was coming. God, you blew one football player in high school and the whole world knew your business. He hadn't even known Dwight's name. His attendance had been so spotty at the time, the guy hadn't even known Guthrie *went* to Sand Cut High.

"Those boys know how to take it without bawling like a baby," Dwight laughed. "I mean, I hear *you* whine like a little piss-boy, is that true?"

Guthrie smiled at him and finished off his beer, feeling the inevitable settling down on his shoulders. He'd wanted to drink, but a fight had just walked in, and who was he to look some gift therapy in the meth-rotted teeth?

"Well, I don't know," Guthrie drawled. "But only someone who liked my lips on his dick would know for sure. Is that *you*, Dwight? Did *you* like my lips on your dick? Because if you *did*, that would make you...." He glanced around the bar like he was telling a secret. "You know," he said, leaning his head in conspiratorially. "*Gay.*"

Dwight let out a howl of rage and charged Guthrie like a bull.

Guthrie took a step to his left and threw Dwight into the wall headfirst. Dwight fell on his ass, but he'd brought in three buddies who didn't like that at *all*, and as Guthrie spun lightly on his heel, he caught a blow to the jaw and the fight was on.

GUTHRIE'S HEAD ached and his arm ached and somebody was bothering him with something cold on the... *ouch*, was that a cut? On the meat of his bicep.

"I don't know you well enough to let you do that," he mumbled, but the chuckle from the man next to him sounded familiar.

"I am disappointed to hear that, Guthrie. I thought we were friends."

Guthrie squinted past the pain in his head, his body trying to process his surroundings while his brain processed that voice.

"Kenny Wilson?" he muttered. "I thought you got out?"

Kenny Wilson had been his one friend in high school. Sweet, scrawny, and bookish, Kenny had been a year below Guthrie in school. Guthrie remembered a couple of fights keeping the older kids away from Kenny as a kid, and when he *had* been in town, Kenny had been something of a shadow.

Guthrie hadn't minded. Thinking on it, Kenny reminded him a lot of April—quiet, sarcastic, kind. He'd been one of the reasons Guthrie hadn't grown up in Butch's shitkickers. When someone gazed at you like you were something, you tried not to disappoint them.

Guthrie squeezed his eyes shut and opened them again, taking in his surroundings. Tan painted bars, tan painted cement floor, hard cot with a clean, sanitized plastic cushion on it underneath him, and a surprisingly warm and cozy wool blanket surrounding him as though he'd been asked to sit up and the blanket had pooled around his hips.

He squinted at Kenny, who was sitting next to him, doctoring his arm, wearing a set of pressed khakis and a baseball hat that proclaimed him a Monterey County Deputy. Kenny had grown up handsome, Guthrie thought muzzily, with a square jaw, a long face, and thick brown hair that had once been stringy. No acne now, and no uncertainty in his plain brown eyes as he stitched up Guthrie's arm.

"I did get out," Kenny said, sounding like he was concentrating. "I got my EMT's license, and then the Monterey County Sheriff's department wanted me to come work for them, and then they found out I was a Sand Cut native and thought I should run the branch. So I'm back, but, you know. Got a badge. Got my certificate. I'm all-purpose law enforcement, and you got me for the day."

Guthrie grunted and shifted on the cot, wincing when *everything hurt*. "It's nice to see you, boy, but I really wish I wasn't in jail."

"Well, even the witnesses who hate you say Dwight picked the fight and his buddies dogpiled on."

"Why aren't *they* in jail?" Guthrie asked grumpily.

"Because *they* heard the siren and ran, sir," Kenny said, sounding almost cheerful. "You, on the other hand, were about to be used as a rag mop, so you had no such option. Here, take these."

"So I get jail?" Guthrie asked. He didn't even question the painkillers and probably antibiotics Kenny thrust into his hand with a cup of water. Jesus, was his head aching.

"Only because the hospital's a ways out," Kenny told him. "But don't worry—I got the names and locations of your assailants. They'll be arrested and taken to Salinas for *actual* jail, and you get to sit in here for your own protection. Good enough for you?"

Guthrie groaned. "Can't I just go back home?" There was only one image behind his eyes when he said that, and it wasn't Sand Cut or San Rafael or even Sacramento.

"Nope," Kenny murmured, finishing with his patch job and soaking Guthrie's arm with antibiotics. "For one thing, you've probably got a concussion, so I want to keep an eye on you until someone I trust can take care of you, and for another, your boyfriend's on his way here to get you."

Guthrie's head gave a giant throb, and he had to struggle to think. "I'm sorry, what was that last part?" he asked.

"That last part," Kenny said, taking his time to tape a gauze pad to the wound, "is that I unlocked your phone with your face while you were out in my jail, and I called one Detective Tad Hawkins of SAC PD. He said he and his work wife will be here around noon."

"Oh God," Guthrie mumbled. "How long have I been here?"

"Well, we broke up the fight around nine last night, and I had the doc come check you out and irrigate your wound—he left the stitching station here so I could stitch it if it didn't stop bleeding, and it hasn't. You may not remember him checking you out, but I was here. You were KO'd somewhere in there, it's true, but he said you were mostly sleeping." Kenny's voice dropped, and he shucked off his gloves and started cleaning up the stainless steel "stitching station" he'd been using to clean Guthrie up. "Apparently, Dwight picked on a tired guy who—according to your uncle Jock—had just had a shitty fight with his shitty father and had tried to get the hell out of Dodge so he could have a drink and cool off." Kenny's gave him a gentle, rueful pat on the thigh, like friends. "So we agreed to let you sleep it off here. Nobody to beat you up, and you got a bed and some shuteye under a roof. How's that?"

Guthrie closed his eyes and leaned his head back against the cinder block wall some more. *Oh, cinder block wall, you and me are friends.* "You called my boyfriend?" he complained.

Kenny's eyes went soft. "Yeah, Guthrie. My friend was hurt and needed backup, so I called his boyfriend. You gonna fight *me* now?"

"No," Guthrie moaned, feeling plaintive. "Nice to see you, boy," he said belatedly, but he meant it. "You, uh, gonna bring me some coffee?"

"Nope," Kenny said cheerfully. "I'm going to have you sleep for another two hours. *Then* I'm going to bring you some coffee and let you get cleaned up. Jock came by to get your truck moved in front of the station so it wouldn't get ripped off. He brought in your shaving kit and your knapsack. I guess he did some laundry 'cause all your clothes are clean. Told me to give you a day or two off, and yes, he knows you're leaving on the fifth to do a gig at a wedding, but he says you need the break. So here we are. Your pit crew. Making sure you don't drive yourself too hard. Now go to sleep, Guthrie. I'll tell you all about the wife and the new baby when you wake up."

Guthrie settled his head down and smiled a little. "New baby," he murmured. "That's good news. Proud to see you again, Kenny."

"Same here," Kenny said, and in spite of the fact that Guthrie was *in jail*, he got the feeling Kenny meant that. That was nice. Guthrie's eyelids fluttered shut, and he dreamed of Tad.

SOFTLY YOU WHISPER

"SO THIS is how we meet again," Tad said, his voice dry, although he was feeling pissed off and achy. He didn't want Guthrie to see that, though. The guy looked shitty enough as it was.

Guthrie, who was curled under a wool blanket on the metal cot that extended from the concrete wall, swung his legs over the edge, his movements jerky and uncoordinated with his recently vacated sleep.

"Kenny!" he hollered. "You promised!"

"Sorry, Guthrie," said the young deputy, hustling in from behind the greeting desk in the tiny department building. "I was filling out your paperwork, and your guy drove like the wind."

"My partner drove like the wind," Tad said grimly. "I think I left my eyebrows back in Sacramento."

Kenny chuckled. "Well, I'm sure Guthrie appreciates it."

Guthrie eyed the two of them from eyes obviously gritty with a night poorly spent. "Fuck me," he groaned, leaning his head back against the cinder block wall of the cell.

"Certainly," Tad said, "but not here."

That earned him a glare. "I am in *jail*. Do you really want to make that joke here?"

"No, Guthrie," Tad explained patiently. "That's why you need to not end up here again."

Guthrie gave him a beleaguered glance. "This was *not* my idea. Did Kenny explain that to you—that this was not my idea?"

"Yeah, yeah," Kenny murmured, handing Tad a large cup of coffee with a lid. "Hold that for a sec."

Following procedure—anybody could see it—Kenny unlocked the cell door and bustled in to help Guthrie to his feet. He did a quick physical checkup, including clucking over a bandage on Guthrie's bicep that was seeping blood, and shone a penlight in Guthrie's eyes, which made him scowl like his head hurt.

"*Minor* concussion," Kenny proclaimed. "No hard physical labor for the next few days. Lots of rest today. Have a doctor change the bandage sometime today or tomorrow." Kenny stood back and folded his arms over his chest. "Jock said he could hold down the fort with your dad for a couple of days, letting you rest before you drive up to your gig. Your guy going to help with that?"

"Yes," Tad said before Guthrie complained. "Yes, we've got a hotel in Monterey, and I can look up a doctor—"

"Got a number for a doc-in-the-box who can help you out," Kenny said, pulling a card from his pocket. "My wife's brother. He'll be good for a favor. He has to be. He still has my lawn mower, and he's an asshole."

Tad grinned. "You said you're a friend of Guthrie's from high school?" he asked, because he and the young deputy had time to chat while Kenny filled him in on the sitch. Tad had *not* liked hearing that Guthrie had been dogpiled by every known felon in the area, but he hadn't been surprised either. What *really* didn't surprise him was the affection in Kenny's voice as he'd talked about how Guthrie—a loner due to poor attendance and family situation and disposition, all rolled into one—had been kind to the other loners in school.

"Yeah, Guthrie helped me protect my little brother when I didn't think he was going to survive." Kenny assisted Guthrie into a tattered cotton hoodie with bleach stains, paint stains, and rips at the pockets and hood, and Guthrie shivered, like he hadn't gotten warm in forever. Well, the jail cell was drafty, and Tad got the feeling it got cold here at night. The Pacific Coast had a tendency toward dampness anyway.

"How's Gordie?" Guthrie asked, like he was finally focusing on things.

"Gayer than you and living in Seattle," Kenny said cheerfully. "Mom wants him to settle down and bring a nice boy home, but he keeps saying nobody'll live up to his first crush."

Guthrie's eyes bulged. "Please tell me he's talking about Mackey Sanders," he said, referring to the rock legend.

"Nope," Kenny said. "All the guys he dates have long hair and brown eyes, Guthrie. You'll have a lot to answer for when he finally finds his clone of Guthrie."

"Kenny," Guthrie said, "please stop talking."

Kenny cackled. "This way your fella'll know you're in demand." He got behind Guthrie and gave him a gentle shove toward the open door. "Now go. Your friend's got your coffee, your paperwork is done, and you've got someone willing to drive you—"

"I have to drive," Guthrie muttered, pausing suspiciously at the threshold. "He's still wounded."

"I can make it twenty miles to Monterey," Tad scoffed. "And I have to. Chris has already taken off to get us a hotel. He's looking forward to clam chowder on the beach, so we'd better not disappoint him."

Guthrie shook his head. "What is it with that man and food?"

"His wife's out of town," Tad told him. "I think he's lonely and wanted to do something exciting. We don't do poker night, so it's bail your ass out of the fire. Now get out of that cell," he added, trying not to let his voice warp. "Let's go do boy's night, and I'll try not to yell at you for looking like hell and not calling me."

"Cell service is *ass* here," Guthrie protested, but he was outside of the jail cell, finally, so Tad could breathe. "I texted you every night. Emails. Voice messages—*oomf.*"

Tad hugged him, minding his bandage and the coffee in one hand, but hard, body shaking. "Shut up," he whispered in Guthrie's ear. "We'll talk about it in the car, but right now let me hold you."

"Yeah," Guthrie whispered. "Yeah. Okay." For a moment—a sweet moment—he rested his cheek on Tad's shoulder. Tad kissed his temple and held him tighter and wondered how he'd gone the last few weeks without taking a single full breath.

GUTHRIE LOOKED his truck over anxiously when they got out to the parking lot, breathing an obvious sigh of relief when he found his guitar and his computer in their places. His phone had been crushed in the melee, but Tad had found a shop in downtown Monterey that would replace it, and Tad could put Guthrie on his plan that might render better cell service.

Which meant they had very little to talk about on the trip if they weren't going to say something real.

"Why didn't you tell me?" Tad said after Guthrie had directed him out of town.

"Tell you what?" Guthrie asked, sipping the coffee like it was the nectar of life.

"That it was this bad," Tad snapped, his hurt undeniable.

"Tad," Guthrie said, sounding like he was warming up for a fight, "I walked into the place for the first time in nearly ten years last night. I had no idea that this place was such a fucking time warp—"

"All of it," Tad retorted. "Not just the bar, but… but *all* of it. Look at you, man. Your clothes are a mess, your hair is too long—you look like you've been camping in the backyard for almost a month. What in the hell are you doing?"

Guthrie made an indeterminant sound in his throat. "It's not as bad as all that," he said, and then, when Tad would have protested, he held up a battered hand. "I swear. It's just, Jock and I are working on the house during the day, and I take nursing duty in the morning and afternoon. We've got Dad in the house with a baby monitor and all the doors and windows open so he can get fresh air. At around five o'clock, I go sit in the truck because it's got the best reception and practice and play and text you, and Jock takes care of Butch, and then we go have a beer on the porch at night. A couple of times a week, somebody comes to watch him so one of us can go shopping for supplies, usually Jock because he almost always needs something from the hardware store. This isn't… I don't know… *homelessness* you're seeing. It's like a really weird construction job is all. Same injuries, same clothes." He gave a humorless laugh. "Same need for a beer at the end of the day."

"Really?" Tad asked, not buying it. "Because Kenny had a different story."

Guthrie made that sound again. "Tad," he said after a moment, "I'm tired. My head hurts. And I am really fucking glad to see you. Can we… can we leave it at that for a bit? What I'm doing is hard, I ain't gonna lie. But it takes more energy to talk about why it's hard than I got right now. Can't we…. Just tell me about the cats. Stupid shit like we don't have time for in text. Tell me how April's doing. About the move. About the wedding. I-I been practicing some songs for Livvy's dads that'll hopefully make their day nice, but I want to hear details. Please? The absolute worst thing about the last few weeks is that I ain't got to see or hear from this whole new family I'm trying to be a part of. Could we just…." His voice cracked, and so did Tad's heart. "Can we do that?"

"Yeah," Tad said, his chest aching. "Yeah, sure. We can do that. Guthrie, you know I love you, right?"

"You came to my rescue, Galahad. I think that's safe to say."

"Good. Then you're going to have to deal with my worry. I'm sorry. You just are. But yeah. You kick back, and I'll talk while I drive this—oh my God, Guthrie, does the power steering work in this thing at all?"

"No," Guthrie said, seemingly forced to honesty. "And there's some other shit going out too. I... I got no time and no money to fix it. Not right now."

"Well, you close your eyes a minute," Tad muttered. "I gotta make a call to Chris. We've got a slight change of plans."

Guthrie fell asleep, like Tad knew he would, and he made plans to drop the truck off and have Chris pick them up. It felt like this would be Guthrie repair day—a chance to patch him up and get him all ready to go to the wedding so he'd have enough energy to come back here and beat himself to death against whatever was going on in his father's house that he didn't want to talk about.

Well, fine.

If they only had a little time to do it, Tad would make the most of it.

AFTER DROPPING the truck off—and taking Guthrie to get his arm looked at by a doctor and not a part-time EMT—they checked into a nice hotel by the beach, and Tad gave Guthrie some time to clean up while he and Chris searched for places for lunch.

"How's he doing?" Chris asked as they scrolled their phones.

"He's exhausted," Tad said honestly. "And other than that, I don't know. He says it's hard, but I haven't heard him talk about his father once."

Chris grimaced. "You... uhm... you might not. When my dad passed...." He shuddered. "I don't talk about that. And you don't talk about getting your sister into rehab."

Tad shuffled his feet, embarrassed, and Chris rolled his eyes.

"Gay men are supposed to be more evolved," Tad told him defensively.

"I'll leave you to it," Chris muttered with deep disgust. "Straight male repression is my jam."

Tad snorted. "Tell that to your much adored autonomous wife," he said. "I'm just saying—he's not okay."

"Mm...." Chris murmured. "Was he ever? I mean... musicians, buddy. It's not always sweet dreams and butterflies in their engine, you know what I mean?"

Tad scowled at him. "Can we pick lunch?"

"Yup. See? Repression—it has its uses."

"I want steak," Tad said sourly.

"Heart disease is something you and your guy can share in the future. On it."

GUTHRIE CAME out dressed in clean jeans and Tad's plaid hooded sweatshirt, which had been worn to death. His hair was clean and combed and pulled back from his face, and the shadows in his eyes had faded somewhat. Tired, yes—but worn, *fatigued*, not so much.

"What're we eating?" he asked.

"Clam chowder," Chris said promptly.

"Steak," Tad muttered.

"Clam chowder," Guthrie said. "Trust me. Nobody comes to Monterey to eat steak. How long until my truck's done, and what do I owe—" He stopped when Tad growled. "Tad—"

Tad growled again.

"We'll talk about the truck later," Guthrie conceded. "I can see it's a sore point. Anyways, I really *could* use the sustenance. Let's go."

And that was that. For the day, at least, Chris's plan of repression and Guthrie's skill at avoidance made for a pleasant time.

THEY ATE clam chowder bread bowls on Cannery Row and then—Chris's insistence—went into Ghirardelli for ice cream, which they ate on the patio overlooking the ocean.

"It's a good thing this is a weekday," Guthrie said, taking a spoonful of their shared sundae. "Otherwise the line for this place wraps around the block."

Tad glanced around, taking in the busy tourist spot and then, over his shoulder, a stunning view of a crystal blue ocean, the rocks and surf below them.

"I can see why," he said softly. "You come out here often as a kid?"

Guthrie shook his head. "Not here. This was for rich folk. But when we were short, Dad would give me the guitar and tell me to play in front of the plaza." He nodded to where a middle-aged woman with a portable electric keyboard was doing a passable Carly Simon impression. "I looked young—pocketed a lot of pity cash."

"Did it get you home?"

Guthrie snorted. "More than likely it got us to the next gig. That was like the ATM stop before the trip."

Tad sighed. "Why didn't your dad play?"

"'Cause he was an asshole and usually got kicked off. The cops only let you go for a set at a time. Jock wasn't good enough." He shrugged. "What can I say. I was their best bet."

"How old were you?" Chris asked casually, but Tad knew that voice—that was his "kid interrogation" voice.

"Well, I took up drums at fourteen," Guthrie said, pondering, "and I knew my first three garage band chords a little after that."

Tad remembered Guthrie telling him that he hadn't been allowed to play the guitar onstage, but apparently here, where he was basically panhandling, it had been okay.

Tad took a giant bite of chocolate and ice cream, suddenly needing it. "No wonder you're so good," he said, trying to keep it light. "I'd be good too if I had to play for food."

Guthrie chuckled. "Yeah, but remember, you're only a real musician if you starve voluntarily. There's a little bit of crazy in there—it's a fact."

"I'll remember that," Tad said, and next to him, Chris murmured, "We're not likely to forget."

Tad knew what he was thinking. Another puzzle piece into what made up Guthrie Woodson. Another note in a plaintive, lonely song.

After chocolate, they kicked around town for a bit, although they didn't really have time for the aquarium. They wandered down to the beach and walked along the surf, or Tad and Guthrie did. Chris made himself scarce, saying there was a store with turkish delight, and he was going to get some for his wife so she'd forgive him for taking the trip without her. It was an obvious ruse to give them some alone time, but Tad didn't mind. There weren't many people on the beach, so Tad reached for Guthrie's hand, relieved when Guthrie threaded their fingers together like he hadn't forgotten they knew how to do that.

"Stop worrying," Guthrie said softly, under the wind. "C'mon, it's not a bad day. Your worry is killing me."

"There's so much you aren't telling me," Tad said, trying to keep recrimination out of his voice. "And everything I guess is just… awful."

Guthrie shrugged. "Listen, when you're changing a dying man's diaper while he's calling you shitty names, your day isn't gonna be great. But me and Jock give each other breaks, and…." He sighed. "Getting to know

Jock again without either one of us worrying about Butch—that's been nice. He's… well, he's not bright, but he's got a good heart. Not his fault he was left in Butch's care when he was as young as I was. I could have been Jock real easy if my mama drank like I think Jock's did. And if I didn't have Jock around to make things better, I wouldn't have been me, I guess. So it's good I'm here for him as Butch dies. Butch is a sonuvabitch, and the world won't be worse when he's gone, but he's been the driving force in Jock's life, you know? Jock needs to know he's got someone. And like I said, good heart. I didn't see it so much after Butch turned his back, but it's been there."

Tad peered at Guthrie curiously. "Where *did* your mother go?" he asked.

Guthrie shrugged, seemingly not curious at all. "Probably anywhere," he said frankly. "I mean, maybe she loved me, maybe she didn't. But if she spent five years with Butch, they must have been years in hell. She ran away to save her own life, and I can't be mad."

"Oh I can," Tad said darkly.

"I asked Jock about her," Guthrie said, surprising him.

"What'd he say?"

Guthrie paused and stared far out to sea, like his mother might be there, over the horizon, calling to him. "That she was real sad after I was born. That Butch couldn't get her to stop crying, so he'd try to beat her until she did. Sounds like postpartum to me, and she had to deal with Butch and me and no help but Jock, and Jock is, like I said…."

"Not that bright," Tad filled in, getting a picture.

"Nope." Guthrie sighed and turned back to their path. "Maybe someday I'll look. But maybe not. I'm not one of those people who think the past has to be resolved. The story for me is always now, you know? And right now, my story is getting this done, seeing Butch to his grave, making sure Jock's okay, and getting to that recording session at the end of August."

Tad blinked. He'd almost forgotten about that. "That's your vision?" he asked, hurt so bad he couldn't feel it yet.

Guthrie turned to him, seemingly oblivious. "That money's gonna be my stake in our future," he said matter-of-factly. "That's gonna be my contribution to the family until I can pick up gigs. I can pay rent so you can get you and April a house. I can help with groceries—all those living things, right? Family's gotta eat, Tad. I love you too, but my weight's gonna get heavy if you've got to carry it all on your back."

Tad struggled with that for a minute, remembering his ex's practicality and how much it galled him and how much Guthrie seemed to live whichever way the wind blew.

He didn't, Tad realized. He'd always had plans. He'd always understood that life was complicated and he had to make his own luck. And Tad thought of April, who was so excited about this move—and about having a job—but still, a dreadful responsibility.

Guthrie doesn't want to be a responsibility.

And Tad wanted to cry, because that had never been the case, but to a kid who'd been busking at fifteen so the family could get to its *real* job, that would be a consideration, wouldn't it?

Tad suddenly captured Guthrie's mouth, hard and greedy, and Guthrie responded.

I need you so much more than you need me, he thought. He remembered Guthrie's song, those lyrics truer than any rational thought Tad had borne about this relationship, and there they were in words and music, for the world to see.

Please love me like I love you.

This was Guthrie proving that he did, and suddenly Tad would have done anything for him, *anything*, if Guthrie had just grabbed his hand and walked into the future without making a plan, needing a cushion, trying so damned hard to carry his own weight.

You're not heavy—you're my wings.

But he didn't have those words, not to say out loud.

So he kissed Guthrie and kissed him until Guthrie groaned and ripped himself away.

"There's kids out here," he panted, glancing around.

Tad knew there weren't, but he also knew Guthrie was trying to be the sensible one.

They'd be alone in the hotel room soon enough, Tad vowed, and there wouldn't be a damned sensible thing about them.

A NICE lunch, but Guthrie'd had a rough night and, Tad suspected, not a lot of good sleep since he'd left Sacramento. Tad and Chris dropped him off at the hotel while they ran to replace his phone and check on the truck. They returned with a grocery-store dinner and some cookies for dessert around eight in the evening, and Chris bid Tad good night with a yawn.

"This boy's had a big exciting day," he said. "What's our plan for tomorrow?"

Tad blinked hard, remembering what the mechanic had said about the Chevy, which had mostly been along the lines of April's "shoot it."

"I'm thinking we pick up the truck, drive back to Sac, and you and I pretend to work since we're driving up to Colton tomorrow night."

Chris groaned. "Killjoy. But yeah, that sounds about right. Up early for coffee and something sweet and not good for us at all."

"Speak for yourself," Tad chided. "My guy needs his vegetables."

Chris nodded. "And a keeper," he said, patting Tad's cheek. He sobered. "Listen, I know it's hard, but you gotta let him do his thing, okay? He's trying to pay his way. You gotta admit, you're both good at taking on responsibility for more than just yourself. I've got the same concerns you do, but he seems to be better at it than he first looks, you know?"

Tad scowled at him, and Chris rolled his eyes.

"Yes, you got called this morning to bail him out of jail. But you got called by a kid he used to protect in high school who took him into custody to keep him safe. Guthrie's got… I don't know. Good karma power. Yeah, he puts himself on the edge a lot, but people are loyal to him. His band, his uncle, that deputy—hell, April and Olivia Larkin-McDaniels."

Sarah the bartender, Tad thought. The kid from his old job that Guthrie texted about music. Seth Arnold, who was going out of his way to offer Guthrie a leg up. It hadn't occurred to him until now, as Chris made the list, that Guthrie didn't need to try to be like Tad to be a hero. Guthrie *was* a hero. He'd done it all on his own. He may have thought of himself as alone, but he'd never really been all by himself. His own good will had given him people he could turn to, whether he expected them to be there or not.

He sighed, letting go of his worry a little. "He… he just looks so thin," he said, feeling weak and stupid.

Chris shrugged. "Well, our future boss keeps promising us casseroles. We'll have to hold him to it."

Tad laughed and grabbed the takeout for the hotel room, shaking his head.

It was hope.

HOPE HE sorely needed when he got to the room. Guthrie was asleep, his hair falling from its ponytail to cover his face. Tad paused for a moment after he set the takeout on the table and shut the door. In sleep, there was a curious untouched quality to Guthrie Arlo Woodson—as though all the shitty luck and barfights in the world couldn't dent his indomitable heart. Good karma power, Chris had called it, and Tad could see it now, shining out from the edges, making him bigger than life.

Tad realized that if Guthrie went AWOL for *years*, not telling where he was going, simply promising to return, Tad would still take him in; grayer, sadder, but trusting, always trusting, that one day, Guthrie would wander in, clothes ragged, bruises fading, that Guthrie shrug telling him that whatever it was that kept him away for the longest time, it wasn't enough to keep him away *forever*.

"Whatcha looking at, chief?" Guthrie asked, his eyes still closed.

"All of you," Tad murmured gruffly.

"When you get tired of looking," Guthrie said, "could you maybe crawl into bed and do that spooning thing you do when you think I'm too banged up for sex?"

"Are you?" Tad asked, smiling, but he was already shucking his sweatshirt and toeing off his boots.

"God, I hope not," Guthrie said, and Tad chuckled softly. He shoved his jeans down, rested them on the same chair that held his hoodie, and then did as Guthrie asked and climbed in behind him, spanning his hand on Guthrie's taut stomach under his T-shirt and pressing his own brief-covered groin against Guthrie's cotton-covered backside.

Guthrie gave a shudder like he was finally getting warm after being cold for a month, and Tad breathed him in.

"Yeah," Guthrie mumbled. "That's the stuff."

Tad could actually feel him drop off to sleep, but he didn't feel the need to go eat the takeout on the table. Not yet. Not yet. Not yet.

He didn't even know he was falling asleep until he woke up two hours later, needing to pee.

HE GOT up and came back, and then Guthrie did the same with a grunt, and when he was done, he rolled so they were face-to-face. There was something odd about his expression, something intense and glittering that spoke of a hardness, a shell, and Tad was suddenly aware that those things he'd been worried about were real.

Their kiss started out searing, frantic, starving, almost violent in its need, and their clothes didn't so much melt away as launch themselves across the room.

Tad was hungry for the taste of him, angry at the separation, and worried—so worried—it gave a tenseness, a jerkiness to his movements that almost scared him. Guthrie had only ever known him as a gentle lover, which was the only kind of lover he'd ever wanted to be. But Guthrie's need and his own ferocious desire worked like emotional napalm, and suddenly they were both on fire.

Guthrie rolled away from him, and Tad was ready to wrestle him to the ground until he saw that lean, battered body bent over the bed while Guthrie dared him with those glittering eyes.

For the first time, Tad faltered.

"Guthrie?"

"Now," he growled. "And don't stop."

Tad had left his shaving kit on the hotel sink, and he was back with lubricant before the coolness of the oceanside night made itself felt on his skin. It wasn't until he was sliding slick fingers into Guthrie and soothing his trembling flanks and backside with his free hand that he realized how wrong this was, how terrified and angry his lover was, how this need went beyond sex and into fury.

"Guthrie?" he asked.

"*Fuck me!*" Guthrie cried, and so help him, Tad's arousal was amped higher by the demand.

As he placed himself behind Guthrie, smoothing with his hands once again, noting how Guthrie's ribs were more prominent, his hipbones sharper, Guthrie grabbed a pillow from the bed and shoved it in front of him. Tad shuddered and thrust into him, his entire body shaking as Guthrie screamed, "Yes!" into the pillow.

He started to rock back and forth, and then to *lunge* as Guthrie's muffled, guttural sounds vibrated the bed. Faster and faster and harder and harder until Guthrie grabbed another pillow and covered his head with it and *howled* with arousal and rage.

Tad's body *loved* it, primal and angry and claiming—this was *his* lover, and he'd *missed* him, and somebody had *hurt* him, and only Tad's touch was allowed!

Sweat stung his eyes and his nearly healed wound ached fiercely, and still he poured his strength, his frustration, his anger into Guthrie, and Guthrie—Guthrie took it, thrusting back and muffling his cries of rage in those damned pillows.

Climax rushed him, ungentle and unwelcome, but it wasn't a call he could refuse.

He cried out and came, hips stuttering in surprise, his fingers digging into Guthrie's hips as the convulsions took him, and Guthrie let out a groan so low in his body that Tad felt it in his spasming cock.

Guthrie's orgasm almost ripped his dick off, and still Tad kept pumping, his body racked with completion when his emotions weren't ready to quit. It wasn't until Guthrie gave a soft whimper and melted into the bed, sliding to his knees, that Tad's final thrusts stilled and he fell heavily over Guthrie's back, landing on his own knees on the hard hotel tile.

His body was clammy with sweat, and so was Guthrie's, but Guthrie was shuddering so much Tad was afraid to let go. He wrapped his arms around Guthrie's shoulders and held on, not sure if he was shaking from sobs of rage or joy or grief or a combination of the three, but absolutely refusing to leave him alone, not now, not when he was naked and hurting and raw.

It took an eternity for the aftermath to ease from their skin, and in the end, the only thing that made Tad move was Guthrie's small voice saying, "I'm freezing."

"Me too," Tad grunted and got awkwardly to his feet. He stood and offered Guthrie a hand up, which he took, leaving them bare and close and face-to-face in the ambient light from the street lamp outside.

Guthrie wouldn't meet his eyes.

Tad hadn't expected him to.

Instead, he feathered a shaky kiss along Guthrie's jaw and murmured, "Now? Now can we talk?"

Guthrie still looked away, over his shoulder, into some forbidden part of the room Tad couldn't see.

But he nodded and said, "Did you bring food? I could eat."

Tad chuckled weakly and wrapped his arms around Guthrie's shoulders. "Let's get dressed, okay? I'm so cold my balls are shrinking."

Guthrie moved away to put on the sweats and T-shirt and hoodie Tad had provided for him. "The hell they are," he grumbled to himself, and Tad chuckled as he found his own clothes.

FOR YOU I'LL WAIT

GUTHRIE HAD seen Larx and Aaron's home when he'd been up to Colton before, but he hadn't seen it in the morning sunlight, with the morning glories wound about an arbor and cut flowers in vases decorating the aisles of chairs. He hadn't seen it with Aaron George, tall and blond and hale and hearty and kind, standing in a handsome blue suit, waiting for his husband, smaller, wiry, with dark hair harboring a few strands of silver.

He hadn't seen Olivia and her sister and stepsister dressed in pale purple, like morning glories themselves, or an entire town full of people watching the two men meet at the altar in front of their respective best friends who were conducting the ceremony.

In short, he'd never seen, nor been part of, anything as bright and shining, as full of sunshine and glory, as the George-Larkin wedding. Even Seth and Kelly's wedding, as much as he'd loved it, had the roar of the ocean, the fight of the wind in it, and that had suited them, because their lives together hadn't been easy, and they wouldn't be, and Seth and Kelly seemed to thrive in the storm.

But Larx and Aaron were working so hard to create a little haven of kindness. Bad things happened there, of course—what happened to Tad had happened to all of them, including to the still thin, healing teenager sitting anxiously in the back near April—but there was hope that the people in the town could make things better.

It was the perfect wedding for two people who were far from perfect, but who wanted to give the world at least one day of sunshine, flowers, and joy.

As Guthrie finished the processional, allowing the last chords to die softly in the early morning August sunshine, he glanced to Larx's arm, where a determined-looking Olivia was clinging with all the force in her white-knuckled fingers. As Guthrie watched from his discreet little stool to the side of the arbor, he could see what seemed to be a ripple or a faint breeze pass along the ruffled fabric of Olivia's full, empire-waisted tunic, and his eyebrows rose.

He saw the exact moment Larx realized his oldest daughter was in labor right before his own wedding.

And then he watched as Larx approached his groom with raised eyebrows of his own, and Aaron George's widened eyes told the same story.

And then they glanced to their two officiates: Yoshi, the diminutive English teacher, and Eamon, Aaron's former boss, the tall and thickly muscled sheriff.

"For obvious reasons," Eamon intoned, "We're going to hurry this up a bit."

Olivia had been seated when the rest of the wedding party had remained standing, and Guthrie stared at her as her husband moved to her side and allowed her to crush his hand.

The wedding vows were lovely—he assumed—but his eyes were on Olivia the entire time. She saw his gaze and winked, and then took her husband's hand and panted her way through her next contraction, and Guthrie felt a stupid shaft of disappointment.

He'd wanted so badly to talk to her.

Oddly enough, Olivia had become one of his closest friends in a remarkably short time. He wondered if that was because, in one way or another, they were both… isolated in some ways. Yes, he was surrounded by people who loved him, but he'd spent most of his life on the road and was having a hard time adjusting to the idea that he might not have to live that way anymore.

And Olivia had changed her entire vision of what her life would be in the span of less than a year. They were both getting used to living a life they'd never thought would fit them, and somehow they'd found each other. Guthrie had hoped… oh, he'd hoped for somebody to talk to.

Somebody besides Tad, because he and Tad had a totally intense way of communicating that was frightening and raw and terrifying in its honesty, and Guthrie needed a friend to tell him that was okay.

What had happened in the hotel two nights before had scared him shitless.

Not just the primal, animal-screaming sex, although that had been such a beautiful purge, Guthrie wished he could stop being embarrassed about it. But besides that, there had been the conversation afterward, the two of them on the bed, peeling each other's hearts open like tangerines.

"HOW BAD is it?" Tad had brought fruit salad, and he sat on the bed cross-legged with the bowl in his hand. Guthrie was leaning against the headboard, wishing he didn't have to eat.

"It hurts," he said. "Can't lie. He says awful shit, and I can either scream awful shit back or take it." He thought of the day before, screaming Butch's littleness, the nothingness of his life into the old man's dying face. "Either way, it makes a body... less. Less of a person. There's no winning."

Tad leaned forward, his hand on Guthrie's ankle, the skin-to-skin contact reassuring at the same time it burned. "What you're doing is so important," he whispered. "There's no way he can make you 'less.' Don't think that way. It's bigger than the awfulness of the person you're caring for—remember that."

SO MEANINGFUL—AND painful and embarrassing. Guthrie didn't want to talk about it to anybody but Tad. But he *did* want to talk about *Tad*. Was it normal to fall in love like this, where even the person's flaws seemed like sunshine? Where the smell behind his neck could be an aphrodisiac and a sedative at the same time? Where the crinkles at the corners of his eyes seemed like a promise of growing old together? Where the thought of letting this person down made your hands shake?

Guthrie had been in love once before, but he hadn't had a chance to find out. He'd tried a couple of times since, and those had ended, mostly because Guthrie's life was always in a state of flux, of wandering, of upheaval. But he and Tad had faced more than flux, wandering, and upheaval, and somehow, some way, he'd fought harder to remain by Tad's side.

Did that mean it was real love, the kind that stuck? He wasn't just working on one dream here, he was working on two—was that allowed? Could he make that recording date with Seth and still have Tad waiting for him with open arms? Did a man like him get the things he wanted most in the world?

Those were the things he wanted to talk to Olivia about. They were the kinds of things he was pretty sure Tad talked to Chris about (although he suspected they discussed diet, fiber content, and bathroom schedules a lot more, because they were stuck in a car together a lot.)

But he wasn't stupid, and he tried not to be selfish. The girl was *in labor* at her *father's wedding.* He kept an eye on her while the dads said their vows, feeling a sunshine burn behind his eyes.

"I get to go through life with a friend, a partner, somebody who gets me, somebody who laughs with me, and somebody who won't leave when things get rough. I know that because we've been through the rough, and baby, you're still here."

Larx was the one who said the words, but Aaron's weren't any worse.

"I thought the sun had gone down on love a long time ago—I'd planned to live my entire life in a sort of perpetual twilight, where I knew what love was but I knew I'd never see it again. And then one day I looked up and you were running on the damned road, which was a death trap, and I realized the sun wasn't gone. It had dipped behind the trees for a bit, but suddenly there it was, right in front of me, and we had a ways to go before night."

Gah! All that poetry from two guys with the most mundane jobs in the world. Guthrie wanted to cry. He'd worked his entire life to be a musician, to be a poet, but apparently nothing made you spout the good stuff like getting your heart broken... and then falling in love.

"And there you go," said Yoshi, obviously proud of himself and happy—and then staring anxiously at Olivia, whose even breathing was not all that loud but had the attention of the entire assembly. "By the power vested in Eamon Mills and me by the internet gods and a very helpful website, we have both seen our best friends married, and hopefully they will only be fifty percent as worrisome as they were before."

"Amen," Eamon intoned. "May the groom kiss the groom, and then may everybody clear a path so Olivia's husband can get her to the first family-mobile so she can deliver the grandbaby of the grooms in a hospital and not the front seat."

There was some general laughter, and then Elton stood, Olivia gripping his forearm tensely, and Olivia took unsteady steps down the aisle. Suddenly her knees almost buckled, and Larx was there to help Elton catch her. Without missing a beat, Aaron was there as well, lifting her up in his arms and bearing toward the vehicles at speed. As the little party hurried forward, Guthrie was shocked to hear Elton call his name.

"What?" he asked, standing and setting his guitar in its case. He'd been prepared to play the recessional, although he'd been pretty sure this was going to be how the ceremony ended the whole time.

"She wants you and me!" Elton called. "Please!"

"Me?" Guthrie asked, horrified. The girl had a whole *troop* of family literally *carrying her to her car* and she wanted *him*?

"*Nobody* who's changed my diaper," Olivia panted. "*Nobody* who borrows my Tampax. And *nobody* who's going to give me shit about seeing my hoochie stretched to the end of fucking days!"

Elton must have nudged her as they cleared the aisle and approached the driveway, where a Subaru Forester was one of the last vehicles parked.

"Except my husband," she corrected, her voice breaking. "Guthrie, please!"

Guthrie was already hurrying down the aisle, pausing where Tad and April were sitting to give Tad the truck keys. "I'll call ya," he said, kissing him on the cheek.

"This is a surprise," Tad said dryly.

"My only qualification is I don't borrow her Tampax," Guthrie replied. "Don't be too impressed."

"She only said that so I'd be forced to entertain at the wedding," said her sister as she hurried up the aisle. "Now move it. We're all terrified of her at this stage, and you should be too!"

Guthrie gave Tad a beleaguered look and started jogging for the cars.

IT TURNED out there was some method to Olivia's madness, although Elton was the one who filled Guthrie in on it as he was driving at a *very* practiced speed on the winding roads toward the already-alerted hospital. There were eighty people in Larx and Aaron's front yard, and a reception at Aaron's place in an hour, after pictures. Olivia had originally told everybody that if she went into labor during the wedding—Ha-ha! Like that was going to happen, right?—she'd leave the place with Elton and give birth quietly, without stealing any of the people from the party. It wasn't fair, she'd argued. All of the plans they'd made, everything it took to get two incredibly busy men to have their own public wedding—and it had to be public, because they were pillars of the damned community and their family and friends were *not* going to let them slink off and marry like they had something to be embarrassed about—and they needed to be there. So even though Christiana and Larx had planned to be there for the birth on any other day, on *this* day, Larx needed to go be the star of the show.

But Olivia still wanted a friend there. And Guthrie had learned over the last couple of months that her stepsister's assessment was damned accurate. Olivia had a huge heart, and she was warm and kind and joyful. But that huge heart was guarded, and her warmth was banked in reserve for the people she trusted, and for some reason, she and Guthrie clicked.

It was, as she'd texted numerous times, as random and as chancy as falling in love. The heart wanted what it wanted when it came to friends and lovers, and she wanted Guthrie there to hold her hand when Elton was busy being the man of the house.

As Guthrie had sent her his poetry and lyrics, he'd realized that yeah, he had a friend, and he didn't want to shake her.

So Guthrie it was.

Guthrie sat in the back of the car and held her hand, listening to her gush about her father's wedding and how the dreamy guy he was marrying had literally carted her in his arms like in the movies.

"Yeah," Guthrie said dryly. "That was something special. How'd you happen to go into labor on their wedding day again?"

"Dumb fucking luck," she panted.

"Total fucking stress," Elton chimed in from the front. "She, Christiana, and Nancy Pavelle—did you see her?"

"Nice lady with the baby's breath in her updo?" Guthrie asked.

"Yeah," Elton said. "She's Yoshi's sister-in-law. I guess she, Larx, and Yoshi are the sarcastic terrors of Colton High."

Guthrie chuckled, and Livvy shook her head.

"You think it's funny, but they're *terrifying*. All the kids are like, 'Omigod, I forgot to turn in my English assignment for Mr. Nakamoto, and now Mrs. Pavelle's threatening to put a snake in my locker!'"

That made Guthrie *and* Elton laugh, and Guthrie stroked her hand as she caught her breath in the downtime.

"What kind of snake?" Guthrie asked at the same time Elton said, "She did *not*!"

"Oh, she did," Olivia breathed, eyes closed. "He was a really sweet corn snake she named Buttons. She set him free but ended up with another kind of snake, rescued, who was so stupid she had to make sure he ate his field mice right or he'd choke on them and die."

"I am boggled," Guthrie muttered. "Tell me more about the magic snake woman who's friends with your father."

"And is sister to Yoshi's mysterious boyfriend," Elton added. "He's super shy—I've only barely met him, but he's got a soft spot for Christiana."

"Everybody does," Olivia murmured. "Just as well the baby came today when she couldn't be here, or the little squid would pop out and love her best."

Elton grunted as though struck, and Guthrie squeezed her hand. "Aw, princess, you know that's not gonna happen. I mean, no denying she'll be the favorite aunt, which is not knocking Maureen, but you'll be the mommy. Lookit you, being all brave and entertaining us and shit. It'll be okay, Livvy. You don't gotta be your sister to be the favorite."

"Sure," she muttered, and her hand tightened over his knuckles, and he had to work with her to keep her breathing even as the next contraction hit.

He wanted a chance to talk to Elton, though, to be in the same room as Olivia, to tell her, convince her that she didn't have to be her sister to be the prettiest. She was perfect all on her own.

"YOUR FATHER'S a fool," Tad murmured, setting aside his food and reaching to tug Guthrie next to him on the hotel bed. "You're a better son than he ever deserved. And I'm so mad at him. I had my mom, and I would have given anything—anything—to have one more day with her. And your dad got all this time with you and he wasted it being a shitty father. Don't worry about not being good enough for him. You're perfect."

OLIVIA'S FATHER had probably told her these things, Guthrie thought, but sometimes, you needed to hear them again and again.

Guthrie and Elton *told* Olivia again and again over the next few hours. Unlike the scatterbrained assholes on television, Elton was a fully functioning emotional human being. He'd read up on labor, knew what Olivia specifically needed, and did his best to anticipate those needs. But it was Elton's job to communicate with the hospital staff and keep his wife focused on the things she was supposed to do—they were partners in parenthood after all.

He said things like, "Livvy, you gotta stay in the present. You do this all the time when you're taking a dump. Know where the baby is in the pipes and breathe around it. You'll be fine."

Guthrie had no such responsibilities. He'd been drafted at the last possible moment for emotional support. He figured it was his job to agree with absolutely everything Olivia said without question and make wildly improbable promises that he could not possibly carry through.

"You're right, Livvy, this is bullshit. Aaron will arrest all the fuckers responsible, no question. Now breathe. Elton loves you, and that's what he said. Yeah, I know he did this to you, but that was an act of love, darlin'. Look at the man—he's got your ice chips, he's got your other hand, now follow his directions, and I'll put a pin in that arrest-the-fuckers thing, okay?"

Then the contraction would pass and she'd be left shaking and rational—thank God—and do her best to relax into the next contraction.

It was rough going. Guthrie and Elton held her elbows and walked her around the hospital room for a bit after she was admitted, and then "the big one" hit and she was in bed, lying on her side, with Guthrie rubbing the small of her back and Elton holding her hand. Finally, one more person stuck their hand up her hoochie (Guthrie could not even *believe* how many people had done that. If men got fingers stuck up their asses in the name of medicine as often as women got hands shoved up their cooters, proctologists would be on the accepted kill lists, and the yearly checkup would be a blood sport) and proclaimed her ready for the delivery room. He and Elton were rushed into caps and gowns and booties. Guthrie felt pretty superfluous after that. Sure, he cheerfully lied a lot—her fuckers list got *really* long by the end of the whole thing. But really, it was all down to Livvy.

And toward the end, in spite of multiple promises not to look because he wasn't that interested in hoochies anyway, he still watched as the tiny miracle was produced from his friend's body.

Red, wrinkled, and squalling was Guthrie's only real impression, and then Olivia was his focus again. He brushed the hair from her face and held her hand while Elton went to check on the baby.

"What is it?" she hiccuped. "Boy or girl? For the present, I mean. I understand you can be wrong about these things for years."

Guthrie laughed softly. "How very progressive of you," he teased. "Elton, end the suspense, would ya?"

"It's a girl," he said proudly, holding the solidly wrapped squiddy thing up to be ogled.

Guthrie was suitably impressed. "Look what you made," he said. "A squid."

"I think there's not enough arms and legs for a squid," she said breathlessly. "I think we have to hope it turns human in a few weeks."

"Let me know how that works for you," he said soberly, and she laughed, weak and a little hysterical but happy.

"You say that like you're not coming back," she said, and he realized with a stab of panic that he hadn't just made this promise to Tad. It was frightening enough knowing he could fuck up and not move to Colton when all this was done and break Tad's heart, but this woman had held his hand while she squeezed out a baby. He was *stuck* now, in this wonderful friendship, caught in the flypaper of amazing family before he even had a chance to fathom escape. "I can't raise this kid alone, Guthrie. Me and Elton are going to need help!"

Guthrie wanted to guffaw. "We just left a giant party of about eighty people who would be *delighted* to help," he chided, and her scowl was terrifying.

"Yeah, but I only want so many of those people in my home," she growled. "Now promise me. Not a bullshit promise. You can wipe the fuckers list out of existence. Promise me." Her voice wobbled, and Guthrie looked to Elton for backup, but Elton was doing the responsible dad thing and accompanying the baby to the washing station and the eyeball station and all the other things they did to babies fresh out of the box before they gave them back to mom.

"PLEASE, GUTHRIE." It was such a simple plea, and Guthrie stared at Tad in consternation. They were naked again, panting, their lovemaking written on their skin again, the night chill of Monterey seeping in through the floorboards of the hotel.

"I already promised," he said, confused.

"It's easy to break promises," Tad said, and Guthrie scowled.

"Not for me," he said. Hadn't he proved that?

"I know that," Tad told him. A faint sheen of sweat was drying on his forehead, and he was so earnest. "You promised we'd make the move. We'd be together. But being with you now—I think you're wondering if it's a dream. If once you have a chance to drive somewhere, anywhere, to get in your dying truck and go, you'll forget that you have family. That you have a place. That people love you. All you'll remember is one more goddamned obligation. Please, Guthrie. Let us be your dream."

"You are," he rasped, and his voice was so quiet he was afraid Tad hadn't heard. "You are," he said again. "You are my dream." And he said it again and again until Tad kissed him to still the shaking that took him over as the reality swept through him, that all that reaching, all that yearning, and it was literally right here in his arms.

"PRINCESS," HE said now to Olivia, "you all have made yourselves our dream. Tad might beat me here by a few weeks, but I'll get here. Trust me, okay? I… I won't have anywhere else to go."

She smiled and laughed a little, and then Elton arrived with the real princess.

"Hello," she murmured, forehead to forehead with Elton, both of them staring at the child cradled in his arms in awe. "I understand you're a girl. Your daddy thought of the prettiest name—"

"Your grandpa thought of it first," Elton murmured. "Trust me, kiddo, you got some awesome people to meet."

The gaze of tenderness, of pride, that Olivia sent her husband then made it hard for Guthrie to swallow. Yeah, these kids were young—so young—but God, he thought they might make it.

"You're killing us here," Guthrie murmured, reaching across Olivia to run a finger along the downy little head. "What'd we name our little princess?"

He heard the name and smiled.

TWO HOURS later, Larx, Aaron, and Christiana showed up in the hospital room, still dressed in their wedding finery.

"Tad's waiting out in the hallway," Larx said softly, since Olivia was sleeping. Elton stood over the bassinet in the corner, having just taken custody of their little princess from Guthrie, who had snuggled that charming creature to his heart as often as humanly allowed since they'd left the delivery room.

Guthrie took that as his cue and stood to go hug Elton, because it felt like the two of them had done something huge together.

Elton grinned at him. "Yeah, Guthrie, you were a part of this. That practically makes us brothers, you know."

Guthrie felt his face heat. "That's a kind thing to offer," he said. "Watch out—I may come back and take you up on that."

"You promised," Elton told him soberly, and Guthrie bent down to kiss the downy little head for the umpteenth time.

"I did," he murmured. "I keep promises like that. Anybody'll tell ya. Give Livvy my love. I gotta leave early tomorrow, so I probably won't see her. Tell her next time I come, I'll have a baby gift, okay?"

"Just you," Elton said happily.

"You're killing me here," Christiana said, holding out her arms. "Give her to me so I can tell her all the embarrassing things about her mother and make myself the favorite aunt of all times."

Guthrie slid out of the room then, and let the family *be* a family, but boy was he glad to see Tad leaning against wall of the hallway when he got out.

"So," Tad said, taking his hand and brushing the hair out of his eyes. "Everybody's dying of suspense, you know. What'd they name her?"

Guthrie chuckled. "Well, they joked about naming her Lumpy Space Princess, but in the end, they went with Emmeline Glory."

Tad made a happy sound. "Aw… that's sweet. That's keeping the family tradition right there, right? Olivia, Christiana—all those royal sounding girl's names for these down-to-earth, strong women. I love it."

Guthrie made a *"hmm"* sound in his throat. "You gonna tell me how the rest of wedding went?" he asked. "After you feed me and before I pass out, of course."

"Sure," Tad said. "You gonna tell me how all of that—" He gestured with the hand *not* laced together with Guthrie's toward the family in the hospital room. "—went?"

"Sure," Guthrie said. "There was some yelling, some crying, and a long list of fuckers that I promised to kill for Olivia, but she told me I could take it all back after the baby was born."

Tad chuckled, and together they turned toward the exit, hand in hand. "I look forward to hearing that," he said. "I need to kiss up to the boss, after all, and knowing his stepdaughter's enemies is a good way to do it."

"Sure," Guthrie acknowledged, "but you're gonna have to find the people who invented stirrups on the beds and the people who said ice chips only and the people who invented the portable IV—because they are all fuckers and need to be stopped."

Tad's laughter accompanied them out of the hospital and into long shadows of early evening. Guthrie was suddenly looking forward to dinner in a hotel room and the sharing of stories as much as he usually looked forward to sex.

That alone was a kind of magic he hadn't been sure existed.

"YOU DOING better?" Jock asked as Guthrie pulled his truck up the drive the next afternoon.

"Yeah," Guthrie said with a sigh. Tad and April had gone back with Chris and Laura, staying long enough to visit Olivia on their way out of town and eat brunch with the family. Guthrie had felt his desertion of Jock keenly, and while his heart was stronger, more ready to see this bullshit through to the end, he resented missing out on those things, and on the ride home with Tad.

And on the time he wanted to be spending with him now.

"Kenny told me your guy seemed okay," Jock said, sounding conciliatory. "Someday, you know, maybe I... maybe you wouldn't be too embarrassed for me to meet him."

Guthrie swallowed. "You can't use some words around him," he cautioned. "And you gotta talk about April like she's a queen. I mean, *all* women, really, Jock, but, you know."

"Don't be crude about your guy's sister," Jock said dutifully, and then he gave a hopeful smile. "I'd... I mean, maybe someday, when this is...." His voice dropped, and he glanced around the yard and the house, which showed a definite improvement from their efforts this last month. "When the house is finished," he said, and then sighed. "When your daddy's not here to pollute the place."

"I'd be honored," Guthrie said. "Now I'm sure you need a break yourself, right?"

Jock shrugged. "I got my girl to help me out, and Kenny Wilson came by too. I ain't been too alone these last few days. And you look better, boy. I was afraid you were gonna get arrested for killing a guy who's gonna be dead in a month, and that'd be no good. So yeah. Come help me give the old bastard his bath and his dinner, and we can have a beer and you can tell me all about it."

Guthrie lit up. "I'm telling you," he said proudly, "it was a bigger adventure than you think."

Highway Runs

THE CATS were the last things to put in the SUV.

After the wedding, August sped by. Tad and Chris had finished their workload with SAC PD and had, with little fanfare, resigned. Chris had been well-respected, but Tad wanted to think their farewell bash hadn't been all riding on his partner's coattails—their cake had been fashioned like a gravel pit, with two tiny plastic figures in suits at the bottom screaming, "Take us back!"

They'd both gotten a little drunk, and Laura had picked them up to take them home. Tad had rolled into the apartment saying, "Guthrie, you'll never believe what Chris said—" only to realize that Guthrie wasn't there yet. That he'd be relocating his entire life up in Colton and the most important person in it would still be missing.

April had found him collapsed on the couch the next morning, his cheeks still wet from his boozy cry.

God, he missed Guthrie.

Their communication had been somewhat less worrisome since their long talk in the hotel room that night, but Tad still knew he was leaving a lot out.

He even knew why. Some of it wasn't even "My life sucks right now, and I'm trying to spare you." Some of it was "My life sucks right now, and I want to concentrate on the happy when I'm talking to you."

Tad got that—but he absolutely hated the thought that Guthrie was suffering, was in pain, and he didn't want to tell Tad.

But finally he trusted that Guthrie *would* tell him before things got so bad he felt compelled to go out drinking in a place that wanted to kill him just for breathing.

Although he trusted Guthrie when he said that wasn't his intention.

"WOULD YOU just believe that I went to a bar because bars are comfortable for me, and all I wanted was a beer and to be somewhere not with that jackass who spawned me? It was just... you know. Bad luck."

Tad had eyed him, splayed under the comforter in the hotel room, his hair falling forward into his face as they recovered from their second round of sex and blinking like he was trying hard to stay awake.

"Guthrie's luck," he said grimly.

"I'm not so special I've got my own brand of luck," Guthrie muttered, uncurling enough to prop himself on his elbow and scowl.

Tad smiled and pushed that glorious hair out of his eyes. "Don't be modest," he said. "I'm telling you, Guthrie's luck is going right next to Murphy's luck in the bad luck hall of fame."

THAT CONVERSATION in the hotel room had been a good one, had unearthed so much of the crap sitting next to Guthrie's heart that had terrified Tad, had worried him.

Tad's life hadn't been easy. Money had been tight, and growing up poor left a scar on a person—there was always a chip on the shoulder, something to prove. There was always a need to be as smart as, successful as, fast as, important as, *good as* the slick kids with all the money who would be living somewhere better when their daddies got them into the prep school. But Tad's mom had been the best, and she'd loved him, and April had been a good sister, and they'd loved each other. Tad had known love was a real thing, and he'd never wanted to do anything with his life that couldn't be achieved with hard work and smart thinking.

Guthrie'd grown up with one caretaker and a father who'd abused him until he'd had to take care in secret, and love was for songs, for scam that was the family business, and not ever for real. He'd grown up in a profession that depended as much on luck as on skill and a family that did its best to fuck his luck. He'd grown up working so hard to make himself better he'd never understood that so much of him was very much good enough, just by being Guthrie. The more they'd talked, the more Tad had understood why Seth Arnold had been so important, even if he'd never loved Guthrie back. Because he'd loved Guthrie as a friend. Because he'd valued Guthrie as a colleague… and as a musician. Because his family—as splintered as it had been when Guthrie met him—had *been* a family, and Guthrie had learned what to shoot for. He'd learned he could be good enough. He'd learned that love was real.

And then he'd met Tad and maybe a lot of his quietness, his keeping things close, was driving Tad crazy, but it was because Guthrie was learning how to make love work when it was a two-way street.

So it was the end of August, and Guthrie's recording date had been moved—something about studio time—and his father hadn't passed away yet, and his whole life was in flux.

But he'd asked April to make a blanket for Emmeline and had even sent a pattern with a hesitant, "Can you make this?" because he thought it looked like what a princess would have. He'd even ordered the yarn on his precious internet time and sent it, because he wanted to be part of it.

Wanted Olivia to know he was coming and, Tad suspected, wanted Tad to trust that Guthrie wouldn't break his promises.

Tad was more secure in them now.

But it still hurt to leave.

He sat in the SUV—as April did one more run-through around the apartment, making sure they hadn't, say, left the vacuum sitting in the middle of the floor—and gave Chris a wave. Chris and Laura, by virtue of having much more stuff, had rented a U-Haul, and Tad and April had taken a small corner of it. There was some concern as to whether or not the truck would go on the winding roads, but Aaron knew where their small housing "development" sat and assured them it was as straight as the roads around Colton got and their truck was well in established guidelines. Tad had laughed at the "development" moniker. The houses were about five acres apart and well off the road, but they were prefabricated, and the county provided services like trash pickup, electricity, and gas. They had U-shaped driveways and peaked roofs to deflect snowfall, and apparently differences in parcel shape or flora and fauna be damned, that meant they were identical.

Tad's house—he was renting for a year with the option to purchase if the job worked out—sat on a parcel with a small stream. When he and April had gone to check the place out the week after the wedding, they'd seen three deer, eyeballing them with suspicion and not fear. Chris—who had purchased his property outright—had already contracted workers to fence in a yard to contain the big slobbering dogs his wife had plans to rescue as soon as they moved in.

There was a service track that wound behind their parcels that they could run on during their days off, and Laura already had plans to teach April how to cook and to, probably, mother Guthrie within an inch of his life.

They just needed Guthrie to get there.

April emerged from the apartment, one hand clenched around a couple of odds and ends she'd found on her last sortie. She gave a thumbs-up so Chris could start the U-Haul and then turned and locked the doors. The expression on her face was both excited and devastated, and as she slid into the SUV, she gave Tad a half-guilty glance before dumping the last few items she'd found on the console between them.

One of Guthrie's guitar picks, probably lodged in the molding by the kitchen table, two catnip mice he'd gotten the day before he'd gotten the call from Jock, and a special ergonomic crochet hook Guthrie had picked up at a store in San Rafael for April when he was still working down there once a week.

Tad checked the haul and swallowed.

"Text him," he said. "Take a picture of the cats in the crates and tell him they'll miss him in the new place."

"That's mean," she said, but she was turning in her seat to get a picture of John Lenny Bruce and McCartney You Fucking Asshole as she spoke. She paused for a moment and took a shot of Tad, who tried to smile, and then she sent the pic.

You'd better join us in Colton, you prick. Email us tonight if we're not getting your texts. We both miss you.

With a swallow she set her phone down on the console and did her belt.

"Ready?" he asked.

"Let's blow this place," she said. They fist-bumped, and Tad put the SUV in gear.

FIVE DAYS before Guthrie absolutely positively had to leave for San Francisco, the unthinkable happened.

His father—almost dead, damn him—snatched Guthrie's phone from his pocket as Guthrie was leaning over to retrieve his untouched dinner tray and dropped the thing into the gears of his electric recliner. As Guthrie stared in shock, trying to figure out how to get the old man out of the chair, Butch, wheezing with glee, hit the button that raised and lowered the thing, and Guthrie heard his phone's components crackle as the chair's gears crushed it into powder.

Guthrie stared at his father in shock.

"The actual fuck," he said, numb. "Why? Why would you do that?"

"I gotta die," Butch cackled. "You don't get to be happy!"

Guthrie blinked. "You think you're going to keep me from being happy if you wreck my phone, old man?" he asked.

"Won't be able to talk to all your fancy friends that way," Butch said smugly. "*You're* gonna be—" He coughed, wetly and laden with blood. "—all alone."

Guthrie could only laugh. "That's it?" he asked. "That's your plan? I've got twelve other options for contacting my boyfriend, Butch. I've got ten other people I can call for help. I... I have a *life*, old man." Suddenly, the secret things he hadn't talked to his father about—although Jock knew them now—came spilling out of him. "I got into a bar fight, and three policemen came to bail me out. You heard that. One of them was my boyfriend, but the other two were *friends*. You can't wreck that by destroying my phone. Nosirree. You're gonna die, and I'm not going to your funeral. Jock might go—you'll have to ask him. But I'm out of here, old man. I'm going to the city to make money with Fiddler. You heard that right too. He don't want you. I was his friend, and he remembers that, but you? You were some redneck who made money off him, and he remembers that too. I'm going to the hills to a family that wants me. Do you know what I did when I was gone? Do you have any idea?"

"Got your knob waxed?" Butch muttered, because that was the extent of his imagination.

"I played for a wedding," Guthrie said, the moment lighting him up inside. "Two men—a sheriff and a principal—walked down the aisle, and their kids were there, and their friends and their entire town applauded, so damned happy to see them together. And then my friend went into labor, and she wanted me in there with her, along with her husband. Can you imagine that? I go from watching your dying, rotting, decomposing animated corpse to...." His voice softened, because he couldn't say this with an edge. "To watching the birth of a baby who is so wanted. So loved. So *cherished*. And I'm asked to be a part of the baby's life. To be an uncle. To be a brother and a friend. I've got all that *beauty* inside me, old man, and you think you're going to destroy that with a *phone*? You watch your television shows. I'm gonna go buy myself a new goddamned phone."

Guthrie stalked out, leaving Butch with the remote control as he took his tray to the kitchen. After cleaning off the tray and putting everything away, he threw some beef and some tomato stock into Jock's Crock-Pot so they could have dinner later that night, and then emerged into the blessedly cool day to turn his face to the sun.

"Good speech," Jock said, walking out of the carport with a bottle of water in his hand. One of the things Guthrie had noticed in the last five weeks was that Jock drank more water and less beer the closer Butch got to the grave. All the activity had leaned him up a little, and his jowls and lines had eased some. He looked like a hale man in his forties now, and not a would-be alcoholic aging before his time.

Every now and then his girlfriend brought them dinner. Guthrie talked to her sometimes, but mostly he let her and Jock have some time alone. It was good to see Jock had a life he was working toward. Made Guthrie proud.

"You know the only problem with it," he muttered glumly.

"No money for a phone," Jock said with a grimace.

Guthrie put his finger on his nose. "Bingo." He'd been eking out the last of his money to pay for gas and groceries since the wedding. He'd been reluctant to tell Tad—moving was expensive, and one good late-night talk was not going to completely erase Guthrie's ethics on taking a handout. Five days. Five days until he signed that contract. Five days. The hotel was paid for, Seth had assured him. All he had to do was be there, on time, with his guitar. "It's fine. I've got my computer— email's a thing. Just…." He shook his head, thinking about the meanness of Butch's act, one of his last on this earth.

"Inconvenient," Jock said with a sigh. "I hear ya. You got any of those numbers memorized?"

Guthrie shrugged. "The top five, yeah. After the old asshole goes to bed, I'll fish the phone out of the recliner and see if the SIM card can be salvaged. That'll be a big help right there."

"Yeah," Jock said softly. "Sorry about that. God, Guthrie. I keep remembering how I looked up to my brother, and now I can't wait for him to die. How awful is that?"

Guthrie sighed. "Just remember he did that to himself. You been… been shaking off his shadow these last weeks, Jock. You keep doing that. The man in the sunlight's a good guy."

Jock nodded thoughtfully. "Good to hear," he said. "Kind of you to say. Look—I'm weedwacking that back quarter. You take over that for me, and I'll take over the whole bath thing for you. You're using your time to get all this shit off your chest. It's time for me and Butch to have our own words." He paused and took a swig of water. "You may not want to listen in on the baby monitor," he said apologetically. "My language is gonna be down at his level, and that's not something I want you to hear."

Guthrie smiled at him fondly. "Appreciate it," he said, turning his face toward the place in the overcast sky where the sun was hiding. Finally he leveled his gaze to Jock. "You got gloves?"

"In the carport by the Weedwacker," Jock said. "And I appreciate it back. This place'll be almost shipshape in a week. You'll be leaving me in a real good place."

Guthrie shrugged. "Yeah, well, we're kin."

THE NEXT evening, Guthrie was sitting in the living room next to Butch, working on his computer and pretty much ignoring the old man as he mumbled at the TV, when suddenly Butch said, "You fuckin' puke. Not even gonna listen to me when I'm dying?"

Guthrie shut his computer and set it very carefully on the end table far away from the old man—he knew what his venom would do now.

"You got something to say to me?" Guthrie asked, steeling himself for the worst.

"You'd better come to my funeral," Butch muttered.

"Nope."

"I've earned it!" Butch whined, tears sliding down his face.

Guthrie turned toward him. "You earned a coffee can full of ashes in a pauper's grave. And either way, you are not my problem once you're gone. Don't you get it? I'm only here for Jock. You… you forfeited any right to me being sad when you're dead by being an awful human being when you were alive. Can't fix it now."

"Who's gonna sing over my grave?" Butch asked, sounding legitimately worried.

Guthrie shrugged. "Maybe Jock'll find a reverend or someone. Not my worry."

"I always thought you'd sing 'Independence Day,'" Butch mumbled.

Guthrie thought about the old Springsteen song, a memorial to the Boss's own troubled relationship with his father.

"I think you gotta remember some tenderness there," Guthrie said. "You never sat me up on your lap and told me to drive, old man. You grabbed me by the arm and threw me in the truck and told me to stop crying. You want Bruce at your funeral, you gotta be a redeemable character. No two ways about it." He was saying these things without heat, without any anger, really, but Butch was weeping, and he started to feel bad, like he was torturing an old dog. The dog may have bit people when he was younger, but now he was just a dumb, pain-riddled animal.

"You're not even gonna respect my last wish?" Butch mewled, and Guthrie almost… almost….

"Fine," he huffed. "I promise—"

To what? To give up his future for duty to a man who'd just the day before tried to destroy his means to communicate with anybody who really loved him? To sacrifice every good thing in his life for someone who'd spent his *entire* life reminding him how much he didn't matter?

"Promise wha—" Butch wheezed.

"Promise to pass that along to Jock," Guthrie said. "He'll be at the service." Guthrie flipped the computer shut; he'd just finished sending out a blanket email to all his contacts, asking for their phone numbers since the SIM card to his phone was as mangled as the rest of the thing.

"Boy!" Butch gasped, genuinely hurt, Guthrie thought, but Guthrie couldn't.

"I'm gonna go make dinner for Jock. You done with your broth?"

"But… but *boy*—"

"I'll take that as a yes."

Guthrie walked out of the room with his tray, dimly aware that *this* was the nine-hundred-pound gorilla he'd feared, and he wasn't yelling or screaming or violent. He was simply done. Any dream he'd had of having a father—his real father—who cared for him, who wanted what was best, had died a sad death in these last six weeks. The man who was washing up for dinner didn't have any illusions of Butch telling him he was sorry and wanting to make up for all twenty-eight years of bad shit in one tear-filled reunion.

But he did have an image of Aaron George scooping his stepdaughter up in his arms so she didn't have to walk fifty feet to her vehicle in labor. He saw Larx bringing his daughter in to hold her new niece and spill the tea about the baby's mom. He saw Elton, holding Olivia's hand and reminding her that she was strong, and they were going to be parents together, and it was going to be okay. And Chris Castro, who took him to IHOP to make sure he took his pain meds and then to make sure he and Tad would be okay, and who apparently hopped in the car to zip to Monterey so he could spend time with his partner and see another city.

Dads. He knew what those were about now. He knew what being cared for could feel like. He'd gone up to Colton to play for Olivia's dads, and he'd done it for free because they were good people—good fathers.

He didn't need Butch. He didn't need to be mad at him for not being who he'd needed.

He just needed to get this shit done and get home to where Tad waited for him, and April, and their cats, and their life.

He had a family, one he'd made. One that would sustain him. One that had driven down here to this godsforsaken shithole and pulled him out so he could breathe.

This was like the worst job he'd ever had since being Butch's son in the first place. He could endure. It was his signature move.

TWO DAYS later he stood in his father's tiny, grimy room—the only room in the house that Jock hadn't fixed up, at least with a fresh coat of paint and some new flooring—and surveyed his father's body.

It was small in death and twisted with pain, the once-healthy flesh converted to sallow, waxy skin. The smell of nicotine oozed from his pores even as the flies started to settle.

Guthrie swallowed hard, wondering if there was any hidden grief in the corners of his soul, but all he could find was a sweet, melancholy relief. It was over, and he wouldn't have to leave Jock here alone to deal with the body.

With a sigh he dragged the sheet up over the head of the corpse to keep the flies from gorging and went to use the landline to call in an unattended death. When the call was made, he went outside, where Jock was already working on the last corner of the yard, hacking the blackberry bushes back to the creek. It was work that demanded hip waders and long gloves, and Jock had been doing it in the early morning to escape the heat, and resting in the afternoon.

Jock stalled the small chainsaw as he saw Guthrie approach and hauled his goggles up over his eyes in the silence. He said nothing but nodded hard, once, and then gathered his equipment and turned to trudge back to the house with Guthrie.

"You called?" he asked, winding the cord of the chargeable saw as he came to it.

"Yeah. They should be here in half an hour."

Jock sighed. "I suppose I should go say goodbye."

"If you like," Guthrie conceded.

Jock sighed again. "You know, all I can think about is how sorry I'll be to see you go."

"I'll be back," Guthrie told him. "After Christmas. You'd better have a tree, and a job, and be all clean and shiny and happy for me. Can you do that?"

Jock practically lit up. "You'll come around Christmas? Wait until you see the place then."

Guthrie smiled to himself, thinking Tad might want to come, and then remembered something important. "He wanted you to sing," he said. It was only a small lie. "Over his grave. He didn't say what—I mean, you can sing 'Born to Run' and he won't know. But that would've made him happy."

Jock's returning smile told Guthrie that maybe he knew the truth there, but he'd take the small gift. "I'll think of that, then," he said. "While we're doing all this other shit. It'll get me through."

GUTHRIE LEFT two days later, early in the morning. The service would be in two weeks, because those things went slow, but Guthrie's truck was on its last legs, and he planned to be in Colton in two weeks, so he couldn't make any promises.

Jock didn't ask for any, but he did haul Guthrie into a big, tearful hug as Guthrie loaded up his truck, his hair fresh from washing.

"Hey, boy," he said, voice choking. "Stay there a minute. I got a thing for you."

He ran into the house and came back with—oh God.

"Jock?" Guthrie asked, surprised. He knew exactly how much money Jock had on a day-to-day basis—between the two of them, they had just enough for Jock to pay the property taxes, buy the supplies to make all the improvements, and then eat.

"It's your daddy's," Jock muttered. "His money, I mean. I… that first day I took his death certificate to the bank and unlocked his funds. There wasn't a lot there. I was his only beneficiary, so I hope you don't mind if I use the rest for his funeral and stuff. But there was enough for this. I figured the old bastard owed you. And I know *I* definitely do. So you keep it. I asked the guy at the store, and he says it's all charged up, and there's every kind of car charger known to man in the box. I-I know you've got to go, but maybe… maybe you can sit at the table for some coffee while you fix that up."

Guthrie stared at the brand-new phone—not a burner but the latest model, with a solid case—and wanted to cry.

"For this, Jock," he said, voice choked, "I'll drink an entire pot."

He reached into the truck for his computer and all the info and dragged it back into the house. Yeah, sure, he'd planned to be out of there by seven in the morning, but God, if big gestures weren't worth the wait.

LIGHTS WILL GUIDE YOU HOME

AARON GEORGE was going to make a difference in Colton, California, law enforcement—but he obviously didn't plan to die trying.

He was safe, up to date, cognizant of working his people just enough to keep them interested and fed, but not so much that they burned out. Tough, compassionate, and funny.

All the things that had made him good to work with *before* they'd fallen down a hole in the world still held.

He and Larx had greeted Tad, April, Chris, and Laura with a barbecue by the pool at Olivia's house (apparently Aaron's house, but she rented), and Tad and April got to hold the baby, coo at the baby, and pet all the dogs to their hearts' content. They also got to swim under the dusty trees, and since swim season was not going to last in the mountains as long as it did down in Sacramento, they were grateful. April, Tad noticed, had bought a sort of long-sleeved swimming costume—something that hid the ravages of drug use on her arms but still flattered her slender frame—and she spent part of the day in shy, quiet conversation with Berto. Mostly, Tad thought, about dogs.

For his part, Tad spent the evening getting unsubtly grilled by Olivia about how Guthrie was doing. It was fun having a friend with the same hobbies, and Tad thought he and Guthrie could settle in here just fine.

But first Guthrie had to, goddamnit, get there.

"So," Aaron murmured two weeks after the barbecue, "you heard from him lately?"

Tad grunted and peered out the window of George's department issue, enjoying the interplay of dappled shadow and gold light against the green of the pine needles, the red-brown of the trunks, and the dazzling blue of the sky. They'd been taking turns on the schedule, partnering up with different deputies and taking different beats. George had spent part of his summer cleaning the department out of most of the people who'd sided with the faction who'd tried to take him and Sheriff Mills out when the whole "falling into the canyon" thing happened. The other deputies Chris and Tad had met had been a little undertrained—and a little resentful of outsiders—but not a lot. They'd mostly been hoping that the two new recruits wouldn't be "too Hollywood" and that Tad, at least, would be "Aaron's kind of gay." Tad had no idea what that meant, but he seemed to be fitting the bill, and he was grateful.

Today he was on a ride-along with Aaron, one of his last before he and Chris got to patrol together, which they'd do for a couple of months before patrolling alone when needed or with various partners. Aaron didn't want to break up a good team, he said, but he also wanted everybody to learn from each other.

Tad was grateful... and excited. It really *was* a different sort of police work. They'd given vagrants rides to a shelter by the freeway that had shuttles to bus stations and vouchers for temporary housing. They'd helped abused spouses either leave their abusers or, in one case, imprisoned the abuser for a good long time.

They'd broken up a meth house and relocated the denizens in a rehab facility in Auburn, with a voucher for the long-term facility April was helping to set up in Colton. They'd even, to Tad's amusement, been part of the local school campaign to knock on the doors of kids who'd had a lot of truancies the year before and talk to the parents about the beginning school year and what could be done to get kids to the classroom.

"I'm not sure how well this is gonna work," Aaron muttered, "but I promised Larx I'd do something after that kid went missing at graduation."

"Well, you do what you gotta to keep the peace," Tad said, which led to Aaron's unsubtle question about hearing from Guthrie.

"About five days ago his father dropped his phone into the gears of one of those electric recliners," Tad said in disgust. "He emails in the evening like he used to text, but you know...." He shrugged.

"Not great at communication?" Aaron asked.

"Well, it's like song lyrics," Tad ruminated, his foul mood about the whole thing coming to the surface again. "There are some great songs out there that evoke a whole host of images with just a few words, right?"

"Yeah," Aaron said. "I'm a closet Swiftie, you know, thanks to my daughters. Between the sound of the music and the meaning of the words, whole novels take place, right?"

"Yup," Tad said grimly. "Except you're never sure if, say, the novel *you're* reading and the novel *I'm* reading are the same. For example, why *did* Billy Joe McCallister jump off the Tallahatchie Bridge? Was his girlfriend pregnant? Did he have a crush on another boy—"

"Or girl," Aaron added dryly.

"Sure, in your world," Tad allowed graciously. "Or maybe people were just swimming and it was a thing, like in Massachusetts where everybody jumps off bridges. Maybe he wasn't *dead*, maybe he just impressed his friends because he *did* it, right? But you'll never know, because you've got all that great imagery but *no discussion as to what it means.*"

"Ah," Aaron said, but he said it soberly.

"Ah what?" Tad asked, wary.

"The filling in the gaps. You know, it happens even when you're in the same house. Life gets busy, something big goes down, and by the time shit settles and it processes, you're both in a slightly different place. You need some time to fill in the gaps. It'll happen."

"You sound very sure of yourself," Tad said sourly, although Chris had said almost the same thing.

Aaron laughed softly. "You're young," he said. "Have faith."

"If one more person tells me to—"

Aaron laughed some more, this time not so softly.

"Where are we going?" Tad asked, softening a little. For one thing, his relationship bullshit was not what this ride-along thing was about.

"This bar/sandwich place that just opened," Aaron told him. "Gonna give them a welcome to Colton and introduce ourselves and give them my personal card in case weird shit happens. From what I understand, it's supposed to be very grassroots hipster, with home-brewed IPAs. They've got the brewery set up in a building behind the bar itself. You'll see. Anyway, there's alcohol and there's food, and there needs to be a friendly relationship with the po-po so it keeps being the sort of place that attracts the people who stay at the local B and Bs instead of the Motel 6 in Truckee."

"You've got local B and Bs?" Tad asked, remembering the night he and Guthrie had spent in the hotel. April had been asked to sleep on the couch in Larx's house, which meant Tad could let go of one of the rooms, but he and Guthrie had spent a sexed-out, euphoric night on one of the worst mattresses Tad had ever experienced.

"Yeah, but they're more for the rich people who come up from the valley," Aaron apologized. "Trust me, Larx and I can't afford them either."

Tad nodded, and one more piece of his new job fell into place. Like a lot of places with tourist appeal, Colton could soon become a place with "summer and winter people" and "townies." That sort of place bred its own discontent, and now he knew what sort of tensions to look out for.

"Understood," he said. "Bodega Bay had that sort of population."

"Tourist and local?"

"Yeah." Tad nodded, thinking bemusedly how sometimes the world spun you right where you belonged.

Caprica—the new bar—turned out to be a nice place. Like Aaron said, hipster, with polished stone floors and a menu that went with a few items, most of them with tags like "organic" and "grass fed" and "free range," but a few appetizers that ran along the fried cheese, mushroom, or zucchini varietals. The people behind the bar were tatted and pierced; the girls had short hair, and the guys had manbuns, and generally, Tad enjoyed the vibe immensely. There was a live-music setup in the corner, although since it was afternoon—and a nice afternoon with great barn-style doors open to the sunshine both in the front and the back, the latter of which led to the brewery—they had music playing over a sound system barely loud enough to hear.

"Huh," Tad said as they walked up to the bar.

"What?" Aaron glanced at him, after getting the attention of the man who appeared to be in charge. A tall, thin young man with a ring in his nose and one in his septum, he had what appeared to be stands of pine trees riding up his forearms, front and back, including his wrists, waved at them and finished his transaction with a young woman who looked like she was taking a break from a retail job and had eaten lunch at the bar.

"Fiddler and the Crabs," Tad said, smiling.

"You like them?" the young man said, striding forward. "They're sort of a hidden gem, you know? Like Blind Blake to the blues, or Tesla to hair bands."

"I'm biased," Tad said apologetically, and then, taking his cue from who he was with, he told the truth. "I'm dating their drummer."

"Oh *wow!*" the bartender said. "Guthrie Woodson? You know him? That's awesome! Do you think you could get him to come up and play?"

"Well, he's cutting another album with Seth Arnold in the next couple weeks," Tad said, not able to keep the pride from his voice, "but after that he's moving up here. I'll have him stop by. I know he loves to perform live."

"Oh my God! Chiana!" He turned to a shorter young woman with buzz-cut bleached hair, an impressively muscled physique, and cascades of flowers on her bare shoulders, biceps, and forearms. "Did you hear that? *Guthrie Woodson* is moving here—"

"And he's cutting a new album with Seth Arnold!" the woman squeed. "Oh my God! Could you introduce us! Could you? Because that would be *amazing*. Oh wow. Corbin and I are, like, *the* biggest fans, right, Cor? You just made our *month*!"

Tad and Aaron laughed, and Aaron was the one who took over the conversation. "As soon as the boy's up here and settled, you'll be the first folks on our agenda," he said, tipping his hat. "But in the meantime, let me introduce us. I'm your local sheriff—there's a special election in a couple of weeks. I'm running unopposed, but I do appreciate a vote of confidence—but mostly I'd like you to know us by sight. This is Deputy Tad Hawkins, and since you're a new business, and one that has alcohol, we wanted you to feel *free* to call us if things get out of hand. We don't arrest people who don't deserve it, but we want folks to feel safe in your establishment." He winked. "You set up a real nice tone here, and my husband and I are looking forward to someplace to go besides the burger place and the pizza place. We want you to feel like we're your friends and not someone you have to be afraid of, right?"

"So nice to meet you, Sheriff," Chiana said, wiping her hands off so she could shake theirs. Corbin followed suit, and the two of them offered a free appetizer their chef was trying out, on the house.

"I'd be happy to pay for that, ma'am," Aaron said, and Tad liked the way he did that without sounding stuffy, while still maintaining propriety. "But yes, some food would certainly sit well. We're both meat eaters, so hit us with your best shot."

They sat and shared their sandwiches and steak frites, trying different sauces and generally enjoying the food while Corbin and Chiana took turns visiting their table and talking about the plans they had for the brewery and how they'd like to institute line dancing on the concrete apron between the brewery and the restaurant and generally making their business feel like a friendly place.

They finally left, and Tad polished off the last of the steak frites and gave a happy sigh.

"This is a good place," he said, gazing out into the sunshine. "We could be happy here."

At that moment, his pocket buzzed and he fished out his phone, his breath catching as he read the message from a strange number.

Jock gave me a cell phone as a goodbye present. May have to return in a couple of weeks and after Christmas. Only if you can come with.

I'm heading for the city—recording starts tomorrow.

So glad to be texting again—emailing is SO boring.

Miss you so much I don't know how I'll sing. Hard to sing if you can't breathe.

Say hi to Livvy and April for me, okay?

Reply when you can. I'll have service for days in a few, but no time.

Love you—G

He stared at the phone, his eyes wide and shiny as he read the message again and again and again.

Like a song he put the things together. Guthrie's father must have died in the past couple of days. Jock had done a great big thing, finding the money for the phone. Guthrie would be returning for Jock. Tad was the first person he texted. He planned to drive himself hard so the recording could be finished soon.

Guthrie missed Tad so much he couldn't breathe.

Tad bit his lip and rubbed his thumbs over them again.

"That him?" Aaron hazarded, breaking into his thoughts.

"Yeah," Tad murmured.

"What's he say?"

"He loves me." Tad stared up at him, shiny, overfull eyes and all, and smiled.

GUTHRIE PUT almost the last of his money in the parking meter three blocks from the hotel—enough for six hours, when he could ask Seth and Kelly if they knew where he could park the truck during the recording session that wouldn't cost an arm and a leg.

He was asleep in the front, leaning against the passenger's side window with one of his blankets folded up behind his head like a pillow when there was a hard knock on the window.

Guthrie groaned and leaned forward, his patter ready on his lips even as he rolled down the window. "Sorry, Officer, I've paid the meter, as you can see, and I'm just waiting for some friends from the airport—oh my God!"

"Guthrie!" Seth said, waving madly in spite of the fact he and Kelly were standing *right there* next to the truck. "What are you doing there? Why didn't you go park at the hotel? Oh my God, have you eaten?"

Guthrie grimaced. This was the delicate part. "Well, you know, valet parking and all. I didn't know where our rooms were—"

"And you couldn't pay the valet price or the food price," Kelly said astutely.

Guthrie grimaced. "And I'm pretty much on my last two hundred bucks," he admitted, "and I was hoping that was the gas to get me home."

Seth's eyes lightened with understanding—but not pity. One of the things that had drawn Guthrie to both Seth and Kelly was that they'd both been there.

"How did you find me?" Guthrie asked before they could say anything. "I mean—"

"We were just shaking off the trip," Kelly said, wiggling his short but powerful body. "And then we saw *this* piece of shit and thought, 'Naw, that couldn't *possibly* be him!'"

Guthrie snorted. "Of course it could," he said dryly.

"Tell you what," Seth said. "Kelly and I will drive with you to put the truck in valet and clear out all your stuff, and I'll arrange for the recording company to pay the ticket, and after I get you checked in, we'll eat on the company dime for lunch."

"Ooh," Guthrie said, appreciating Seth's strategy. "Who's all mister practical now?"

Kelly rolled his eyes. "He knows how to live on the company dime, believe me," he said. "But part of that is the company is always stupid excited about paying for him." Kelly's smile was all pride. "I'm pretty excited about not having to pay San Francisco prices, and no amount of 'Oh, but we'll buy your tuxedo and pay for your town car' is going to cure me of that."

Guthrie chuckled and scooted over, opening the cab so they could both scoot in and he could drive to the hotel. "They pay for your town car?" he asked, legitimately impressed.

"It's *amazing*," Kelly said, ignoring Seth's blush. "It's like he's avoided getting a driver's license his entire life so the symphony could feel all badass by getting him a car. We both nod our heads like, 'Yeah, okay, sure,' like town cars were even a *thing* when we were growing up. I mean, until we went back East, the best thing I ever rode in was Seth's dad's restored caddy."

"It's sweet," Seth said, and Guthrie laughed some more, because Seth said that with all sincerity when the caddy was probably the only vehicle Seth knew from the entire *fleet* of cars on the road.

But that was Seth and Kelly, and Guthrie relaxed into their company as he pulled around the block and into the hotel's valet parking. As he grabbed his guitar and his knapsack with his computer—and Seth and Kelly took his drum set—and he realized this was really all he owned in the world besides the truck, he tried to take the lessons Seth and Kelly had learned in stride. Nobody but Guthrie had to know he had two hundred dollars in the bank, *maybe*, and the only people who did know would love him for who he was anyway.

TWO WEEKS later, he, Vince, Amara, and Seth sat in the studio and listened to the final notes of the final song fade plaintively away into the silence, and then everybody—Seth's agent, Adele, their sound engineers, the grips who'd helped arrange and care for the instruments—*everybody*—took a deep, shuddering breath before erupting into applause.

"My God," Adele said through a suspiciously tight throat. "I can't... I can't even believe what you kids did here. Did you hear that?"

"Yeah, baby," Vince said, low-fiving Kelly, who had stayed in the engineering booth through the entire process, probably picking up pointers through osmosis. "You bet your ass we did."

Guthrie, it appeared, was the only one nervous about the album. "Are you sure?" he asked again. "That was an awful lot of... you know. *Me* on that album." In fact, six of the ten arrangements were penned by Guthrie Woodson. Adele had been breaking her back trying to write and rewrite the contract, making sure particularly that Guthrie would be on the receiving end of bonuses if any of his songs broke big.

"Oh baby," Adele said, her throaty smoker's rasp a comfort. "You're going to break that album wide open. 'Road Like a Ribbon' is going to go nationwide, you have no idea. This is going to be...." She held her hands to her chest. "Wow. This must be what Travis Ford felt like when Outbreak Monkey cut their second album. I might even be in a place to *call him* and ask. You… guys, this… this is gonna be *huge*."

Guthrie smiled weakly, overwhelmed. "I'm… I don't know what to do with huge," he whispered. The last two weeks had been, as he'd suspected, a sleepless whirlwind. The band—they'd decided to rename it the Hot Crustaceans—had practiced, jammed, fiddled, tweaked, and delivered on that tipsy Christmas promise to make music together they could be proud of, and to enjoy the hell out of each other while they did it. Guthrie had called that first text to Tad pretty much right. He hadn't had much time to eat, much time to *breathe*, once the band hit the studio. One of the things the four of them had in common besides their young college years together was an absolute work ethic. For every one of them, the final decision was "What's best for the song."

Nine times out of ten, the answer had been "More Guthrie."

Guthrie, caught up in the tide of creativity and excitement, hadn't thought to contradict his friends until now, when he realized what "More Guthrie" might mean.

But now, in the breathless hush following what Guthrie had to admit had been an extraordinary musical experience, it was starting to seep in.

Adele approached him gently, which was probably why she was Seth's agent, because she could do things like that. "Baby," she said softly, "we send the rough cuts to the executives digitally this afternoon. Tomorrow morning, before you check out, I should have your signature on the final contract. The money should hit your bank account in a week." She glanced around at all of them. "That's not just for him, you know. This is gonna be some serious green. And I know none of you are stupid—you've all been responsible with your pay so far, so you won't let me down now—but I'm saying." She smiled gently at Amara. "This could be 'taking a year off to have a baby' money."

Amara held her hand to her mouth and looked desperately at Vince, who nodded.

"This could be 'get your sisters an apartment of their own' money," she said, eyeballing Seth and Kelly. Then she turned that tender attention back on Guthrie. "And you. I've only known you for a couple of weeks, but I already know what your dreams are. You and your guy, you can live a quiet life while you perform at the local tavern, and every time you get a wild hair, this album is going to be your ticket to making any music you want. This money here—you spend it wisely and this is freedom money, Guthrie. And I'll help you with whatever you need. But right now, you all deserve a night on the town at some place we need to buy Guthrie a tie to eat at. You need good wine and sparkling chandeliers and some goddamned happy, 'cause every damned one of you deserves it. How's that?"

The engineers and production crew had to make the cheers, because the musicians were all busy staring at each other in wonder and trying not to cry.

AT DAWN'S buttcrack the next morning, they all met in Seth and Kelly's suite, Guthrie with all his stuff ready to take down to his truck, as they signed the final contracts. Guthrie's bonuses made spots dance in front of his eyes, and he thought he should send Jock a riding mower as soon as the check cleared.

It was everything he ever wanted; except the one thing he *really* wanted was four hours away, waiting on his call.

"This should clear in the next three days," Adele said seriously. "I wish I could make it *right now*, kid, 'cause from the looks of you, I don't know how you're going to get that death trap of yours up to Colton, but three days is as soon as I can get." He felt a pressure on his back pocket then, which felt like a grope but couldn't possibly be, because Adele had integrity like a rock. As she turned to embrace Seth, Kelly, and the others, Guthrie put his hand in his back pocket and pulled out three hundred dollars, with a Post-it on top.

Don't argue—let me get you home.

By the time he could even *think* to argue, they were all trooping to the elevators, Kelly manning the luggage rack because—his words—he didn't trust all the music geniuses not to spill their instruments all over the hotel.

When the valet arrived with his truck—embarrassingly loud, and oh God, was it belching black smoke now?—they all helped him load it up before they called for their town car: Vince and Amara for the airport, Seth and Kelly to go meet their family, gathered in Sacramento for the occasion. Kelly and Seth hugged him tight—so tight—and Seth whispered, "Please, Guthrie, go be happy. For us."

"For me too," Guthrie said, pulling away, and Kelly grinned.

"That's what I like to hear. Now go before your truck just up and fucking dies."

It was as good an exit line as any.

SADLY, THE truck barely made it back to San Rafael before it—Kelly's words—up and fucking died. There he was, cruising along the freeway, when the unsubtle *bwa-bap-bap-bap-bap-bap* that had started on his way to Sand Cut from Colton grew louder.

Home, his brain was shouting, *Home! Holy shit, Guthrie, he's waiting for you. You haven't seen him in nearly six goddamned weeks. You've barely talked to him, texted him, known him, but you are scant hours from home, and you can't stop. Can't stop. Can't stop. Can't*—fuck!

That last *brap*! had been so loud it shook the windows, and suddenly the car was losing power.

Oddly enough, Guthrie's luck seemed to be turning for the better because the final gasp—slowing to twenty miles an hour, belching black smoke, backfiring, the whole nine yards—began about four miles from Eugene C. Calhoun's auto dealership. According to Guthrie's phone, he pulled up to the service bay about fifteen minutes after the repair guys arrived and forty-five minutes before Eugene C. Calhoun himself.

The truck sputtered, backfired, and quit, leaving Guthrie to stand up on the brake and wrench his shoulders on the defunct power steering to get it to coast into position as the mechanics stared in surprise.

"Oh, Guthrie," said the head mechanic as Guthrie tumbled out of the heat-clicking vehicle. "It's great to see you, man, but I know that sound. The only thing to do for this thing is hold a funeral."

Guthrie's heart was thundering in his throat. *Home! Tell this asshole you need to get HOME!*

"Take a look, would ya?" Guthrie begged, and at that minute, Martin came trotting out of the office, a genuine smile on his face as he pulled Guthrie into a bro hug.

"Guthrie! My dude! What's up?" His nose wrinkled as the black smoke hit him, and he took one look at Guthrie's truck and grimaced. "Oh man. She's dead, isn't she?"

Guthrie sighed and tried not to cry. He and the band hadn't slept in two weeks—and it had been great! Felt like living on music! But now, with home so damned close he almost couldn't breathe, he wasn't sure he had enough sleep to pull it together.

"I am three days from having enough money to buy a brand-new truck," he muttered. "Three goddamned days. *Shit!*"

Martin surveyed the dead Colorado with a now-practiced eye. "How much *do* you have?" he asked. "Because I can give you $800 in trade for that thing. There's a used truck in the back—just came in. Calhoun hasn't seen it. He'd never know you bought it. Only problem is, we need more than the trade-in for a down payment." He grimaced. "You know the drill, but I can get it for you under blue book."

Guthrie smiled at him, focusing for the first time on the young man who had apparently blossomed since Guthrie had walked out nearly three months ago.

"You selling cars on the floor now?" he asked, impressed.

Martin shook his head, blushing like the kid Guthrie had known. "Naw, but one of the new salesmen doesn't know his dick from a hole in the ground. I'd put it under his name and do the paperwork myself. He won't get much of a commission, but the sale will show up and make him look good. He won't argue."

Guthrie gnawed his lip, thinking of the money in his back pocket and knowing it wasn't enough. He could take a bus? But what would he do with his stuff? The thought of calling Tad and having him come down to bail Guthrie out one more time didn't sit with him. He had his pride, god*damned* if he didn't, cash in his back pocket notwithstanding.

God. Three days. *Three days.* The thought of puttering down here in San Rafael while he waited for the check to clear made his head hurt, but that might have been the lack of sleep and, well, the whole last month and a half catching up to him. He couldn't *think*.

His pocket buzzed, and automatically he pulled it out, surprised and pleased to see Olivia's text.

Tad said you're almost done with the album. WHEN ARE YOU COMING HOME?

And maybe because he was tired and maybe because he was in the moment with his beloved truck's carcass still trickling smoke in front of him—maybe because he'd seen this woman vulnerable and emotional and she'd trusted him with that time. And maybe because he wanted to see Tad so goddamned bad his chest hurt, and all that guardedness that had kept him alive for so long didn't seem to serve a purpose anymore because the people he loved could see right through it. Hell, people he hadn't known three weeks ago were shoving money in his pockets to see him through to when his ship came in. How much pride could he have?

Maybe it was all of it, but suddenly he could admit that he needed to see his lover, and he needed to talk to his friend, and he needed the downpayment for another goddamned truck.

Workin' on it, darlin', he typed.

Her response was immediate. *Working on it how?*

Having a little bit of car trouble.

His phone buzzed in his hand.

"It died, didn't it?" Olivia asked.

He grunted, the words paining him a lot more than his own father's death, truth be told. "Like a shot horse," he said, staring with mournful eyes at the poor old dinged-up machine with the primered quarter panels and the egg crate in the flat bed.

"Where are you? It doesn't sound like you're on the side of the road, so maybe you *can* be trusted with your safety, but you're not *here*, so I need to know."

"I'm at my old job," Guthrie said. "I got a friend here who can sell me a used truck at a loss. It's just…." Oh, this hurt. "Three days, Livvy. More money than I've ever seen in my life hits my bank account in *three days*, and in the meantime, I'm looking at buying a bus ticket and renting a locker for my shit—"

"You can stash your shit at my place!" Martin said indignantly, overhearing, at the same time Olivia said, "Oh bullshit. You've got two choices. One is hang in there while I get Elton to go pick you up—he's in town going shopping, but he could be there in three hours." She grunted. "I'd go down with you, but—" In the background, not too far away, he heard a whimper and a grunting noise, and his cheeks heated as he realized she was probably nursing that baby *as they spoke*. "Every two hours. Like clockwork. And she eats like a *horse*. It would turn a six-hour trip into a ten-hour trip, and that would make everybody batshit."

Oh God. She and Elton, probably working at a sleep loss. A three-hour trip was nothing… unless you had a newborn baby at home.

"Livvy, don't be dense," he said. "You guys need your sleep and your gas money and your peace. You're not coming down here to get me—"

"How much do you need for the down payment?" she asked brusquely.

He was so surprised he blurted the amount, but he added, "But I haven't even seen the truck!"

"Is this your friend from the dealership? You think he's being square?"

Guthrie grimaced because he'd hit Speaker since they were in the auto bay, and it was hard to hear, and Martin had heard that, but the kid rolled his eyes.

"Yeah, Livvy. I trust him, but I don't know if the truck is going to last me—"

"Well, it doesn't have to go for ten years, does it?" she asked acerbically. "It just has to get you here and jockey you around until you get your feet under you. You worked there. Is it a good price?"

"It's a steal," he said frankly. "Hell, it'd be a steal for my dead truck, but if this thing runs—"

"Purrs like a kitten," Martin confirmed. "I was in the service bay when they did the checkup." He gave a sweet little smile. "I know it's hard to believe this at a new-and-used car lot, but I wouldn't do you wrong. You, uh...." His abashed look was 100 percent genuine. "You, uh, gave me the confidence to ask Tracy out, you know? I owe you, brother."

"You're dating?" Guthrie asked, honestly pleased. "That's sweet to hear."

"*Guthrie!*" Olivia snapped on the other end of the phone, and Guthrie remembered what he was doing. "Go check out the truck. Me and Elton have some leftover funds from the insurance settlement on the Kia—"

Oh shit. "Livvy, I can't take that—"

"Three days?" she said, and with a cold shiver he saw all those zeroes heading into his bank account. All those promises.

"What if something goes wrong?" he babbled, suddenly afraid. "What if the banks go belly up, or Seth's studio suddenly hates the album? What if Seth's agent rethinks this entire thing and decides I should be paid like a studio musician? What if the album flops and they want all the money back—"

"Guthrie," Olivia said softly, "stop. You signed a contract. The money is being transferred. That's what you said, right?"

"Yeah," Guthrie said through a dry throat. Until all that had come bursting out of him, he hadn't realized how terrified he was of having *everything*, Tad included, yanked away from him, the goalposts moved one more time, his life locked in flux like some living ghost's as he moved from gig to gig without a home.

He'd never realized how much more he wanted than that until *right now*.

Suddenly "just enduring," his signature move, was not enough.

"Honey," she said, "even if it all got bolluxed up, you still need a vehicle to get up here and fix it. Go take a test drive and let me talk to your moneyman, and we'll see what we can do."

"Here," Martin said, taking the new phone from him carefully. "I heard that. Olivia?"

"Hiya!"

"I've heard a lot about you, darlin'," he said, and Guthrie dimly realized Martin had gotten that word from Guthrie himself. "How's that baby?"

"Chowing away," came Olivia's voice, tinny now with the little bit of distance. "Let's discuss how I'm about to throw away my money on a friend."

Martin winked at Guthrie. "You and I both know he's good for it," he said. "You at a computer?"

"Yup!"

"Well send me your info, let me get Guthrie set up for a test drive, and let's see what we can do."

GUTHRIE WAS never sure what sort of magic Martin worked to make that deal happen. He had his test drive with a clueless recent college graduate who had babbled about T-bills and investment portfolios as Guthrie took the truck through its paces around San Rafael. He was pleasantly surprised at what he found.

The vehicle was more than decent—steering, suspension, engine noises, body. So clean. There were dings in the bed that meant it had been used, but it had obviously been cared for. The 100,000 miles on the odometer wasn't a lot for a truck like this—they were used for hauling, and this one would be good for another 200,000 more, Guthrie guessed. The truck that had just died—why hadn't he named her again? Had he been that afraid of connections when he was eighteen?—had garnered nearly 500,000 miles before coasting into the service bay, and Guthrie figured it had earned its rest. Hell, it was almost a dignified way to go.

Maybe this new one could even match the old one and—the thought still filled him with wonder—if it didn't, Guthrie might not be forced to drive it into an early grave from sheer desperation.

"So," the young salesman said, "are you getting it?"

Guthrie tried to breathe past the panic and remember the truth. The truth was, Olivia had probably already made the deal. All that remained was Guthrie signing on the dotted line. The truth was, even if the last two weeks were a fever dream, he knew how to make a living wage, and he'd find some way to pay his friend back.

The truth was, he could get to Colton in three days, exhausted, trail sore, almost frantic from missing Tad, with his pride in his hands along with the truth that he had no trust, no faith at all in Tad, in their friends, in the life and family they'd already started to forge together, or he could get there tonight, maybe have time to shower at Livvy's, maybe be able to get something to eat since he'd skipped breakfast, and having a good story to tell, and then nothing—nothing—but time to remind Tad why he was worth waiting for.

And he'd have more than his pride with him. He'd have proof, maybe, that he trusted in the world, trusted in the home Tad had promised to make them, had faith in the people Tad had put faith into. He'd show up with more than pride. He'd show up with a whole heart ready to put, giftwrapped, into Tad's hands so Tad could see it opened.

"I think Martin has the paperwork," he said, his voice coming from far away, his relief at having made the decision enough to weaken his knees. At the last minute, he remembered his sense of self-preservation. "Any way I could get it in a different color?" he asked, only partly to give the salesguy shit. Ugh. The days of electric-lime paint—had he slept through those or just been poor enough to miss them on the road?

He anticipated the practiced smile of apology, and when he got it, he was ready to move in for the kill.

"Well, maybe not," he said, "but is there any way the service guys could remove the lockbox in the back of the old one and reinstall it in the back of this one?"

And the salesguy was so excited to offer something to seal the deal, Guthrie got it for free.

MARTIN AND Olivia had hammered down the terms and conditions by the time Guthrie weaseled into the office from the back entrance, and while the salesguy watched on, seeming a little bit bewildered, Martin walked him through the paperwork. At one point, Guthrie tried to cut Olivia's loan down by offering the cash Adele had thrust in his pocket that morning.

Martin literally shoved it back at him.

"Oh my God, Guthrie—no. Just no. Pay it back to her, if you need to, but seriously. Take the cash, get a cup of coffee from the bistro at the corner, and wait for the lockbox to be installed."

Guthrie tried to scowl at him, but he couldn't. "They got good sandwiches." He yawned wistfully, and Martin rolled his eyes before pulling out a set of keys from his own pocket.

"Better yet," he said gently, "this one's for my car—you know my Honda—and this is my apartment. I just moved in with Tracy. She'll be at work in five. Hug her on the way out. I'll text you directions, you go nap on the couch for two hours, and I'll tag you when the truck's done. It's ten minutes away."

Guthrie opened his mouth to protest, but a yawn came out instead. Martin smiled and pressed the keys into his hand.

"You never did tell me," he said. "Did you make that recording session?"

Guthrie grinned at him. "It's where the money's gonna come from," he confided. "Look for the Hot Crustaceans—the LP should drop right before Christmas."

Martin sucked in an excited breath. "Oh God. Really?"

Guthrie nodded, and his heart must really have opened in the last three, four months, because his excitement spilled right on out. "I got six tracks on it," he said, biting his lip. "Like, Fiddler—erm, Seth—he picked through everybody's stuff, and there's ten total, but he picked *six* tracks of mine, and we worked 'em, and they did…. God, they did magic stuff to my music, but the lyrics and percussion's mine, and some of the guitar—"

"The voice?" Martin asked. "Did you do vocals?"

His grin broke free. "Yeah," he said. "And… and Martin, I think you might… I think it might hit. I got no guarantees. You might be the only one to buy it, but—"

Martin squeezed his eyes shut in excitement. "It's gonna be huge," he said, and Guthrie heard nothing in his voice but happiness for a friend. "It's gonna break *huge*, and every time it plays over the loudspeaker, I'll tell anybody who'll listen that Guthrie Woodson's my friend, and he even slept on my couch on the way home from cutting a legend." He opened his eyes and reached out to shake Guthrie's hand. "My friend Guthrie. It'll be epic."

Guthrie's eyes spilled over, and he couldn't blame the tiredness—not on this. "Thanks, brother," he said, and Martin pulled him into a hug.

"Go get some sleep," he murmured. "Paperwork's done. I'll text you when your lockbox is installed and it's all shifted over. If you want to get sandwiches on the way here, *that's* what you can do with your three hundred dollars. How's that?"

Guthrie nodded and accepted the kindness with a full heart. "It'll be epic," he said. "Let me get my laptop and knapsack. The rest is my instruments—"

"We'll treat them as gently as we'd treat Saint Peter's testicles," Martin said, his eyes dancing.

"I'm stealing that," Guthrie promised, impressed by the wordplay. "Epic."

THREE HOURS later he was on his way.

The nap really *had* done him good, and as he settled into the cab of the truck, a new coffee in the cupholder, his phone playlist hooked up to the Bluetooth—which was such a better setup than his old truck he couldn't even believe technology had improved that much—he remembered to text Olivia that he should be there in Colton around six, maybe seven.

Come to Larx's house, she replied. *We're doing dinner there tonight. We can give you directions to Tad's, and you can call from the landline.*

Thanks, Livvy—that's kind.

Is the truck as ugly as you said it was?

Electric lime green. Thank you, darlin'. I can't thank you enough.

One word. Babysitting. Now stop texting and start driving. Love you!!

Love you back.

He set the phone in the holder and wondered about all the people in his life he had to love. He hadn't known that in April, when he'd gazed out at the audience and seen Tad looking back at him, those gray-green eyes catching at his heart.

But he knew it now. Knew he wasn't riding through the world alone. Knew that if he fell, he'd have someone who'd care enough to help him up. And knew that if someone he loved fell, he'd be there ready to do the same.

Funny how knowing something like that made you free in the world. He'd spent his life on the road, from gig to gig, and he'd never felt like he had wings until now, Golden Earring's "Radar Love" pounding through his new sound system, urging him to fly home.

ALL THE PROMISES WE MADE

"Hey, Livvy, what're we eating tonight?" Aaron asked as he led Tad through the front room of the house. Dozer had already gotten his customary greeting of lots of body wiggles and happy woofings, and now it was time to let him out back to pee.

"Beef stroganoff," she said happily, her back toward them as she fussed with something on the stove. "I'm sautéing the beef now, in wine so cheap, it giggles when it breathes."

Tad laughed, and they both watched as she almost dropped the bottle of wine.

"Oops!" he said. "Didn't mean to startle you!"

"Oh!" She turned and gave him an odd smile. "You're eating here tonight? Aaron, watch out for the car carrier!"

"Not my first rodeo, Livvy," Aaron said, neatly sidestepping the carrier that sat back from the kitchen table. He checked inside on his way to the door and gave the sleeping baby's cheek a tap with a blunt finger.

"Of course not," she said. "Just, you know, startled to see Tad."

Her surprise was almost panicked, and Tad wasn't sure what to do with that. "If that's okay?" he asked, looking at Aaron, who had invited him since April was having some sort of crafting thing with Laura and Rosie Mills, Eamon's wife.

Aaron shrugged. "Larx said so. Livvy, didn't he tell you?" He let Dozer out, and the dog ran outside with a mission obviously in mind.

Olivia shook her head. "No worries." There was a new element to her expression—a deviousness almost that Tad couldn't decipher. "I'm making plenty, and the three teenagers are all out—" She made a fluttering motion with the hand not holding the wine bottle. "—working or going to a football game or, you know, raising hell and getting laid."

Aaron snorted. Tad had gotten to know the three "teenagers"—Aaron's son, Larx's youngest daughter, and Larx's foster son—in the past couple of weeks. The two boys were fresh out of high school and working while attending junior college classes in Truckee, and Christiana was involved in every club known to man or guidance counselor.

"What about Jaime and Berto?" Aaron asked.

"Berto's with April, Laura, and Rosie," she said, "and Jaime's with Christiana—something about physics club." She shrugged. "It's just us grown-ups. Tad's definitely welcome."

Reassured, Tad chuckled. "April didn't tell me Berto was going to be there. That's sweet. Maybe she'll teach him her yarn thing, and they can do that together." He sobered. "I understand handcrafts are good for trauma and PTSD too."

"He's looking forward to it," Olivia said earnestly.

"I'm gonna go shower and change," Aaron said, letting the dog back in and taking note of the knapsack in Tad's hand. "Feel free to use the guest bathroom to do the same."

"Thanks," Tad said with relief. He'd locked his weapon in the lockbox in the SUV, and he did feel like relaxing with friends for an evening. It was easier to do in jeans and a hoodie. The shadows were growing long, and the evening was cooling off in the mountains in late September, and Tad was looking forward to huddling in the soft fleece sweatshirt—new, in forest green, with Colton County emblazoned across the front in white and yellow.

He disappeared, familiar with the house now that he'd been in Colton for nearly a month. He emerged twenty minutes later feeling a lot less road-dusty, hearing Larx's and Elton's voices in the kitchen as they bantered with Olivia.

"And how was our princess today?" Larx cooed, and as Tad rounded the corner, he saw Grandpa Larx had taken the opportunity to pull the baby from the car carrier into his arms.

"I'm doing fine, thanks," Olivia chirped. "Saved the world a couple of times, did the bills, created food for a human being from my own body—all in a day's work."

"How's *my* princess today?" Elton asked, standing behind her and wrapping tender arms around her waist. Tad watched as she melted back against him.

"You know how I am," she murmured. "We had a whole long talk about it."

"That's my super-princess," Elton said back, and Larx glanced up from the yawning baby.

"Is there something here I should know about?"

Olivia glanced around the room, and seeing Tad coming from the hall said promptly, "Nope! How you doing, Tad?"

"Almost human," Tad said. "Thanks for the use of the shower."

"Aaron gets *very* particular about sweating in his khakis," Larx said, shaking his head. "I try to tell him it's no different than blue jeans and a button-down, but he begs to differ."

"Well, we're gonna make you work for it," Olivia told him tartly. "You know the drill. Set the table." Her eyes flickered to the clock. "Add a plate, okay?"

"For who?" Larx asked, and his eyes sharpened again, particularly at Olivia's insouciant shrug.

"Kirby," she said. "He might get off his shift early." She met her father's eyes then, and Tad recognized family eyeball semaphore when he saw it.

"All right," he said, reaching into the cabinet for plates. "What's going on? Nobody lets a rookie off an EMT shift early."

"Nothing," Olivia said, eyes wide-open and guileless.

Tad knew that expression. April used to wear it whenever she'd stolen his T-shirts from the laundry pile because she liked the way they fit better.

At that moment, Olivia cocked her head, and a coy smile played with her lips as the crunch of the gravel drive could be heard under large tires. "I think our guest is here now," she said, and then she gave a gentle nod of the head. "Tad, do you want to go let him in?"

Tad was turning as she spoke, and part of him was thinking, "But I'd know the sound of his truck," while the rest of him was hearing the strains of "Radar Love" pouring out of an open window.

The music shut off just as Tad flew out the door and into the yard.

He was climbing out of the door of a newish green Chevy, knapsack over his back. He paused for a moment to check his long hair in the side mirror, and Tad saw one shoulder dip a little in uncertainty, in nervousness. He was biting his lip as he turned toward the house, and in the fading twilight, Tad still saw the exact moment he caught sight of Tad, standing midway down the walk, staring at him in surprise and, Tad wasn't ashamed to admit it, raw hunger.

"Dozer!" Aaron called sharply from inside the house, and Tad heard the door close behind him. The sound urged him forward down the walk to where Guthrie, wearing the now much-worn plaid flannel hoodie and faded-but-clean jeans, was approaching much too slowly.

"You're here," Tad said, eyes raking over him, taking in the thinness, the exhaustion behind the eyes, and most importantly, the shining, brilliant smile.

"You noticed," Guthrie said, drawing nearer. "So're you."

"I was invited to dinner," Tad told him irrelevantly. Oh God. He looked *so good.* He took another tottering step, feeling his eyes burn. He'd put this moment off in his head, not dwelling on how close they were, so afraid of the pain of one more day he hadn't realized it was almost here.

"So was I," Guthrie said, drawing close enough for Tad to pull in his body heat, the sweat from the drive, coffee on his breath, tiredness, and... joy. "They were going to give me directions home after dinner."

"Don't need directions," Tad murmured, twining his arms around Guthrie's neck. "You're here. You're home."

"Only home I need," Guthrie whispered back. The knapsack dropped to the ground, and he stepped into Tad's body, rubbing his stubbled cheek against Tad's.

For a moment, that was it, that breathless moment of remembering, growing accustomed to each other's warm bodies, heartbeats, smells, and then Tad turned his head and took his mouth, warmed and found when he'd been lost, held and safe when he'd been alone under the pine trees, dreading the onset of night.

GUTHRIE WAS sure he somehow owed Olivia an apology; he wasn't sure how good his dinner conversation had been. He did recount the death of the old truck, and that had garnered some general laughter, and he'd thanked Olivia and Elton for the thousandth time.

Tad had chided her for keeping the secret of Guthrie's arrival, but she'd laughingly said the real surprise had been Tad's presence for dinner, so it wasn't her fault. Aaron and Tad had talked at length about Caprica, the brewery with the open slots for live music. Almost like his very own personal agent, Tad had negotiated a three night a week stint for him, solo.

"What am I supposed to do with the rest of my time?" Guthrie asked.

"You'll find something," Tad said with assurance. "There's businesses here or in Truckee. There's even gigs in Truckee. You might not have to work another day job if you don't want to."

"Since your boyfriend's health and dental program is as liberal as I could make it, probably not," Aaron said, and that had made everybody laugh too.

So dinner had been loud and excited—but small, Guthrie was made to understand. He'd lucked into a small dinner this night, which was the only reason the family excused him and Tad early.

But maybe the fact that they'd held hands at the table for the entire meal—and even a dessert of fresh peach cobbler—had given them a pass too.

Guthrie had followed Tad through the black night of the mountains with tingles rushing down his skin. Now that he'd touched Tad's hand, kissed him, held him so tight his breath had hitched, he had the patience for excitement, the emotional reserves to be thrilled.

He wasn't just following his lover through the night for a hookup or a moment.

He was following Tad *home*.

There'd been a bustle when he'd arrived, as Tad took him through the ranch-style home and showed him where *everything* went. Guthrie followed along while he took turns petting and releasing (and then petting and releasing and then petting and releasing) the now gigantic kittens, who seemed to remember him fine. There was a study where his instruments went, along with Tad's desk. There was the garage where the egg crate and the sleeping bags went. There was the hamper in the hallway bathroom where Tad dumped out his threadbare canvas knapsack, and the mudroom for laundry, which Tad vaguely gestured toward as he hustled Guthrie—holding April's much-loved blanket—down the hall.

Guthrie would see the bedrooms and the kitchen later. After… after….

He and Tad fell into each other's arms like tumbling into a canyon. Clothes melted, and breath mingled, every kiss more sacred than the last. It wasn't until Tad's hands, cupping Guthrie's cheeks as they sank onto the bed, wouldn't stop shaking, that Guthrie realized what this moment was for Tad, and how badly he'd been missed.

And what Guthrie needed to do for Tad that maybe he'd learned in the last four months.

"Here," he'd whispered, taking the lubricant from Tad's still shaking hands. "Here. Let me."

Tad—always so good at planning, at giving orders, at organizing the world, fell backward onto the mattress in the moonshine streaming through their peaked window and gazed up at Guthrie with such hunger— and such trust.

But Guthrie *could* be trusted. He wasn't at the mercy of the world anymore, tumbling like a shoe in a dryer. He'd wrestled with his past and come out the better man, and he'd made good on promises to the future. He'd learned to trust people in his life, and his reward?

He was trusted in return. He wouldn't hurt the people he loved— not for the world.

His mouth on Tad's length was urgent but not hard, and his fingers, slick and stretching at Tad's entrance, were gentle but insistent.

Tad let out a wordless cry when he was ready, and held out his arms, clearly having faith that Guthrie would fill them—and fill him.

Guthrie did, sliding into him gloriously, awed and humbled by the feeling of his lover's flesh embracing his own. The tears still came, but they were tears of joy, and he pumped his hips and let them fall, because a man should never hide his joy from his lover.

Tad's shuddering climax felt like a stream of stars, pulling Guthrie's own orgasm along in their wake. They cried out together, softly, their skin so sensitized it only took Tad's lips on his chest, his shoulder, to send him over again, and it only took his come, pumped into Tad's entrance, to send Tad into the same river.

When they finally washed ashore, Tad wouldn't let him go fetch a cloth, wouldn't let him leave the bed at all.

"Later," he murmured. "Later. Just… just stay and hold me now. God, I missed you."

"Me too," Guthrie said, his voice throaty and choked. "God, it's gonna take me a week to leave to so much as get milk, you know. I am *so* here to stay."

Tad chuckled a little and then buried his face into Guthrie's chest. "Good," he whispered. "'Cause I'm planning to marry you someday."

Guthrie smiled, thinking of the permanence of that. "Good," he said. "Looking forward to it."

"You topped," Tad said a minute later, putting the obvious up for discussion.

"I trust myself now," Guthrie told him, the words resonating in his chest.

"Yeah?"

"Yeah. You know that nine-hundred-pound gorilla I was so afraid of?"

"Yeah."

"I set him loose. You know what he did?"

"What?" Tad asked, but he didn't sound worried.

"He talked about all the beauty in my life, and how there were people who loved me. Mr. Hyde...." He swallowed. "My father—he died knowing I wouldn't sing at his funeral. And I had people in my life who would sing to me every day. That's... that's some damage there, not gonna lie. But it could have been worse, and... and worse didn't happen."

"So you trust yourself," Tad said in understanding.

"I trust myself to pay Livvy back, to be a part of her family, not to let your sister down." His voice dropped, because sex was still private. "Not to hurt you when we... uhm...."

"Yeah," Tad said, stroking the outside of his arm.

"That."

"That."

They were quiet then, and Guthrie's eyes started to close.

"We should get up," Tad said, surprising him into blinking.

"Why?" Oh God, what had he forgotten?

"April's going to be home any minute, and she's going to make sounds even the cats can't hear when she sees you back."

As though summoned by thoughts and prayers alone, they heard the rumble of Tad's SUV down the long driveway. Guthrie and Tad laughingly rolled out of bed and ran to the bathroom to wash up before Tad made Guthrie put on his pajama pants and a new fleece sweatshirt.

"The stuff in my knapsack was clean," Guthrie mumbled, noting that he had an entire underwear drawer to himself, and socks as well.

"The stuff in your knapsack needs to be buried in the backyard or set on fire," Tad laughed.

"Except for your hoodie," Guthrie said soberly, picking it up from where it had fallen to the floor.

"Yeah," Tad said fondly. "That we're keeping—"

And then the door opened, and April cried, "Oh my God is that new truck *Guthrie's*!" and the two of them tumbled out of the bedroom to greet her.

Their lives together would be busy and even a little crowded, but as Guthrie embraced a sniffling April, who wouldn't stop patting his shoulder and practically sat in his lap as he told her about his trip, he caught Tad's eye.

Tad smiled gently and said, "I'm making hot chocolate. We're gonna be up a while."

Busy was okay, Guthrie thought, watching him. They could do busy. Guthrie would do a lot to have the people he loved around him, and now he knew how much that could be.

And so did the man he'd marry someday, the man who trusted him to be that guy like Guthrie trusted Tad.

All the love songs in the world boiled down to this. To know your family would be there, a gathering of love and kindness in the dark, a light in the window, people to listen to you sing.

Guthrie wondered what sort of music he could make now that he knew this, and the world opened up in his heart.

Continue Reading for an Excerpt from
String Boys
by Amy Lane

Now

THE WIND hit Seth solid in the chest as he emerged from the back entrance of David Geffen Hall. Oh my God, the Hudson was unmerciful! Temperatures tonight threatened to sink to the thirties, with a healthy dose of sleet to seal the ice in any unwary traveler's veins. It wasn't even December yet—not even Thanksgiving.

It was Seth's first winter in New York, and his heart felt as cold as the wind.

"Hey! Seth! Come on! You said I could crash on your couch!"

Seth looked up and smiled gamely. "Yeah. Sorry. Just not used to the winters, you know?"

"You look sad," Caleb said perceptively. "You know, the offer still stands. I, uh, don't have to sleep on the couch."

Seth's heart felt too heavy for Caleb's usual flirting to even elicit a smile. "Definitely the couch," he said, pulling the solid wool of his coat up to his chin and making sure the violin case he was cradling against his chest under the coat was secure.

"Your performance was good," Caleb said earnestly, his pale face shining in the light from a nearby streetlamp. Together they were walking toward the 66th Street Subway Station. Seth's agent had managed to find an apartment on the Lower East Side—tiny, cramped, and stifling, even in April when he'd moved. It still boasted just enough living space for one person.

Of course, in New York that meant Seth had a bunk bed that he shared with his friend Amara, who was alternate flute when they needed one. Caleb could sleep on the couch.

Amara was home in Sacramento, where Seth yearned to be, visiting her boyfriend and her family. But Seth had two more weeks of performances on his contract.

He had tickets to Sacramento in December. *You've got to try*, he told himself. *Maybe if he sees you, he'll remember we're stronger together. It doesn't matter if he told you it was done.* Then, as he always did, he heard, *You'll never stop trying.* The insidious little voice gave him hope, and he warmed up some.

"Thank you," he said absently to Caleb. "That's kind."

Seth was a soloist, which was something he wasn't supposed to be in his twenties—everybody had said that as he was coming up. You had to be *really* good to play solo, to be first chair, to get a job in an orchestra, to play in New York at all. Seth had lived his life assuming he wasn't the guy who got to do those things special. It was always a shock to realize that every other violinist in the world didn't get the same opportunities he had.

Kelly had always said Seth was meant to walk among the stars… but that had only seemed possible when Kelly was there.

"It's not kindness," Caleb argued. "It's pure envy! My God—it's like the only part of you engaged is the part that connects with your violin!"

Seth shrugged. Old news. His family all knew what was in his heart, and that had always been good enough for him. Without Kelly there to understand the things Seth didn't say, it was like the good parts of Seth weren't there at all.

As though summoned, Seth's phone buzzed. He stiffened, there on the sidewalk as they approached the stairway to the subway station, because he knew. When it was Kelly texting, he *always* knew.

He pulled it out and read the message, biting his lip.

He's got maybe a week. Please, Seth, for Matty. Please come home.

Seth stopped and shuddered, his heart finally converted to ice.

But that didn't stop him from writing the message. Didn't stop him from pressing Send.

Not for Matty. For you, Kelly. All you had to do was ask.

"What is it?" Caleb asked, sounding worried. It didn't take a genius to see Seth was upset.

"I should pack," he mumbled, trying not to lose his head. "And I have to trade in my ticket for one on standby. I need to go home."

"Home?" Caleb sounded incredulous. "Seth, I don't even know where you come from!"

Seth shook his head, trying to keep his breathing even. Always, always, that amorphous threat, the long arm of the law reaching for a moment Seth couldn't remember—but it had never been enough to keep him away for this long.

"I come from a shitty school in a cow town," he said, knowing his voice was sharp and not sure how to fix it. There was more to his home than that; there must have been. He'd risked so much to return, time and time again. The last time, though, the time Kelly had frozen his heart, had been the time he'd risked and lost it all.

"I never fucking left."

Then

THE OLD school multipurpose room let in the most terrific draft, and the parents in the audience shivered. Wrapped in coats, mittens, and scarves, the collective assembly of the inner-city school tried to exude as much goodwill as humanly possible, while the babies in the many carriages in the aisles all whimpered or grizzled from cold or tiredness, and the younger children fidgeted, anxious to get their little hands on the free cookies lined up on the folding table in the corner of the cafeteria.

The program had started with the choir and progressed to the band, and the little ones had endured quite enough of hesitant voices and shrieking flutes, thank you very much.

Then Mrs. Joyce, sainted woman that she was, stood up and beamed at the mothers and fathers—some of them young enough to remember when she was *their* principal—and everything settled down as it should. Mrs. Joyce was a bosomy woman with skin of rich dark teak, who wore her tightly kinked graying hair back in the same bun she'd worn for the last thirty years. *Nobody* wanted to feel the weight of her disappointment fall upon their heads.

"So our next performance is entirely unexpected," she said warmly. "Mrs. Sheridan, our retired orchestra teacher, was given a donation of nine violins last year. She asked a friend to restore them, restring them, and tune them as a donation to the school, and then she picked nine volunteers—volunteers, mind you—who wanted to play the fiddle. The first hands that shot up were all young men, and we call them our string boys. Everybody, please give it up for Mrs. Sheridan and our string boys!"

BEFORE THE introduction, Seth Arnold peeped through the dusty scarlet curtain surrounding the stage and surveyed the crowd with a cynical eye.

His best friend, Matty Cruz, shouldered his way underneath Seth's chin and did the same thing.

"Our mom's here," Matty muttered, trying to sound bored. "She had to bring the twins, but still...."

"Dad's here too," Matty's little brother, Kelly, chimed in, making the curtain gap wider. "See? Leaning against the back wall?"

Matty's shoulders relaxed. Their parents were separated, like a lot of parents, but their father was still trying.

Seth nodded at his best friend soberly. "That's good," he said, letting a little smile grace his lips. Matty and Kelly still believed parents could be kind. Seth was relieved his father wasn't in the crowd. He'd gone to great lengths not to let Craig Arnold know where he'd been after school for the past ten weeks.

When Mrs. Joyce got to the part about the boys being volunteers, everybody behind the curtain let out a silent groan.

Volunteers, Seth's scrawny ass.

They weren't volunteers. They were *sacrifices*, that's what they were! Mrs. Applegate, the new teacher, fresh and shiny and straight out of teacher school, was having such a heinous time with Seth and Matty's fourth-grade class—the class with twenty-seven boys and eight girls—that when old Mrs. Sheridan had come piping into the principal's office about wanting to teach *somebody* the violin, Mrs. Joyce had grabbed the first boys she could find, to give Mrs. Applegate a break.

Matty's little brother got stuck on the end because the musicians needed after-school practices as well. Since the boys walked to and from school together, period the end, Kelly got to pick up a violin too, even though he was only in third grade.

The main reason—the *only* reason, really—they'd all been so eager to keep up with the violin was that it saved them from having to deal with Mrs. Applegate's sorry attempts to teach long division. Mrs. Joyce had taken the boys into the computer room after their rehearsal and let them participate in online math tutorials. Even though the computers were dinosaurs and the room was freakin' hot, even in the wintertime, the math tutorials were still better than knowing Castor Durant was beating up three kids a day just because Mrs. Applegate couldn't keep track of the chaos.

Or it *had* been the only reason.

Last week, Mrs. Sheridan had dismissed the other boys to math tutorial and kept Seth in the multipurpose room for a moment.

Mrs. Sheridan was an old white lady. She had gray hair in braids around her head, like white ladies in the movies, and wore antique white blouses with ruffles. She might have ended up an unfortunate victim, just like Mrs. Applegate, but she was just so danged… nice. Consistently kind. Not stupid, just… nice.

And she'd politely asked Seth to stay in the room, and asked him to hold the violin under his chin like they'd been practicing for the last ten weeks.

"Now, Seth," she said gently. "You've done everything I've asked. Everything. I'm so proud of you. But I want you to do me a favor here— just a small one. Could you pull the bow across for the first note in 'Twinkle, Twinkle, Little Star' for me? Just once. Slowly. And I want you to close your eyes and hear the note as you make it."

She'd asked them to do this many times, and Seth fought off the temptation to roll his eyes before he closed them.

It was such a small request, and she always got so happy when they did what she asked.

How hard would it be to do what she asked now?

He held the bow loosely in his hand, making sure his fingers didn't brush the string, and kept the violin firmly under his chin. Then he let out his breath, and on the inhale, he dragged the bow slowly and surely across the string.

And almost forgot to breathe entirely.

For the first time since he'd come to the cafeteria, happy to be let loose from the everyday routine, he got to hear the noise he had the potential to make.

And it was lovely. Pure and perfect, beautiful in a way the music his dad played on their boom box at home had never been, the note wavered in the ancient multipurpose room with its cracked linoleum and missing ceiling tiles. And even though his eyes were closed, he suddenly saw his battered surroundings with an air of faded grace.

His bow finished its journey, and he let out his breath again and opened his eyes, stunned and in awe.

Mrs. Sheridan was beaming gently at him. "That was exquisite, Seth. Would you like to practice a little more, to see if you can get that sound again?"

Seth nodded at her, his eyes enormous. What the hell? He already knew how to do long division anyway.

So this night, the night of the winter concert, Seth was not particularly concerned that his father wasn't in the audience. He just wanted to make that noise—the pure one—the best he could.

"You ready?" Kelly asked, pulling his attention away from the audience for a moment. "You have to do that solo thing."

At eight, Kelly Cruz was about the cutest thing Seth would ever see. He was missing two teeth and had dimples on his little round clay-tinted cheeks. His mom had combed his loose curls tightly back, and only a few springlike strands sprang across his forehead, making him look impish. Adorable but capable of great mischief, Kelly was the one who spent hours occupying his twin sisters so his mom could talk on the phone, which was her job and helped them make the rent.

Like most of the students at Three Oaks Elementary School, Kelly and Matty weren't just one thing. Seth had shown up in the second grade with his speech all prepared. His father had gotten a job in California, and they'd moved up from Arizona, where he'd needed to say, "My mom's dad and mom are mostly black, and my dad's mom and dad are white. And my mom was mostly black. That's why I'm pale brown." Everybody in his old school had asked. But when he'd shown up at Three Oaks, nine out of ten kids had a complexion between his own pale tan and Mrs. Joyce's dark teak, while the few all-white kids showed up like a freakish neon pink. Nobody had seemed to care, and Seth had been grateful.

Kelly and Matty's dad was half Mexican and half white, and their mom was half black and half white, but they'd only told him that while they'd been playing cars at their house, because it was something to say. Not because they expected Seth to ask them so they could rank themselves by who was the most white.

And unlike in Arizona, where everyone had expected his dad to leave him with his mom's parents when his mom died, nobody in California asked about that either.

Seth liked Sacramento.

He could disappear.

Except he wasn't disappearing on the stage this night. Or if he did, it was the best magic trick ever, where he could play that violin and it would speak for him. Nobody had to see the boy attached.

All they would notice was that sound—that pure string sound, like the violin was crying—that he could make when his body was loose and his soul was dreamy and everything in the world was made of light.

Kelly's charming smile, his perpetual goodwill, told Seth that was possible.

"Yeah," Seth told him, smiling back quietly. "I'm ready to make that sound."

Scan QR code below to order now

Writer, knitter, mother, wife, award-winning author AMY LANE shows her love in knitwear, is frequently seen in the company of tiny homicidal dogs, and can't believe all the kids haven't left the house yet. She lives in a crumbling crapmansion in the least romantic area of California, has a long-winded explanation for everything, and writes to silence the voices in her head. There are a lot of voices—she's written over 120 books.

Website: www.greenshill.com
Blog: www.writerslane.blogspot.com
Email: amylane@greenshill.com
Facebook: www.facebook.com/amy.lane.167
Twitter: @amymaclane
Patreon: https://www.patreon.com/AmyHEALane

BONFIRES

AMY LANE

Bonfires: Book One

Ten years ago Sheriff's Deputy Aaron George lost his wife and moved to Colton, hoping growing up in a small town would be better for his children. He's gotten to know his community, including Mr. Larkin, the bouncy, funny science teacher. But when Larx is dragged unwillingly into administration, he stops coaching the track team and starts running alone. Aaron—who thought life began and ended with his kids—is distracted by a glistening chest and a principal running on a dangerous road.

Larx has been living for his kids too—and for his students at Colton High. He's not ready to be charmed by Aaron, but when they start running together, he comes to appreciate the deputy's steadiness, humor, and complete understanding of Larx's priorities. Children first, job second, his own interests a sad last.

It only takes one kiss for two men approaching fifty to start acting like teenagers in love, even amid all the responsibilities they shoulder. Then an act of violence puts their burgeoning relationship on hold. The adult responsibilities they've embraced are now instrumental in keeping their town from exploding. When things come to a head, they realize their newly forged family might be what keeps the world from spinning out of control.

Scan QR code below to order now

CROCUS

AMY LANE

Bonfires: Book Two

Saying "I love you" doesn't guarantee peace or a happy ending.

High school principal "Larx" Larkin was pretty sure he'd hit the jackpot when Deputy Sheriff Aaron George moved in with him, merging their two families as seamlessly as the chaos around them could possibly allow.

But when Larx's pregnant daughter comes home unexpectedly and two of Larx's students are put in danger, their tentative beginning comes crashing down around their ears.

Larx thought he was okay with the dangers of Aaron's job, and Aaron thought he was okay with Larx's daughter—who is not okay—but when their worst fears are almost realized, it puts their hearts and their lives to the test. Larx and Aaron have never wanted anything as badly as they want a life together. Will they be able to make it work when the world is working hard to keep them apart?

Scan QR code below to order now

SUNSET

AMY LANE

Bonfires: Book Three

Larx and Aaron have faced a lot together—small-town prejudice, work injuries, and pregnant daughters. But finally two of their teenagers have graduated and Larx is making moves to lessen his workload in anticipation of Aaron being elected sheriff in the fall. Maybe, just maybe, they can start planning the wedding they've longed to have.

Then a student goes missing and Aaron's mentor takes a bullet during the search. Larx and Aaron backburner their plans and jump into what they do best—taking care of their people.

They don't expect to be the ones who end up in danger.

While Larx and Aaron struggle to get out of their perilous situation, their family is galvanized into action. Just like Larx and Aaron's relationship, their rescue is going to take hard work, ingenuity, and a solid sense of humor, but the people whose lives they've touched are up for the job. Nobody will rest until Larx and Aaron are safe and sound— and ready to ride off into the sunset toward the beginning of the rest of their lives.

Scan QR code below to order now

SEAN'S
SUNSHINE

AMY
LANE

The Flophouse: Book Three

As a young detective, Sean Kryzynski expected violence on the job, not to get stabbed coming back from lunch. Add an angsty bedside breakup, and by the time he gets home from the hospital, he's over everything, including his irritating, hot-as-balls nurse, Billy No-Last-Name with the big, cynical brown eyes.

Billy's whole porn-model flophouse is experiencing a wave of altruism and adulting—people getting real jobs and going to shrinks and doing good works. Billy opts in too—he wants to be a good guy—but his assignment is taking care of the world's most exasperating, headstrong patient. At least bunking with Sean means Billy has his own spare bedroom and some peace and quiet to do classwork.

The porn model and the policeman seem to have no common ground, but Billy's experience herding his younger siblings helps him manage Sean with unexpected empathy—a skill Sean has been working on too, because he wants to be a good cop. Eventually they chip away at the walls around each other's hearts and discover a real connection. If not for their incompatible day jobs and inconvenient pasts, they might even be falling in love….

Scan QR code below to order now

AMY LANE

SWIPE LEFT, POWER DOWN, LOOK UP

Busy soccer coach Trey Novak doesn't have time for the awkwardness and upheaval dating can cause, but when his cousin stands him up for a lunch date, he meets someone who changes his mind.

Dewey Saunders is dying to get a real job in his field and start the rest of his life, but a guy's got to pay rent, and the coffee shop is where it's at. When the handsome customer in the coach's sweats gets stood up, Dewey is right there to commiserate—and maybe make some time with a cute guy.

Trey's making hopeful plans with Dewey when his professional life explodes. He and Dewey aren't in a serious place yet, and suddenly he's promising to make sports a welcoming place for all people. When Dewey puts himself out to comfort Trey after an awful day, Trey realizes that they might not be in a serious place, but Dewey has serious promise for their future. If someone as loyal and as kind and funny as Dewey is what's offered, Trey would gladly swipe right for love.

Scan QR code below to order now